CAPTAIN VINEGAR'S COMMISSION

Philip Glazebrook was born in 1937. His books include *Journey to Kars*, which describes a lonely journey taking him through the Serbian and Greek provinces of the old Ottoman Empire, and through the ruined classical cities of Asia Minor as far as Turkey's frontier with Russia and the fortress of Kars. These travels in the Levant furnished the picturesque background for *Captain Vinegar's Commission*, the idea for which had grown out of his fascination for nineteenth-century accounts of adventurous Eastern journeys, and for the heroic character of the men who undertook them. His fifth novel, *The Gate at the End of the World*, is the sequel to *Captain Vinegar's Commission*.

Philip Glazebrook's novel *The Walled Garden* (originally published under the title *The Burr Wood*) is also published in Flamingo. The author lives with his family in Dorset.

CAPTAIN VINEGAR'S COMMISSION

Philip Glazebrook

FLAMINGO
Published by Fontana Paperbacks

First published by Collins Harvill 1987
This Flamingo edition first published
in 1990 by Fontana Paperbacks
8 Grafton Street, London W1X 3LA

Flamingo is an imprint of
Fontana Paperbacks, part of
the Collins Publishing Group

© Philip Glazebrook 1987

Printed and bound in Great Britain by
William Collins Sons & Co. Ltd, Glasgow

PART ONE

I

IN THE AUTUMN OF THE YEAR 1842 an active boy might have been observed ascending a hillside in the Western Highlands of Scotland, whilst a rough-coated little dog of the terrier kind dragged along on a length of twine at his heels. The boy was not a native of these wild haunts. His father, who was dead, had been English, an officer in the King of Naples' army, and this last month was the first spell of time that Tresham Pitcher had spent amongst the high hills which had been his mother's home.

How he loved the place! It seemed as if the landscape of his mind – the background to the adventures of his imagination – had come into being around him. In Clapham, which was where he lived in his step-father's house, it was necessary to close his eyes to reality, to the thin blackened trees, to the house-fronts, the traffic, the stained London clouds, if the figures from old times who rode through his head were to have enough sky over their heads and sufficient wilderness under their horses' hoofs. Here too his father had walked, on the sporting tour which had carried him into Tresham's mother's life with the long romantic strides she had conveyed well into her son's mind – and it seemed to the boy that the print of his father's footsteps was discernible in these wild places, amongst the footprints of Sir Gawaine or other heroes of Malory, as it was not on the common land at Clapham. In the month he had so far been here, staying with his two stepsisters and his mother at her father's manse on the seashore, the suggestive desola-tion of the scene had so worked its way into his mind that he lived freely in the world of his imagination.

'Come on! Come on!' he cried out into the wind at his grandfather's dog, Gaisgeach, elderly and stout, which started out eagerly enough on these adventures with him into the hills, but which needed coaxing, even pulling, once the sixty acres of its master's glebe had been left below. The dog was useful, though, for turning into whatever companion imagination required. 'Oh, come on, Gaisgeach!'

The wind flattening the deer-grass stripped away the words from Tresham's lips. The wind scratched the silver coils of the river in the strath below. The wind buffeted his ears and shrieked against the upthrusts of rock which broke through the slope he ascended. He was climbing towards the shoulder of a dark hill, the most seaward peak of jagged and tumbled mountains which rose against hurrying sky and flying cloud above his head. There was no limit to imagination in these wastes. In January a British army had been lost in its entirety in Afghanistan. He had read of its destruction and slaughter with a kind of breathless appetite for horror. Hard to picture in Clapham, here the wintry passes between Cabool and Jalalabad lay all around him. Behind the wind he heard the shrieks and death cries, and the clash of the long Afghan knife on rock; and his soul which longed for adventure shivered with delight. 'We knyghtes adventurous ofte suffren grete woo and payne,' said the knight he loved best in Malory, and he longed to suffer with them. He imagined he was wearing his father's sword, which was indeed his, but was kept for him by his mother, who always replied 'Not yet' when he asked if he might keep it for himself. He strode onwards.

> Bold strides he took and long
> That beat the sounding moss
> And clattered rude on sullen crags.
> Meanwhile the Foe –

What foe?

Silence. Over a crest he had dropped into the sudden shock of silence out of the wind's reach. He heard his boots squeak on the deer-grass, his thoughts loud in his head. The gloomy peaks rose above him as before out of the silence like images of eternity. Between those peaks and himself he saw into the glen which lay between. Two little lochs divided by a ridge of sand glittered darkly down there, and a clutch of hovels fringed their shore, stone walls and turf roofs scarcely visible in the stony landscape. The fever was in them, he had been warned. Was that the foe? His father had died in Italy of fever. Also in that village by the loch, so he had heard, dwelled an old woman who had murdered the gauger, the government excise-man. No one would lay a hand upon her for fear of her magical powers. Was she the foe? What was the cause of the dread he felt in the silent hollow which he crossed with frantic haste? Sliding into view over the shoulders of other mountains as he walked came a remote summit slim and steep as praying hands. In a minute he would be in the wind again, or in the sound of running water from a burn whose course he could see cutting through the heather fifty yards ahead, and silence and dread would be blown away together. Then he heard a thin long scream.

He ran forward, jerking Gaisgeach after him, till the roar of the little burn over its stones, where he flung himself down, washed through his mind louder than fear. He lay looking into the brown bubbles, trying to undo the coils of the scream which had fallen on him like a snake from a tree. He watched the pebbles through the amber window of water. But the scream – the scream, and what he had seen besides – would not be dowsed.

What he had seen was cudgels beating a cloak. But the cloak had screamed. Horror iced his blood. Printed on his mind was the fierce energy of the two figures laying blows on the cloak on the heather, and their faces red as meat. He saw them in the burn water. Nothing protected him from their reality. He had to go forward: quickly he had to make up someone brave enough to go forward. His brain rocked with fright. Gaisgeach was no good. With shaking hands he undid the twine which was round the dog's neck and set him free. Then he stood up and looked.

Towards him with flying hair, and rags blowing about skinny limbs, ran a girl who dashed over stones and peat-hags with amazing lightness. Behind her heavily as bloodhounds blundered the laird's two sons, older boys than himself, whilst a little wizened imp of a child, a ghillie's boy, skipped after them on his stunted legs shrieking with crazy laughter. All three of them were armed with three-tined forks, the leisters used for spearing salmon.

As the girl flew by like a seabird Tresham ran at her hunters. The boys pulled up short as the apparition jumped out of the burn shouting in his high English voice. Then they came on laughing. Tresham dashed at them and struck out, hurting his knuckle on the cold corrugated flap of an ear, missing the big red faces. He wasn't hit, but was pushed in the chest with sufficient force to throw him down. The bare legs and kilts of the two boys thrashed past. Looking after them Tresham saw that the girl had not run on, but seemed to be waiting to be caught. Wondering at this, he forgot his third enemy, the ghillie's boy, and never heard the lame child creep up to deliver to his head a blow from the leister which knocked him unconscious.

*   *   *

It is a difficult matter to decide at what point – with which incident – to begin the story of a man's life. No doubt every day and every action could be made significant by its interpretation. The event just described in Tresham Pitcher's boyhood was quite out of the usual line of his experience; but, in his behaviour, and still more in what he made of the event afterwards, this encounter with the laird's sons on a Scottish hillside tells more of his character and nature than could be learned from the account of a hundred more typical days of his life, in which he worked at his Greek in an attic room of the Clapham house, or gazed out of the window at the unsatisfying scene which met his straying eye.

With his stepsisters the case is different. A biography of either May or Eliza which began in Scotland would give altogether a wrong emphasis. Neither in their lives nor at their deaths were the wild places of the Earth, or its wild tribes, to hold any of the significance which such scenes and such peoples were to hold for Tresham. Where he looked for so much from landscape, and responded so gratefully to what it supplied in the vital matter of breathing life into his imagination, landscape for them never rose above its humble rôle of 'the view', that background to walks and gossip which might occasionally be sufficiently noticed to be rhapsodised over, or to be improved into a watercolour drawing executed upon the best principles of fashion.

In this spirit they had been out drawing waterfalls on the day in question. Long before they came to Scotland, Bartlett's engravings of *Caledonia* had shown them what a Scotch waterfall should be; and the steamer carrying them north from Glasgow to Inverness had stopped especially at the falls of Foyer, on Loch Ness-side, so that tourists could view without exertion the heart's blood of the wilderness

[12]

pumping horridly into its chasm. Nothing could be more agreeable for their albums than a sketch of the falls of Ardessie, once the height of the drop had been extended, and the angle of overleaning rowans made more dramatic, and mountain peaks moved about the paper until the composition was sufficiently 'aweful' and 'sublime' to lie upon a Clapham parlour-table. They drew and chattered, and May helped with Eliza's trees, not trying quite her hardest as she did so. Scotland was infinitely comical to them, now that they had forgotten the agonies of the journey, which they had made sure would kill them a thousand times. Especially was their step-mamma's papa, Pastor McPhee, and his manse, comical to their view. Fancy there being no looking-glass! – and none nearer than Inverness, so the old witch in the kitchen had told them. And no iron nails but what the packman brought, and no spoons, even, but what the tinkers melted down from horn! There was nothing, and the only agreeable sensation was the superiority they were able to feel to the place and to all in it. The people were no better than beasts. With the Pastor they had gone one forenoon to a settlement on the wild loch shore and visited a sick woman in her hut. Shrouded in peat smoke which had blackened the stone interior, behind a plaid hung from a rope, the thin white creature coughed herself to death. Tresham had stared and stared from the hut door where he had stood grasping the dog tightly and seeming to absorb the scene of misery through widened eyes until May had pulled him away. Now May and Eliza went visiting with the Pastor no more, but drew the waterfalls, and giggled over the queerness of the manse.

They were sitting this afternoon by a bright fire of birchwood in the parlour, warming stockinged toes freely in the knowledge that Pastor and Step-mamma were out visiting the parish in his sailing boat over the sea loch, when they heard the front door into the passage unlatched, and a staggering footstep enter the house. Eliza ran across the little room, half firelit and half lit by afternoon light struggling through its small window, and opened the door.

'Why, Tresh, whatever have you done now? May, May!' she called, poking her face back into the parlour, 'May, come quick!'

Her elder sister May was putting on her boots at the fireside. She was sick and tired of Tresham's fibs and to-dos. 'Put on your boots, Eliza,' she said.

Eliza ran back lightfooted and began to drag on her boots with flustered fingers. She was nearly sixteen. At last both sisters were shod, and could rustle into the passage where their stepbrother crouched on the flagstones with his head in his bloodstained hands. The girls lifted him to his feet and pulled him to a wooden chair where they sat him down with his back to the window. He did not speak. Eliza's fingers explored his head, May clucked her tongue over the drenched and peat-stained condition of his breeches and jacket. Bloodstains streaked his face and neck, but the blood – to Eliza's relief when she examined her fingertips – was dry. There was a lump on his head, the scalp was broken, but no other injury they could discover. Had he fallen from a crag, slipped crossing a river, been attacked by some wild beast? All Tresham would moan out was 'No! No!' and shake his bloody head slowly. At last May snapped out:

'Oh, for pity's sake, Tresham! Try and be a man! If this is to do with one of your silly stories – is it? Is it? You aren't hurt, you know,' she added.

Tresham had walked with them to Ardessie, and she had allowed him to go on alone, up into the wilderness which was threatened by the hard, high line of the hills ever present above the manse, whilst she and May were sketching the falls. She might have known he would get into some scrape for which she would be blamed.

'Oh, May, he is hurt though!' cried Eliza, putting her arm round the boy's shaking shoulders. 'Come, Tresh, and we'll clean your poor old head and put you into bed, and you shall tell us all about it when you choose. Was it –' she dropped her voice – 'was it an adventure?'

Tears now filled Tresham's light-coloured eyes. He nodded his head. Eliza hugged him, which squeezed the tears down his cheeks, and down hers too, as she supported him along the stone passage and up the stairway. May followed carrying his jacket and bloody neckerchief well away from her dress.

Later that evening the two sisters sat waiting by the loch shore for the return of their step-mamma and her father in the Minister's sailing-craft, *Swallow*. A fine clear light fell between clouds on the sea. The girls sat amongst the rocks above *Swallow*'s anchorage, leaning against one another for warmth, the light in their faces. A fresh wind dashed the sea-fret on the stones, the seaweed lifted and fell on the breaking wave, the sound and scent of the shore charged the atmosphere with the sea's presence. To the east, behind them, slopes rolled upward into cloud and gloomy mountain. Somewhere up there was the high ridge of shale which overlooked the spot where Tresham had been injured, and from which he had walked down to the manse in its clump of trees. Had the girls considered the matter, they might have realized that his return to the manse in such condition – a walk of three hours at least – was a heroic feat of endurance.

But the girls were not discussing Tresham any more, nor the view, nor Scotland at all. Their world, both of reality and of imagination, was contained very sufficiently within that Clapham landscape which their stepbrother considered so pinched. Of course, they had always lived there, at Laidlaw Villa, whereas Tresham had first opened his eyes under Italian skies, and had first looked upon a southern world lit by a meridional sun. Eliza and May couldn't imagine this: they couldn't be bothered. A picture had formed in Eliza's mind, put together from Heaven knows what ingredients and misunderstandings, of Tresham's father on foot in a tattered uniform, with an enormous sword clanking at his side, trailing along a dusty lane under grape-laden vines, whilst Step-mamma in a colourful costume followed him on a donkey with Tresh in her arms. This was her idea of Tresham's early years, and of her step-mamma's career before she had come to the respectable decencies of Laidlaw Villa; but of course the picture was too disreputable to speak of, even to May.

No, as they sat by the shore between mountains and sea, the sisters had been discussing the prospects, for and against, of making the acquaintance of the family of a rich brewer who, having bought a tract of land on Grove Road in Clapham, was now engaged upon enclosing it behind a wall. Within this wall was rising a large and wonderfully turreted villa, all stucco and plate-glass and opulence, which was said to contain, of all exciting ideas, a ballroom. An agony which the girls could hardly bear was the fear that a ballroom might exist in a private house not a mile from their home, and its owner be unknown to them. They had seen the brewer himself setting out for business in a four-wheeler; they had seen, and even brushed against, his daughters at the

[15]

counter of the circulating library; but how to bridge the gulf between seeing and knowing was the puzzle.

So intense and deep were their speculations that the *Swallow* had swept up the sea loch under a spread of white canvas, and was standing-to off the anchorage, before they knew she was in view. They first heard the clap of her mainsail, and the Minister's deep, strong voice over the water giving orders to the boy who always sailed the dangerous sea-coast of his parish with him. Now she slid forward under her fore-sail through the slapping waves, a graceful undecked eighteen-foot craft rigged fore and aft, the Minister at the tiller whilst the boy, Ruari *beg*, crouched in the bow to catch up her mooring-buoy with his boat-hook. All was action, colour, and sea-borne sounds. Beside her father in the stern, alert, sat a cheerful-looking little woman wrapped in a boat-rug, eyes and bright round face alight with interest in the scene. The moment the boat-hook caught the buoy, and Ruari drew alongside the rowboat attached to it, the Minister's daughter was on her feet and darting actively over *Swallow*'s gunwale into the dinghy, where she caught up the oars and made ready for her part from old days in landing *Swallow*'s crew.

May and Eliza, who had been watching her agility with amazement, ran down to the shore as she rowed the dinghy in. 'Well done, oh, well done, Mamma!' they cried.

Whilst Ruari jumped ashore with the painter onto gull-whitened rocks, the Minister's voice came rolling in with the breakers like the tones of a bell-buoy:

'The truth of it is, she is wasted in London, wasted entirely, your step-mamma is.'

His daughter said nothing, shipping her oars as Ruari beached the dinghy, but her eyes shone. Neat and quick she stepped ashore, and stood clasping her hands where the foam of the sea flecked her boots. 'I do love it so!' she cried out to them all, to the girls and Ruari and *Swallow* and the sea. 'I do so love it all!' she repeated, laying her head against her father's sea-cloak as he stepped ashore and took her arm.

'Mamma – !' Having forgotten Tresh, Eliza spoke with sudden alarm as she remembered him – 'Mamma, poor Tresham has been most dreadfully hurt!'

'Tresh hurt?' Mrs Wytherstone turned with the question to her elder stepdaughter.

'Eliza, what a noodle you are!' scolded May, buffeting her sister's arm. 'Tresham has tumbled over a rock and cut his head, Mamma, that is all it is. Pray, Mamma, don't be upset.'

Mrs Wytherstone shook off the hand May had laid on her arm. 'Upset? Tresh hurt and you two chattering here?' She gathered up her skirt and was off across the moor towards the manse with the rapidity and directness of a bird's flight, which soon shrank her figure to a 'dot under the mountains.

Tresham lay in bed awaiting developments. The pines at the window darkening the room seemed like an oppression continued from the moment he had opened his eyes and found sky and dark hills staring down at him where he lay in the heather. With his fingers he had touched with a creeping sensation of horror the loose flap of hair and flesh on his head, and had brought down his bloody hands to stare at. *For God's love let me not die in this forest.* The wind blew over him as indifferently as water flows over a creature it has drowned. He was aware of the hostile desolation of the landscape, and of himself in its midst alone. He felt the sharpness of fear. He knew he had no courage. There was only the courage of the stalwart he had invented, who had rushed at the laird's sons and struck them. But that was himself – he remembered the cold wrinkled ear his own fist had struck. He had invented another part of himself. He got upon all fours, and then upon his feet. Pain struck hammer-blows in his head which shook his vision. He began to climb.

Anyone who had watched the boy get to his feet and climb towards the mountain ridge he must cross, under gloomy slopes amid a waste of scree – anyone who had watched his long and lonely wandering walk down from the heights, must have wondered where the courage came from that kept the speck of life moving across the vast scene hour after hour until he reached the white-washed manse among its pines.

Tresham could not now remember the walk. He remembered the fear: such sharpness – such reality – that he almost wished he might face it again. And he remembered finding himself dumped at the manse door as if the bold knight who had rescued him from his extremity had flung him down on the step from his saddle-bow and ridden away.

Then had come Eliza. 'Whatever have you done?' He had blamed her in his head for not asking the right question, which would have freed the right answer within him. So he had moaned and answered nothing.

Now he lay in bed in the little room like a cupboard at the head of the stairs waiting for his mother. She would know what had happened to him without laying upon him this necessity to tell what was ineffable.

He heard the door unlatched, a step in the passage, a rustle on the stair. There darted through his mind the attitudes he might strike to dramatise his state. He shut his eyes. She was in the room, on her knees at his side. Her hands lay cool as shadows on his forehead. No need to speak, or open his eyes. She would tell him what had happened to him, just as she used to tell him into the darkness stories and adventures as he fell asleep in Italian lodgings during their old wandering life together.

'Dear Tresh, what have they done to you?'

It was a beginning. She knew it was the forces of an enemy – the enemy – though she had not spoken the adversary's name. He waited for more. Her hands found the wound on his head which the girls had washed, and examined it, and seemed satisfied. She smoothed the covers over him.

'I so wish you'd come with us in *Swallow*,' said she, kneeling again, 'such a beautiful sail, and the wind so cold, and the spray flying over us.' So she told him where they had been, and of porpoises sliding through the waves, and of the white sea-splash of plummeting gannets, until her words painted on his eyelids the scenes she described, and painted out the horrid and weird confusions of his own experience. He almost fell asleep, as he had fallen asleep so often amongst scenes which her words created in his head.

'Now here is Grandfather,' he heard her break off to say; 'I'm sure you can tell him just what happened, to set his mind to rest.'

He tried to slip into sleep, but the effort woke him to full awareness of the little room now overfilled and dominated by the Minister. 'Well, child,' began the solemn voice, 'the girls have been telling us you've been attacked just now. Who was it attacked you? And where did it come about?'

Sternness was indivisible from the Minister's voice. Tresham felt his eyes prised open by his grandfather's will. In the craggy head looking down at him the two eyes were large and gloomy as the two lochans in the hills where he had fought the enemy. Tresham's eyes appealed to his mother.

'Should he sleep first?' she suggested.

'Hush, Hannah!' said the Minister, raising his hand. 'Wait, and the child will speak.'

Tresham felt his mouth too prised open. 'I saw,' he began, 'there were two of them hitting a cloak I thought, but there was a scream. No, there were three, three boys. The cloak turned into . . .' He felt the dissatisfaction of the poet whose muse offers only inadequate words to convey the inchoate but significant image. 'Then she was running. I couldn't stop the two boys. Then I hit them. Then I was hit. They weren't sticks, you know, they were those forks for salmon they were hitting the girl with.'

'Leisters were they?' said the Minister. 'Now, there were two boys, were there, or three?'

'Oh, you see, there were the two from Eileann Lappich, and then the lame one that's always with them.'

'The laird's boys, is it you mean, and wee Murdo with them?'

'Yes.'

'And they were beating – a maid, you say? Or a cloak?'

'I saw them I thought hitting a cloak and then next I saw the girl running.'

'So you went to stop the boys running after her?'

Tresham nodded. Had he done that? He could remember the fear – vivid, shocking – but not the action. The Minister paused. He passed his hand over his jaw. 'Were you not frightened?' he asked. 'For they're great louts, those two, and wee Murdo is one of the Devil's own.'

'I did do it,' Tresham asserted.

'So . . . And then one of them knocked you down, did he?'

'Except I was – or yes, he did,' Tresham agreed, afraid to add that he had been knocked senseless in case he didn't understand what 'knocked senseless' meant, and might give the Minister an opening to find him out in a lie.

'And what of the maid?'

He saw again how she had stood on a peat hag awaiting her pursuers in a way he didn't understand. He said, 'I don't know if she ran away.'

[19]

'You didn't wait before you ran off yourself, you mean?'

Tresham shook his head on his pillow trying not to sob.

'Father dear,' put in his mother, 'the child's head was split open by the blow, look. You shouldn't make him feel he might have done more, surely? But what is to be done?' she went on. 'Those dreadful boys! Shall you see the laird? Oh, it's all so difficult for you with the laird as he is too!'

He ignored her. 'This all fell out on the hill above Craigour, is it so, where you told the girls you were going?'

'Above the two lochs.' He saw them clearly, and the ridge of sand between, and the dark huts on their shore with the smoke blowing flat. If only he could tell!

'You had a long trudge home, did you not? It is well the mist was not down on Ruigh Mheallain. And the dog Gaisgeach,' he added from the stairs which he had begun to descend, the very scrape of his boots on the treads sounding too loud and forceful for the little house, 'he came home with you did he, for he's not about?'

Gaisgeach! He hadn't given the dog a thought since freeing him in the burn. As unexpectedly as the muse speaks to the poet there came into Tresham's head the dramatic stroke which would well have expressed – had only it happened – the horror and fear he had felt of his adversary on the moor.

'Oh!' he said, raising himself in his bed. 'I haven't said the worst thing! They stuck their leisters right through Gaisgeach and killed him!'

The Minister's descent of the stairway stopped. He turned. 'Leistered my Gaisgeach!' he cried in a great voice. 'Leistered my poor Gaisgeach?'

All was consternation. The girls shuttered their faces in their hands and screeched. Mrs Wytherstone embraced what she could reach of the Minister's broad back.

'Was he dead? Did you leave him on the hill?' he asked.

'He wasn't there when I woke up,' said Tresham. 'Nothing was there.'

'Woke up?' His mother caught at the words anxiously. 'Dear Heaven, did you swoon?'

'Yes, I swooned,' he said, and smiled at her. That was exactly it.

'Swooned' was the word. She knew after all what had happened to him and how to tell it. A feeling of peace and well-being came upon him. Their consternation and alarm filled him with satisfaction. Before their confused voices had descended the stairs he was asleep.

*   *   *

An hour or so later Mrs Wytherstone and her stepdaughters sat comfortably in the parlour below. There was light enough at the window for her to see the print of the duodecimo volume of poems in her hand; the girls sewed at the Minister's linen; the peats crumbled and glimmered in the hearth, adding a reddish tinge to the room's illumination. Unmatched chairs and a plain table took up the floor. The little window did not encourage gazing out; for gazing at within, there was a steel engraving of Martin's *Fall of Nineveh* on the wall, a muzzle-loading gun in a corner, a coil of rope on a peg behind the door and, upon the shelf over the fireplace, a stuffed sea-eagle in a glass case bearing a plate inscribed 'To The Reverend N. McPhee from Capt. M. Pitcher, Coire Chaorachain, Sept. 19th 1826' – which was the date of Mrs Wytherstone's first marriage, to Tresham's father, and the white-tailed eagle a bird he had shot the summer previous to his marriage on his sporting tour of North Britain. Apart from the Minister's own sanctum across the passage, walled with books and likely to have a new sail for *Swallow* half-made on the floor, there was no other downstairs room save the kitchen. Mrs Wytherstone, who had left off reading Alfred Tennyson and had been considering the room's contents in silence, now said:

'How comfortable we are, my dears!'

'Except for poor Step-grandpapa,' said Eliza, looking up.

'And poor Tresh's horrid wound,' put in May, 'and Gaisgeach dead.'

'And except that poor Papa is in London,' added Eliza, looking down again at her sewing.

Mrs Wytherstone sighed. What they objected was perfectly true – the Minister had set out to walk to Eileann Lappich, four miles off at the head of the sea loch, to interview the laird as to his boys' crimes –

the dog she believed dead – her son's head was split open – her husband was certainly absent – and yet they were wonderfully comfortable, far more content than ever they were around the parlour table at Laidlaw Villa. And her stepdaughters were just as comfortable as herself, but they had scored a point, they had made her sound heartless. So she sighed. The 'step' between them was indeed, she thought, like an uneven piece of paving in their relationship, on which the foot jarred if every word was not watched.

It was the journey from London – its extent, and the trials of the road – which made her feel so satisfactorily isolated with all that was needed for contentment. Thrown together in isolation, the family had shown strengths uncalled for at home. In railway trains and in boats – and most of all in the abysses between train and boat which appear in the best-laid plans of travel – resources of unity and good fellowship had drawn them together. Mr Wytherstone had been most anxious for them to journey by rail wherever railroads extended, for he believed in the future of steam travel. Working for a firm of tea merchants in the City, he had caught something of the 'railway fever', even investing (his wife feared) in volatile railway stock. So she had put aside her own love of the sea, which she shared with her father, until they had struggled on the rails by various lines as far north as Glasgow, where she put the whole party into a twenty-seven-and-sixpenny cabin on board a paddle-steamer bound for Inverness by way of the Crinan and Caledonian canals. She had not been at sea since returning with Tresh across the Channel after her husband's death at Rimini seven years ago, and this two days' voyage, with the girls who had never been to sea before, had put the party into a happy mood of interdependence and gaiety by the time they stepped ashore in the cold northern light of Inverness.

Of course, they were no sooner safe in Napier's Hotel, hardships of travel over, than different expectations and intentions separated the family again. Except for Macdonald's Tartan Warehouse the shops fell very far short of the girls' standards. Tresham was disappointed at having missed the mail-coach journey from Perth. That route still ran the risk of attack from caterans; even the guide-book admitted that Sir Hector Munro returning from India a few years ago had been waylaid in a snow-wreath in the pass of Slochmuick and held to ransom, and to have travelled through the scenes of such lingering shades of the Middle Ages would have fed his imagination richly. The steamboat, clanking and hissing among the mountains on its way through the canal, banished any mediæval terrors haunting the misty crags.

Knowing her son's disappointment, Mrs Wytherstone made up for Scotland's apparent tameness by repeating to him many a dire tale of the savage north dredged up from her own childhood, which she told him privately when they were alone together, perhaps at the boat's rail, or before he went to sleep, for she didn't want him to think that their own old intimate wanderings together in Italy – 'our travels' – were threatened by this excursion with his stepsisters. Such stories continued into today, and into these very hills, that barbarous crimson thread which had always fascinated his mind. They had been told to her mother, who had been born on the isle of Lewis in 1797: at which time, and in which place, the shadows of the Middle Ages had indeed not entirely cleared away.

Hannah Wytherstone had lived as a child in Edinburgh, before the Act of 1823 which, by providing Government money for churches and manses to be built in the Highlands, had obliged her father (and many other comfortable Lowland clerics) to migrate to a remote parish amongst the northern tribes, there gradually to change their ways, and adapt their dress and sermons and theology to fit what their wild parishioners required. She had moved with her father to Wester Ross, where she had lived until carried off in marriage by Captain Pitcher. Now she sat with her book on her knee, looking at the white-tailed eagle which her husband had presented to her father in place of herself. To reach this parlour, even from Inverness, had entailed catching the mail from Dingwall, driving thence in a four-wheeled gig to Achnasheen, where a night was spent at the abominable inn, and so at last in a humbler gig by rough roads a full day's journey into the wilderness of peaks and sea lochs lying along the western coast, where they found the manse at the foot of a dark hill, in mist beside a rainy sea.

The clatter of the latch, and a draught of air which brightened the peats' glow, announced the Minister's return from his meeting with the laird. Though they waited in expectation, he did not come into the parlour. After a few moments Mrs Wytherstone rose and put her Tennyson on the table, saying she would speak to the servant about their dinner, usually eaten at five o'clock but today delayed. However, she didn't go to the kitchen. Rapping on the closed door across the passage she enquired in a low voice, 'Father?'

There was silence for a moment or two. Then the door was opened to her. Her father stood amid books and stores and cabinets holding the bundle of rag and sacking on which Gaisgeach had always lain in this room for company.

'I should not care so for a dog,' he said painfully, shaking his head while the tears glistened on his bony cheeks.

Mrs Wytherstone touched his hand only, and knelt down at the hearth to blow a little fire into the peats. She knew that her father's sense of wrongdoing in having cared excessively for a dog was more painful to him than the dog's loss; he could be hurt harder in his conscience than in his heart. That was his nature. To sympathise with him therefore over the dog's death would have been to compound his sufferings, and attract probably a stern rebuke to herself. So she comforted him indirectly by blowing up the fire in his grate, and waiting for him to speak. She was used to ministering to awkward men. In a little while he said, 'They deny it utterly.' Then he was silent. A flame crept out of the peat which his eye was upon. 'I had the boys called before me there,' he went on, 'and they denied my asseveration utterly. Denied the fight, the maid, all of it.'

'And did their father believe them?' she asked cautiously.

'Why would he not? Their tale was likely enough.'

'What was their tale of it?'

'Och, 'twas a long rigmarole you could barely make out for their hemming and hawing and sucking away at their teeth so hangdog before their father, the two louts that they are. But the drift of it was this, that they'd been away up behind Ardgour with the leisters taking salmon for the house, as they'd been bid, and hieing home they took away a cloak or a plaid from a shieling to carry the fish in, and the maid whose raiment it was said she'd come down with them and take it from them when they'd done with it. Oh, aye, and there were fish not dead in the cloak which they beat with their leisters, so they said, when I told them that your boy had said he'd seen them beat the maid on the ground.'

'And Gaisgeach? Did they deny that?'

'I wouldn't speak of the dog to them,' he replied slowly, adding 'but I hold them guilty of it in my heart.'

'So you don't believe them? You do believe Tresh?'

'What would keep my old Gaisgeach from me but death?'

Mrs Wytherstone sat back on a footstool and clasped her knees. Her father, having pitched the dog's bedding into the basket of peats to be burned, put a chair where the dog used to lie, and himself sat down at his writing table which was spread less with papers than with physic bottles and with unusual stones picked up from mountain or shore on days when he felt a lively interest even in the geology of his parish. Such days and moods were infrequent. It required only an untoward incident to tip him into despondency and bitterness now with all his work, and with its frustration (as he saw it) by the irredeemably brutish condition of his parishioners, and by the laird's contrariness, and by nature herself as she showed her enmity in mist and flood and storm. Though there were many books in the wall-shelves, there were none open on desk or table, and indeed no chair placed by window or fire for reading. He had been a scholar: had learned the Gaelic as an academic subject in Edinburgh – which, when discovered by his bishop, had led to exile amongst tribes which spoke no other tongue.

'Shall I tell Jenny you will eat her supper?' Mrs Wytherstone asked.

'I will have to walk up to Craigour tomorrow to find who the maid was, if I can,' he said, ignoring supper. 'If those children of the Devil up there will tell me a word of the truth, that is. I wish to Heaven they had all been cleared away out of the glens, so I do,' he continued angrily, with a sweeping gesture of his hands, 'cleared away as they've been in Sutherland, and made to dwell where the fear of God may be put into them. It is often I wish the glens hadn't a smoke in them, so I do, for the sheep is a better creature than the drunken beasts up there this day.'

'Still, Father,' she said, 'there is improvement, you know. The roads and the inns are as good as Italy, quite, and a hundred times better in the fifteen years since I lived here.'

'Your "improvements" are not for the rabble in the glens,' he retorted. 'Roads and inns and decency are for those who come when the rabble is cleared out. If you had no clearances you would have no improvements, depend upon it. Do you know there are fifty stills in the

[25]

parish? Fifty illicit stills making whisky! Small wonder there is never a man sober, nor a woman either, and criminal relations between them in every hut. Aye, the sheep is a purer creature, so she is.'

'Jenny came from the glens,' she reminded him, thinking of supper.

'Lot came from Sodom,' he replied, 'but his city was destroyed as Jenny's must be. But come,' he said, suddenly more cheerful, 'come and we will eat of Jenny's stoved hen before that is destroyed. For a stoved hen she will have for our supper this night as sure as it is Tuesday.'

He took his daughter's hand and opened the door into the passage. Both of them heard a scratch at the outside door of the house. The Minister's eye lit up; he took a stride, and flung open the door. In trotted Gaisgeach, stubby and resolute. Ignoring them, he made directly for his usual spot in his master's study and, squeezing under the chair he found upon it, dropped with a weary flop of bones onto the boards of the floor.

Mrs Wytherstone would have run and petted him and looked for injuries, but her father flung shut his study door. 'Leave the dog!' he warned harshly. 'And, mind, I will not have him touched while I am away.'

'Away, Father?'

'Of course,' he said, pulling down his cloak from its peg on the wall. 'Did you suppose I would leave the laird believing his two sons are liars, when it is my own grandson is the liar?'

When he had gone, Hannah Wytherstone hesitated at the stairs' foot. Should she go up to Tresham and waken him, and warn him, and help him? Where did her loyalties lie? She had struggled earnestly before in this house – at the foot of these very stairs – with conflicting loyalties, one the almost gravitational pull towards her father, the other her attraction towards Tresham's father when he had come amongst them on his sporting tour. She had stood before at the bottom of these stairs, considering the two calls on her heart, and wondering how much wickedness there was in her yearning to mount them.

By the time the Minister had again walked the four miles to Eileann Lappich the long September evening had begun to fade at last into

[26]

dusk. The tide was at its ebb as he crossed the mud-flats at the head of the sea loch, the wind had dropped with the setting sun, and all around his rapid-striding black figure a wet light gleamed on the sand. Ahead of him the rising shore, and massy trees sheltering the laird's policies, loomed dark as night.

There was nothing comfortable between Minister and laird at that time. By the Veto Act of 1834 the patron of the living, the laird, had been obliged to have his choice of incumbent confirmed by the heads of families in the parish. Thus the autocracy of the laird had been eroded, allowing the Minister to rival his power. Now, however, the House of Lords decreed the Veto Act unconstitutional. Rather than fall back into the absolute power of the lairds, many ministers, half the ministry indeed, contemplated seceding from the Assembly altogether, and forming a Free Church supported by parishioners.

Should he secede? Abandon benefice and manse? And would he take his wild parishioners with him if he did so, and would they support him, or would they cling to the coat-tails of their laird after all, out of fear and custom, and accept whatever creature of his own he put up in their pulpit? In that case where would he find himself, for he had not a penny piece but what he earned? The questions bothered his mind just as the cloud of midges in which he walked bothered his eyes. He tried to think what was best for the parish. He tried not to despise his parishioners. He even tried to think charitably of the laird.

Before the Veto Act he used to compare his position *vis-à-vis* the laird with the position of the Bishop of Jerusalem *vis-à-vis* the Turkish pasha of that city: both were Christian incumbents dependent upon a heathen civil power. Now it was so again. All power lay with the barbarous pasha of Eileann Lappich in his castle amid the circle of oaks which the Minister now approached. Matching the fluttering of apprehension in his heart, jackdaws like flakes of night spilled out of the tower as he strode into the yard.

It was a tumbledown affair. Four storeys of rough stone, narrow windows piercing it more or less at random, were capped with a slate roof, blue slate which now rather beautifully shone in the clear sky of evening up there above the trees. Grass, ferns, even rowan trees, grew crazily out of the tower. The arched doorway was reached by a flight of steps into the first storey of the building, and up these steps and in through that arch the Minister walked, relying upon the clash of his boots to announce him.

He found the family eating in a hall stinking of mutton-fat candles. The clatter of their knives on plates echoed on bare stone walls, and did not cease with the Minister's entrance. But the midges at least had left off tormenting him. He greeted them all, the two sullen boys, their large swollen-faced mother with her shifty wet eyes, and the popinjay at the table's head. He alone, the autocrat, laid down his knife to mock the Minister's greeting by raising a finger to the spot where his forelock might have been had his head not been bald and freckled.

'Is it you, McPhee, back again?' he said. 'Better stop for a mouthful to eat this time round. Better stop all night indeed – stop a week if you want, eh, and then you can finish your business without wearing out your boots.'

The Minister listened with a smile affixed to his features, leaning his weight on his hands on the table board, and watched the little man crowing out his mockery.

'I thank you,' he replied in lofty tone, 'but I have no need to take meat or rest when I step from my house to yours, for you are the nearest to me of all my parishioners – as this world measures distance.'

'So, then,' the laird said, sticking out his legs in their plaid trousers and folding hands on his stomach, 'how can I oblige you, man, if not with food or a chair? I suppose what it is, I suppose you've found out the truth of what passed on the hill at Craigour this day, eh?'

The Minister replied in his sternest voice, 'It has been shown to me that I spoke hastily in my accusing.' The confession rang round the hall like a further and graver accusation. 'Though I have no doubt that your two boys here are not blameless,' he went on majestically, 'nor do they stand guilty of all the wickedness I laid against them in my heart, and so I am come, as I am bound to do, to beg their pardon.'

'There, my boys!' squeaked out the laird in glee. 'The Reverend Mister Norman McPhee begs your pardon!' The candles guttered in his shout, as the two great bare-legged boys shifted on their bench without looking up at the Minister or their father. 'Though I'm glad to hear he doesn't think you blameless, or I might have had call to beg your pardon myself for the drubbing you had of me just now. So, Mr McPhee,' he went on, 'your wee grandson from London has

[28]

changed his tune has he? Was it he tried to bed with the slut in the glen, was it? And my brave boys fought him off her?'

The Minister's knuckles whitened where he leaned on them. 'I have learned of other circumstances,' he said, 'and I came to tell you I had so learned. Now if you will allow it I will leave you.'

The laird waved his hand in the air, and took up his fork again to go on with his meat. 'Goodbye, McPhee! Will you send the brat over to me for his beating, or will you beat him well yourself for his damned lies against his betters? For we must set an example of truth-speaking, must we not, among my poor savage people as you think them! Goodbye!'

The Minister, having bowed to them all, had already stalked out of the smoky hall, with its candle-sconces on the walls flaring ruddy pools on the stone. Out of the tower's windows as he strode away there spilled a clamour of laughter which pursued him under the trees, and made a Christian spirit hard to nurture on his long walk home in the dark.

*　　*　　*

Dearest Step-papa [wrote Tresham next day in the room to which he had been confined], I cannot tell you what a delightful visit we have made to Grandpapa's. Of the railing we did I could write you a volume. The speed sometimes would have astonished you, but I was not a bit alarmed. At Leeds we saw a pile of stones of 120,000 tons which had been broken by the paupers of the place, is it not sad work for them? On the railways and on the steamboat we never left off saying how wise of Papa to advise us to go by steam, for afterwards the coach seemed quite slow and dull. I was glad we had not come in the coach from Perth to Inverness. I have attended to the geology of the mountains most particularly as you wished it. Here on the sea-coast you may see the transition plainly from red arenaceous sandstone to light grey and even white crystalline quartz rock inland, resting on vertical strata of gneiss and mica schist. The mountains are very fine. But I do not just gaze at them, I learn all about them I can, as you see. I have not forgotten what you told me the man at Oxford said, see, I can write it down for you – 'Geology gives that intellectual foundation which is required to make the testimony of the eye fruitful and

[29]

satisfying'. I love to walk among the mountains. I have found besides rubrus chamaemorus and betula nana the pinguicula lusitanica and nymphae alba. The lichen grows on the birch trunks so that the old trees exactly resemble stones. You would smile to see how they plough the ground here, with what they call a cashcroom I think. They fish for lobsters too, but they do not fish as hard as Grandpapa says they ought, that is done by others who come from Moray to steal away the cod and ling. I enquire about all these matters because I attend to your precept, not to Wonder but to Question, and so to proceed onto the firm ground of Answers. I walked up a mountain yesterday expressly to add a piece of granitic rock to my collection and an ugly incident befell. As I walked I saw three Boys attack a Maid and throw her down and beat her, and when I ran up though I fought stiffly they threw me down too and beat me. They stuck big forks they have for salmon into Grandpapa's dog called Gaisgeach which means Hero. They hit me on my head so that I swooned. Of course it is a trifle and not a great Adventure but they did not believe me. But I showed them the marks on Gaisgeach and they had to believe me then. Only they didn't. But now Mamma and Grandpapa do not quite agree and I am shut up upstairs. Of course the marks were nearly gone when I showed them, but Mamma could see the fork marks. I have not neglected to work at Greek which I will do now. I have read the half of Xenophon now for the School entrance. I think the fork marks on Gaisgeach would have quite satisfied Grandpapa was he not disposed to take the word of the Laird over the Truth, for his position depends upon the Laird you know.

Your affectionate stepson,
T. Pitcher.

II

THE WINDOW OF TRESHAM'S ATTIC ROOM in Laidlaw Villa faced north
over the oblong of garden lying behind the house. At a table in the
window he sat over his book. He defeated the Greek words one by one
and forced them to contribute their mite of sense to the narrative. By
these laborious means he had followed Xenophon and his mercenaries
across the Mesopotamian deserts to Persia; and he felt he had crawled
after them on all fours every inch of the way. He was bored by the
book's contents till he hated every inkstain and blemish upon the book
itself. However (and this was Tresham's strength) he knew that he had
made himself master of those contents thus far, and could satisfy any
examiner who questioned him on them, so that he no more despaired
of finishing the task before him than his stubborn inner spirit had
despaired of reaching the manse door the day he had been knocked
down on the hill. It was necessary to labour through the book in order
to enter the great School which his stepfather believed to be the key
to superior fortune; and within himself was a spirit capable of the
task. As to the 'superior fortune', he had no opinion about that: he
concerned himself with the journey and not the objective.

If he looked up, he would see the garden below, its painted summerhouse at the end of the grass walk, the thinnish screen of trees which
half obscured with their leaves the hazy, smoky view over London
lying to the north. It was possible in a clear light to glimpse the coloured
sails of barges on the river. This hint of voyages – firing memory of his
own travels by sea that summer – could scarcely be resisted whenever
it crossed his mind that the sails might be there to be seen if he looked
up. So he looked up. Smoke lay in windless drifts too close upon the
dark mass of the city for the river's course to be traced through it, and
he saw no coloured sails. The grey gravel plains of Mesopotamia cannot have looked more dreary to Xenophon's Ten Thousand, or more

unlike the sea-girt isles they pined for, than the scene from his window looked to Tresham.

In the garden below, the cat was stalking a sparrow. He watched. The creature, a black cat belonging to Eliza, crept along on its belly firing out through its eyes such beams of malevolence that Tresham could not believe that the doomed sparrow, dusting himself on a path, was unaware of the evil one stalking him. He had wings, why did he not fly away? Alarmed, Tresham rose and leaned over his table to knock on the window glass – but he saw in the summerhouse his step-uncle, a clergyman; and he saw that his step-uncle too was watching the cat. Tresham could not interfere. There sat the Reverend Marcus Wytherstone, knees in black breeches apart, a hand fondling the gold chain across his waistcoat, florid and portly, intent upon hunter and victim.

The cat sprang: dust flew: wings fluttered. The cat was loping off, prize in mouth, when she found a malacca stick hooked round her neck. The Reverend Marcus had moved rapidly, and struck surely. Angrily the cat scratched at the stick, lost the bird, clawed at it, missed, and cantered off in the wispy style of the species.

What power! thought Tresham looking down at his step-uncle. To interrupt the hunt – to clap his hands or rap the glass – would have been nothing: but to save the victim in the very jaws of its fate seemed to Tresham very grand. The victim, for one thing, knew that its life had been spared, and knew the identity of its saviour. And the adversary with the morsel in his mouth could never be sure of victory with such a power at hand. He was thinking these thoughts when he became aware that his step-uncle was signalling to him, beckoning him down into the garden with the malacca cane which had been so fatal to the cat's hopes. By way of reply he held up his Xenophon. He saw his uncle's lips puff out a disdainful rejection of the excuse. Happy with this permission he hurried down through the house. Even in Mr Wytherstone's own house his clerical elder brother was a superior power.

Mr Wytherstone, of course, was at business in Mincing Lane. May and Eliza were at the haberdasher's. His mother, busy at the linen-cupboard with Meg the maidservant, called out to Tresham as he ran downstairs, 'Tresh, dear, should you give up your books so early?'

'Uncle Marcus wants me.'

'Well, dear, Uncle Marcus isn't . . . it is Step-papa must be obeyed – obliged, you know. Your examination is so important to him.'

'I shall pass it, Mamma.'

'Uncle Marcus – has he told you to call him "Uncle Marcus", by the by?'

'Yes, Mamma.'

'It sounds so . . . but there, if he likes it. Yes, he has offered to take us all to the Tower, the girls as well, and it would be a blow if you weren't done with your books in time for such a jaunt as that would be.'

'But Mamma, we've been on our own to the Tower, you and I.'

He looked into the linen-cupboard, but darkness concealed the expression of her face when she replied rather vaguely, 'Ah, have we, my dear? Perhaps they aren't quite aware of where you and I have been on our rambles.'

'I'll read like bricks, depend upon it, and I'll be ready.'

Full of love for his mother's innocent duplicity, he ran on downstairs. There were few of the sights in London, which were interesting to her curiosity, which she had not taken her son to see on their gallivants together, from the ballooning at Vauxhall to the Elgin marbles at Montagu House. It was understood tacitly between them that these expeditions were a shared secret: secret journeys for which they planned and provisioned, the objective of no importance to Tresham beside the private delightful fact of the two of them on their travels together. They walked the streets, or sat in an omnibus, or ate their meal in a chophouse, within a cocoon of shared adventure continued in his mind from days beyond precise memory, though recalled by the word 'Italy', before their wanderings had fetched up at Laidlaw Villa. This vagabond feeling of freedom, and of a kind of precariousness which went with it, was sharpest among the flares and shadows of the walks at the Vauxhall Gardens, a dangerous landscape full of collisions with stumbling figures, and harsh voices, and violent music, and the uprush of fireworks through the dark, where his hold on his mother's hand was tightest, but his awareness most vivid.

When he reached the summerhouse he found his uncle reading. One stout calf in its black stocking rested on the other knee while his hand caressed his snowy stock and his attention seemed altogether absorbed in the quarter-bound octavo volume held up to his face. Tresham waited. From beyond the garden wall came the continual uneven rolling of iron-shod wheels on the road, with which was mixed the hundred differing inflexions of weariness, or lameness, or high spirits, in the horses pulling the traffic. Now and then all sound would cease, and into the queer silence would come the hasty rapid rush of one set of hooves and wheels alone; and then once again would resume the treadmill grind of wheels smiting stone. This is what the world really sounds like, said Tresham to himself as he listened, surprised at the strangeness and unfamiliarity of it after his lonely morning with Xenophon and his own thoughts.

The boy's hands grew larger, his coatsleeves shorter, in the awkwardness of waiting before his uncle's chair. However, if there was a good deal of annihilation in being ignored by Uncle Marcus, there was (as the sparrow had found out) a sense of being restored to life in attracting his notice.

'Remarkable!' he cried, laying down his book. 'Remarkable fellow! Burns, you know, his travels into Bokhara, and I don't know where else besides. You shall read them. Such courage and so forth as the fellow has. Remarkable!'

'I should like to read them, sir, when you have done.'

'And so you shall. Did you know, by the by, that that other fellow, great Eastern traveller, Mr Fraser – did you know he lived at Inverness? Yes, yes, at Easter Moniak just by, with all the other Frasers, I suppose. I say so because of your Scotch journey. And did you go in for view-hunting as May and Eliza were telling us they did? Can you draw? Or did you shoot and fish as your papa used to do?'

Except his mother, no one spoke of his father to Tresham – no one here had known his father – and he loved to hear the name freely used, as his Uncle Marcus sometimes did, for it seemed to release his father from his tomb at Rimini, and put the idea of him into circulation again. 'We tried at fishing in the sea from Grandpapa's boat,' he said, 'and I should have liked to fish in the river where Papa caught ever so many salmon. But Grandpapa didn't care to ask the laird if I might.'

'Well, you shall come and shoot with me when you are a little older, at Rainshaw. And fish too, as soon as I have made a lake. What do you say? Shall you come and fish in my new lake?'

[34]

'I should like it awfully, sir.' The sparkle in his eyes expressed how gratifying was the invitation.

'So, in Scotland you were busy collecting up stones, is that it?' the clergyman next asked, laying his fingers together in an arch on his waistcoat. 'I have looked at the letter you wrote to your step-papa, do you see,' he explained.

'Step-papa wished me to take notice of how the mountains are formed.'

'Quite so. But I fancy from your dear mamma that you liked to wander abroad on the mountains a good deal, too, did you not – whether they was formed of arenaceous sandstone or plum pudding!'

Tresham said nothing. Grown-ups knew so much more about you than they had learned by fair means: they handed about your letters, and revealed what you had confided, and always betrayed trust. So he said nothing. His step-uncle continued:

'Was it the views you cared for, then, or what was it took you upon the mountains? Come, you see I am interested.'

'Not the views quite – ' Tresham's resolution to give away nothing more broke down at once in face of interest – 'it was being far up and ... and the mist trailing, and the sound of water when you came to it. And then going so far and so high I thought I was lost.' He looked cautiously at his step-uncle, half afraid he had made himself foolish.

'Very good, very good! There's a deal more sense in that than there is in arenaceous sandstone. Never put science above feeling. It's a dull dog who will put what the mountains are made of above the grand notions it puts into his head to walk about upon them. Your step-papa don't, you know, not at bottom. He may talk as he did last night about fixing upon the facts, but at bottom that's all humbug. Yes, yes. Why, bless me, do you suppose he is in tea for the facts? Not a bit. Did you ever hear him speak of his idea of operning up the India trade by pushing tea over the Karakoram into the bazaars at Kashgar? Did you not? Well, he keeps it from you, no doubt, but that is why he is in the tea trade, depend upon it – for the romance of the thing! That's what keeps him in Mincing Lane – and keeps us all at our posts, if we're worth tuppence. You enquire of him how many tangs a jing you may expect large-leaf Bohea to fetch at Yarkand, and see if his eye don't light up! You see if it don't.'

[35]

He laughed: and Tresham couldn't tell whether the whole conceit about his stepfather and the tea trade was a piece of mockery or not. Then Uncle Marcus went on, with the air of expansiveness flattering to a child:

'If I was in tea I should fix my thoughts upon Kashgar too, I dare say, shouldn't you? Well, well, I go on upon these things and I dare say I'm a bore.'

'No, no,' said Tresham, 'I'm not bored a bit.'

'Having no family, do you see, and caring little for company at home, I don't know what bores people and what don't. Xenophon now, I suppose that bores you, don't it? Well, if you can master what bores you, and make it serve your purpose, you'll have learned a great lesson. A great lesson. Geology, now, and Greek – and Mincing Lane too – are such stuff as the mountains are made of, so to say, which you must get your foot upon if you are to enjoy the fine views and noble sentiments of your mountain walks. Ah well. Tell me, now,' he said suddenly, looking into Tresham's face, 'what about this dog of your Grandpapa's?'

'Gaisgeach?' Tresham was taken aback.

'If that is the dog you say was speared on the mountain.'

'He was, they did.'

'It wasn't the girl was attacked? You didn't see her ill-used? It wasn't something too wicked to tell, that you saw?'

Tresham hesitated. His eyes gleamed at the chance of being understood. But he remembered the deceit of grown-ups. 'No. It was only the dog.'

'If you say so.' A look of petulance, at a trap fruitlessly sprung, tightened the clergyman's lips.

Tresham added: 'It's true it was worse than I told. But not about her. There was just more than I could say.'

'Just so.' Uncle Marcus nodded, his eyes softening again. 'There was more to it than could be told by telling what occurred. Is that right?'

'That's right.'

'Well,' said his step-uncle, tapping the book on the table, 'half old Burns here is yarns, I don't doubt, but if he succeeds in making me understand what I should feel if I was to travel through the wilds of Turkestan, what care I if he's yarning? He's telling me the truth, ain't he, no matter if he takes a liberty now and then with the facts. It don't do to set up facts above the truth.'

Tresham grasped through this exegesis that what had happened on the hill above Craigour – and what he had made of it – was understood by his step-uncle, and allowed. Then, with a chuckle, Uncle Marcus issued his warning:

'Poor Burns, though, poor fellow, took himself in at last, with his swell talk, for I believe he persuaded himself the Afghans were not to be feared, not by him at least, and that was how he came to stop amongst them too long at Cabool last November, and was pulled in pieces for his pains. Maybe a yarn doesn't hurt, if it puts your listeners in the way of grasping your true meaning, but believing your own yarns – we won't call them lies – leads you into all manner of pickles. All manner of pickles.'

He took up his book and began to read, vanishing from Tresham as suddenly as if he had stepped into a balloon and been carried away to the Turkestan of Burns's *Travels*.

Adolphus Wytherstone's door key, rattling in the lock on his return from Mincing Lane each evening at six o'clock, caused every heart in the house to sink. This he did not intend, and might have been surprised and saddened to learn. If he was a tyrant, it wasn't because he had seized power, or even wanted it. A tyrant's power had been wished upon him by the females of the household as an easy way of accounting to their consciences for the distance between themselves and him. In his own heart he thought himself neglected, slighted, overlooked by his family, who seemed to be too busy about the occupations they followed without him to include him into their lives when he came home. If he asked what they had done with the day, the girls would twist their hands and look sideways, irritating him; yet, if they rushed to tell him some event, an invitation come in the post, or an encounter with so-and-so at Mr Batten's Circulating Library, or a mishap to a horse at their gate, he could not pretend much interest. He resented the necessity of getting money, to which he attributed this separation from his family, and the habit of resentment had become engrained into his nature.

[37]

All day life went on in the private amiable ways of the family, the girls walking to the windmill, or peeping over the wall into the paradisiacal grounds of The Shrubberies, or sewing if wet; Tresham in his attic or consorting with the gardener's boy; Mrs Wytherstone busily up and down stairs: but the rattle of Mr Wytherstone's latch key sent through each the tremor which Ulysses' men may have felt when Polyphemus returned at evening to the cave in which he kept them prisoner, and made ready to eat one of their number.

His younger brother's domestic tyranny, however come by, did not in the least affect the Reverend Marcus Wytherstone.

'Well, Dolly,' he said when his brother came upstairs into the drawing room that evening, 'sold any tea, have you?'

Adolphus didn't answer this. He walked to the window with its view of sooty trees, where he stood for a moment rubbing thin hands with his back to his brother. Their blood-relationship might have been guessed, though Marcus was rosy, and glossy, where his brother was grey and pinched and rather threadbare. Consciousness of this cheapness beside his brother was amongst the causes of Adolphus's peevishness in Marcus's presence. For a moment he couldn't even remember whether it was deliberately insulting in Marcus, or merely customary between brothers, for the man to remain seated like that, one fat leg cocked on the other, when he himself entered the room after toiling all day in the dust and heat of September.

'I should have thought,' he said, turning from the window as if some spectacle in the roadway had disgusted him, 'I should have supposed, Marcus, that you might have wearied of finding anything comical about the tea trade, in the twenty years I have been obliged to earn a living in it.'

Marcus chuckled, and held out the newspaper he had been reading. 'Do you want this, do you? Nothing in it, riots and so forth, Peel fiddling with the tariffs.'

'I'm surprised you call the riots "nothing",' said his brother, taking the paper, but throwing it onto a table and continuing to pace the room. 'Kent will have the worst of it, you see if it don't. You'll have a few rick fires in the parish, shouldn't wonder.'

'I doubt it, Dolly, I doubt it. No unemployment with us, do you see, or none to notice.'

Adolphus gave a sour little laugh. 'Employing them all yourself, are you? On your building and your lake-making, eh?'

'Why shouldn't others do the same? Other landowners. Employ the poor fellows the farmers have turned off.'

'I suppose, Marcus,' huffed his brother, 'I suppose not every parson in the land wants a lake in his view, or a tower full of books in his park – ever think of that? – no, and couldn't afford to pay for them neither, not even at starvation wages.'

'Come, Dolly, that's unworthy in you. I don't pay starvation wages, and you know I don't. Not I. Allow me a little virtue in my fancy. And I'm only making a few repairs to the old place, you know, to keep it weathertight,' he went on, ignoring his brother's satirical laugh. 'I've to compete with the railways for labour now, for one or other of these great railway nabobs has started out driving a line into the parish, did you know of that? Yes, yes, we have the navvy encampments a few miles off now, and a deucedly unsettling influence on the parish they are too, I can tell you, with their liquor and their poaching ways.'

'And their work.'

'Yes, they bring work, no doubt of it. Confound them. For there's no doubt either but that things would go along a great deal quieter with us if they wasn't parading through the county offering high wages and an outlaw's life to all who'll take it.'

'Ah, things would always go along a great deal quieter if there wasn't any progress, Marcus.'

'I'm not so sure as you are that upset is progress.'

'I dare say not, no, for you've a great deal more to be upset than what I have.' It was the unassailable good humour of his brother which brought out all the tartness in Mr Wytherstone. And why indeed should he not be good-humoured, with the family manor-house and the rent of seven farms to live upon, as well as the stipend of a rich benefice of which he was patron as well as incumbent? In his place Adolphus would have been good-humoured too, he was sure. It was the constraint of fitting into the mean space which life allowed him, like the figure of a saint cramped into a lancet window, which crabbed Mr Wytherstone's happiness. There, Marcus only smiled off his last peevish remark!

'I believe it's your romantic nature the railways appeal to, Dolly,'

Marcus was saying, 'I do indeed. Tea whirled about the globe on the wings of steam, eh, isn't that it? Isn't that it, ma'am?' he added to Mrs Wytherstone, who now came into the room. He had risen from his chair and now watched her stretch up and kiss her husband. 'Now then, Dolly,' he went on, 'if you won't admit to being in love with the romance of steam, we shall be forced to conclude that your interest in railways is plunging your money into railway stock, you know.'

'Upon my soul, Marcus!' burst out his brother, pushing away his wife's embrace. 'You do provoke me! What is it to you how I manage my affairs? Precious little you know of having dependants, and poverty. Precious little!'

'You won't serve your dependants by risking your capital in some tomfool railway scheme, that's certain,' retorted Marcus.

'Capital?' A spot of colour had appeared in Adolphus's grey cheeks. 'What capital have I ever had, pray? And how can the trifle a man in my place may save – how can such a trifle serve to dig his dependants out of the pit his poverty has buried them in, eh?'

'Pit? Poverty? Come, Dolly –'

'Yes – pit! Poverty! What do you know of it at Rainshaw there? It is a pit, I say! Oh, the girls may dig themselves out, no doubt, a girl may always make a fortunate match. But what of Tresham? Is he to fail as I have failed, for want of a fair start?'

'But if he is to go away to this great school – '

'And how is it to be paid for? Eh?'

There was silence, until Mrs Wytherstone said in an agitated voice, 'Oh, my dear, perhaps he should not go away to school, after all, if it means risking everything. Might he not stop with us at home, and go on at Mr Pritchard's?'

'He is your son and not mine,' said Mr Wytherstone coldly, 'but I should have supposed you would appreciate what I intend for him. However, if you are indifferent to his future, I suppose he may as well apprentice himself to some trade or other at once.' He took up the newspaper.

Marcus's broad back was at the window, looking out, while he jingled the money in his breeches pocket. Mrs Wytherstone sank into a chair. The fear that her husband was speculating in railways stock haunted her day and night. In every report of ruin by the railway fever

[40]

which she read, she saw the spectre of uncertainty and homelessness returning to claim her after these comfortable years at Laidlaw Villa. Poverty! He thought this was poverty! He should have seen her – Heaven forbid! – the night in the post-house at Dôle when it had been necessary to raise by any means the *vetturino* fare for her onward journey, and no means remained. Her dead husband's possessions had been sold already, save his sword, which she would not sell. Tresham was asleep in her arms in a blanket hopping with fleas. Round her by the flare of torches raged drunken ostlers and shouting postillions. Bread, a corner to rest in, the promise of a place in tomorrow's *vetturino* – to gain these marvellous riches for herself and her child she was desperate enough for any act. And he mistook *this* for poverty!

*　　*　　*

Laidlaw Villa
Scone Walk
Clapham,   August the 27th, 1845

My dear Marcus,
　　You will be surprised to receive a letter from me, and I assure you that only the unhappiest circumstances have compelled me to take the course of appealing to you. The appeal is made, not to your generosity (that would reduce me to the extremity of begging), but to your concern for justice, which, I am sure, will allow that, whilst I have fared but meagrely in the world's goods, into your hand has fallen by the chance of primogeniture all the good things to which we were both born.
　　I will put the matter shortly, for it is as painful to me to record the way in which I have been deceived, as it will be painful to you to read of such wickedness as has been practised against me. I have long wished that the money which I have set aside, by great frugality in my living, for giving to my dear Wife's son an opportunity in life less straitened than my own, might be expanded into a sum sufficient to provide endowments for my own daughters May and Elizabeth. With every man upon 'Change making his fortune by railway speculation, why should

[41]

I not take the opportunity of thus providing for my children?

I took up Stock, therefore, after judicious enquiry, in the Ruabon and Wrexham Grand Junction Company, being assured that the Line was required as well for the movement of coals as for the movement of Welshmen, that it had been surveyed, and that work upon it would shortly commence. I was widely congratulated in Capel Court on my bargain, and was, indeed, importuned on all sides to part with some of my Stock.

After many months of silence, and growing concern, I learned from a small paragraph in one of the Railway newspapers, that the Line was not to be proceeded with. Attempts to dispose of my Stock at Capel Court were now greeted with heartless mirth. The scrip was valueless. The villains behind this scheme to defraud honest men of their savings had long since decamped with my funds.

I will be quite frank. I had invested all that I had by me, some £400, residue of that £650 left to me by our dear Mother, which I had resolved to employ in the purchase of a superior education for Tresham, as well as further moneys borrowed to increase my holding in the Line. Of all this I have been defrauded. The £400 is a loss I must stand. Further to it, I owe £500, with interest, to the merciless tribe of Jews who, having advanced me money eagerly enough in my prosperity, now gorge themselves upon my misfortune.

I must withstand, as I say, all these punishments for the fault of having attempted to assist my children, just as I have withstood all the misfortunes of my life. For myself, I have long ceased to look for justice in this world. Is there, however, any particle of equity in a society which suffers the child's hopes to be blighted with the parents, when remedy within his own family lies to hand? Is it not a wrong, that Tresham should be obliged to leave the great school in which he is become a luminary, and should lose all opportunity in life, because a vindictive world has destroyed myself? – is that not a wrong which a Christian would consider it his privilege to set right?

You professed a partiality for Tresham when you saw him here some years ago. I believe you would be gratified by his development. You have no offspring of your own, and, of course, an ample income from our family's possessions. You will, I am sure, grasp at this opportunity to continue the boy's education in a school which will furnish him with all the advantages lacked by his unfortunate stepfather, who is also, my dear Marcus,

yr affec. brother,

A. Wytherstone.

PS A further severe vexation has come upon me just now, which I tell you only to show how a man, once down, must consider himself within reach of harassment by any who care to try it, even criminals and tramps. In the severe weather last Winter, an old vagrant, who had laid himself down under my garden wall for warmth (the wall being heated just there for the stone fruit by a flue from the hot-house stove which I installed on your advice) succeeded in pulling all down a-top of himself, and so perished in the fall. Aside from the expense of rebuilding my wall, the tramp's demise – one might say, his culpable suicide – has been the source of much irritation to me by the authorities, who pretend to believe that the wall had been deliberately rendered into a dangerous state by the insertion of flues!
A.W.

If, by the way, you should wish to renew your acquaintance with Tresham, before deciding as to his future hopes, he would run down to Rainshaw before the end of the present Holiday.

III

——•——•——•——•——•——•——•——•——

ON A FOGGY AUTUMN MORNING IN 1845 Tresham Pitcher and a school
friend drove through the London streets on their way to the terminus
of the South Eastern Railway at London Bridge. Tresham was
travelling by the railway to stay with his Uncle Marcus in Kent, and
his friend was come to see him off.

'I hope it ain't a bore, Cropper, old fellow.'

'Of course it's a bore, Twesh – but not half such a damned bore as
stopping at home.'

Cropper was a great swell in both boys' eyes, lying back in the four-
wheeler with his hat-brim on his nose. Tresham had been staying
with Cropper's people in Park Street for a day or two, glad to quit
Clapham for the West End, so the two of them were very intimate,
and Cropper had enquired all particulars of his friend's uncle's place
in Kent.

In his replies Tresham had allowed fancy a free hand. He had
described an establishment of servants and horses, sport over a dozen
farms, a mansion of the olden times lying at the centre of it all. To
admit that he had never seen Rainshaw Park, after hinting at his easy
intimacy with his rich uncle, had been impossible; it was in this point
alone, his connexion with a landed estate, that his own circumstances
outshone Cropper's, and he was obliged to consolidate upon his
strength, if he was to keep in the swim with heavy swells like Cropper
at school.

When they reached the London Bridge station the boys strolled onto
the platform followed by an urchin lugging Tresham's bags. Under
the station roof smoke and fog and steam mingled in a gritty cloud
which was pulsed through for Tresham with the rush and excitement
of departure. He had not known how it would quicken the blood in
his veins. Supposing such feelings, like all natural response, to be

incorrect according to Cropper, he concealed them.

'I say, Twesh,' said his friend, tapping the wood of the carriage with his cane, 'you sure you ought to twust this contwaption to take you into Kent?'

'Oh, Lord, yes,' Tresham replied as he stepped languidly aboard without daring to examine the tall-funnelled black engine fuming like a dragon at the platform end. 'I've travelled ever so far on the railways, you know. When I ran up to Scotland the other year, to my grandfather's place, I railed where I could. Get the boy to give me my bags, will you?'

'Here, you, put the gentleman's baggage aboard and look sharp.'

The two swells stood aside for the ragged boy to lift the bags into the train. Though wanting to help him, Tresham accepted that whatever line his friend took in such matters was the proper one. His sense of the privilege bestowed on him by two years' attendance at a great school – his awareness of the distance between Clapham and Park Street – showed itself in his conviction that what other boys did naturally was correct, and what he would naturally have done was probably a solecism. Cropper was awfully watchful for slips.

'Wailed up to Scotland? Did you? Oh, I dare say you told me. I say, old fellow, you do get about the shop, don't you? Quite the twaveller.' He looked up respectfully at Tresham, who had now closed the carriage door, and was leaning upon it.

Tresham saw – he saw in a flash, amongst the smoke and reverberations of his departure, and in his friend's respect – he understood how it was that travel frees you from identification with one dull spot or another. Like a butterfly on its way between two cabbages, the traveller appears to be a part, not of the cabbages, but of the light and air between.

*   *   *

The train ran into the station nearest Rainshaw Park after a journey of two hours or so. Misty autumn sunlight had succeeded the fog of London, and Tresham had been looking out eagerly at scenes of wood and orchard which the smoking train dashed through. Part of the

[45]

delight of speedy travel – the rushing scene and flying perspectives – was that no object, however boring in itself, remained long enough in view to bore the traveller. Nor were thoughts static and wearisome at a train window. Causes and consequences disappeared like houses and haystacks – Cropper had vanished behind, Rainshaw was in the mists ahead – all that existed was himself in this rocking, rattling reality. Now the journey was over. The platform, when he stepped down upon it with his baggage, was like the harbour quay of a foreign land, after the fluxing seas of travel from the London Bridge station.

Off rushed the engine in explosions of steam and thunderous blasts of smoke driven upwards, the clanking carriages dragged after it, the speed already terrific by the platform's end, under a bridge – gone! Peace poured in upon the scene, the very sunlight repaired itself where the smoke had driven holes in its rays. Tresham felt that he had been propelled through the clouds and dropped into another epoch.

In the yard outside the station, where he waited with his bags, the bustle occasioned by the train had already subsided, carts and traps departing between the hedgerows, stationmaster and porters disappearing within the new brick building set down amid fields and hopyards, silence returning. Then a gig drove into the yard, and the dry little gingery man with the reins called to him, 'You for Rainshaw?'

'Yes,' said Tresham.

'Get up, then.'

'Take my bag, will you?'

'You can put that on,' the driver said.

For reply Tresham threw the carpet-bag up at him. Obliged to catch it, dropping his reins, the man's surliness was corrected. No one is a better judge of when he is being slighted than a schoolboy used to holding his position only by the unsleeping exertion of dominance over those who challenge it. They drove out of the yard in silence.

It was a drive of three miles to Rainshaw. This Tresham discovered, and the man's name, which was Branch, but otherwise he asked no questions, and Branch volunteered no information. Wide views of the landscape were not revealed from the crooked road they took between the fields; the gig was carried forward into a misty scene in process of creation around them, and of dissolution behind them. The autumn sun glowed down mildly and sadly upon what was near, and upon the mist which vaguened all beyond. Woods, farms, orchards, came into being as they passed, warm scenes complete with dogs lying in the dust, children staring, women entering sheds with clanking pails; they passed a hopyard which, opening its long green arbours to his view, carried Tresham back almost beyond memory to glimpses of Italian vineyards; then these things too were gone into memory and mist. Ahead lay Rainshaw, waiting, like all else in the landscape, for his arrival to bring it into existence out of the mist.

'Our gates, these.' Branch's voice was a little warmer, that of a sour man attempting sweetness. 'No lodge nor gatekeeper this end, see. Only goes nowhere Squire ever goes, this road. Only goes to railway mostly.' Evidently he did not like to ask Tresham to get down and open the gate, after the carpet-bag incident.

Tresham jumped down. He swung open the gate and the gig entered the park. A grove of beech trees on a bank overhung the spot, so that it was not until the gig had ascended out of their shade that a prospect opened across parkland to the façade of the house. Tresham looked eagerly at his destination. Oaks clustered near, everywhere the great oaks clustered and watched from the slopes of the park. Behind the bulk of the house, and its slim tall chimneys rising from slate roofs, was a screen of trees melted together by mist into green vagueness. The impression that the scene gave to Tresham was of dignified old age, and old timber, dozing under the beams of a declining sun.

Confusing events now rushed in on Tresham, as they often do on arrival at journey's end, breaking in upon the dreamy equilibrium of travel. He was aware of the gig's wheels on gravel under the entrance front, of a woman in a dark dress at a porch door. Then he was in a wide shadowy room smelling of woodsmoke, columns supporting its ceiling, dark furniture against panelled walls, the sound of his boots rather loud on oak floors. Ahead of him the woman – Mrs Poynder, she had said was her name – opened a door into a further narrow room which was walled with bookcases whose glass fronts reflected light from an arched window beyond. Against the light of the window was outlined his step-uncle turning the leaves of a folio spread on a lectern.

'Mr Tresham is come, sir,' said his guide.

The parson turned, looking surprised. 'Bless me, is it today?' he said, and, coming forward, held out two fingers to Tresham. 'Don't

[47]

touch anything, don't touch anything,' he went on, not unkindly. 'I dare say you're all over smoke and dirt, are you? See he has plenty of soap, Mrs Poynder. Confounded railways – wish they were at Jericho! I suppose you've had a bad journey? He'll want to rest, Mrs Poynder, so take him up directly. We'll meet at supper, and then you shall tell me all about it. These are the tombs at Palmyra, you know,' he said, tapping the open folio of engravings, 'you shall look at them, if it would amuse you. There may be a detail or two to suit a little building I'm putting up for myself, that is what I hope. Well, well. We shall see.' He re-applied himself to the engravings, and Tresham allowed himself to be led out by Mrs Poynder.

He next followed Mrs Poynder's rustling figure out of regions of carpets and comfort into one of hollow-sounding stairs and sparse furnishing, past countless doors and turnings, and views along silent passages, and cobwebbed windows allowing a glimpse of roof or sky, until she opened a door and showed him a small room under a sloping ceiling, with his bags forlorn upon its floor.

'Tom the boy will come for you when supper is served,' she said, and left him.

It did not occur to Tresham to wonder why, in a large and empty house, he had been allotted an attic under the roof. He was used to attic life. A chair, a bed, a candle in a brass stick, engravings of sea-battles of Nelson's time on the plaster walls; hot water fumed in a jug in a china dish, and the soap his uncle had prescribed lay near. Mists of evening having closed in around the house, the view from his window showed him nothing to satisfy curiosity. Sparrows quarrelled and rustled in the topmost leaves of a large magnolia. Sundry tappings and hammerings which he heard and felt in the fabric of the house must come, he surmised, from the scaffolding he had noticed over a part of the entrance front. The rush of his journey had cast him up high and dry on this remote and silent shore.

He was used to attic life, recognizing the world, so to speak, as he looked down upon it from a high angle. In the remoteness and silence he felt himself expand tendrils and feelers which would be at risk of being trampled upon or mocked in the hurly-burly downstairs. How it contrasted with life at school, though! In his attic at Laidlaw Villa the image had come into his head of an iron hoop bowled along the road, kept upright and rolling by noisy, hasty blows on its rim - this was himself at school – and of how the hoop, unsustained by the strife and din beating it along the highroad, would wobble, and totter, and fall into the dusty silent side-road of his own life alone. Which was best, the delicate expansion of thought and feeling in a quiet attic, or the vigour of sustaining yourself upright and rolling in the midst of life, the iron hoop on the highroad?

Stopping with Cropper in Park Street had been life in the highroad indeed, and so had the rush of his journey, and holding his own with old Branch in the gig; now, in this dim quiet space under the roof, the hoop wobbled and wavered towards collapse. A listening stillness pressed in from all the great empty house at the door.

At last the hall-boy Tom came for him, heard far off ascending stairs and approaching along corridors. Tresham followed him back through the silent, darkening house into the panelled hall. A door led into the dining room. Here, in a lofty bow-windowed room, Tresham found his step-uncle seated at the cloth with his back to the fire, already eating, and reading from a book on a stand beside his plate. He looked from Tom to Tresham with the air of one who finds the plot hard to follow, but quickly rallied, filling a plate for Tresham himself from the dishes on the table, and furnishing him with a book-rest to match his own taken from the immensely large mahogany sideboard.

'You may choose a book if you like it,' he said, indicating a heap of volumes on a round table in the bow window before taking up his napkin again and sitting down to his food and wine across the cloth from Tresham.

'I don't think I'll read just at once,' Tresham said.

The parson considered this with surprise. Then he resumed turning the leaves of his own book, and eating with his silver fork.

Tresham too began to eat, taking in the size and dignity of the room with covert glances. Its height, and plasterwork, and tall windows and heavy curtains, were the work of a later age than the hall; but its character was given to it by the portraits with which the walls were crowded, the faces and figures of innumerable men, women and children of the last two centuries. The stares of so many eyes upon him as he ate impressed Tresham mightily with the ancestry of his step-uncle. It seemed to explain the gloss of the man seated under this

[49]

gallery of forebears, that so many men and women had gone into his making.

'It is the habit of a lonely life,' said the rector suddenly, looking up from the page, 'reading at table. I could not change it.'

'Oh. . . pray. . . I shouldn't. . .'

'Or, that's to say, I could change it if I chose, of course,' he went on, 'but then I should have to change back again when you were gone away, and perhaps I should miss your company.' With that he resumed reading.

From time to time he would look up, now asking Tresham to throw some coals on the fire 'to save little Tom running in', now speaking of his book (an account of the Bokhara victims' fate), now holding out some treat or spectacle to be seen on the ramble he proposed taking next day to show his guest the place. Tresham saw that the book-rest was a ruse to save him making conversation when he had nothing he wished to say, and decided that he too would have a book open beside him at the next meal. Not bookish, he had no dislike of books, though he read them roughly, bending them open very wide in his big hands as if to dig out all he wanted the more easily. He thought how peaceably meals would go on at Laidlaw Villa if his stepfather stayed behind a book instead of wreaking upon his family all his petulance and acerbity.

More than he had been in London, Tresham was struck by likenesses between the two brothers. As a visitor at Clapham Uncle Marcus had been so inveterately cheerful, and richly dressed, and good-humoured, that he had seemed a world away from the gloomy tea-merchant; but here at home the parson's coat too was an old one, on his head he wore a skull cap like a scholar in a play, and he gave off hints of the testiness and petulance which Tresham knew so well in his stepfather. Aware of their similarities, Tresham could see how the brothers' different circumstances had allowed the expansion of the parson, and had obliged the diminution of the man of tea. If the well-to-do squire amongst his portraits and silver was testy at table, why, it was an allowable fad in such a man to read a book; had there been a whole family in the house with him, he could have shut himself up in his library – and not have forfeited a reputation for tolerance or affability by doing so – whilst wife and children disported themselves as rowdily as they pleased elsewhere. Wealth and a large house had dignified certain family traits into eccentricity, whilst poverty and cramped quarters, in his stepfather's case, had vitiated the same traits into disagreeable vices. Hard even to think of all these proud ladies and gentlemen looking down from the walls as ancestors of his stepfather, and his two stepsisters. They seemed to endorse only Uncle Marcus's blood, and rights. Without question, the squire of Rainshaw Park could do as he liked.

In keeping with these impressions it seemed to Tresham that the large undertakings he was shown next day – called by his uncle 'the repairs' – were a simple assertion of the squire's undoubted right, or even duty, to put his whims into practice.

Setting out from the house in the morning, they stood on the slope below the house's north elevation, and looked down upon a scene of peaceful activity. Below them the parkland, emerging from woods and groves of trees, made a shallow valley half a mile across through which a stream meandered amongst rushes. At the valley's end a dam was being constructed to contain the stream and form a lake. Eighty yards across, and twenty or so feet in depth, the dam was building out from both sides of the valley at once. A company of eighteen or twenty labourers were digging, and barrowing, and tipping, clay from two pits onto the dam's two wings. The clay was raw yellow, a violent colour in the landscape, and the barrows had cut two yellow weals in the turf between clay pits and dam. Round the clay pits, which glared like pots of ochre paint, women were sitting with children amongst the men's discarded shirts, and other children were tumbling about at the dam, or playing in the stream. A large solitary oak had been felled in full leaf in the middle of the valley, where the lake's water would be, and men were at work cutting up this fallen giant. The rasp of the saws, the cries of children, the creak of barrows – there was a harmony and serenity about this community at work under an autumn sun in the sheltered valley.

It impressed Tresham vastly. Such work going forward at his instructions magnified the powers of the man he stood beside so that the whole landscape, the oaks and wooded slopes themselves, seemed to radiate out from him in obedience to his ideas of order. There came into Tresham's mind a recollection of his uncle saving the sparrow from the cat's jaws in the garden at home.

'What should you say,' asked the squire, leaning on his stick and looking down at his works and his labourers, 'what should you say if you was to waken up one morning and find you had a labourer's life before you?'

Tresham laughed; then, realising from a glance at his step-uncle that the question was seriously intended, he replied, 'I should say, I had hoped I was fit for something better.'

'Better? That man does best, who best performs the part allotted him.'

'Then. . . then I hope I am to be allotted a better part.'

'Your famous school makes you hope for one, does it?'

Tresham met the eyes turned keenly and sardonically on him. 'Yes, it does, sir. A fellow finds out his worth, you know, if he can keep himself afloat there. The swells in the Sixth – why, they're such capital fellows they could succeed in any line they chose!'

Uncle Marcus knocked over a thistle with his stick and walked away down the slope. Over his shoulder he said, 'If your school makes you believe you may choose to play what part you fancy, then I fear it deludes you. Indeed it does.'

'Well, "deserve", Uncle Marcus,' replied Tresham, catching him up; 'I hope to deserve a better part than a labourer's when I come away.'

'And if you shouldn't get one, will you agree that you didn't deserve to, hey, will you? I think not. I fear not. Such a school as yours teaches a boy to quarrel with his lot, if it don't suit his liking.'

'But sir, sir, don't you allow that it's by quarrelling with his lot that a fellow may better himself? Or none would rise.'

'I don't know about rising. There wasn't this to-do about "rising" when I was young, nor quarrelling with your lot either. No, it is by showing himself capable in the task he is allotted that a man improves himself, that is what I allow. Now then. Suppose your time was up at school, eh, and you was to come away with all honours, well then, what should you propose doing, hey? To make your way in the world.'

Tresham cast about blankly in his mind. He had not specified to himself the exact means of transport which would continue in the world his successes at school. 'I suppose I should look out for someone to suggest something. Some fellow I had made a friend of,' he added, falling back upon Cropper and Park Street as the needed transport upwards.

'Pooh! If toadying is the only work your school has fitted you for,' said Uncle Marcus half jovially, 'why, I think you had better make an honest labourer of yourself at once. Ever used an axe?'

They had reached the workmen's equipment by the nearer clay pit, and the rector picked up an axe.

'I never tried it, Uncle Marcus.'

'Should you like to learn?'

The axe held out to him stirred an instinct within Tresham which he had forgotten he possessed. Here was the weapon, there the challenge. How keenly he had once felt the significance of the grim blade. He took the axe. 'I should like to learn above all things!'

'Come, you shall have your lesson from my woodmen here,' said the squire, and the two of them walked towards the green felled oak and the bearded men.

*   *   *

Upon the Gothic porch which he had added to the entrance front of his house the rector had caused to be engraved the words *Nisi dominus aedificaverit domum vanus est labor*. At first sight Tresham felt inclined to mock this sentiment as a pressing into service of God to approve the rector's self-indulgence in expanding and Gothicising the house. As near as his nature allowed, Uncle Marcus even seemed a little ashamed of the works, referring to them always as 'the repairs'. Yet (Tresham saw) he *was* repairing the homogeneity of the house, which centuries of random additions had impaired with differing styles and materials and rooflines; once stuccoed, and battlemented overall, his house, 'repaired', would present a unified front to the world. Unless God build the house, the labour is vain. . . The words ran in Tresham's head as he explored the old mansion in the next days, or looked out of its windows, or stood gazing into the glow of the hall fire in its bed of whitened ash.

Perhaps because of its size, the house seemed to him unnaturally

[53]

still, its silence a medium to be pushed through like water, which closed in immediately upon a shut door or a departing footstep. On their wooden scaffold workmen were creeping about the façade, tapping, hammering, chipping; adding here creneallation to a gable, there knocking out a pointed arch to Gothicise a window. These living sounds of work, and the workmen's voices coming in at unexpected windows, heartened the dim silences of the interior. The way to his attic became known to him as if he had never taken any other way to bed; closed doors, and little secondary staircases, and the passageways into whose mouths his chamber-candle cast a wavering light, all revealed their secrets to exploration as the days passe. Mrs Poynder's taciturnity no longer seemed unamiable to him, and the queer, jerky companionship of his step-uncle, now offered and now withdrawn, became as familiar as the portraits in the dining room. 'We will have a talk about it some of these times,' the rector was sure to say, thus postponing any topic raised, almost, and returning to sigh over his book as he ate, moving his legs uneasily under the table and exclaiming, 'Ah, poor fellow! Poor fellow!' (His table book was still Captain Groves's account of the imprisonment of Stoddart and Conolly at Bokhara.)

Tresham too read a good deal. The rector, having corrected his tendency to crack books' spines by opening them too fiercely, let him choose what volumes he liked from his library. In this way, seated by the hall fire or turning the pages of the folios of engravings his step-uncle especially prized – Wood's *Palmyra*, Roberts's *Holy Land* just coming from the press – he wolfed down much food for his imagination. One picture especially, a painting in the manner of Claude over the library fireplace, drew him to peer into it whenever he found the room empty. It was a landscape of mountain and sea and plain and columned temple, in which grave melancholy figures stood under sunset-gilded trees, beneath an azure sky of eternal summer, into whose light rose far-off summits tipped with snow. It appealed, like the axe, to an instinct buried in his nature; a landscape of happiness, and fulfilment, worth searching all the world to find.

An hour or two of the mornings he spent learning to use an axe from the woodmen. But it did not satisfy him as he had hoped, or even elucidate whatever mystery the took, or the craft, held for him. It was hard work, and he cared for it less and less as time went on, as though familiarity drove out of the implement and its use the half-grasped magic which had dwelt in the idea. He rather wished the grim black old axe was his own, though, to keep by him for some unspecified future use or need. But he did not know whether the axe was his step-uncle's property, or the woodmen's, and he had to be content with its coming to be called, after a few days, 'Mr Tresham's axe' by the men.

Meantime the rector came and went between business-room and library, or his dam and his 'repairs', and little Tom kept the fires alight, and Mrs Poynder alternated between concern for the house and concern for the parish. She might have been a poor parson's wife, thought Tresham when he listened to her discussions with his step-uncle:

'Well, what is your receipt for the soup, Mrs Poynder?'

'Forty pounds of beef, sir, a bundle of leeks, a peck of peas,' read out Mrs Poynder from the paper held aslant in her hand to catch the light in the dim, pillared hall.

'Forty pounds of beef? For how many families is this?'

'Why, our usual thirty-eight, sir.' She was patient, knowing she would have her way.

It had been settled that Tresham was to stay a week, and in the course of that week only one incursion was made by the outside world into the world of Rainshaw. Many men, and women too, came as a matter of course to the rector's business-room off the hall (where he passed a part of each morning), but these were all his tenants or parishioners; on one morning, however, a thin gentleman rode up to the door, and had his horse taken from him by Branch, and sent in his name. The rector despatched Tom to fetch Tresham, and to carry a tray of wine and biscuits into the drawing room to this Mr Gulliver. The meeting was brief, uncomfortable because Gulliver was an uncomfortable, lanky old man, who stared hard at Tresham in intervals of sucking down his wine and crunching up biscuits. Tresham couldn't make out why the old man had ridden six miles on a wet day in order to talk about canals, and disagreeably too. He had brought a dog with him, which had run off hunting from the front door, and this, though it didn't perturb Mr Gulliver, agitated the rector extremely into a ringing of the great bell on the house roof, and a sending out of all hands to hunt down the miscreant, and a running in and out of the drawing room himself with a telescope under his arm to watch how the hunt fared. Meanwhile Mr Gulliver talked of waterways to Tresham, and asked him his views as to the likelihood of canals fighting off the challenge of the railways for the traffic in freight. In the end, when the dog had turned up, Mr Gulliver and the rector spoke privately for a few moments in the new porch whilst Branch brought the horse round. Nothing was afterwards said of the visit – except for the rector's comment upon the usefulness of having a porch to one's house on a wet day.

Only once in the week did Uncle Marcus himself drive out. The parish church was in his park, amongst a handful of tile-hung cottages and farm buildings where two lanes met, embowered in oaks out of sight of the house. The village itself lay two miles off, so that for an hour before the service the congregation, in twos and threes or walking singly, could be seen crossing the park by the footpath from village to church, many of them sauntering down the slope to view the progress of the squire's dam since the preceding Sunday. Tresham was much struck by the freedom and independence with which the villagers walked about under the house windows from which he watched them, not sure that he wouldn't have wished them to have looked small and to have hurried along the line of the path in single file, in keeping with their humble place. The rector drove himself and Tresham to church in the gig, which he stopped half-way to send his step-nephew across the turf to look into a tree-ringed pond.

'Just step over and see if any of the boys have set lines, will you? They do it on their way to church, you know, and take up the fish after. I don't care about it,' he said, 'but I don't choose that such scallywags should think they make a fool of me. Just throw them on the bank there.'

They drove on, and a boy from the farmyard by the church took the horse. The rector was dressed in his usual clothes, black breeches and gaiters, black cutaway coat and white stock, and he did not read the Service, which was taken by his curate, Poat. He did, however, let Poat put him into a white gown to mount the pulpit steps to deliver the sermon, a commentary upon one of the Epistles of fifteen minutes or so which he gave without notes in his usual speaking voice. Tresham, listening below, considered the soundness and unity of this man's life. It seemed a structure in which no part was at variance with another.

Nisi dominus aedificaverit. . . Looking up at the figure in the pulpit floating in the dark spaces of the church, as suddenly as a sunshaft through one of the windows there shone into Tresham's mind the idea of Faith. All was made clear.

Faith sustained his step-uncle. Hence the order, hence the whole-ness, hence the peace. In the dark mouth between pulpit and sounding-board the rector wagged like a tongue speaking with Faith. He believed, and was content. He believed the world ran upon a design of equity and order requiring only his regulating touch here and there – the sparrow restored to life from the cat's grasp, works for his parishioners – to go along as sound as clockwork. He believed in this world and the next. Tresham was aware of his step-uncle in the pulpit above him, sustained there by Faith like the Ark on the waters of the Flood, con-taining within himself all that was necessary for the elect to survive. And who was elect? Whoever believed: that was the distance at which the Ark floated from the shore. Could he swim to it? Could he believe?

Suddenly as it had shone out, the irradiation faded. His step-uncle had ended his sermon, the pulpit was empty, an empty mouth under the sounding-board, and Poat's voice creaked out prayers. There was left in Tresham's mind, though, the question burnt into his thoughts by the departed light: Can you believe? He did not ask himself, Is it true? but, Can you believe?

After the service he walked round the bluff of land on which the church was built, looking out over wooded folds to the south. Boughs had dropped from the trees among the gravestones, the church itself was neglected and out of repair, ivy-grown, the smudge of old yews leaning against it. A heap of ragstone against the southern wall showed where some structure had tumbled away altogether. These stones Tresham recognised.

'Uncle Marcus,' he enquired on their way home in the gig, 'are you using the stones of the church to build your Tower?'

Now this Tower was another of the rector's projects. At the spot in his park to which he intended that the winding waters of his lake would reach, he planned a stone tower copied from the tombs at Palmyra to house, in an upper room, the books he loved concerning travels in the East, for which there was no more room in the shelves of his library. When showing Tresham the work in progress he had explained it by

[57]

his desire to give to unemployed masons work fitting their skill and dignity. 'I should have thought very ill of myself if I obliged a mason to take on a labourer's work at the dam,' he had said. 'No, no, if a man has turned himself into a mason, why, he must be given mason's work.' Anyway, in the heap of ragstone tumbled off the church Tresham had recognized his step-uncle's quarry for his Tower, and now asked him about it.

'Fortunate I found a use for them,' the rector replied, 'couldn't be left in a heap there, had to be moved.'

'Uncle Marcus, when the Tower is finished, shall you spend much time there, do you suppose?'

'Much time? I don't know. I don't know.' He drove in silence for a while up the slope of the park road from church to house, through the shadow of oaks alternating with sunlight. 'There will be at all events the idea that I might. There will be that. An idea of going.'

The rector's fascination with remote and dangerous travels seemed to Tresham an aberration in his character – in the unity and soundness he had been thinking of in church. Was it the one chink which the rector allowed his imagination to put its eye to, inside the well-caulked Ark? For he had never been abroad, so far as Tresham knew, and the Asia he read of was utterly at variance with all he had experienced or enjoyed.

'Should you have liked to travel in the East?' Tresham asked.

'I don't know about "liked". I might have been a missionary. Such a fellow as Wolff. If I hadn't been obliged to give it all up when the estate here came and tied up my hands.'

From what he had learned of Mr Wolff, and that eccentric clergyman's wanderings about the East to circulate the Word, Tresham could conceive of no being more different than was his step-uncle. Yet the rector saw himself as having followed one possibility among others, in becoming what he was: an idea of fluidity which Tresham hadn't believed a mind like his step-uncle's would contain. A wandering missionary in the East, outside the Mussulman's structured world, instead of the linch-pin of this orderly English creation of oak and park through which he drove his gig!

'So you always did intend yourself for the Church, though, Uncle Marcus?' He had learned that the rector did not object to being

[58]

questioned; preferred it to the trouble of initiating topics himself.

'I'll tell you how it was, Tresham,' he replied, sitting still in the gig in the stable yard which they had reached, and pulling off his gloves. 'You see that mulberry, do you?' He nodded towards an old tree shading the grass between stables and house. 'Now then, it was near forty years ago, under that mulberry where he was sitting, on an old seat used to be there, my father said to me, "Marcus, how would it suit you to take up the living here and go in for the church? For you don't want your brother Dolly always pulling away at your sleeve as parson when you're squire here," he said. And he put Paley's *Evidences* into my hand. Branch,' he called out to the old man who had turned up to take the horse and gig, 'Branch, what have we done with the old seat used to stand under the mulberry in my father's time?'

'That got broke up time you had they mummers come,' Branch retorted as he led the horses away.

'And Paley gave you. . . Faith?' Tresham asked.

'Ah,' replied his step-uncle, 'we'll have a talk about it all some of these days. I shall take a turn about the garden now. I always do on Sunday, you know, for it is the only day of the week when the blessed garden ain't full up with fellows gardening, and looking at me like a thief if I eat of a bunch of my own grapes!'

On Tuesday Tresham was to leave, going back to Laidlaw Villa for a day or two before returning to school. Approaching departure began to tinge Rainshaw with the declining sunset light of nostalgia, as he anticipated how he would feel on looking back upon the place when he had left it. His step-uncle speaking of his own youth amongst these scenes caused Tresham painful envy of the long settled future Uncle Marcus had looked forward to. How easy it would have been, and how pleasant! The idea was like stepping into the Claude landscape of sunset and dreaming shore in the library, and closing some door in the paint for ever behind him. Alas! – instead he must leave. On Monday evening he went out on his own to walk in the rough weather about park and woods for the last time.

An autumn gale had blown away into memory the mist and peace and mild sunlight of the first days of his visit. From the valley the felled oak he had worked on was gone, timber carted, a blackened ring in the turf marking where the brash had been burned. Rain had made the tracks between clay pits and dam into slippery ruts along which labourers struggled with barrows, sacks covering their shoulders, whilst the trees which had once shaded their families now roared and strained like furious giants. The stream was ruffled dark by the wind where he crossed it. He said aloud into the gale:

> O fountains! When in you shall I
> Myself eased of unpeaceful thoughts espy?

As he climbed the slope two further lines followed in his mind:

> O fields! O woods! When, when shall I be made
> The happy tenant of your shade?

To have a life in prospect as owner of these fields and woods! He hurried on as if he could outrun the pain of such thoughts, or as if the wind on the ridge of the park which he was climbing might blow them out of his head. On he walked, over the ridge, through a wicket in the paling and so into the chestnut woods. The track he followed was one made by woodmen to haul out the chestnut when it was coppiced, this one disused and overgrown, its ruts marshy. Leaves danced and whirled, the wind strode over the wood and shook the trees. Still he walked on, further, deeper into the wind-battered shaggy woods than he had ever walked, hoping for recovered spirits before turning back.

Birch and thorn and oak, relics of the old English forest, were now interspersed with the coppiced chestnut. The depths of these woods were an older landscape altogether than the windows of the house overlooked. It was strange that it was here, so close. Winter, too, seemed nearer, in brakes of holly and thorn – perhaps was always here, winter sheathed in summer as the sword in the scabbard, the truth within the fable. The edged steel of winter was never far off in the dark of these woods, he felt.

The raging of the wind, the rushing of the wind in his ears, kept him from all suspicion of what lay so close at hand. The muffled thump, the beat of a monstrous heart, he heard without comprehending. Suddenly the track ended. It had lost itself some way back in brambles and thorn, but here it ended in a palisade of stakes. He looked over this defence.

The wood vanished. There was a void, a chasm, beyond the stakes. Across twenty yards of space the trees resumed. Over there, in the stormy dusk on that cliff edge, he saw fires, smoke, huts gleaming with light. Between his own cliff edge and that, an abyss. He looked down. Steeply the slopes plunged to dreadful depths. Now his eyes and ears filled with the frenzy of the scene. Noise – the thumping of a steam-engine – burst up from the cutting. Frantic work seethed like bubbles in a black cauldron down there. The demon of work threw up tentacles to grasp the rim of the gorge, wires and ropes and rails which hauled up buckets and barrows, and tipped them, and plunged them down again empty into the smoke and din and glare. Thump, thump, thump beat the steam-heart of the monster clawing its way through the earth. Blasts of its uneven ugly breath, with the smell of steam and the clank of beaten iron, were blown over him at one moment by the wind; at another, the wind's roar in the trees was the only savage sound accompanying the scenes of pandemonium below.

He stepped back from the paling and the cliff edge. Had the demons down there seen him, they would surely swarm out of the gulf and pull him down. Out of these terrors and back to the park! Away, quick, by the path he had come!

And yet – fascination laid bony fingers on his arm as he turned away. A torrent of life flowed down there. Hideous, but the vital force. He knew it, and could not come away. Now he saw that the lights and huts across the gulf marked the navvies' encampment. Figures crossed the clearing, an opened door showed a flare of light, somewhere a man fell and cursed, the music of a fiddle came clear on a gust of wind. A woman stood on the edge of the pit facing him. He felt her eyes on him. Did she hold out her arms, or was she managing clothes and hair in the gusts? Afraid, he lived more keenly than ever a woman's eyes had made him live before. Two men were approaching her from behind, huge men as shaggy as the trees. He held out his hand to warn her. She ran along the cliff-top in the clearing where the navvies had laid waste the wood for firing, and was gone. Was she crossing the cutting? Was she coming? After her blundered the two giants, and the wind spoke in his ear with their drunken laughter.

Fear showed Tresham that he had never done a brave thing. Once on a mountainside he had made up a hero to fight for him. In those

[61]

days he had been in touch with old heroes and brave deeds, so that one had sprung forward to take the sword from his hand and fight for him. But now no hero stirred in his imagination. He turned and ran.

Through the darkening woods, with the hollow roar of the wind behind him, he ran for his life till he came to the wicket-gate into the park. Here, under open sky, it was less dark, the wind's rage less furious without trees to shake. His heartbeat slowed and his thoughts quietened. No creature from the railway cutting would venture after him here, surely. He walked on till he came to the clay pit above the half-built dam.

Work was finished for the night, the men gone. Work – ! he remembered the orderly and peaceable activity, the women, the children playing, the summer sky. It wasn't the real work of life. Work was what he had seen and heard clawing and thumping through the earth towards him from the other side of the woods. That was reality. What you fear most, is most real. Whatever challenges you, is the adversary. And at some time, in some place, the tryst has to be kept.

So he thought, looking across the valley at the old house on the hillcrest opposite. Its outline in the dusk was that of a ship riding out the gale, its prow the eastern bow windows, its mast the tall chimneys, its staysails the steep-pitched roof gables. There sailed the rector in his well-caulked ark. It was a lonely shore on which Tresham knew he stood, and watched the ark he knew he could not swim to, and heard the beat of the steam-engine clawing through the earth towards him.

*   *   *

Rainshaw Park
Kent,   September the 15th 1845

My dear Dolly,
          Tresham has just left me, travelling at his own insistence upon the Railway, that Bane of our Age. You will not have known that a Branch line was projected to run past us here, and much work done, cuttings dug, embankments raised, the whole landscape in Turmoil, to say nothing of morals depraved, etc, etc. I am glad to say that I am now reliably informed that the Venture has run short of cash, and Works will be suspended, many investors no doubt like yourself landed in Queer Street. I had at

any event obliged the Contractor to circumnavigate my Estate, despite the offer of bribes to a vast amount aimed at overcoming my Principles, so I am left with no Monuments to Greed, thank God, in the form of abandoned Works.

You will understand that I am little disposed to sympathy towards your own Gambling in railway Stock, though of course regretting that your Budget should be further pinched by the inevitable consequence of deep Play, especially if undertaken with money not your own. You are too Romantically inclined, it was ever your fault, for I recall you as a child investing your money through old Whibley on a contender in a pigeon-shooting Match, for no other reason but that his name was Nightingale. It is I fear a penalty of your over-sanguine Nature, to meet with those who outmanœuvre you. You will have remembered Savage's lines, and must endeavour to profit by their Truth:

> Even Calamity by thought refined
> Inspirits and adorns the thinking Mind.

It is the penalty of my position that I must regard the Estate and its income as Responsibilities entrusted to my stewardship on behalf of the Family itself, and not as mere Riches to be handed out on a whim to one or another improvident relative. I must look first to satisfy the needs of that which is at the Estate's heart, namely, the people and buildings found upon it. On the first count, I have been obliged to put numerous works in hand for the employment of those made idle or destitute by the Activities of Chartists, Trades' Unions, Land Reformers, and all those other scoundrels who have claimed to be True Friends to our working men. It is left to private gentlemen to correct the recent errors of Church, State and Agitator, but the bill is a heavy one. As to the buildings upon the Estate, here too I face a long bill for repairs, as the house must be kept weathertight, not for my own comfort, but in case I do not always remain a Bachelor.

Besides these concerns, I have private troubles with which I will not burden you, save to say that my Curate, Poat, a most vexatious fellow, is I find a pervert, and must be sent away. His flight to Rome is awaited eagerly by my Enemies, amongst whom I fear must be numbered the Archdeacon, who badgers me about my Sexton's drinking, and will seize any opportunity to interfere in the Parish.

It will be readily apparent to you, now that you know my position, that I have no money to spare for the object solicited in your letter, namely your stepson's continuance at his School. However, shortage of money should not signify, if I believed the cause a worthy one. I do not. My belief is, that such Schools are concerned only to turn out upon the world spurious imitations of what used to be a genuine Article, namely the educated English gentleman, so as to satisfy the aspiration of a class enriched by Industry or Trade, to have 'gentlemen' for sons. A knowledge of the Classics, nowadays, (which used to expand our Fathers' understandings by steeping them in the best productions of the Ancients) is sunk to the parrotting of a few tags in a House of Commons filled with the sons of brewers. Your stepson's school is a mere manufactory of such Brummagen 'gentry', and I should not spend my money at such a shop even if money were plentiful.

Instead of acceding to your demand, therefore, I have asked a Mr Gulliver to the house whilst Tresham was with me, a neighbour and fellow-Justice who has places at his disposal in the Inland Waterways Board. I believe he may be prevailed upon to offer one such place to my nominee, and, since Canals are sure to outlast the craze for Railways, Tresham will have bright Prospects. The position of clerk will seem a humble one, no doubt, to a boy whose expectations have been raised by mingling with the sons of rich Tradesmen at school, but abilities will show themselves in the most modest circumstances, as I do not doubt you have found out in Tea.

My kind remembrance to Mrs Wytherstone and the Girls, your affec. brother
M. Wytherstone

IV

———————————

IN THE MIST OF A NOVEMBER EVENING brick walls loomed over the narrow streets of the town. It was very cold. By arch and street and gateway hurried the figures of boys coming and going in the mist. On a corner, under an iron lantern affixed to the wall, glowed the red coals of a brazier, a man's figure stamping the ground beside it and blowing on his hands. Chestnuts were roasting on a grid over the embers, and one or two boys, attracted by the scented warmth given off into the dusk, stood near, or counted up their money with careworn expressions.

Through the nearby archway, as yet unseen, voices approached. There was a deliberate, ringing loudness about them which warned of their owners' importance; and the shrinking away from the brazier by certain small figures confirmed the approach of a ruling class.

Into view they now swaggered, four of them arm-in-arm, large, muddy, swathed in long scarves, little caps on their heads, clattering out of the mist in a swirl of voices and laughter like victors from battle.

'I say, there's that wogue with his chestnuts!' Breath curled out of Cropper's mouth.

'Let's take some.'

'Who's got some tin?'

'Oh, send a boy. Send one of these scugs.'

Round the coals they clustered, warming hands, gingerly pulling hot chestnuts off the pierced top and eating them with cheerful hunger.

'How is it these fellows roast 'em just right, which you never can do at home?' asked one.

'Send for the tin, do,' said another voice, 'he wants paying.'

'Want paying, do you?' Cropper seized the little man by his shoulder. 'Come on, fellows, let's shut up his shop for him!'

'Here, you, boy!' called out sharply the voice that had suggested paying the man. 'You cut along to my house and fetch some money

[65]

from the fag you'll find making toast at my fire. Quick now! You know who I am, do you?'

'I know you, Pitcher.' Shrinking away, the small boy turned and ran into the mist.

'The tin'll be here directly,' said Tresham, hoping to quell Cropper's move to overturn the brazier.

'You treating us, Pitcher?'

'Thank you, sir, you're a gentleman, sir,' breathed the ragged chestnut-roaster, ducking his head humbly. 'Will I put on a few more of me nuts, will I, for your honours?'

When the boy who had been sent for money re-emerged from the mist, he had with him a spindly stranger in an old-fashioned hat and a caped top-coat. The boy, anxious to be seen running as Pitcher had ordered, hovered between that duty and the duty of leading the stranger up to his masters. To Pitcher he handed over some coins, saying, 'Oh, Pitcher, I say, I found this gentleman looking for you in your room, Pitcher, and Farr said I should bring him on here.'

'You are Tresham Pitcher?' As he stepped into the rays cast through the mist by the coals, the stranger's cadaverous face was reddened, and his spectacles made to gleam. 'I am your uncle,' he said, removing a glove. 'Norman McPhee, your mamma's brother.'

Tresham took his hand, rather at a loss for words and what to do, in face of his friends watching in silence. This new uncle, however, stepped towards them with hand outstretched. 'I take it you are my nephew's friends, and I'm pleased to be acquainted. I'm down from the city of Glasgow, where I've a post in the College.' Shaking hands all round, he did not seem to be aware, as Tresham was, of the shabbiness of his round hat and the worn cloth of his coat. 'Tresham here I've never set eyes upon,' he went on, 'and it isn't for long we will meet today, for I've to take the coach directly. You'll walk with me to the inn, will you, Tresham?'

'I fear it's impossible. We're forbidden to be out of our houses after dusk.'

'So, now, is that the case?'

Tresham willed him to go, and to take with him that thin Scotch voice trickling out of him to wash away the ground under Tresham's feet.

[66]

'Well, I must go alone. But I have a letter for you, Tresham, in my pocket. Aye, here it is. Your step-papa asked that I should bring it to you and talk to you of its contents.' He held up the letter.

'Oh, never mind that. I can read it well enough, I suppose.' Tresham reached for the letter and crushed it into his breeches pocket. 'Now, sir, the inn where your coach starts is – here, one of these boys shall show you your line,' he said, and told off a small boy to point the way.

When Tresham came back into the circle round the brazier, where his friends were eating the chestnuts and spitting out shell, giggles and low voices were stilled.

'I say, Pitcher,' said one, 'I thought your uncle had a landed estate, you told us.'

'I don't believe that fellow's my uncle in the least,' said Tresham with noble unconcern. 'Never heard of him in all my life. Now then,' he asked the chestnut-seller, 'what's the bill for feeding these fellows?'

'He's Scotch, mind,' a voice warned the man, and all laughed.

'Come, here's enough for the whole box and dice of it!' said Tresham, throwing the man a silver coin, and linking his arm through Cropper's to walk away into the mist.

Tresham and Cropper came into Pitcher's room together after sluicing off the mud of football, and threw themselves into two chairs facing the fire. In the fireplace at their feet crouched a small boy blowing rather hopelessly but with tireless vigour at a feeble glow amidst the coal.

'Look here, you wetch,' said Cropper, kicking his backside, 'you get that fire going sharpish, or we'll give you a licking. We'll fweeze to death, hanged if we won't.'

The boy blew harder than ever, the seat of his trousers and the soles of his boots presented humbly to the room. Suddenly he stopped and looked round, his face flushed with blowing. 'Oh, I say, Tucker, I found a letter in your togs when I was cleaning them. I put it on the table.'

Tresham put out his hand. Farr jumped up and fetched the letter and gave it to him, then resumed desperate endeavours at the fire. Tresham read the letter casually while Cropper talked. 'I say,' he said,

[67]

'here's a go.' He got up and walked across the room, the letter in his hand.

'What's a go?'

'This letter. The governor's been plunging in railway shares.'

'Oh Lord! Who hasn't? Got any eggs we could eat, have you?'

'In the cupboard. He's taking it mighty hard, though, the governor. Lashing out all ways. As if. . . as if everything depended. . . but that's rot, of course. And it can't – ' Can't matter to me, he wanted to say. Me, myself, all this, can't be dependent on him and his wretched affairs. Selfishness – that buoyancy chamber within a man designed to keep him afloat when holed – selfishness limited the damage, for the moment, from his stepfather's torpedo. 'It's all rot,' he repeated.

'Of course. Just so long as he pays to keep you here, I suppose.'

'What? Devil take it! – ' Tresham snatched up the letter and peered into it fiercely. Then he crushed it in his hand and sank in the chair by Cropper's. 'By God, Croppy,' he said, 'I believe he means to let me down after all.'

'Does he now! Here's times!' Cropper got up. 'I say, Pitcher,' he said from the cupboard he had opened, 'your wetched fire ain't ever going to be fit to cook upon, so I'll just take a few of these eggs along to some other fellow's fire.' From the door, his hands full of eggs, he said, 'If I was you I'd give Farr a licking.'

Tresham came to life in his chair. 'I don't know about that,' he said with spirit, 'but I'm damned if I'll disappear into the Inland Waterways for ever!' He got to his feet. His heavy energetic stride made the room small. 'That won't do,' said he to Farr in the grate. 'That'll never burn, that won't. Get up.'

Farr got up and looked into his master's face fearlessly. 'I'm sorry,' he said. 'I never could make a fire go.'

'Never fear,' said Tresham. 'You run off and get some paper and sticks, and we'll start again.'

When Farr came back with kindling he found the coals taken out of the grate, and all made ready for a new beginning. Tresham built a pyramid of sticks over the paper, laid one or two coals, lit the paper, and sat back on his heels beside Farr to watch the creeping flame steal along the sticks until they began to emit a wreath of smoke into the chimney.

'This is the moment it can go wrong for you,' said Tresham, 'see? The flame's sinking. Now what you do – '

'Is blow?' asked Farr.

'No, no, blowing ain't a bit of use!' Tresham took up the towel he had brought in from his bath and held it across the upper half of the chimney-opening. Draught soon brightened the flame, sticks began to crackle, the fire to roar. 'You see?' Tresham watched the fire take hold.

But Farr watched Tresham. 'I say, Pitcher,' he let out, 'it would be an awful shame if you was to leave.'

'Leave? Who asked your opinion? Didn't they ever tell you what happened to eavesdroppers, Farr?'

'I wasn't *listening*. I just heard you say about the railways and your papa. My papa has to do with railways as well, but – '

'But he makes money by them, does he?'

'Well – I think so. He's in Constantinople now because of building a railway,' Farr volunteered, looking sideways to see if an original contribution to the conversation from him was acceptable. The way the corners of his mouth turned up, and his bright face ringed with curls, gave him a look of good nature hard to snub, and Tresham said:

'In Constantinople? There are no railways there, surely?'

'There is one near, yes, Papa built one, oh, ever so long ago, just a short one, somewhere on the Black Sea to bring up the coals from the mine to the sea. He built it, and then the Sultan sent him away, and now he has gone back to see all about it. Papa has built ever so much in foreign countries.'

'And does he live abroad, your papa?'

'Now he doesn't, no, now we live – now he's building a house for us in Wales, you know, but it won't be finished for ever so long and we only live in a bit. It's a castle,' he added, again peering at Tresham to see if this might not be too much.

'It sounds as though he has a very jolly life of it, your papa. I shouldn't half mind seeing Constantinople.'

There was a silence while Tresham fed the fire and Farr watched. Suddenly in his high voice Farr asked, 'Is it true you killed a man with gunpowder? That's what all the fellows say about you.'

Tresham looked into the eager uncertain face in the ruddy light. A

[69]

sense of something unusual in the air had precipitated the question, and the same sense of crisis – of the ship torpedoed under him – made Tresham answer honestly.

'Well,' he said, 'no, not exactly, in spite of what the fellows say.' He told Farr of the garden-boy at Laidlaw Villa, whom he had discovered selling peaches to the greengrocer, and whom he had obliged, as the price of silence, to procure for him gunpowder from an uncle working with explosives on the railways: then he told how he had packed the heating flues within the garden wall with this gunpowder, and had tried to bring down the wall by detonating it: and how the experiment had unaccountably failed. Three months after, however, in a severe frost, the wall had fallen, crushing to death a tramp who had no doubt known of the hot flues in the brickwork and had sought their warmth. 'And that's the truth about the man I killed with gunpowder,' Tresham finished, feeling as though he had already set about dismantling the image of himself which he had been at pains, at school, to create. 'I dare say it's a blow you haven't been broiling eggs for a murderer all term, ain't it?' he asked Farr.

'Oh, I don't mind a bit,' said Farr. 'Shall I try and cook you some eggs now, do you think?'

'Just stop where you are, there's a good fellow, and tell me about your papa at Constantinople, will you.' Paint what pictures you like, he wanted to say, only that I mayn't have to look inward, or forward, by the light of that letter from home. And so little Roland Farr painted in his two sisters and his brother, and the carefree life they seemed to lead in their Welsh valley under the moors close to the sea, where their castle was slowly rising – and Tresham listened, as he looked into the fire, until the image Farr painted was clear enough to step into, like the picture on the wall of his step-uncle's library.

Next morning, ignoring the school timetable which no longer seemed relevant to his life, Tresham walked away from the school buildings over the football field to a slow, clear stream which formed the boundary of school ground. Here he took from his pocket his stepfather's letter to try what reading it out of doors would do.

Laidlaw Villa
Clapham   November 7th 1845

My dear Tresham,
        It is my painful task to inform you that I have been
defrauded of a large sum by the wickedness of the Directors of a
Railway Company which I had been prevailed upon to support.
        I had taken pride in those successes, which my sacrifice
has enabled you to enjoy; and I had looked forward to seeing you
in that place, which my efforts would have purchased for you:
it is not to be. All that you might have become must be immediately relinquished, by your withdrawal from the school. Pray
inform your Headmaster. It is however possible that family
influence may obtain for you a Clerkship in the Inland Waterways.
        Yr affec. stepfather, A. Wytherstone.

Tresham no longer felt aggrieved, or unjustly used, as he had done in
the heat of first feeling: what he felt now was mortification, that he
had ever deluded himself that he stood upon solid ground of his own
making. Never again. Never again would he cut such capers on thin
ice and be made a fool of. When Crates the Cynic was asked, amid the
ruins of his city, where he would dwell in future, he struck his own
forehead and declared that for his part, from now on, he would inhabit
that city within himself which no future Alexander could overthrow.

Beside the stream tall wreckage of thistles stood stiffened with the
sugar-icing of the frost. He walked slowly, thinking, the stream
gliding at his side, his footsteps spoiling the frost's sparkle on the
grass. Where would he go now, and with what aim? He stopped to
watch an ant scrambling rapidly among the prickles of a dead thistle
leaning over the stream. A thread of fibre broke, leaf and ant fell
together on the glassy current. How the ant struggled, like a bird in a
cat's claws! He might have saved it. For what? For 'this deceivable
world'? He thought of the tiny creature at peace on the bottom of the
stream, the water flowing above it like the wind over the moor, and he
let the current carry it away.

Remembering Malory's words about 'the deceivable world' he
walked on. 'And the more that God hath given you the triumphal
honour, the meeker you ought to be, ever fearing the unstableness of
this deceivable world. . .' Across the field, from the sunlit spires and

towers of the school buildings, a bell had begun to toll, iron strokes urgent and uneven, like the strokes of a boy beating his iron hoop along the road. Tresham didn't attend to the summons. Fearing nothing the bell threatened, he found it unreal. On he walked by the stream, thinking of Malory as he had hardly done for years.

The sun-touched stone pinnacles and upper works of the great school floated above morning mist quite as real as the towers of Camelot, or the fantastical outline of Constantinople, as he pictured it. But no more real. The bell's notes might have been the herald's trumpet sounding in the ears of a knight-at-arms on the lea below a castle, or the call of the muezzin heard by a traveller across the Golden Horn. . . The horizon of possibilities was infinite.

The bell ceased. In the silence, like its grimmer echo, he heard in his mind the clank of iron, and the beat of the steam-engine, as those sounds had gushed out of the railway cutting at the back of the woods at Rainshaw. That was real. That was what he feared. Then that was the tryst he ought to keep. *Gawaine, it is a long time since you were knighted, and in these years you have done little for your maker.*

*   *   *

Mr Wytherstone laid down Tresham's letter on the parlour table beside his chair, and closed his eyes. He thought of poking the fire, for he was cold after the omnibus ride from Mincing Lane, but he found he had not the energy. He heard his wife rustle to the table and take up the wretched letter for the twentieth time. He hated Tresham for putting into his few lines such inadequate comfort for his mother. It was dated 'November 18th, The London Bridge Railway Station', and began:

> My dear Step-papa,
>   I send my traps home to you by this carrier, but will not come quite at once myself. Pray beg Mamma not to alarm herself, I shall be all right. As for going away from school, it does not signify. I think I will be a Missionary. I have borrowed a little Money from a fellow here so I am all right.
>   Your affectionate stepson
>   Tresham Pitcher

He found that he did not feel, himself, pain or anxiety over Tresham. But he felt bitter resentment. It even opened his eyes.

'A missionary!' he hissed out. 'Well, of course he is no stranger to knocking about roads abroad and so forth. I don't doubt but this freak for becoming a missionary has its origin in hankering after a gipsy life.'

'Tresham's father was not a gipsy. He was not a gipsy, Adolphus. He was a soldier. He was a colonel.'

'Yes, in Italy.'

'What do you mean to imply, Adolphus?'

'I mean to imply nothing. But I never heard of a man who wasn't a scamp going for a soldier to the King of Naples.'

'Do you not know that my first husband's mother's family were Treshams of Treshamstown, they were indeed, and quite as old a family as the Wytherstones can claim to be!'

'In Ireland, yes, I dare say.'

'And what is wrong with Ireland as the seat of an old family, pray? My dear, you seem to suppose that apart from the English, the world is peopled entirely with gipsies. But I suppose it is because you have never been overseas. As for Tresham wishing to become a missionary,' she added, 'I shouldn't in the least mind it, if only he could come to us first.'

'Shouldn't mind?' Energy of anger jerked him upright. 'Shouldn't mind him throwing in my face all I have made of him, and setting out for Africa with a grubby collar and a carpet-bag full of bibles? Oh, no, I dare say you shouldn't mind him disgracing me!' He lay back weakly again.

'Adolphus, your own brother is a clergyman.'

'A rector in the Church of England. Yes. Not a missionary. A missionary is a very separate item. Perhaps he got a taste for it up there in the wilds of Scotland, perhaps that was it, eh? Perhaps he's going to join himself up to one of those wretched Scotch churches that are always squabbling up there.'

There was a silence. Then, softly, anxiously, Mrs Wytherstone asked, 'Adolphus, do you think he might have gone to Scotland? To my father? Oh,' she said, hugging her arms about herself miserably, 'if only I knew where he has gone!'

[73]

V

——————————

Laidlaw Villa
Clapham
December 12th 1845

Dear Farr,

I am obliged to you for lending me the Money, some part of which I now return. I did not need as much, for I could not realise my purpose, but you are a good fellow to lend it. I may call you a good fellow now that I am come away from school, I suppose, as I could not have done when you was my fag. Such Rules as used to regulate my conduct seem a trifle comic already!

I went down into Kent but could not find what I wished. I had seen an encampment of Navvies and Railway works near to my Step-uncle's place, and it was my purpose to have joined them and found work ·there. Then I would have become a Missionary if I found out I could live amongst the Navvies and get Work with them. But when I reached the Wood where they had been I found it empty and the Works idle. Only, in a hut, I found a young Woman, who had been rather ill. I could not help her. She had a baby. I did not know what to do. I told her to ask my Step-uncle for Relief, but I fear he don't care about the Navvies who are not his People. I gave her some of your Money and came away. I came up to Town with the Railway, and, my word if that ain't fun. The rushing of the engine full upon you as you stand waiting is the most thrilling sight out. I never could tire of Travel, which is why I should have liked to be a Missionary.

So my Railway Works have turned out a Bubble, just as my Stepfather's have done. I hope the Railways which support your family are more to be depended upon, for I often think of you all at your castle in Wales as you told me of it that evening.

Now I am to be put in for a place in the Inland Waterways Board, where I shall be a clerk if I succeed and have £90 per annum. The waterways reaching all about the kingdom, and the barges constantly moving upon them, make up a most romantic picture to my mind. At all events I am determined to like it. Of course it will not do to play the Great Man as I did at school, but since I found out how one may be let down, I won't care for such swagger again. I leave that to Cropper now! I hope the poor fellow is not still so short of tin as he said he was when I asked him for the loan of a guinea! I will send you the rest I owe, eleven shillings and sixpence which I spent on the young Woman and railway fares, when I receive my first salary. I do not care to trouble my Stepfather for it.

Perhaps you will write and tell me how you go along, I should always be pleased to hear. Don't let Cropper lick you if you are to be his fag as I suppose.

Your affec. and grateful friend
T. Pitcher

Board of Inland Waterways and Navigation
April 18th 1846

Dear Farr,

Herewith, as promised in my last, the half-a-guinea I have owed you since your kind advance of same on my coming away from school November last. As you have not written to a fellow, I cannot know if the continued loan has incommoded you. I think of your papa jawing with the Sultan of Constantinople, though, and feel sure you do not want for half-a-guinea!

Well, I have joined the Waterways, as you may see from my heading, and am living in guinea-a-week lodgings at Creech Lane, in Bishopsgate, as an independent gentleman upon £90 per annum, which will rise in due time to no less a sum than £110! That's if I stick by it, which I intend, though I confess there are times when the eternal copying of papers seems a worse grind than ever was the copying of a set of hexameters for old Quiggin at school.

You should only have been by when I was examined for my place, though! There was a lark! My name was put in by one of the Secretaries, old Gulliver (the old Gull, we call him) on the interest of my Uncle, the Squire of Rainshaw, and about Christmas I was called up to be examined by the Chief Clerk, a fellow named Cuff with watery eyes and a big set of whiskers who tries to look very fierce at us all. Can ye read and write? enquires Cuff, peering at me very keenly. O, well enough, says I. And d'ye know your tables? Cuff asks next, looking fierce. Well, you know the mathematicals ain't taught us at school, so I ventures out with A little, Mr Cuff. And Geography, and Trigonometry, and French, d'ye know them I s'pose? asks Cuff. I think I know them a bit, says I, feeling sure I shall be ploughed as soon as the first question is put. Ye'll need to know a dooced deal more than a bit, sir, (says he, very threatening) – Aye, when I examine ye tomorrow ye'll need to be perfect, perfect d'ye hear! And with that he stamps out of the room, and I stammers after him, But Mr Cuff, today is the day I am to be examined, not tomorrow. D'ye tell me that's so? (says he with a mighty surprised air) – well, sir, tis fortunate for ye, for had ye come tomorrow I fear you would not have come so well out of it. So I was shown to a desk, in a large room crowded with others, and one or two fellows lounging at the fire gossipping of actresses, and here I have been ever since.

There certainly is no need of the accomplishments old Cuff threatened me with, nor yet of the Greek and Latin we crammed at school, for all we do from morning till night is copy papers, and such dull papers too! If they was about waterways I shouldn't mind it, but they ain't a bit. At least I suppose they are at the bottom, but you can't make out anything of the romance of the thing – the dip and splash of the oars, so to speak, or the fine free lives those fellows on barges must lead – through the triple-ply dullness of the stuff we copy about bills of lading and I don't know what besides. Nobody attends to the work, but comes in late, and lounges at the fire, and goes away early. They are a second-rate set. I have been to one or two evening parties at the invitation of this or that fellow, but they see no refined company, and I very soon wearied of the experiment.

The company I see is not in the least refined, either, for I must tell you that Creech Lane, where my lodgings are situate, is a vicinity much favoured by American sea-captains, who lodge there in quantities whilst awaiting a ship or a cargo in the Port of London. It is on account of Creech Lane being lined with a double avenue of fine linden-trees, as I believe are the streets of Yankee seaboard towns, which reminds them pleasantly of home.

In my lodging-house is accommodated the family of such a Sea-captain, who remain there while he is upon a Voyage, and, through them, I have met with others. Their conversation is highly delightful to me, full as it is of storms and adventures, and remote shores, and savage tribes. Refined they are not, for the spittoon, the pipe, and the punchbowl, are all in high demand as the stories circulate, whether ladies are of the company or not. The Sea-captains' ladies are another feature of the case, for of course they remain to languish while husbands sail away, as languishes the sea-widow in my own lodging-house, who is as beautiful as her manners are free.

If such company be dangerous, I prefer its dangers, and its spittoons, to any amount of the 'refinements' otherwise open to me through my family, where I sometimes go to yawn my way through a conversazione where there is no one worth conversing with, or a dance where there is no one worth dancing with. The éclat which I had with my Stepsisters whilst I was at a great School, has altogether passed off now I am become a clerk, and, instead of thinking me rather above them, they have come round to thinking me decidedly beneath them, though I have not changed one whit.

I do not know why I write you all this, except that I have an infinity of Time upon my hands, and the fondest memories of your Charity when the blow fell upon me about quitting School. Perhaps you will write me a line to tell me how you are going on, and whether you still continue with your object of going up to Cambridge, which you told me of during our talk that night? I wonder if your papa is come home from Constantinople?

It is often as hard to discern any purpose, in working here, as it is hard to trace the existence of real waterways, and real barges, behind the screen of dull paper, and duller men, which generally occupies our time. For our Chiefs are a very middling set of men, taken up with squabbling with one another over imagined slights to their vanity, which is exorbitant. It is as hard work to admire them as to admire the beaks at School – but then, at School one does not intend becoming a beak, whilst in the World, I suppose, ambition should urge a man towards resembling his Chief. I frequently believe, when listening to the adventures of the Sea-captains, that such capacities as I have, or would like to develop, would be better employed in signing-on for a voyage before the mast in a Yankee clipper to the Ivory Coast, than in copying bills of lading all my days, until I become as dull a dog as old Gull and am made into a Secretary.

Well, old fellow, I have put in the day most agreeably in chatting with you thus, and must now take my hat from the peg and go home to the Sea-captain's lady. Perhaps you will take the time to let me know how you are going on, and the news from School.

Your affec. friend,
T. Pitcher

Trinity College,
Cambridge

April 4th 1848

Dear Pitcher,

I write this in great haste to beg a favour of you. Pray forgive me for never having replied to your letter sending me back the money two years ago. Do me this favour and I will explain all.

The fact is, I have come back before Term to Cambridge from Wales in hopes of reaching Town for the Monster Meeting for the Charter at Kennington on April 10th, which I never would have been let go to from home, for Papa is awfully fierce against the Charter and Mamma is worse. But I do not know London a bit, and should be sure to be lost before I was half-way to Kennington. Then I thought of you, and of how you would be sure to know your way, and how we could talk as we went along. The fact is, I don't know another fellow I could ask. And I am most awfully keen to see Mr O'Connor and march with those grand fellows with the Charter to the Parliament. Events are so thrilling in Europe just now, and this is all we have in England. Pray be a good fellow and say you will come. There are to be half-a-million of us, all stout Republicans like myself! They say the Queen has fled to the Isle of Wight, and all the Nobles are arming their Retainers and barricading themselves within their houses.

Your affectionate friend,
Roland Farr

[78]

I did not write before because whilst I was at school your letter seemed to be so much that of a man-of-the-world that I could not reply in a way that pleased me. There you have it! R.F.

Board of Inland Waterways and Navigation
September 19th 1848

My dear Farr,

As I told you in April, political events I regard as a thorough bore unless there is a prospect of losing one's head or one's income, which never seemed for one moment at risk during your Monster Meeting's collapse in the rain that day – though I own that I liked the comedy of seeing poor Mr O'Connor helped into his cab by the Police, and the sundry other amusements we saw. But I confess that recent events in Europe have roused even me. Did you read of the 10,000 French slaughtered in the Faubourg St-Antoine? And now Austria marches against the Magyar rebels! I suppose Windischgrätz will succeed as he did at Prague, but such doings stir the blood most awfully, and make me very disconsolate with my bills of lading. Are they to be copied in England – or, rather, in Ireland – do you suppose? If they was, I shouldn't hanker after a berth in a ship to the New World with some of my Sea-captains, for we should be sure of finding adventures enough at home.

At any event, because of these possible convulsions to old England, and because I have a six weeks leave due to me, I plan to make an expedition – alas, no, not to Paris or to Buda-Pesth! – an expedition through England by these Waterways, which the Board has buried beneath such mountains of paper and such quantities of ink that I begin to doubt if real water and real barges exist in them. I shall thus combine some business for the Board, in visiting sites most easy of access by water, with more or less adventurous travels of my own to discover in how revolutionary a state the country may be. I am preparing myself for my ordeal by two hours work a-day in a skiff I have acquired, under the eye of a Yankee boatswain!

I shall make my journey alone, by river and canal as far to the West as Glastonbury, then Northwards by Swindon and the Severn canal to Gloucester and Shrewsbury and beyond. If I find myself in Wales, about the commencement of December, may I address myself and skiff to your Castle, like a knight of old with his steed?

You have not wrote that you got back safe to Cambridge that day of the Charter Meeting, but I suppose that you did. Write now, like a good fellow, and say that you will be at your Castle in December, and give me your views on the chances of Count Kossuth and his Magyars, whom I suppose you support against their Austrian masters.

Your affectionate friend,
Tresham Pitcher
PS Today is my 20th birthday!

VI

- - - - - - - - - - - -

AGAINST THE WINTER'S SKY rose a wide Welsh moor crossed by a road which climbed and fell over its ridges until the grey thread could no longer be traced across the misty waste. Now seen upon this road, now only heard from a hollow in the moor, there crawled a cart pulled by a grey pony. Light, and colour, had faded out of the landscape with the onset of dusk and coming snow, but as the cart plodded closer across that cold and dreary upland, and began to descend towards the shelter of trees, it could be seen that two men were seated in the cart, whilst a boat, a rowing skiff, was roped upon it behind them.

Where the road entered the trees it made a sharp descent, the cart pressing on the pony's quarters. The passenger threw off his covering of sacks and jumped into the road to walk.

The carter showed no signs of life. The passenger, Tresham Pitcher, who had fallen almost into a trance of cold and inaction upon the moors above, now slammed along with his boots ringing on the ground, and looked about him with revived interest in the altered scene as he descended. To the slope clung crooked little oaks straining uphill like a tribe of old dwarfs labouring to climb out of the valley below. Down the road he followed his bobbing skiff on the cart. With the driest of whispers the few shrivelled fingers of leaves in the oaks stirred in a current of air from below. It was a milder breath, perhaps (thought Tresham) from the sea. He stepped out with fresh vigour at the notion of reaching his destination, and passed the cart.

Now beeches replaced the oaks, tall and Gothic grey, pillared alleys opening to left and right. They grew out of greensward and bracken and lichened rock, and drifts of their fallen leaves fringed the road, which here doubled back and forth through the steep wood as it lost height. Tresham was looking eagerly for a glimpse of the sea, or of the house, when he realised that what he had already seen, and had taken for a natural outcrop of stone damming the valley below, was in fact the Castle. His stride broke, startled. Pigeons clattered out of the trees. From the valley came the sound of running water, which trickled into his head with words:

And at the nyghte they came unto a castel in a valeye closed with a rennynge water and with stronge walles and hyhe.

He waited for the cart. He felt a reluctance to end his journey, with the end in sight. He looked down on the fantastic assemblage of roofs and towers filling the valley below, too indistinctly seen in the dusk for him to tell what was finished, or ruined, or half-built. No gleam of light, no sound of life, gave an indication that the place was inhabited. A few flakes of snow now began to materialise out of the sky and float silently through the trees.

When the cart reached him, Tresham climbed onto it again. With his skiff and his battered bags, riding up to the door on the carrier's cart, he felt more fully equipped for the character of adventurous traveller than he might have felt on foot and alone. 'This is Ravenrig, I suppose?' he asked the carrier for reassurance in hearing his own voice. 'Sir Daniel Farr's?'

Upon the bundle of sacks and cloaks the round hat nodded. When the cart reached level ground, it turned to approach the castle. Even at dusk the eye of the traveller was made to perform feats of airy climbing and exploring amongst porticoes, and mullions, and oriels, and the faint glow of stone rising into towers, and turrets capped with slate, upon the mass of building confronting him between the valley's wooded slopes. All the windows were dark except in the north wing of the great façade, where light streamed out in profusion through many windows, and touched the outlines of urns and balustrading on the terrace without.

'Drive up to the front entrance,' said Tresham, 'then after you may take the boat where the servants direct you.'

A mighty door within its arch of stone soon faced him. A peal on the bell: the disagreeable sensations of waiting, and the tramp of feet within, confirmed his wish that journeys, however miserable, did not have to end in arrivals: and the door was drawn open. Lit by his lantern stood a robed native of some Eastern land. Into this black-bearded countenance under its huge turban Tresham stammered out who he was. Without a word the Easterner stood back that he might enter. As Tresham did so, he remembered his skiff.

'Oh, look here, I have a boat in the cart there. Where shall the fellow drop it off?'

'Boat?' The Turk – if Turk he was – leaned forward and fairly shouted the word into Tresham's face.

'A small boat. A skiff.'

'Skiff, skiff,' said the Turk, trying the word over in guttural tones. 'I will see skiff.' He tramped out to the cart with swinging lantern and was soon examining the frail-looking boat, which the carrier unroped. Left in darkness at the door, Tresham could only wait. When the Turk came back, after issuing orders to the carrier, he said, 'Good, is good. Is like kaik.' Then he swept indoors and away, calling out, 'Come! Come! Follow!'

The lantern lit its bearer's robes, and spilled out rays into the emptiness of one room after another, and showed the stone walls of corridors and the colours of tapestries, and climbed a spiral stair, until at length the Turk, pausing to sweep his hand over beard and moustache, threw open a heavy door and led Tresham into a room which seemed to blaze with light in the traveller's eyes after the dimness and uncertainty of his approach.

An hour or so later, when the family and their guests had eaten dinner at the round table in a hall which occupied a floor of the one inhabited tower of Ravenrig, Tresham was able for the first time sufficiently to withdraw his faculties from grappling at close quarters with the company, to take stock of his foothold amongst them. It was unearthly, a dream, after the rough and lonely life he had led for weeks past on his travels, to find himself a part of this brilliant scene. He said so to Lady Fanny Farr, his friend Roland's mother.

'My dear Mr Butcher,' she said, turning on him the lustre of her attention out of large dark eyes, 'your adventures fascinate me, I wish to hear every detail, I am most impatient, we are all most impatient. Of course Roland has showed me your letter – you won't mind that? But I must tell you, this room you admire is not to be our dining hall when the castle is finished building. Not a bit of it! This room is to be. . . oh, I can't at all recall what it is to be, when dear Mr Bounty – beside me here – when dear Mr Bounty our architect is done with us. Some of the old tapestries we may remove' to the large dining hall,' she said, indicating grey-green needlework faintly colouring the stone walls above them, 'and some of the arms, I suppose. Now, Mr Butcher, do you see those trophies of arms above the door there? The mail suit and the long swords crossed below? Now, would you not say those are Circassian? I am convinced they are Circassian.'

Tresham looked up to where the edged steel patterned the stone above the Gothic arch. 'They certainly have very much of the appearance of Circassian arms,' he said sagely.

'You think so? Not European?'

'You know, I dare say,' said Tresham, 'you know there is a tribe of Lesghians in Circassia who wear a Crusader cross on their mail shirts and use swords inscribed in mediæval French? Perhaps those arms are some of theirs.'

'How fascinating. How fascinating.' Her eyes glittered on him, then she called across the table to her husband, 'Daniel! My dear! It seems that my trophies are Circassian after all. Mr Butcher is quite an expert, and he puts it beyond doubt.'

At this Sir Daniel, a short, square man with determination firmly stamped upon his features, looked rather fierce at Tresham through his gold-rimmed eyeglasses and asked, 'I don't know how close to Circassia you ever was, Mr Pitcher?'

'Never closer than Italy, sir. But my uncle who is squire of Rainshaw has any number of books of travels to those parts, and I – '

'Squire of where, you say?'

'Of Rainshaw in Kent.' These questions were the first words Sir Daniel had addressed to him, and Tresham felt them as a challenge to his substantiality and worth. Lady Fanny, however, had laid her hand for one flattering moment on his sleeve, and rushed on: 'I cannot tell you the relief it is to us that Roland should have found a sensible friend. At Cambridge he has fallen in with such a set of Radicals and Revolutionists you cannot conceive of it. So he says – is it true? – or is he quizzing us, do you think? Such dreadful rows he has with his poor papa, though, over the news from Europe! What are your views, Mr Butcher? I am for the Magyars – but can one be for the Magyars without being a Revolutionist? Have you visited Hungary? There will be time for us to find out all about you because you will stop with us, I hope, until. . . until you must go away. That he is the youngest makes it natural for Roland to be Republican, you know. Oh yes. The youngest child always wants to turn things upside down so that he may end up on top, is it not so? Are you the youngest child in your family, I wonder? I say that Roland is youngest, though Enid of course is his twin, but girls run ahead, do they not? You will like Enid, I know – not a bit the contrary character of Roland. Enid, my dear!' she called out to the slight and shy-seeming girl in a cloud of hair across the table, 'I wish you to pay particular attention to Mr Butcher whilst he is here. I have told him how excited you were over his adventures in the letter Roland read us.'

Enid only pouted out her lips towards her mother, ignoring Tresham. It struck him how no one corrected her for calling him 'Mr Butcher', as if they had learned the futility of trying to set right her misapprehensions.

'It is so delightful for the children to have a visitor,' she went on, 'they see no company here, there is no company here. Why we are building a castle in such a place I hardly know,' she added, staring rather blankly, as though paths she tripped along in the maze led her always to this blind alley.

Whilst she had her hand upon the sleeve of a new captive, though, such flatness only lasted a moment. With her attention on him, Tresham had time or thoughts for little else. On his other side sat the elder daughter, Lucinda, who replied very indifferently to his remarks, and turned back to a low discussion with her brother Edmond, eldest in the family. Opposite Tresham sat Roland, and when Tresham looked across at his cheerful bright face in the candlelight, and his cluster of curls and arched brows, he was astonished that this boy – who had blacked his boots at school – should all the time have had at his back, like a secret, the magnificent reality which now surrounded him. It was as though a low door often passed was discovered to lead into a treasure chamber.

For the scene, to Tresham's eyes, was indeed magnificent: fires blazing in two vast chimney-places, the sconces, the trophies and tapestries, the coffered ceiling gilt and scarlet and blue above the round table loaded with silver – it was journey's end. Not least intriguing was the Turk, who served only Sir Daniel. In his fantastic and wide-spreading turban he stood behind his master's chair, looming above him, and seeming to shade him, like an item of ceremonial equipment, a State Umbrella perhaps, employed to enhance the dignity of a Ruler who, travelling light far from the seat of his power, has been able to bring with him only this one symbol of the absolute authority possessed in another place. Not here, for all its magnificence, was centred Sir Daniel's world. This was merely a conquered province. Rather than taking part in the talk, the visiting ruler seemed to Tresham to ponder his own thoughts in the shade of his Turkish umbrella, though responding with his attention, and with sufficient good humour, if addressed by one of his children. Such attention sent a thrill of alarm through Tresham, which lesser creatures of the jungle might experience when the king of beasts turns his yellow eyes this way and that. He remembered the tone of voice in which Sir Daniel had asked, 'I don't know how close to Circassia you ever was?; it seemed to have the timbre of the lion's roar in it. Here was a formidable adversary!

'Children! Daniel! Mr Bounty!' called out Lady Fanny beside him as they all rose at the finish of the meal. 'You all know how I dote upon theatricals, and none of you will let me have any – well, now, a charming idea has come to me, which I hope our new friend will indulge me in – ' here she laid a hand on Tresham's arm – 'and it is this. We are all quite upon tenterhooks to hear of his travels, and why should we not have a chapter of them each evening from his own lips, do you follow me, as if he was a travelling minstrel of the olden time with a ballad to sing of heroic adventure? Would not that be grand? I don't doubt we should be well amused, for in recounting how he has come here in that scamp Jenkins's cart he has been wonderfully droll. Is it settled? Mr Butcher, will you allow it?'

*   *   *

Bright eyes – Lady Fanny's and her daughter Enid's in particular – had sparked Tresham into a desire to appear in a leading rôle before them, and he had nonchalantly agreed to recount his canal journey to them. How he regretted it next day! His head was full of it as he climbed the sand dunes which sheltered the end of the Ravenrig valley from the sea. His apprehension of Sir Daniel as a formidable adversary had resolved itself overnight into a thorough dread of exposing himself and his tales to that powerful scrutiny. He mustn't disappoint Roland, or Enid, or Lady Fanny. And the journey had not disappointed him: it was a question of so selecting, and shaping, and relating its incidents that he might convey to them all – to Sir Daniel too – his own saitisfaction with his adventures, which he had felt very strongly sitting amidst the splendours of Ravenrig last night, at journey's end.

He paused in his climb up the sand dune and looked back. In the hollow of the valley's end, beside the stream, stood a low white cottage sunk into bracken and wintry grass. At its door stood Roland beside his twin sister Enid on her white pony, both of them bending forward to see whatever it was that an old man in rusty black showed them so tenderly in a basket he held. An extraordinary idea came into Tresham's head, from his childhood, forgotten for years: that he was a changeling, not the ordinary child everyone took him for but the heir to mysteries, whose true nature only his mother knew, and was often on the brink of telling him. It was the streaming white hair of the old man, or the basket, or perhaps the sea's presence beyond the sand dunes, which put the idea so vividly into his mind. Then it was gone. Behind the cottage the valley curved away between steep woods towards the unseen castle. Above the cottage, above the woods, the moor was whitened with snow. The stream flowed clear and fast over stones at the cottage door, but its waters were unheard by Tresham, drowned in the steady thunder of the sea shaking the sandhills. Nor could he hear what was said at the cottage door, or see into the basket so carefully grasped. What might he have been, if he had been a changeling? Heir to Uncle Marcus? He found that the idea of Rainshaw had diminished since he had seen Ravenrig, and what Roland was heir to. He turned his back on the valley and toiled up the soft sand. What he would have given the world to be exchanged into, at that moment, was some heroic traveller whose exploits would spellbind the company, and reduce the leonine Sir Daniel into a lap-dog. Oh, wretched travels!

He had walked along the valley with Roland beside Enid's pony. It had been suggested at breakfast, in a pleasant upper room of the tower where he had found the four children of the house seated round a table, Lucinda behind tea-making apparatus, Edmond reading a letter, Roland and Enid arguing. The ceiling of the room glared white with the reflection of snow lying out of doors.

'Shall you go out shooting?' Edmond had asked him as he sat down. 'There will be capital sport with the woodcock in this snow.' Then he resumed his letter.

'You must have been awfully glad it didn't snow upon your boating,' Roland said. 'Or maybe it did?'

'Oh,' said Enid lightly, 'I don't suppose Mr Pitcher gives a hang for snow.' Tresham couldn't tell whether the dance in her curiously slanted eyes mocked him or not. When she talked to you she held her face at a high angle, and looked at you aslant, like a young horse inclined to bolt.

'Enid!' exclaimed Lucinda. 'I don't know what Mamma would say if she heard what language you use when she is not by.'

Enid laughed. 'I don't suppose a hang or two will scandalise Mr Pitcher, Lucy, who lives so much amongst sea-captains. You see, Mr Pitcher, I know all your secrets from Roland. The sea-captains are only the least part of it, I assure you.'

Her nursery naughtiness was spiced by dwelling in the body of a young woman, which she seemed to disregard. Walking beside her pony along the valley towards the sea, later in the morning, Tresham couldn't help imagining how it would be if she took a turn for real naughtiness, and abandoned the nursery for the bedroom with those eager manners, and kissed instead of teased. Roland rested his hand on her pony's neck, and she rested her hand on his. This seemed to Tresham very enviable.

What was not enviable in Roland's lot? Ravenrig, when he had looked back at it rising to close the valley behind them, had seemed a castle of fantasy, a dream, every crochet and tower and battlement powdered with snow this morning against a sky of blue intensity that gleamed like the mediæval Heaven of old illuminations. How could Roland have come from this idyll of stone and trees and running water to squat in Tresham's grate at school and blow up his fire with such meek humility? All the superiority which Tresham had then enjoyed fell away from him in this place. Instead, the pain of longing, for he

[88]

knew not what, squeezed tears out of his eyes, which the sea-wind encrusted on his cheek as he climbed the yielding sand dune.

There lay the sea, the limitless flux of water surrounding the island. Journey's end. And how was the journey to be described? Certain grim scenes only, from the island behind him, came into memory's eye: cold dawns, wintry woods, low spirits, darkness, the antagonism of nature itself and all he met with. That was the reality. It must be transformed. Courage, pace, adventure – that was the nature of the journey, more true than mere reality, which must transmute the raw material of fact and incident so that his listeners heard what he believed he had experienced. Below him the cold dull waves broke on the stones, broke and receded, broke again with their monotonous chant. And this was supposed to be the sea! The Θαλασσα of Xenophon's poor soldiers! How much it needed changing, before it could figure as the element of adventures and romances. There it lay, the restless unhappy sea. He looked at it without satisfaction, as if he had not known that this boundary to his travels existed.

*   *   *

Roland was pacing up and down his mother's sitting room in the afternoon when Lady Fanny came in, followed by Mr Bounty the architect, who was carrying before him a fluffy little dog on a velvet cushion, as though it formed part of the display in an hieratic procession. There was a certain pampered whiteness and softness of skin about Mr Bounty suggestive of church ceremonial. Finding that Roland stared at him, and did not give up his ground, he withdrew. Roland resumed pacing. Unpinning her bonnet, Lady Fanny said into her looking-glass: 'Oh, my dear, don't be a bore striding about so. And where is your friend? I hope you haven't left him with Enid, giving her ideas?'

'He ain't a Liberal, you know,' said Roland sarcastically.

'Liberal, no, he isn't. Something a good deal worse.'

'What do you mean? Do you mean a Radical, Mamma? What do you mean?'

'I mean he is nothing at all, nobody.' Their eyes met in the glass. 'What is this about his uncle being a squire?'

Roland looked away, and would have recommenced his pacing, but checked himself. 'I know nothing about it, Mamma,' he said.

'Then you should know. You should know who your guests are, before bringing them amongst us. If you don't care about me, you might think of your sisters, at least. Where is he now? Is he with Enid? And pray do stop him telling us about this tiresome boating tonight, Roland.'

'You asked him to tell us.'

'Oh, I know I did! What can have possessed me? Do you think Lucinda might play the harp to us instead? No, I believe that is almost worse.'

'Mr Bounty might be asked to perform, do you think?'

'Now, Roland, that is wicked – !' Nevertheless Lady Fanny giggled, and clasped in her arms the little dog which had jumped onto her lap. Her giggle made Roland quite as happy as her caress made the dog.

*   *   *

Dinner at the castle was at six o'clock, but still Sir Daniel, who had not been seen by Tresham all day, did not appear amongst them. His place was laid, his chair empty, the Turk absent. When asked after her father, Lucinda replied that no doubt he had been out on the estate to oversee the rebuilding of farmhouses or the unloading of materials onto the quay he had established a few miles away on the coast. He was always 'improving', she said.

'And Lucy – ' across the table came Enid's eager voice – 'and Lucy, the people have taken up his word, haven't they? "Improving". Tell about the tenant we heard saying to Mamma that he'd done some improving, and now was going to "improve even more" – didn't he?'

Tresham was stirred to find himself watched and attended to by Enid. But he wished she would talk to him, and look at him, directly. It seemed as if she needed to hold a brother's or a sister's hand before addressing him. Lucinda put an end to Enid's intervention with her cold stare. Then she said to Tresham that her father suffered occasionally from the tertian fever which had hung about him since his early days in the Levant.

'What was his business, just, in the East?' asked Tresham to keep alive the conversation (for Lady Fanny was as absorbed in Mr Bounty as she had appeared to be absorbed in himself last evening).

'Really, Mr Pitcher,' said Lucinda, 'I do not quite know all the details of Papa's concerns. Tell me, pray, have you asked Mr Bounty to show you over the works here? There is little else to amuse a visitor, I fear.'

Altogether the dinner passed slowly for Tresham. Little thrills of agitation would make him uncomfortable when he thought of his ordeal ahead. All these diverse attentions and turned-aside faces must be captured by his narrative. And Sir Daniel would not see his triumph. He rehearsed the opening words he had settled upon, even whilst talking dully with Lucinda. Slow as it passed, dinner at last ended, and Lady Fanny rose to her feet. Now she would call upon him: the blood coursed through his veins.

'Come, children, Lucy, Enid, we will leave the gentlemen to their wine. Not too long, Edmond, pray.'

She had forgotten. Disappointment overshadowed relief. As he rose, there came a strong flat voice across the hall:

'Ain't Mr Pitcher going to give us his account of how he has come among us? Mr Pitcher, I've come down particular to hear you sing for your supper, the way the minstrels Lady Fanny talked of did. Now then.'

In the stone arch of the doorway stood Sir Daniel, the Turk behind him. The challenge had come.

'By all means, if you wish it,' Tresham replied, striving to keep his voice from shaking, 'if Lady Fanny hadn't intentionally forgot?'

Enid said, 'Oh, Mamma doesn't forget by intention.' Laughter put the children on his side. All sat down, dresses rustling, men drawing their wine towards them. He was aware of the sparkle of the table like the stretch of the lists between himself and Sir Daniel.

'Five hundred years ago,' he began, in the words he had fixed upon to get himself started, 'when Lady Fanny's minstrels used to go among the castles telling their stories, they liked to begin by joining up their English adventures to the old stories of the ancient world, and making out, for instance, that it was some of the old heroes from Troy who had founded Britain. Then Achilles and Hector were our English knights' ancestors, and the minstrels' stories just a continuing of the *Iliad*.'

'And is your story to be?' asked Lady Fanny.

'No, nothing so grand. No, Lady Fanny, I tell you that – I remind you of it – as a basis for saying what I do think is true, of myself and all other travellers. I think no one goes on a journey without adding himself to a list of travellers which began with the Argonauts, and went on with Arthur's knights, and won't end till the world ends.'

'Gracious!' said Lady Fanny. 'What a charmingly romantic view of something as dull as a journey.'

Tresham took a sip of wine, glad his hand didn't shake. Their faces looked up at him like flowers to the sun. The sense of mastering words strengthened his nerve. 'Now,' he said, 'I'll leave out my preparations –'

'Why?' asked Sir Daniel, looking up from the dish of rice which had been set before him by the Turk, and which he had been eating very unconcernedly. 'Tell us it all. Why did you make this journey? Were you bade?'

'Not bade, no. What I suggested was agreed to.'

'And why did you suggest such a thing, now?'

'I was like a child who wants pictures in his book, sir. I wanted to see these waterways I'd worked at for two years. Not one of those office fellows had ever been upon a barge, or opened a lock, or pushed his boat through a cut with his feet, or even knew how it was done.'

'And they let you go for such a purpose?' Having finished his rice, Sir Daniel now waited with hand outstretched for the Turk to put a peeled orange into it. No one else had been offered an orange.

'No,' Tresham admitted, 'there were things gone wrong here and there which needed looking to, and no one wanted to leave London in winter except me, so they let me go upon their business as well as my own.'

Granted attention, he told of his preparations, and of his setting out one autumn morning on the Thames, and of the long days' rowing, and of dry nights in his tent under a hedge, and wet nights in farmers' barns. But the adventures (he thought to himself as he talked) – the adventures! How was he to concoct out of the little incidents of the journey such adventures as would put into their minds the true picture he had of himself – the picture of a Traveller who had overcome as many obstacles, and demons, and ordeals, as Ulysses and Sir Gawaine rolled together? Lady Fanny's voice broke in.

'And what was most unpleasant about it all, Mr Butcher?' she enquired, with the unmistakable air of a listener who will consult a watch, or yawn, if not allowed to speak.

'Unpleasant? Why, most unpleasant was rowing on a wet seat, I suppose. There is no remedy for that.'

'But . . .' complained Lucinda, 'truly did nothing unpleasant happen to you? Nothing uncommon? No real adventure? One hears England is so – '

'Oh Lucy, you goose!' cried Enid. 'How stupid you are! There are no adventures of your sort to be come by nowadays!'

'My sort; I'm sure I don't know what you mean by my sort.'

'I mean romantic adventures, of course, you stupid!'

'Enid – !'

'Now girls!' interposed Lady Fanny. 'We had better let Mr Butcher continue.'

'Miss Enid,' said Tresham, wresting her bright eyes and flushed face onto himself, 'Miss Enid, I do assure you there's life in the world yet, and adventures too. I could tell you a dozen.'

'Pray not a dozen,' said Lady Fanny, 'but one, if it is amusing.'

'Perhaps this will serve you, then. You must know that there passes about upon the roads and trackways of England on every day of the year a perfect army of men looking for work. Sometimes one comes upon them in gangs – when I own I dodged them if I could – and sometimes, more often, I would meet with a single navvy on the tramp, with his tools on his back and his lurcher at his side, when I hadn't the least objection to sharing my barn or my crust with him, or sharing his "tommy" as they call it, for often they are Irishmen and have a good many tales to tell. I knew nothing of their world, beyond what I had once seen of a shanty camp across a cutting at my uncle's place, which had rather haunted my dreams. Why,' he went on, 'the very existence of this army of men on the tramp was a wonder to me, for it's half as if that whole class of men, and stout fellows too, had been called to arms by a clarion we don't hear asleep in our beds, and were marching to join colours we don't see through our windows. For you don't meet with these navvies in the towns, and you don't meet with them in the railway carriages nor the coaches either, but they're there all the same, tramping and gathering about the lanes, quite as proud and free as any men living.

'Well, one cold morning a few miles from Gloucester, when I was coming down to the water from the barn where I had passed the night, I was hailed by one of these Irishmen who came running out of a wood with his cap off as if the Devil was behind him. I dare say I was as wild a looking figure as himself, for I had a rough beard then, which I shaved off before coming to you. He certainly took me for such another one as he was – my skiff was under a hedge and I hadn't pulled it out yet. Gabbling out words I couldn't follow, he laid hold of my arm to pull me back with him into the wood. Well, I went. Such a wood it was, too – I wish you could see it as I do – dark, you know, and wintry, with such brakes of thorn and briar as you fancy covered all England in old days! On we pushed into the wood until we came upon a clearing under some oaks, which I took for a charcoal-burner's place of work at first. But I saw a couple of kilns and I knew they were for lime – burning chalk for lime, you know. On one of the kilns I saw what I took for odds and ends of old clothes. Two bundles. At one side of the kiln a pair of boots and moleskin trousers, at the other an old sock cap and half of one of the velveteen coats the navvies wear. Nothing between, where the heat of the skiln was. I was close before I saw there was a pair of legs in the trousers, burned clean off, and a head in the sock cap at t'other end, burned off just as clean. The lime, the heat of the lime, had burned the poor fellow through as neat as mice eat through a cheese. The two of them had come on the glade the night before, and had laid themselves down to sleep in the warmth of the fires. Very likely they were drunk. In the night one of the poor fellows creeps closer and closer to the kiln till he lays himself down on top of it to drive the cold out of his bones. In the morning his tramping-mate finds him in two halves and comes hallooing through the wood for me.'

There were stirrings and shocked sounds. But Sir Daniel said, 'Such was the yarn the Irishman spun you, at all events, Mr Pitcher.'

'What do you mean, Papa?' asked Roland.

'I mean, if one had murdered t'other, what surer way than the action of quicklime to cover up his crime for him?'

'Very well,' said Tresham, as if he had considered this objection, 'but why show me his victim's remains?'

'Because, my young friend,' said Sir Daniel, 'because he figured a young gentleman like yourself being taken in by his tale would be the best support such a rigmarole could have when you and he went off to tell the Justice all about it together. Didn't he beg you to go with him to find a Justice, eh?'

'No,' Tresham decided to say, 'no, he didn't.' Sir Daniel, who had been complacently cracking walnuts, swept the pile of shells irritably aside. Tresham expected further shots from him, but instead Lucinda asked:

'What did he do, the Irishman?'

'What did you do?' asked Roland. 'I shouldn't have known what to do.'

'Called for a constable,' suggested Lady Fanny. The children laughed, but Sir Daniel cut into it to ask his elder son, who was staring into his wine:

'And you, Edmond, what should you have done, I wonder? If you'd found yourself for once away from home and obliged to look out for yourself?'

'What? Are you still at the Irishman?' asked Edmond mildly. 'I daresay I should have wished the man good morning and left him to it.'

'Pray ask Mr Pitcher what he did do,' urged Enid across the table.

'The truth is,' said Tresham, 'if you make such a journey through England as I have done, you pass between two worlds, one above the water, so to speak, where constables may be called and Justices appealed to, and one down below, where you may as well expect to settle matters by calling a constable as expect a constable to settle your quarrel with a Nile crocodile. If you venture below the water, why, you must shift for yourself.'

'I take it, then, that you didn't call a constable or take the Irishman before a Justice, as you considered yourself out of reach of such remedies,' said Sir Daniel, who was wolfishly throwing walnuts into his mouth again. 'So what did you decide upon? How did you "shift for yourself"?'

'The Irishman, sir, proposed that we dig a grave and bury his comrade, and so we did, and I borrowed the dead man's shovel to lend a hand with the work.'

'You buried him?' exclaimed Lady Fanny.

'We did, and hard work it was too, with tree roots to be cut through and frost in the ground. There now,' he said into the silence his story had obtained for him, 'there's evidence for you of the two worlds I spoke of, that a clerk in the Waterways may find himself burying the two halves of an Irishman in a Gloucestershire wood, once he steps out of his office to discover if his waterways are real or not.'

'And when Mamma asked what was unpleasant,' said Enid in awe-struck tones, 'you said a wet seat!'

'Unpleasant ain't much of a word, Miss Enid. Unpleasant means a wet seat, or midges, yes, it does. But my morning's work in the wood showed me a world I didn't know of, real enough, too, and myself caught up in the midst of it. That ain't "unpleasant", that's – why, that's the very purpose of making the journey, I suppose, to find your-self in as deep water as that, with no constables to save you.'

His vehemence carried them with him; except Sir Daniel. 'You mistake the purpose of making a journey, Mr Pitcher, if that's what you suppose.'

'What is the purpose, Papa?' Lucinda asked.

'To take along with you some benefit not to be found where you're a-going, Lucy, that's the proper object of making a journey.'

'I don't see – ' began Tresham.

'Law and order, Mr Pitcher,' supplied Sir Daniel. 'That's the bene-fit you should have took with you. Yes, by calling a constable into this wood of yours, which you say is beyond the reach of law – by carrying the Irishman off before a Justice – by making the exertion, sir, to extend the rule of law where it wasn't to be found – that should have been your purpose. Aye, that should have been your purpose, not complimenting yourself upon your facility for living outside the law yourself. I think, Mr Pitcher, you've a very degenerate view of the purpose of journeys, I do, indeed, in spite of your bringing up the Argonauts and such. Life and the world ain't put into your hand so that you may amuse yourself with sensations, no, no! Come, we will all go up together into the drawing room – that is, with your permission, my dear,' he added across the table to his wife, already on his feet, the Turk pulling back his chair.

Through the Gothic arch the party defiled up a flight of stairs into the tower room above, now in use as a drawing room. There was here, temporarily, a very heterogeneous assemblage of objects of art put down pell-mell all about the floor and on the tables: curios from the

East, statues, fragments of marble, armour from the ancient world as well as alabaster and ivory and arms from the Middle Ages, all loomed or glowed or gleamed in the light of candelabra. Through the weird interior landscape of these oddments, waiting dispersal to other rooms and galleries, Tresham walked away from the fire into the recesses of the room. He appeared to examine the objects of art, but really nursed his mortification. What value was there in amusing the rest of the company – even Enid – if he had not impressed himself upon Sir Daniel? What were the plaudits of the stalls, in face of censure from the Manager?

'Mr Pitcher!'

It was Sir Daniel's voice. He was seated apart from the others, his Turkish servant busy with brazier and copper saucepan in a fireplace beside him. Tresham walked towards him between columns and statues.

'Sit down, Mr Pitcher. Yusef makes me my coffee as it is made in the East. Because it seemed an affectation I tried to give it up. But I cannot like European coffee. See, he boils the water over the fire. Then he will throw in the coffee. It must be brought just to the boiling-point three times. You shall try a *finjan*.' He spoke in Turkish to Yusef, who, his eyes a-glitter, handled his materials and blew up his fire with a conjuror's dexterity. Tresham felt himself fascinated into this circle of influence around the glowing charcoal, whilst powerless voices and laughter receded almost out of hearing at the room's other end. When he was sipping the sweet, thick coffee from a little cup in a filigree holder, Sir Daniel asked him, 'Tell me, Mr Pitcher, why do you suppose that such excitements as burying an Irishman are better worth your while than the satisfaction of a copying clerk with his day's work well completed?'

'Because, sir – well, you must be a little stouter of heart, I suppose, for the one than the other.'

'Ah – stoutness! But a clerk, to be a good clerk, don't have much call to be "stout", surely?'

'It is my very objection to being a clerk.'

'So you have ambitions?'

'My ambitions were knocked on their head when I was taken away from school.'

'And so, you strike back a blow, do you, by this running after adventures on the canals?'

'If that is how it appears to you, sir.'

'Don't mistake me, I am not disapproving of stoutness; no, no! But I am sceptical. I have a sceptical nature – a state of things brought on by having been knocked on my back, my young friend, more times than you can dream of! Now look here. If you have ambition, well enough; then adventures are incidents along the way to be endured whilst steering your proper course. But adventures – dangers – excitements – are no proper ends of themselves, not they. If you have no aims but those, why, pretty soon you reach the limit, and you do not survive. You do not survive.'

He looked hard into Tresham's face through his eyeglasses. Then he said, 'Now, sir, you said it was at Blixworth you changed from the Severn Canal onto the Grand Union, I believe?'

'Yes, at Blixworth.'

Sir Daniel shook his grizzled head. 'Not possible. The link is on the canal map, right enough, but it don't exist on the ground, for it never was built. No, sir. Somehow you came, I know, for here you are with your skiff amongst us. But you have not come quite honestly, that I know too. Never fear, it does not harm me and I shan't make a noise about it, for to be honest I've taken a liking to you, and no man living admires boldness – stoutness, as you call it – better than what I do. But boldness employed with a proper end in view. Mind, I don't say the end must be a grand one. But it must exist. Else it is mere adventure. Mere longing for recklessness. And that has but one finish – an early grave. No, I never would employ a reckless man about any work of mine, not until all others had refused it. But a bold man – well, all the proper work of a man requires boldness, I believe.'

'Even a clerk's work?'

'I'm sure such work will not always be yours, Mr Pitcher.'

Hands which looked too square-fingered for the task unhooked the gold wire of Sir Daniel's spectacles from behind his ears. With the removal of his eyeglasses his scrutiny of Tresham ceased, and his attention withdrew into a musing stare focused upon difficulties visible to himself alone.

*   *   *

[98]

Some of the difficulties preoccupying Sir Daniel became plain to Tresham next morning, when he stepped out onto the terrace. For in place of yesterday's busy scene, all work on the castle had ceased: no tap of masons' hammers, or creak of bricklayers' barrows, or any activity whatever broke the silence of the scene or the whiteness of the snow fallen upon the unfinished works.

'Mr Pitcher!'

It was almost a whisper, Enid's voice directed at him from above. He looked up. She was at a window, tying the strings of a bonnet drawn round her face.

'Roland is in the stable yard and would like you to go to him, if you please.'

'Shall you be there, Miss Enid?'

'You should wear a greatcoat, for he intends driving.'

'I have none. Nothing respectable.'

'I will bring one of Papa's.'

Her face was gone. At last she had addressed herself to him directly and with an urgency which made him sparkle as he hurried under an archway in search of Roland. Some adventure was afoot! Out of the yard rattled a pony-carriage, Roland driving his mother's pair of ponies, Enid beside him. She threw down to Tresham the bundle of furs in her arms and squeezed up against her brother to make room for him beside her.

'I'll walk up the hill,' he said, settling the long fur coat on his shoulders, and striding out to keep pace with them.

'You see Papa's men, the men building the castle, have struck work?' asked Roland excitedly as they hurried along. 'They held a meeting in the village and decided.'

'Are we going to the village?'

'No need. Sparrow's there.'

'A friend of yours?'

'Sent by a friend. Sent by about the grandest fellow I know, Truefitt of King's,' said Roland proudly. 'Truefitt knows ever so many fellows of Sparrow's sort, ready to dart off where they're needed and organise labour.'

'Organise it to strike work?'

'Organise it to sell itself at a just price, Pitcher,' Roland corrected

[99]

his friend earnestly as he drove along. 'That's fair, surely?'

On the steep road out of the valley Tresham strode ahead, wondering what they were up to. With Sir Daniel's warning in his mind, as to the need for purpose, he tried to settle what his own line should be. Mischief, in supporting Sir Daniel's enemies, might be forgiven a son and daughter, but would not be forgiven a stranger. He would stay aloof, watch, decide where his advantage lay. It made him feel mighty mature, deciding his actions all according to plan, as he stood waiting for the two children to catch up with him through the trees in the pony carriage.

'So,' he said when they came up, 'where are we going, if not to interview your strikers?'

'Well,' answered Roland, 'Papa has brought in a gang of his navvies, they're some of the fellows he takes about on his works abroad, and they are to be landed at the quay this morning. Sparrow sent me word of it and told me to go to them. To tell them. If I can.'

'Papa's idea,' put in Enid, 'is to break the strike with them, you see.'

'Ah. And you – '

'I have to send them away,' said Roland. 'Come, climb up with us.'

Enid again made room on the seat for Tresham. He realised that he hadn't taken the place earlier so that he shouldn't be squeezed against her. Yet to squeeze against her was his keen desire. He jumped into the little carriage and sat down as nonchalantly as he could. But the 'maturity' he had prided himself upon a moment or two earlier, in respect of these two 'children', was blown into atoms already by her warmth against him.

When they reached the moors Roland turned the ponies westward towards the sea. The road climbed and fell across the snowy uplands. They drove in silence, the sea a wide grey gleam ahead. After a while Tresham spoke to Enid – spoke softly, because she was so close, because Roland's thoughts took him away from them: 'Does your mother know where you are gone with her ponies?'

'Why did you make your journey in winter?' she asked instead of replying, the words rushing out with her breath warm and scented on his cheek. 'I have been meaning to ask,' she added, 'if I saw the chance to.'

'Because . . .' He was silent. How could it be said? 'Because it is only in winter you find the landscape I have always imagined.' Such thin words to explain his love for the wintry woods which lead to the end of the world. Don't you feel it here, on the moor? – he would have liked to have asked. Or here? – and laid his hand on hers so that she should feel what he felt. If he only knew the words to tell her, or how to touch her, she would believe. The moment passed. The opening she had made, closed. 'Summer is over,' he said rather savagely, in his disappointment with himself. 'My summer, at least. It was in Italy, with my father, when I was a child.'

'You speak as if one summer was all we might have,' she said, looking steadily ahead, speaking low.

Her words seemed to cast a gleam of light on the road ahead. By that gleam he asked the answer to the riddle from yesterday: 'What did the old man in the cottage by the sea show you in his basket?'

'Only a lobster.'

He looked at her profile. Aslant and mischievous, her eyes danced. 'A lobster? Am I to believe you?'

Before she could answer, the pony carriage checked under them and Roland exclaimed, 'Look! There they come!'

Over a crest of the stony road had appeared, marching towards them, a column of men. Their tramp had a cheerful ring to it which would have disheartened a foe. Enid's hand flew out of her muff and laid hold of Roland's arm. He had stopped the ponies, thrown the reins to Tresham.

'I had better go and speak with them, I suppose.'

Roland spoke in a quick, strained voice, for once unsmiling, and lightly leaped down onto the road. Tresham watched him walk away. In his long, waisted greatcoat with its furred collar he looked a slight, delicately-made figure to be defender of the road in face of the marching column.

When the navvies were ten yards from him, he held up his hand. Hesitant as it looked, the gesture brought the tramping column to a confused, colliding halt of clashing boots and shovels. All were rigged out in coarse strong cloth, cloaks over their shoulders, low-crowned hats on their heads and their tools on their backs. Out stepped a strong, swarthy fellow who strode up close to Roland and swept off his hat, the black curling hair springing out all ways. He dropped the butt of his tool-bundle on the stones with a crash. Flat and loud he said to Roland:

'Now, sir, are you come to guide us on to Mr Farr's?'

'No, I am not, I am come out to stop you.' Roland's voice was very clear and boyish above the shifting feet and mutters of the men.

'Mr Farr altered his mind?'

'My father ain't much apt to alter his mind.'

The note in Roland's voice offering friendship was rejected by the man's rejoinder: 'You his son? Give us what orders you got from Master, then.'

'I have no orders from my father. I am come because I think you can't know you have been brought to break a strike of workmen building the castle.' He had raised his voice so that it carried to all the thirty or so men on the road. 'You won't take the bread from fellow-workmen's mouths, I'm sure.'

'Speak you to me, my lad,' warned the black-bearded leader. 'My gang does as they's told to do. A strike, you say?'

'Yes, for a shilling a-week and –'

'They in work, as asks this raise?'

'They were until they struck.'

'"They were until they struck"! Then what great fools they for striking, with work all up and down the land scarce as gold. You hear, mates, do you? We ain't taking their jobs from them, it's work they laid down we'll be picking up. Come, my lad, out of our road!' He shouldered his tools, as did his men, and all closed upon Roland's slender figure.

'Wait!' Roland pushed him in the chest and appealed over his head. 'Wait! – don't you see? – if you don't combine with your brother-workers my father will reduce your wages too once you've come into his power here!'

'We'll take our chance of that,' called out a voice from the ranks. 'Mr Farr has dealt square in every land I worked for him, and I'll deal square by him in bloody Wales.'

'But it's not to my father you owe loyalty, you fools!' cried Roland. 'It's your own brother-workers you must stand to!'

'When 'tis my brother pays my wages I'll stand to him first.'

'Clear away off our road, my lad,' warned the black bear of a leader, who had thrust away Roland's hand from his chest.

'I will talk to my father's men if you – '

'Your father's men!' His hand seized the frogging of Roland's great-coat and held him fast. 'And you was not your father's son I should make you smart. This gang of us – my gang you see here – a railroad in France we made for your father. Bridges in Germany we made for him. I been in Hungary with him. He brought me safe through all such heathen lands. I reckon we know more of loyalty than ever his son knows. Twenty tons of muck a-day each man of us here can shift. Now then. You clear off the road and let men to work.'

'I will not! You are impertinent!'

'None of those games, my lad,' said the labourer, for Roland had struck out at him when he found himself pushed backwards. 'You are your father's son and shan't be harmed, though.'

With one mighty arm he had picked Roland up, and now approached the pony-carriage with the evident intention of dropping the boy into it. Enid turned eyes full of ardent appeal onto Tresham. He flung the reins into her lap and jumped down onto the road.

'Here, you ugly fellow, I am not Sir Daniel Farr's relation,' he called out to the approaching navvy, 'so perhaps you've no objection to harming me. Put Mr Roland down on his feet. Thanks. There now, Farr, if you care to talk to these fellows, I will undertake that our bully boy here don't interfere with it.'

Roland walked rather uncertainly past his friend. Tresham saw him go, and heard the ponies shift on the stones behind him. His eyes never left the face of the black-bearded navvy opposing him. He saw the man's stumps of teeth, and the spittle on his tongue, as if they were the last things he might look on in this world. The sword was out of its sheath! Never had reality been so sharp, fear so keen. Wave after wave of bright blood surged through him. Seconds elapsed. Then his adversary shifted, tugged at his hat, looked away.

'Ach, ye're a child too,' he said.

Tresham turned his back on him and sauntered to the pony-carriage, where he climbed up beside Enid. He felt he had won the place close to her which she prepared for him.

'I don't know if Roland has done jawing, has he,' he said, looking back for the first time at the column of men on the road. He didn't care what Roland had done with the time, only that he had won it from that

[103]

ruffian and given it to Roland. He took the reins from Enid and stilled the shaking of his hands by resting them on his knee. The thrill in his nerves was as beautiful as the trembling of music on harp-strings. Gradually he declined from that intense pitch into ordinary perceptions of the world outside himself. His passage through that wonderful region guarded by fear was over. Roland had taken the reins and turned the carriage. Away they drove at a sharp trot from the body of men huddling uncertainly in the midst of the snowy moor. Soon his heart beat in its old dull way, and his hands grew steady as stones.

Enid and her brother and Tresham found only Mr Bounty taking luncheon in the dining hall, eating of a duck rather disconsolately. He waited whilst they ate, recounting anecdotes of persons in Society unknown to them, and followed them up into the drawing room after. From the oriel at the room's end to which Enid had been driven by his voice, she suddenly called.

'Oh, look, whatever can Papa and Lucinda be at?'

Roland and Tresham went to look. On the terrace below the unfinished south tower Sir Daniel and his daughter were unrolling what appeared to be a canvas sail.

'What are they doing?'

Sir Daniel, in a short, square-tailed blue coat and a forage cap, was attaching the canvas to a rope hanging from above, and instructing Lucinda in the knot to be used. Then he began to climb a ladder placed against the unfinished building. He stumped up the rungs in sure-footed style, though the long ladder bowed and shook at each step. Then he disappeared onto the roof. Soon a pulley-wheel turned, and the canvas sheet attached to its rope began to creep up the face of the building.

'I believe I see their dodge,' said Mr Bounty, who had joined the watchers at the oriel window. 'I told Sir Daniel that the roof that ain't slated over ought to be covered up, if heavy snow's expected, and I dare say he's at it.'

'Then why hasn't he told the men to see to it?' asked Roland. 'He's a bit long in the tooth for larking about at such a height. He don't see a bit well, you know.'

'The men are on strike,' said Tresham.

'Well, some other fellows. The gardeners ain't on strike, surely. I say – ! You don't think the fellows up on the road there have refused him, after all? Do you?'

Enid said, 'But Roly, we can't have Papa on the roof.'

'Oh, Lord, he's as neat on his pins as the cat,' said Roland rather unhappily, craning up at the roof again.

'You can't let him alone up there, Roly. You can't. We'll have to fetch men. I'm sure we could get those workmen from this morning to come if they thought Papa had put himself in danger.'

'But Enid – don't you twig to him? It's what he wants, to bring the men in. And after I'd made them see sense.'

'Sense! I don't know what the sense is in killing Papa, which is where your games will lead at last. I shall go and help him, at least.'

'You won't call it games when England is in arms as half Europe is!'

'I shan't call it games when Papa is lying dead at the foot of the wall,' said Enid energetically as she ran across the room. 'I shall call it murder, so I shall.'

She was gone through the door. At the hearth to which he had returned, Mr Bounty poked the fire. Roland searched Tresham's face. 'If I have made Papa's gang keep off,' he said, 'what is Truefitt going to say if we bring 'em in now?'

'No harm to your cause in you and me giving a hand,' said Tresham. 'We should look pretty sick sitting by the fire if he was to tumble down three storeys.'

'Come on!' Slipped from the leash of his republicanism, Roland dashed after his sister.

The terrace outside was full of the noise of a rising wind echoing off stonework, and flapping canvas with which the girls were wrestling. High above stood the figure of Sir Daniel calling down instructions. He was outlined beside the pulley-wheel against a sky full of coming snow, and appeared to be standing on the narrowest of unfinished walls like an angel on a pin. Having looked up, Roland looked quickly down in terror.

'Papa, take care! Take care!'

'Ah, you have come, have you, Roland, and Mr Pitcher too. Come up, will you, and we shall be done in half the time.'

'I don't believe I can climb it, old fellow,' said Roland quietly to Tresham. 'I don't care a bit for heights.'

'You go ahead and I'll be a rung or two below you.' Tresham took his elbow and compelled him onto the ladder.

'Pray, pray take care!' called Enid from her work with the rope. Since Roland wouldn't look at her she appealed to Tresham: 'Must he go up, Mr Pitcher?'

'He must. It is nothing. I will look out for him.'

When they reached the roof they found Sir Daniel working the pulley from a platform of scaffold behind the outer wall of the façade. Over the exposed wooden ribs of the tower roof he had been drawing, and lashing, the tarpaulins. Bridges of plank led across the abysses, and Tresham crossed one to help him. Clutching the ladder-top, Roland called:

'Papa, surely the gardeners might be brought in for this!'

'Oh, I see! You are to decide who shall work and who shall not, are you? To suit yourself. Thank you, Mr Pitcher, just pull your rope t'other way. And Roland, what if these poor fellows you've filled up with ideas of combines and strikes – what if they don't just agree with you as to drawing the line? Eh? For by Heaven there's many and many a man in Europe wishes he might halt what he's begun when the consequences are not quite comfortable to him.'

'You are thinking of Hungary, sir?'

'All Europe – all Europe! Now throw your rope over, Mr Pitcher.'

'Papa, do take care!' called Roland, who had not left the ladder-top.

'Roland, I have run about the rigging of a sloop in a Black Sea storm, you know, and shan't be upset on a roof.'

'Is the gang of fellows you landed at the quay not coming?' Tresham asked as they worked.

'Snave and his men never was coming here,' replied Sir Daniel. 'Here we have a roof over our living quarters all snug, at least. No, it's down to Tehane they've gone where the farmhouse stands open as a pie-dish. And Jones there and his family nowhere to lodge but a barn till we have the farmhouse roofed in. That's where the gang I brought in are gone. All your blackguardly Sparrow has done,' he shouted to Roland, 'all he's achieved is he's left an honest family facing a snowfall without a roof!'

'But Papa, if you break – '

'Come, Roland, lend a hand here – work whilst you talk, will you! It's all talk and no work with you agitating meddlers.' When Roland had edged his way across the planks and joined them by the flapping tarpaulin his father put a rope-end into his hand. 'Now then, belay that lashing on the beam there and make fast,' he told him, and then exclaimed, 'What, can you not tie a bowline? Was you never taught knots, either of you? Come, boys, you shall learn a bowline at least.' As he bent the rope into shape he talked to them. 'I believe a man knows his own interest pretty thoroughly without meddlers and agitators telling him what it should be. That's as I've found it. Aye, and with one man that comes to me I'll make a fair bargain for his labour. But with men as combine in a union with a meddler for their head I'll not bargain. I'll not be blackmailed by such. Now, Roland, you pull tight on the rope. How would it be if a union of bakers was to double the price of bread? Well, if a baker can't choose what price he sets on his baking, why should a labourer choose the price he sets on his labour-ing? No, no, he must charge what the market will stand, or make up his mind to be starved, that's all. Now, there's a bowline tied by Roland – well done, sir! Is your side made fast, Mr Pitcher? Capital. Come, the girls shall send us up another tarpaulin and we'll finish off over there.'

They looked over the edge of the parapet down to the terrace below. A tarpaulin was hooked ready to the pulley-rope; nearby, shrunk to child's size by the height from which they saw her, Enid was skipping with a length of rope whilst Lucinda looked on. Their laughter came up on a gust of the wind. The scene arrested Sir Daniel. 'Is it Lucy dancing?' he asked, peering down, his hand on the battlements.

'Enid skipping, Papa.'

'Ah, whichever!' he said. 'Whichever, 'tis a picture worth all Bounty's castle and more. Long may she skip.'

The pulley creaked as he wound up the canvas, work began again below and above. The wind was blowing strongly now, seizing the tarpaulins, whistling among the chimney-stacks. The effect of airy height up there, almost of flight through the rapid sky, was wonderful. Above the woods sheltering the valley the snowy moors could be seen; blanched outcrops of moorland overlooked the black woods like the tents of a besieging army. The harder and colder became their work on the roof, and the wilder and darker the weather, the more cheerful became Sir Daniel. With his rapid energy, in his square blue jacket, he might have been a seaman making all fast in a rising storm at sea – skipper of a sloop-of-war, say, reefing down his sails to carry on work come storm or mutiny.

'Wouldn't we combine well into a Union, sir?' shouted Tresham as they worked. 'The three of us on the roof here, and Miss Farr and Miss Enid sending up supplies?'

Sir Daniel gave a gruff laugh. 'We should, until Sparrow came among us and lathered us up to strike.' He was sitting against the parapet waiting to wind up the pulley, his hands square on his knees. 'Once we struck work we'd fall out though, sure enough. Thieves and revolutionists never can agree. See how Kossuth and Görgei disagree upon every question! Aye, I wish you could go to Hungary now, Roly, and see for yourself what pickles these revolutionists of yours are in. I'd send you, did I not think you'd be sure to work your way into some scrape or another.'

'But Papa, your friends at Pesth were Nationalists, surely?'

'Count Szechenyi was my employer, certainly. A fine man, and a patriot – a patriot, mark, not a Nationalist. I admired him much. Why, he put steamboats onto the Danube – a hundred schemes! I worked for him on the Theiss. And now what has become of him? He's gone mad, that's what's become of Szechenyi! The events of the year have sent him out of his mind! Any man who supposes he can harness an insurrection for progress and not for destruction – any such should go and look at the wreck of Szechenyi through the spy-hole in his cell at the Pesth madhouse. I'd send you for two pins if your mother would allow it. Come, here's our last tarpaulin,' he said, getting to his feet as the pulley-wheel began to creak. 'Poor Szechenyi! No, his long hopes of progress are in rags. Better not look beyond the work itself if you want satisfaction. If he'd hoped for nothing beyond a sound profit from his steamboats and his canals, he'd not be locked in a mad-cell today.'

Tresham considered these words as they lashed down the last tarpaulin. Following the great contractor along the plank bridge to the parapet when all was done, he asked, 'So you have had no purpose beyond completing your contract in all you've done, is that it, Sir Daniel?'

'Limited, I grant you. But I have made it out, and I keep to it, and I steer the ship by it. You, sir,' he said, turning fiercely on Tresham from the head of the ladder, 'what was your purpose, in confronting my ganger Snave on the moor there this morning?'

'Purpose?'

'Aye, purpose; do you think like Roly here, that I mayn't bring in men to undo the damage done by that blackguard Sparrow? Do you have a philosophy about it, sir, that leads you to try and stop Snave on the road?'

'I saw my friend being bullied by a ruffian,' answered Tresham coldly. 'There was no need of philosophy.'

'So your purpose is to go about the roads stopping people being bullied, is it, like the knight in a story? Don't you enquire into the rights and wrongs of the case? I fear you are an incorrigible adventurer, Mr Pitcher, I do indeed.'

His forage cap disappeared down the ladder, followed by Roland. Tresham was alone on the roof. The wind strode down from the moor and chased scurries of snow across slates and canvas. The blast cut him through, but as much with exhilaration as with cold. Reluctantly he left the wild storm-voices in spires and towers and creaky vanes, and began to sway down through the dusky mid-air on the ladder like a spider down the gossamer thread it spins out of its own self. An incorrigible adventurer! It was as though something he had invented had been praised.

*   *   *

The snow was melted from the castle's valley when, a week later, a four-wheeled gig carried Tresham rapidly away over the moors at the end of his stay. Rather to his disgust, his companion was Mr Bounty, now settling plump limbs under rugs and comforters beside him for their journey across snowy wastes beneath the mountains' misty summits. Tresham left Ravenrig with regret; he had come away on this day because it was the day he had named in his letter to Roland before arrival, and to stick to it, he thought, kept up his character for independence.

[109]

In the mild climate of this wooded cleft in the moors Lady Fanny's indolence and affability cast a spell of dreaming timelessness on visitors. Tresham had felt it. Walking with her round the garden she was making – yew and stone and the ever-running water of the stream were its chief components – he learned the strength of her passivity. There was to be no carrying in and out of orange trees here, so that the illusion of a Mediterranean garden might be contrived. What would grow well, she grew, wanting no fragile effects, settling the castle into its landscape as she settled her family into the castle, there to make their home.

And yet you could see – even Tresham understood, though he had no experience of such women – what withering effect the spell of indolence had cast over those who stayed too long in her temperate valley. There was Mr Bounty, for instance, trotting about at her heels with her dog on its cushion; and there was poor will-less Edmond, past trotting anywhere except out on his own with a gun. Roland, because his character did not please her – though he tried piteously not to irritate or bore her – Roland had never been subjected to her spell as had Edmond. Tresham saw all this, and determined to leave on the day he had settled upon. He sometimes fancied, looking up from the castle, that the tribe of dwarf oaks clinging to the moor's rim had been guests who had left it too late to escape unpetrified from the valley of the enchantress.

After dinner the night before, Lady Fanny had drawn him down onto a seat beside her to ask, 'You surely don't think of leaving us tomorrow?'

'Tomorrow is the day I had settled upon, Lady Fanny.'

'Ah, before you had known us. Now will you not stay?' She called to Edmond, 'Edmond, were we not saying how unhappy we should be at losing him?'

'Yes,' agreed Edmond, who had one leg cocked over another in a chair nearby, 'I don't know why he don't stop on over Christmas.'

'At least you cannot treat us so abominably as to go away from us tomorrow,' said Lady Fanny.

But Tresham knew, by an instinct for self-preservation, that it was the stranger with the unsapped will who teased this affable, indolent woman into trials of her power. He had left, though it had been tempting to stay. The castle was a tempting place.

A day or two earlier, idling in the drawing room from table to table amongst the curios and antiquities, he had come upon the architect's plans for Ravenrig out of their morocco case, and had been interested to examine them. Having seen the extent of the castle from its roof, when he had worked up there, he had wondered at the labyrinth of rooms and stairs and corridors and courtyards which must lie below. Here on the plan Gothic lettering named each room for him. More than rooms, they were activities; it was like the plan of a clockwork machine, which only required winding up for the house to start working – for knives to start being cleaned in the Knife Room, the balls to move over the table in the Billiards Room, dinner to appear in the Dining Room, and all the little cog-wheels to start their interconnected spinning. The confidence of predicting on paper all the workings of this complex machine was what struck Tresham. The stability such plans expected! The order! It made him jealous as he pored over the ramifications of floor upon floor, from cellars to attics. Then the door of the drawing room opened and Sir Daniel strode in rubbing his hands.

'Well, well,' said he cheerfully, standing very squarely before the fire with the tails of his green cutaway over his arms, 'I believe we have Sparrow on the run – eh, Lucy dear?'

Lucinda had followed him less ebulliently into the room. 'I do not understand how Roland takes up with such creatures,' she complained, sinking into a sofa.

'Come Lucy, don't mope,' said her father, whose morning's work had evidently been meat and drink to his spirits. 'Reckon up the pluses. We have worsted Sparrow, and if he don't cut and run I shall eat my hat. We have taught young Roly a lesson – leastways, events have taught him a lesson. And I have enjoyed myself immensely! The men will be back tomorrow, Bounty, depend upon it. Is that Bounty? Oh, it's Mr Pitcher, is it. Halloo, Mr Pitcher, you didn't run over and see the fun, then, of all of us contending?'

'I should have had no purpose in going, sir, except to see the row.'

'I thought a row was purpose enough for you fire-eaters!'

'You see I have learned by what you told me on the roof.'

'I'm glad of it.' Sir Daniel had fitted on his eyeglasses and now looked hard at Tresham. 'By Heaven, though, it was a bold thing to stand up to Snave, you know, for he could pretty well crush you, I suppose. Aye, it was bold. If Roly was always to have you by when he gets into scrapes I should be glad, very glad. You know he is set upon making an Eastern tour? He has talked to you of it?'

'I know he's been pretty much taken with the travels he has read in *Eothen* and Mr Warburton's book.'

'*Eothen*!' exclaimed Sir Daniel. 'Imagine! There I have been these thirty years in and out of the Levant – telling my children of it – collecting all manner of stuff from it – living it, breathing it you might say – and not a one of my children thinks of going off there, nor even of making enquiry about it of me. And then we have *Eothen* appears! A young fellow knocks about the Levant a week or two, and writes a pretty book about it, and there's Roland can't wait to be started after him, as if the East was come into his life all of a sudden! Well, we shall see. He's at Cambridge yet. Now, looking over Bounty's plans, are you? Like 'em, do you? Think we shall be comfortable?'

Tresham's jealousy returned. 'You have to be awfully sure that things will go according to plan, to build such a place.'

'Ah, indeed, a man must believe that things will go according to plan, Mr Pitcher, or nothing would be worth a toss. Now sir, suppose we was in Hungary this minute, and we was to see out of yonder window the Wallacks coming down the carriage-drive with their scythes to take off our heads, do you know there ain't one thing in this room, not one object, we could snatch up and take with us to buy bread in exile if we was to escape? Not one thing we could carry off, if you look about you. Now suppose I had gone in for jewels, eh, and gold masks and medals and coins and such. Well, when we saw the Wallacks a-coming for our heads, why, we'd snatch up a few jewels or a handful of gold, and off we'd run to Vienna, or wherever we thought was safe. Now then, that don't do for me. That's no plan to live by. No, you must settle with the fellow you live a-top of so he don't come for your head with his scythe, and then you must build your house according to plan and put your valuables in such form as you can't carry off. That's trust. That's what's wanted. I've lived in the East, Mr Pitcher, under the Sultan where no man is secure – I've lived in Hungary, too, where the Magyar notion of security is to set down his castle where he can best

bring his guns to bear on his peasantry – and I've come to build my
castle here, and fill it with what you see, which can't be carried off,
because here in this kingdom you can make your bargain and count
upon it holding. Yes, I do believe in matters going according to my
plan, by Heaven I do!'

'Don't you, Mr Pitcher?' enquired Lucinda's silky tone.

Believe in stability, and order, and life according to plan? When a
failed railway company could take it all from you in an hour? He turned
to the window to hide his bitter unbelief in such things for himself.
He said, 'From your castle windows I can believe in it pretty well, Miss
Farr. Yes,' he added, 'I see a set of fellows coming down the carriage-
drive now with their scythes, but I dare say they have only mistaken
the haymaking season.'

'Very English to make a joke of it all, Mr Pitcher,' warned Sir Daniel.
'Who hasn't seen disorder, don't value order at a true rate. I heard of
a friend of mine t'other day,' he went on, 'well, "friend" hardly, but
a noble Magyar I knew well. He'd been unluckily away from his home
in Transylvania when the Wallacks rose, but on he hastened, and
found himself seized by his own peasants who were in his castle before
him. Where was his wife and his seven children? he asked, but they
gave him no answer save horrid grins which filled him with dread. If
ever you saw a Wallack grin, Mr Pitcher, you'd begin to know how his
heart sank in him. Low as beasts, lowest race I ever saw. Well then,
he was told that no harm would befall him if he did as he was bid and
dressed himself for his dinner, when he should meet his wife and
children. So dress himself he did, and came down, and there upon the
table was all the shining meat covers off the kitchen wall from greatest
to least in a row, with the light of the torches winking in the copper.
He sat down and asked that his wife and children might be brought,
and they lifted up the covers, and there they were. There was his wife's
head, and his seven children's heads, each on a dish in its blood with
the eyes starting out at him. But they wasn't done yet. They obliged
him to taste of each dish before they killed him, or so it was told me
by his valet, who watched all from a gallery, and saved his own skin
by the fact of being a German.'

'Papa, pray do not speak of such horrors!' begged Lucinda.

'I must speak of what happens, Lucy, if I hear jokes about scythes.

And if I hear such stuff as Sparrow serves up and Roland swallows down. In face of that I must speak of where the road leads to. There's Sparrow's ideas at one end of the road, and there's the eight meat covers at the other, that's the truth of it. That's the truth of it. And ruination for the country all along the way. Who's to risk capital in Hungary now? It's all gone to the mischief. Ruination. I'd sooner have a shilling in my pocket than a guinea in Hungary any day. Aye, I would.' He fell to brooding, rocking to and fro before the fire and staring with an unseeing eye into the long depths of the room afforested with the columns and statues and glooms and glitters of his collection of weighty objects.

No doubt, thought Tresham, his host's preoccupation with Hungary was on account of commercial ventures at risk there. Of course the settled order of constables and Justices – and England parcelled out amongst the rich into noblemen's parks and railway companies quite as sure of their future as the labelled rooms on the Ravenrig plans – of course such order was essential to men who profited by it. Still at the window, he thought of the feeble Sparrow-led protest of Welsh workmen so easily snuffed out. Suppose they had come marching down that carriage-way armed with scythes – ! He thought of Snave facing him on the road, and his blood raced. Imagination showed him the gloomy Transylvanian mountains at dusk, the nobleman riding hard for his castle, torches, savage laughter, the long table with its row of shining covers. . . Ah, if he'd even been the valet, what a chance to act the hero and rescue his master, cut a way clear, ride for dear life!

But in England there was only Sparrow piping away on a soap-box to a half-dozen of Welsh workmen in the rain. And O'Connor helped into a cab by a policeman after the Chartist fiasco at Kennington. That was all there was in England, bounded by the dull grey sea he had found beyond the sand dunes like the moat around his prison.

Sir Daniel had not remained for long brooding before the fire over commercial mishaps in Hungary. He was very soon ringing bells for servants and writing off letters 'for immediate despatch'. He was in motion again, in action, going forward. Tresham, though, in the four-wheeled gig on the moorland road beside Mr Bounty, was going back

– back to Creech Lane, and his landlady's niece, and the brown London light in the room at the Waterways, and common clerks and streets and fog – back to that hopeless order, after his glimpse of the sea. They had gone some way before Mr Bounty spoke.

'Pleasant folk, eh, our friends at Ravenrig?'

Tresham didn't reply. Bounty at first had been cold to him; then, finding that Tresham was pretty much at his ease amongst the children of the castle, had begun directing at him attentions in the form of anecdotes showing off his own very superior position in Society. Tresham had not known he was to have Bounty's company in the gig until the little man had come bustling out of the castle lapped in furs and had hopped into the vehicle before him, crying out in his high voice as soon as the servant had wrapped him in rugs, 'When you are ready, Pitcher'. Having allowed his skiff to be sent the day before by a cart going to Pentre Bridge to collect materials from the railway there, he had no choice but to accompany Bounty, though he wished he had held out for the sturdy independence of the carrier's cart by which he had come. However, as soon as the wheels had begun to turn, his spirits had risen; now, with snowy wastes of moor and mountain ahead of the eager horse and flying gig, and the sensation of being once more upon his travels, whether forward or back, happiness broke irrationally in.

'Yes – simple, but pleasant,' repeated Mr Bounty, patting his old-fashioned white hat with his gloved hands. 'Sir Daniel is a very simple fellow – even rough – though I flatter myself it makes not a penn'orth of difference to me. When Lady Fanny asked me to build a house for her I said to her, "My dear – " of course I had known her for years, years, known her father the old marquis too, used to see him at Brighton oh! twenty, thirty years ago – "My dear, let me see this Sir Daniel of yours, let me see if we rub along together, and I shall tell you right enough whether I shall take the work on." The trick was, to put one's hand upon Sir Daniel, for he was never about.'

'Never about where?' asked Tresham.

'Oh, at Constantinople I dare say he was about! In Pesth one might have met him any day of the week, no doubt. Perhaps in those towns up in the North he was about. But was he in Mayfair? Was he at one's friends' houses? Not he. You know his history, of course?'

'I know nothing about it.'

'You don't? Then perhaps I shouldn't – but, after all, I am only telling what all the world knows. And there is nothing disgraceful in it, I suppose, now that the old notions of what made a gentleman are gone to the Devil. Well, Daniel Farr – or whatever his true name may be – Dan Farr – '

'Is Farr not his name?'

'Oh Lord no! I fancy his true name would have a good deal more of the Israelite about it.'

'He don't strike me as a Jew,' said Tresham.

'No? Well, he's learned to disguise it from people who meet him a first time, I dare say. At all events, whatever his name, Dan Farr shipped out to the Levant as a boy, worked his passage in a Smyrna brig, so I've been told, and made himself useful to some of these half-bred families who have the Smyrna trade in their pockets, merchants and consuls picking up the Turk's leavings, you know. He must have known what he was about, for he was put in by one of those fellows, a German I think – German or Austrian, a banker – to work up some coal-mines on the Black Sea, building a railroad, this German fellow was, to carry the coals down to his ships, and Farr soon had the whole affair in his own hand, running about everywhere overseeing everything, and putting a fortune in his pocket while he was about it. Then the old Turk – I heard this at Sir Stratford Canning's, mind, so I shouldn't like it repeated – the old Sultan when he saw this Englishman, as he took Farr for, when he saw this Englishman working up the coal-trade he took fright, thinking of how such gentry had served the Moghuls in India, beginning with trade and ending with conquest, so the old Sultan ordered up the German banker and told him to send Farr packing, bag and baggage.'

'And Sir Daniel went?'

'Beg pardon? Oh, Dan had to cut and run all right, or a bowstring might have put an end to him then and there. He was too sharp for that. He had the German, Novis I fancy the banker's name is, he had Novis undertake to put funds out of the Turk's grasp into Austria, or Hungary – into other concerns this Novis fellow has, at any rate, where the Sultan couldn't put his hand upon it, and then Farr threw off the Eastern dress he'd worn all those years, turbans and so forth, and dismissed his hareem if he had one, and fitted himself out with a tall hat and kerseymeres and made his bow in London as a wealthy young man – for he wasn't above twenty-six or seven then, and this was in the Regent's time.'

'And then he married Lady Fanny, I suppose?'

'Lordy, what a to-do there was about that! Upon my soul, the old marquis took it hard! He did take it hard, seeing his daughter throwing herself away on a Levant merchant. But there was always a something you couldn't quite look down upon in Dan Farr, even at his roughest, and I don't know how he did it, but he contrived to make himself agreeable to the family at the last, and married he was to Lady Fanny, who had turned a good many coroneted heads before he came upon the scene.'

'When you say you wasn't able to meet with him, do you mean they didn't live in England when they got married?'

'Live in England? For a spell they did, in a villa down at Twicken-ham, I believe it was. Or Wimbledon. It might as well have been at Timbuctoo, for I never was in it, the fashionable world didn't go to them. Babies were born and so forth, little Twickenham babies, and there Lady Fanny lived amongst them. Pretty soon the story of Dan Farr's losses got about, though – you've heard all about that, of course?'

'Never a word.'

'It was ever so much talked of. 1830? '31? That would be about the mark.' Relating gossip had made Bounty comfortable. His dry voice warmed to its work, his cold protuberant eye lighted, his gloved finger drummed on his rug-wrapped knee to recall a name or a date. He had succeeded in shrinking the tract of moor and mountain into mere painted scenery on drawing-room walls. 'Well – first we heard a whisper of Dan Farr's losses, next thing we knew he'd disappeared. Gone. Levanted. It was Lady Fanny's brother Tom Hastang, Lord Hastang you know, who was rather an intimate of mine, queer fellow, dead now, died at Boulogne – it was Hastang told me all about it. You never knew Hastang, I take it?'

'No, I never quite did,' said Tresham. The recognition – the ad-mission – that he knew nothing and nobody had begun to weigh rather heavily, so that he tried to make his negative sound conditional.

Mr Bounty looked for a moment hopeful of discussing Lord Hastang; but the fresh scent of Daniel Farr's lost fortune sent him after it once more. 'Well, Farr had gone after his money, that's what it was, of course, as it always is with these commercial gents – Novis, the banker fellow, he wouldn't trump up the funds Farr had put with him, and whatever Novis had used them for was fast going to the Devil. That was how Hastang told it, poor fellow, standing there chalking his cue at Brooks's, for he was a great billiards player was Hastang – though it did for him in the end, that and the other. Farr was away the deuce of a time. Seven years, eight years. He was heard of at Constantinople, he was heard of at Aleppo, he was heard of at half the dirty towns of the East – seen by fellows on their travels, you know, dodging into some pasha or other's audience hall in his turban and wide trousers again – and then when that Hungarian fellow Szechenyi came to be talked of with his steamboats and his chain bridges and his rebuilding of Pesth, why, there was Dan Farr bobbing about at his elbow. Then it seemed nothing could be built in Europe or the East without Farr having his hand in it, so poor Hastang used to say as his own fortunes went down the hill.'

'That was about the time he asked you to build him a house, was it?'

'Asked? I don't know much about asking. I suppose I met Lady Fanny somewhere and consented to look at the site when I had the time for it. Farr had bought up the Ravenrig property then, done it *in absentia*, or else he'd slipped in and out of England on the sly in those years, and he wanted the old house pulling down and a new one putting in its place where he might set up for a squire as these nabobs will. It was the Lears' old place before. I'd known old Colonel Lear for years, of course, before his trouble came – you know him ever, did you?'

'I think I met –'

'No, you'd be too young, it was '37 or '38 he shot himself. Of course there's always been a feeling Farr turned his widow out of Ravenrig, but I don't hold to that, no, the place was sold and paid for before old Lear ever took a pistol to his head. Maybe Farr moved a bit quick, maybe he did, but she'd had his money and she couldn't keep the house too, that was how Farr looked on it, no doubt, as these mercantile princes do. If I was Farr I don't believe I'd feel the widow on my conscience, nor the Colonel's death neither, I don't indeed. I know people blame him, but I don't, I don't. I'd never have consented to take on building him a castle else.'

'What was Sir Daniel's connection with Colonel Lear shooting himself?'

'None in the world. None in the world. But if you buy up the property of a family that's come to grief you never do make yourself liked, that's the fact of the matter. That's what was behind the strike of workmen, of course.'

'What, you mean the Lears put the men up to it?'

'The Lears had no need to move. Feeling did it. Feeling for the old ways, the old family, don't you know. Against some new nabob come bustling about the place spending his money.'

'Spending it on them, though,' Tresham objected. 'Rebuilding their farms. "Improving even more",' he said, quoting Enid and thinking of her eager face as she had said it.

'Don't make a ha'porth of difference, that don't. Hang me, I've seen it all so many times, in building model villages and so forth – you move the rural population into their new quarters, and it ain't five minutes before there's an outcry for the slum they've left behind 'em, and the old landlord who kept them in it, and the old ways of keeping 'em in filth and misery. Why, bless me, Dan Farr there thinks he's facing up to revolution and I don't know what all, with his strike, but what he's really run up against is new money ousting old and the true-blue peasant who don't like it. Of course with these troubles come upon his interests in Hungary it ain't a wonder if he expects revolution every time the garden-boy don't touch his hat to him.'

'I suppose his affairs are awfully scuppered by the Hungarian war?'

'Aye, and I fancy business in Turkey ain't going just according to Cocker neither,' said Mr Bounty with a glint of satisfaction in his eye. 'You notice the headless statue he has, did you? In the ante-room on its own there? Fine thing, very fine. Farr calls it "my Phidias", though whether it's by Phidias or not I shouldn't like to say, and Newton of the British Museum won't give his opinion either, except to say it don't come from Palmyra, which is where Farr says he came by it. Well – they say – I've been told – the head of that statue exists, and somehow or other – don't ask me how – Farr is pretty much in the hands of whoever it is possesses the head. Of course, if head were joined to body it would be worth a mint of money, but they say there's more in it than money – there's faith and honour at stake, and all that kind of thing. Maybe it's this fellow Novis has the head, who knows. He seems to be the evil genius of the piece. Anyway, I fancy some trouble has come upon our friend Farr which has to do with that statue, for I've found him with his hand upon it more than once, looking fierce as the Devil. These commercial fellows are apt to come unstuck at the last, that's the fact of it. Ah well, Lady Fanny's provided for, so Hastang always said, and the castle is pretty well paid for, I suppose.'

He ceased speaking, refolding comforters about his throat to keep off the raw air. In the silence, the grandeur and magnitude of the landscape through which they were passing reasserted itself upon Tresham. Palmyra! He thought of the engravings of the ruined desert city which he had seen in his step-uncle's library. Was it possible that certain hints of Eastern travel mentioned at Ravenrig might materialise into a real journey? Up here amid snowy wastes all seemed possible. Exhilaration lifted his mind high amongst the fierce mountain peaks so that empty valleys, and silent snowfields, and distant travels, lay below him in imagination like the kingdoms of the world.

It was not long before the road began to descend, and watery woods to smudge the snow, and the roofs of houses to cluster thickly, until the town of Pentre Bridge could be seen below them filling the valley with smoke, and barking dogs, and the clank of iron beating iron. Mr Bounty sharpened up immediately. 'Well, well,' he said, 'at last! A weary way, a weary way. Should you care to stop a winter there, eh?'

Looking at the houses and people and vehicles they were plunged amongst so suddenly, Tresham said, 'Do you remember the story of the man who'd spent a year, as he thought, in Estregalles, and when he touched his own shore again he crumbled away to dust, because it hadn't been a year but a hundred years, by his own world's measure?'

'I don't,' said Bounty. 'Where was the place he'd been, your fellow?'

'Estregalles. Avalon.'

'Well, Lady Fanny has London to look forward to once a year, at all events.'

'Does Sir Daniel come up to town?'

'He does, yes, but he don't go about much. He's a fish out of his water is the fact of the matter – though east of Temple Bar all's well, I dare say.'

'And they all go up? – the girls too, I suppose?'

'I should hazard it's on account of the girls he consents to keep up a house in town. For they won't make matches to please him from Ravenrig, that's sure.'

'They have a house, do they?'

'A very moderate sort of house in Berkeley Square.'

The thought of a match made up for Enid in Berkeley Square gave Tresham an unexpected jolt. He had supposed without thinking that she was part of the surroundings he had found her in, and would stay put. The gig now was rattling down through streets heaped with dirty snow, and the question of destinations arose.

'I shall go to the inn at the bridge,' said Mr Bounty. Arrival in even so small a town as this put him in command of the outfit, and made Tresham a mere passenger beside him. 'They know me, decent folk, and they'll give me a sitting room, you know, and some mutton chops – devilish good, Welsh mutton – and take care of me till my railway train goes out. Honoured if you care to join me, of course.'

Awkwardness – the payment for sitting rooms and mutton chops, his rough travelling clothes beside Bounty's furs and broadcloth – threw Tresham out. In Bounty's indifference he saw how little impression he had made on the man. He said he had better look out for his skiff at the railway station.

'Just tell the fellow where you want setting down,' said Bounty, quite as if the castle gig was his own.

Tresham said nothing, and got down from the gig in the inn yard whilst Bounty was helped out the other side into the inn servants' welcome. 'Goodbye, Pitcher,' he called, his attention already on mutton chops and other comforts in an upstairs parlour. 'Look me up in town if I can be of service, Albany finds me. Goodbye to you.'

Instead of lengthening his step as he should have liked, and striding away to fresh adventures, Tresham found himself stealing off with his carpet-bag, downward into a stratum beneath Bounty's notice, unsure even of how to take leave of the gig's driver. On the bridge he paused, trusting in the river to hearten him. Shrunk by frost, its meagre black water crawled under the arches. He thought again of the knight in the story who had crumbled to dust on touching his native shore after sojourning in Estregalles.

In his bedroom at the castle that morning he had lain watching the early light of the sun weaken and strengthen by turns on the ornaments. It was a room, he felt, prepared for visitors far grander than himself. Above him, the ceiling was adorned with a plasterwork wreath, garlanded leaves and flowers supported between *putti* in low relief, and the effect of the waxing and waning of winter light was to give to these leaves and to the angel-faces an appearance of dancing life, as if wind rippled real flowers, and sun played upon real children's faces. They were the children of the house, and the garland they supported between them was all the interwoven mysteries and beauties of childhood which they shared here. So linked into one another's were the hands, or so busy with the flowers, that no hand was free to reach out to a stranger. What did the basket contain, which the old man showed them at his cottage-door by the sea? As he searched for an empty hand amongst the angels, or a smile directed downwards, sunlight was quenched, animation dimmed, and he was alone.

He was alone on the bridge, crumbled to dust, the wonderful realities of that favoured valley all behind him. He had touched one angel-hand, though. In the pony carriage with Enid for an hour he had shared the wreath of flowers. *You speak as if one summer was all we might have*. A mysterious promise that summer would come again? He did not tinker with the scene, the sensation. Into memory he dropped it whole, like a miniature-portrait of the beloved, or a flower between the pages of a book. It was as if all his feelings about the castle – about Roland – about that valley by the sea and its mysteries – were freed to flow in one direction, towards Enid.

Aware that his loitering figure on the bridge might be under observation from Mr Bounty's inn windows, and might be pitied, Tresham put his bag on his shoulder and crossed the river, just as if he was setting out upon fresh adventures.

VII

——————————

THERE WERE INDEED TREES in Creech Lane, where Tresham lodged, but that the trees appealed to American sea-captains, as he had told Roland Farr, was a piece of embroidery which had come into his head as he sat writing the letter, for he had never yet met a seafaring man in the neighbourhood. There was a chestnut outside his windows, its sooty trunk well known to him from his sitting room, its branches familiar in every detail from his bedroom, and, although he liked the tree for its response to the seasons, he hated the tree's indifference to himself and to his own plight, as the man who cannot sleep hates the clock for striking the hours.

One evening shortly before Christmas, opening the front door and passing softly upstairs, he reached the landing without being intercepted. The gas, however, was lighted in his sitting room, and he heard the rustle of skirts towards the door. Darting up the second flight he gained his bedroom. She as yet left him alone in his bedroom.

Washing his face, removing his boots, he wondered at the alteration in his feelings at hearing those skirts rustling. They belonged to his landlady's niece, a country girl orphaned by cholera the previous year, who had been pushed into cleaning the house and serving the lodger so as to repay her aunt's charity in housing her. How eagerly Tresham had made himself nice last spring before hurrying down to be ready in his sitting room when Charlotte-Anne brought up his supper, in hopes that she might be tempted to stop in the room with him! She was a young female like hundreds he saw on his way to the office or back: but, unlike them, a young female in the house with him, in the room with him, whose hands set his table and made his bed, and whose person lay at night under the same roof with him. Though desire may be engendered by a view of the unattainable, once aroused it will fix itself pretty readily upon the lesser objective within reach. But alas, it may be very quickly dissatisfied with its conquest of what lies to hand.

Very far from hurrying downstairs, Tresham sat on his bed with his boots off wondering how long he might stop up here in peace without molestation by the tedium of the Charlotte-Anne within the conquered body. It was to stop her following him upstairs that he at last went down. But in his sitting room he found not the vulgar expanses of Charlotte-Anne, but the little elderly figure of his mother's Scotch maidservant in black bonnet and shawl.

'Meg!' he cried. 'My mother's not ill?'

It was not illness, but Tresham's failure to reply to a letter summoning him to Clapham which had brought Meg to him. If he went back with her he would fall into his stepfather's jaws, but would avoid the jaws of Charlotte-Anne. 'Very well, Meg,' he said. 'Give me a minute to change my coat and we'll start directly. If the servant should come up with my supper, tell her it won't be wanted.'

What sins might his stepfather have found him out in? Never fear – the prospect of action instead of passivity, the streets instead of his sitting room, caused Tresham to pull on his boots again cheerfully, and set out from the house with Meg under his arm in high spirits to walk to the Regent's Circle for the Clapham omnibus.

Mr Wytherstone's summons had wakened a general sense of guilt (which was why Tresham had ignored his stepfather's letter), but when he came to think about the matter in the omnibus rumbling through the streets he found that he had no real weaknesses *vis-à-vis* Laidlaw Villa save the terrible weakness of Charlotte-Anne. Perhaps she had written. His fists clenched themselves at the thought of his mother reading – touching – a letter from such a creature. How had he let it happen? In a smelly omnibus climbing the Clapham hill in December beside his mother's old maid, when girls' charms had disappeared under winter wraps as completely as swallows gone to Africa, it was easy enough to swear off a Charlotte-Anne.

Very different on a sultry night in summer, though, when he returned to Creech Lane after wandering in the carnal city. He knew that. What point, though, in vaunting resolution and independence, if not against falling alive into other people's hands, as he felt himself to have fallen into the red hands and arms of Charlotte-Anne, and to be caught there in the horrid scent of poppies which clung about her.

When summer came, he would be strong – if summer ever came again.

The silence and the darkness when they got down from the omnibus at Clapham shocked him as usual. The gas-flare and rattling wheels of London had given way utterly to unlighted ways and the wind off the common. Approaching Laidlaw Villa, Meg laid her hand on his arm.

'Neither of the two of them knows I went out for ye,' she said, 'for I wish it to seem ye came on your own hook, as the saying goes. I'll slip round the back now, then do you knock away at the front and I'll open to ye.'

Meg had come from Edinburgh, where she had worked in the Minister's household before he had gone to the parish in Wester Ross, and she was very protective – partisan – towards Mrs Wytherstone. Once when Mr Wytherstone had rung a bell, as she thought too peremptorily, for her, she had seized the bell from him and rung it in his face until he had retreated from the room. Tresham recognized that in tricking him back into childhood and dependence, as she had done by her journey to Creech Lane, Meg was acting as agent of his mother's will – though not a word on the subject would have passed between them.

When he was admitted, and climbed the stairs – 'Look now who's come to see ye!' called out Meg running before him – he found his mother sitting over her needle in a puddle of lamplight. Lines of age and care he had never noticed shocked him: then, in a twinkling, it was his mother's face again, known from earliest days, alight with love for him. Tea was sent for. His stepfather put down the paper and listened whilst he stood before them on the hearthrug and told them of his travels.

They allowed him to be famous. They listened to his tales, and let him boast of the Farrs' wealth and of the splendour of Ravenrig, almost as long as he liked to go on. When tea was brought, and he broke off, his mother said, 'Such adventures! Tell me, Tresh, I want to hear about your friends at the Welsh castle, now. What sort of people are they?'

'What do you mean, Mother?'

'Your mother means,' said Mr Wytherstone, 'your mother means – how did you get along with Sir Daniel? – did he take a liking to you? – is he likely to offer you anything – '

'I'm sorry, Dolly dear, but I didn't mean that at all,' said his mother. 'I meant – oh, should we have liked them? Are they simple people?'

Tresham laughed. 'I don't suppose you become about the biggest fellow going in that line by being simple, Mother! No, they're none of them simple!'

'Then,' she said quietly, leaning back in the buttoned sofa, 'then, Tresh, if they are not simple people, they are not like you.'

That he knew what she meant was like an arrow in his heart. He turned away, looked into the fire. In his mother's sense, Enid was simple. She was without guile, and so was Roland. But he did not want to admit it, for some reason. He asked, 'May is out, I take it?'

'On a visit to Eliza and Walter at Sydenham, poor May,' said his mother. 'I hoped the children might put her in spirits again, but everything in life seems to remind her of her loss.'

'Hardly a loss, Hannah,' said her husband. 'That blackguard had promised nothing.'

'By Jove, if he'd promised – !' Tresham made a show of indignation on his jilted stepsister's behalf, though secretly her mishap with the rich brewer's son from The Shrubberies seemed to him to serve her right.

'People out of some liquor-shop!' burst out Mr Wytherstone, reddening almost to the hue of his brother Marcus. 'Of course I know where it is – I can't send her about in a carriage, so any half-bred brewer don't think he need treat her like a lady, that's where it is.'

'Oh Dolly, dear, it wasn't your fault, you shouldn't think so much of not having a carriage, indeed you shouldn't. It was no one's fault. Those people at The Shrubberies, now, they are not simple people,' she added, 'and poor May has found it out to her cost.'

She did not need to look at Tresham for her parallel with the Farrs to be apparent. She resumed sewing while Mr Wytherstone, still in a rage, disputed the hearth-rug with Tresham and said to him rather stormily:

'Now sir, it's about your future – what's to be done with you – that I wrote for you to come here, which you've done at last. I have worked at it pretty thoroughly since – '

'Pray, Step-papa, don't put yourself – '

'Just listen, will you, Tresham? Just listen for once, without climbing upon your high horse. Now. There is no use telling of the quantities of letters I wrote which went unanswered. I wonder at the lack of feeling, though. Family, colleagues, friends – oh, it's all one nowadays, feeling is knocked into the gutter in the scramble after places.' He had driven Tresham off the hearth-rug, and was as tempted to preach as is a parson by an empty pulpit. 'If I'd consulted my feelings as a gentleman, by Jove, I shouldn't have carried on with the work, I should have left you to be a clerk all your days. But I've succeeded at last. It ain't all I could have wished. No; the military line was my first intention when I'd come down to trying India, but I could get no-where, nowhere.'

'Step-papa – India is a very large step.'

'Don't interrupt me. I had written to a cousin of your father, some kind of Company servant he is, to see if he knew of a position going begging, and back came a letter at last – a week ago, Hannah? – back came his letter to say his son had just dropped dead with the fever and he was willing to attach you to himself in the boy's place. It wasn't a very feeling letter, but there, we shan't hold that against him if he's as good as his word.'

India! The idea loomed up in front of Tresham like a genie escaped from a bottle. He got to his feet and took two or three energetic strides, all the little room allowed. India!

'Well, sir?' His stepfather had raised himself on tiptoe when Tresham stood up, as if in hopes of overtopping him still in height. 'Well, sir?'

'India! It is an awfully large step. It does need thinking of.'

'Thinking! I have been thinking of it for a year. Do you suppose I have done it without thinking?'

Mrs Wytherstone, who had bent more assiduously over her needle since India was mentioned, now looked up and implored her son: 'Of course you must think. You must think most earnestly, Tresh. Dolly,' she said, turning her sad, large eyes up at her husband, 'Dolly, you have puzzled so long over how to succeed in placing Tresh that I am not sure you have quite thought what is best for us all. Do not be angry. It is so.'

He looked down at her. It was clear he understood all the pain behind her words. 'Oh, very well. Think of it then, Tresham. You'll come up to us for Christmas Day, I suppose? Very well, on Boxing Day I shall write off to your father's cousin. I suppose you could undertake to leave pretty well at once? Goodbye, my boy, I have a little writing to attend to upstairs, but you stop and talk with your mother now you've come at last.'

As his stepfather left the room a curious feeling came over Tresham, which he didn't analyse, of being left at his mother's mercy – at the mercy of love. He did not sit down. Knowing her mind so well, he said, 'As to the fever, that's a chance a fellow must take. There's a girl at my lodgings orphaned by the cholera here in England, without all the trouble of going to Calcutta to catch it.'

'A girl at your lodgings? Does Mrs Skinner take in females?'

'No, no, Mother, not a lodger – she's a servant, she's Mrs Skinner's niece, I believe. Some sort of niece.'

'What is her name?'

'Her name? I don't know her name, I never saw her above once or twice in my life.' Tresham walked impatiently about the room, looking into the pictures, whose glass reflected the firelight. His mother's enquiry as to Charlotte-Anne had the effect of hardening his heart to go to India.

'Be content with England, Tresh.' She might have read his mind.

'Mother, it is you fed me on travels and adventures.'

'Ah, in books. Leave them in books, where they do no harm.'

'No, I'm not thinking of books, I'm thinking of your journeys with Papa, and the banditti and the Corsairs and everything. Remember?'

'I was young, Tresh. And for your father adventures were the breath of life. We were both young and didn't think of danger, or fever.'

'And I am young now, Mother.'

He would have added, And I should like to have my sword to take to India, but did not like to tell her that his mind was made up to go. What constraints there were, in living amongst people you love! He wished for himself the liberty of living amongst strangers to whom neither loyalty nor love is owed, where only the selfish motive need be consulted. That seemed to him to be independence.

'You will stay the night, and go down to your work with Step-papa in the morning?'

'I won't, Mother, no.' Better even the red commercial arms of

Charlotte-Anne Skinner, than the confusion and pain of love at home.
'Don't stir,' he said as he kissed her. 'I shall let myself out.'

*　　*　　*

A dark, draughty day in January found Tresham Pitcher being driven
in his step-uncle's gig from the railway station to Rainshaw. At the
edge of the park old Branch got down to struggle with the gate, which
seemed likely to fall into pieces, whilst Tresham held the reins. The
mossed-over track was only traceable across the park ahead of them
by wheel-ruts shadowed by the low light. 'Squire don't go nowhere
less and less,' Branch said in explanation of the tumbledown gate.
'Now that's railroad or nothing, he don't go no more to London.'

'The railway line they were building at the back of the woods, is that
finished?' Tresham asked.

'That never came to nothing. They do talk of going along with that
somewhen, but she's all growed over with now, that is, for she weren't
never properly wanted, didn't go nowhere, see.'

Tresham saw in his mind the gulf cut through the wood, heard the
beat of the steam-hammers, the gale in the trees. Saw the navvies'
camp, and the woman across the gulf. . . Branch had climbed up beside him and begun to drive up the slope into the park. There was the
old ark of the house anchored on its crest amongst the trees. Gleams
which fell between the clouds chased over its stone and slate and
windows, and brightened the great dark oaks, and flashed on the lake
water, and sped away greening the turf with their flying footsteps.
Now soft, now loud, the wind's gusts scattered through the air the
slow and measured tolling of a bell.

'He has a burying on,' said Branch, wagging his head at the church's
grey tower between the trees.

'Is he taking it himself?'

'He has to, don't he? Reverend Poat won't touch it.'

'Poat still here, is he? I thought he'd gone over to Rome.'

'Good as. You know squire, though. Won't turn anyone off.'

'Stop a bit, I'll go down to him,' said Tresham, obeying an impulse
to jump out of the gig. A memory of his step-uncle in his pulpit

prompted the action. Towards the few mossy cottages at the church gate, now under the oaks, now under the sky, he walked down the park between manor and church, through the small landscape of his step-uncle's life. Over the shed door in the farmyard his step-uncle's horse looked out at him. The funeral bell had ceased, the door in the ivy-roofed porch was closed. He lifted the latch and went in.

The latch of the door clashed loudly through the still and icy shadows of the church. The cold, as it seemed of centuries of winter, laid its hand upon him. In the chancel the outline of a coffin on two stools was a deeper shade among shadows. Indistinct as the coffin – wavering like the candlelight – rose and fell a muttering voice to the black hammer-beams above. In his stall his step-uncle was reading the Burial Service in such light as he could catch on the page of his book. Opposite him was seated – was slumped in a choir stall – a very much dishevelled old man as well plastered with clay as if he had wrestled with Death in the pit. He was asleep, breathing stertorously.

Tresham felt himself trapped in an awkward scene. In a moment he realized that his step-uncle's voice, hardly altered from his muttered reading of the old words, was addressing him:

'Deepen the grave, will you? Deepen the grave. You will find a spade somewhere about.'

Relieved to be made part of the action, Tresham walked out into the churchyard, where he soon found the open yellow pit with spade and pick cast down on the heap of clay beside it. To have work to do under the sky was a blessing. He threw off his coat and jumped down into the grave.

The work soon warmed him – soon exhausted him, indeed. Was everyone ever born buried with such labour as this? He leaned on his spade so deep in the earth that the gravestones thronging the church-yard loomed over him against the sky. Then he resumed digging. He felt a regret – an artistic regret – that he had not made more out of the sheer labour of burying a man, in his tale of burying the lime-burnt Irishman in the Gloucestershire wood.

'That will do.' Uncle Marcus's voice came out of the sky. 'Take my hand and I will pull you up. Never mind the mud, take my hand.'

The grasp which pulled him up became his step-uncle's greeting, a firmer and warmer grasp perhaps than the rector might have extended if not required to help his visitor out of the grave. 'You are very welcome, very welcome,' he said hastily. 'Now, come, the coffin is a light one. I don't doubt we can manage it between us.'

'I can run and get a man from the farm – if you should like it, that is.'

'We'll do it ourselves, if you please. There is a handcart somewhere about we will find. I don't want the farm men quite knowing all Fettle's disgrace do you see. They'll find it out, of course, but I don't care to be the means of discovering it to them.'

Leaving his coat where it lay, Tresham followed the rector's hurrying black gown into the church. He was now as well plastered with clay as poor Fettle, whose snores reverberated like organ notes from the chancel. Why were there no mourners? Where was Poat? Was Fettle drunk? His step-uncle's well-ordered kingdom seemed tumbling about his ears since Tresham's visit to him four years ago. He helped Uncle Marcus lift the coffin, light indeed, onto a handcart found in some recess, and then himself pushed coffin and cart creaking after the rector into the churchyard.

Winter trees rocking in stormy gusts seemed warm and living things after the death-chill of the church. Whilst his step-uncle read from the fluttering page Tresham looked out over the grave he had dug at the wooded folds under a rapid sky. There lay safe England, his step-uncle's kingdom. Ahead of himself, over the sea, lay 'lands both wild and strange'. A shiver of excitement made him stir his feet and feel the cold. Would it be disrespectful to the dead to pick up his coat where it lay by the coffin, and put it on? Who was in the coffin, to be buried so deep in the grave he had dug?

When the time came for the committal, he and the rector lowered the coffin by means of ropes till it glimmered in the pit. The service over, he warmed himself filling the grave until his step-uncle emerged from the church wearing top-coat and breeches and low-crowned hat.

'I shall leave Fettle,' he said. 'Let him find himself in church when he comes to his senses. Wretched man. Come, I shall ride up to the house if you don't mind walking beside me. Poat has left me in the lurch, of course. Ridiculous man.'

'I thought he might have gone over to Rome.' He held open the churchyard gate.

[131]

'He wasn't quite clown enough for that ever. No, no, he sent word he had taken some illness or other. Rome, yes, I thought I should have to get rid of him over that nonsense, but I let him be, let him be, and of course it passed off. Just step into the stable and throw the saddle upon Pricklefish, will you.'

Curate's apostasy and sexton's drunkenness were treated just the same, thought Tresham, as he saddled the old horse – both were let alone, that is, in hopes that no apple-cart was permanently overturned. Conservatism and charity were both served thus. He wondered how frequent were scenes like the one he had come upon, in which Uncle Marcus was obliged to deputise for all the weak or wayward parish officers his policy sustained. He led the horse out for the rector to mount.

'Thank'ee, thank'ee. Glad you came down, Tresham. I shouldn't have got the poor creature easily into her grave without you.'

'Who was it we buried?'

'Oh, a poor girl, a sad case. Drowned. Drowned with her little boy. In my lake there. Of course it was said she made away with herself, but I wouldn't have it, I wouldn't have her denied a resting-place among us at the last, poor soul. And she may have been trying to save the child who had strayed into the water. It may have been as I suggested. But I doubt it. The boy, you know, was caught tight in her arms when they were found – ' the rector dropped his rein and made a circle of his arms as if he hugged a child to him – 'and tight in her arms I buried him. Of course it's why Poat wouldn't come, wretched man, in case she'd taken her own life.'

'Who was she?' The lake in which she had drowned had been a green dell in the park when he was here before. 'Who was the girl?'

'I don't know who she was. Well, yes, I know who she was well enough,' the rector conceded, as if to deny her an identity would be as uncharitable as to deny her a grave. 'We had an encampment of these navvies, you know, a year or two back now, they were supposed to be building us a branch line we didn't want, and it all came to nothing, of course, as I expected. She was one of them, one of their women I take it. A bad lot, I'm afraid. The child had no father. I believe she lived out there in the woods where the work came to a stop, in some sort of a hut there, I'm told, where the navvies' shanties were. So I believe. Why, boy, you have lost all colour! Are you ill? Here, come, you get up on Pricklefish and I'll walk!'

'No, no – I – just – ' Tresham resumed walking up the road between wood and park.

'Well, directly we are home you shall take a glass of wine. I dare say the railway speed has knocked you up. I can't do it, you know. Now they have taken off the stage I don't get up to town. If I can't go by land I won't go at all, as I've told them.'

'Your idea of being a missionary in the East might have fagged you a good deal more than the railways, sir, don't you think?'

'The East? Fagged me? No, no – it is the velocity, you see, that is where steam knocks you up. However,' he said, 'the accidents are so fearful that the railways are sure to be put a stop to. No doubt of it.'

Tresham had his reasons for pursuing the theme of Eastern travel, and asked, 'I dare say you regret not having gone to the East when you were young, do you, sir?'

'Can't say I regret it, no. The East retains all its interest for me, without my having ever gone out there. Who knows but what I shouldn't have cared for it at all if I'd run all over it. No, I'm glad I've stopped at home. Then one may believe any traveller's tale, you know, without constantly wishing to set the fellow right, as they do in the journals.'

'Yet, of course,' said Tresham, pacing down the gravel carriage-drive beside Pricklefish, 'of course, some fellows must go, or there would be no travellers to write the tales.'

'I believe some of the rascals don't go half so far as they make out, though,' rejoined the rector. 'There's Captain Spencer now, filled up two volumes with *Travels in Circassia* if you please, and I'm told he contented himself with viewing the shore of the place from the deck of a yacht! So Mr de Hell says in his book. However, here we are at home. We will talk about it all some of these times. You go in and tell Mrs Poynder you are come, and she'll take away your clothes and brush off the clay. I've been thinking perhaps I had better just trot down before dark and see if Fettle is come to himself,' said the rector, turning his horse.

The 'repairs' to the house were complete: the date 1848 was engraved in a weathervane on the stable clock tower to mark their completion. The light was already fading as Tresham walked between the elms of the lawn and the shrubbery of Portugal laurel and laurustinus towards the house, impenetrably sombre in all its finished gloominess of crenellations and narrow windows and Gothic porches thrust out here and there like defensive works. All its shutters were already closed up against the night. Not a gleam of light leaked from it anywhere.

So forbidding did the entrance front appear, with the wind rustling the magnolia leaves around the blank eyes of its windows, that Tresham did not immediately sound the iron bell, but walked on to the park railings to look down onto the lake. Grey as a sword the water glistened with the last light from the sky. How sharp and bitter cold that blade must have felt to her. How fortified against her the house must have appeared on its crest above. In she had walked. If the rector had made no lake, she would have hanged herself from an oak. If Tresham had not come, another stranger would have deepened her grave. There was no pattern. Even if she was the woman he had seen across the gulf – even if she was the girl he had found so ill in the deserted camp, when he had crossed the gulf from school and given her two shillings of Roland Farr's money – even so, there was no pattern. The horrid gleam of the supernatural, which had shocked the blood out of his face when he had heard whose body they had buried, was now extinguished. So he hoped, entering under the motto on the porch and ringing the iron bell.

'Uncle Marcus,' said Tresham at dinner an hour later, checking the rector's escape into the book on his reading-stand, 'I have an idea of going to India.' No answer. The fire burned cheerily, the silver winked, the portraits looked down. His step-uncle helped himself from dishes on the table, pushing them afterwards towards his guest. Had he heard? 'Uncle Marcus, what it is, I have been offered a place attached to my father's cousin which I think of taking up. I hope you don't think me ungrateful as to the Waterways,' he said after another pause, 'but the truth is I never should make anything of myself at that work.'

His step-uncle said, 'Made them out a report they didn't care about, I hear.'

'I set down some facts I found out on my travels.'

'Ah. Yes. Yes, Gulliver struck me as a man who has had a pack of facts loosed upon him, when he spoke of it.'

'There is no question of my being turned off, you know.'

'No, no – it is hardly possible to be turned off by the Waterways Board, I take it.' As he ate, his eyes stole towards his book.

'My stepfather has taken such immense pains, sir, to put the Indian place in my way. You can't conceive how he has worked at it.'

'I can indeed. It is the only work he cares about. Your step-papa, Tresham, holds to the belief that it is influence that's all that counts in life. Stuff and nonsense!' He drank off a glass of wine, and went on, 'Now, of course, if Providence puts a plum in his way, it is a very foolish fellow who don't catch it up. But that ain't at all to say he mightn't have got other plums of his own if he'd been obliged to work for them.'

'You think a man finds himself in the position he deserves?' You drinking your wine amongst your heirlooms (Tresham thought) and your brother pinched between Mincing Lane and Laidlaw Villa?

'I think a man finds himself in the state of mind he deserves,' said the rector, 'content or not with his fortune, that's to say. Now, if you don't care for your work at the Waterways, and show it by your contempt for the views of the men set above you, why, I'll take a wager the same history is repeated at Bangalore or Timbuctoo. It ain't finding the position, that ain't the trick, as your stepfather believes. No, its accepting your place in the scheme of things, and accepting the rate at which you advance, that's where it is. I daresay you say to yourself, "Oh, India's a great way off, it will be well enough to think of all that when I come to it" – but come to it you will, and it won't differ much from the Waterways, not in what affects you, for a man don't come up against one set of troubles at London, and another at Currachee – no, he runs up against the same troubles in all places, for he takes them about with him in his own character. That's the truth of it.'

'But mayn't it be, sir, mayn't it be that discontent with his lot is just the spur to a man getting along in the world?'

'It is the making of a deuced uncomfortable life, depend upon it.'

'I'll take my chance on not being comfortable. I ain't afraid of that – not half as afraid as I am of sleeping away my life at the Waterways, at least.'

The rector did not contest this view. His hand reached out to turn a page of his book, which he must have been reading with half an eye all the time. In a bid for his attention Tresham said:

'My plan is, sir, that I should walk to India.'

'Walk, eh?' He was not impressed.

'Or ride. Go overland at all events. I have thought of it all. I should go first to Vienna, then by the Danube to Buda-Pesth, and see a little of Transylvania on the way to Bucharest. Then the Black Sea to Constantinople. Then through Asia Minor into Syria, Palmyra, the desert to Baghdad on the Euphrates. Across Persia by a northerly route to Mashed, or I could go south – '

'Wait a bit! Are you proposing to yourself to see the world, or are you proposing to get yourself to India? Eh? And you will find Baghdad upon the Tigris, not upon the Euphrates.'

'I should certainly like to see something of the world on my way to India, yes, I should.'

'You should like to put off getting there, I suppose, and put off taking up work there – ain't that it?' His shrewd gaze silenced Tresham. Then he looked at his book, saying mildly, 'Well, well – walking to India! I wonder, I do indeed. We will have Arrowsmith out after, and you shall show me your line on his maps.'

His book, Tresham saw, was Spencer's *Travels In European Turkey*. His uncle preferred the tales of a man known by him to be a liar, to the company of a real prospective traveller through the Sultan's dominions! Never mind, he would be patient, for his visit to Rainshaw was made in hopes of obtaining a loan of money to make his land-journey possible. He too had a book – Mr Fraser's account of his capture by the tribesmen of Koordistan – which he opened on the stand beside his place.

Before dinner was over his step-uncle showed that he had not put Tresham's journey out of his mind. 'I suppose you have considered it all, have you?' he asked. 'Fitting out and so forth. What money you shall need. Companions. Language.'

'I believe I have thought pretty well what's needed, Uncle Marcus. I hope my friend Roland Farr goes with me.'

'Your friend wants to walk to India too, does he?'

'He wouldn't stay in the East, he has too much to come home to. He is the son of Sir Daniel Farr, you know, of Ravenrig.'

[136]

'Oh I dare say, I dare say. As for having much to come home to,' went on the rector, 'it ain't impossible but that you yourself might have not inconsiderable reasons for looking to England for your future home, some of these days.'

'Then I'm sure I don't know what such reasons are, Uncle Marcus,' said Tresham, looking boldly into his step-uncle's face, 'for I know of nothing considerable coming to me in any land.'

The rector pushed his silver about the table in a way that almost showed discomposure. 'This place, you know,' he said, 'my property about here, it lies entirely in my own hand, to leave as I choose. Of course I may marry and have a dozen children. If I don't, though, then there's my sister and my brother have nothing but a pack of girls between them. I promise nothing, mind, but it bears thinking of. It bears thinking of.'

At hearing the words – at the idea, the hint, of inheriting Rainshaw which swelled out of his step-uncle's mouth like another genie in the candlelight – Tresham suffered attack from envy and yearning sharp as rats' teeth. No, he would not build on such chances. He would not lay himself open again to destruction of the card-castle. He thought of the Cynic Crates' resolve to depend on defences which no Alexander could throw down. So it would be with him. He replied, 'Of course, as you said, a fellow is a fool who don't catch at a plum if chance puts it in his way, but my own feeling is, that no fellow is worth a rap who lies all his life with his mouth open under a plum tree.'

'Oh, I dare say, I dare say.'

Though the rector returned huffily to his book for what remained of the dinner, Tresham was satisfied he had answered rightly to temptation.

All the same, it wasn't possible to put the idea of inheriting Rainshaw out of mind. Mrs Poynder – and Tom the hall-boy now grown into a footman's place and dignity – had shown him to quarters very different from the attic of his first visit, and when he went up there to sleep he recognised his accommodation, and the number of wax candles burning in it, as being all of a piece with his step-uncle's hint of inheritance. He had a bedroom reached through a comfortable little sitting room all his own, with a fire in the grate, and books, and engravings of nursery rhymes, and an easy chair or two, and a writing table between shuttered windows. A bronze clock had been wound up and set going, surely by the rector himself. It was tempting. It was the sort of apartment to be kept open, and run down to from town, and grown into a comfortable fit by the future owner of all.

Tresham, however, he hardly knew why, blew out the many candles and went down two steps into the chilly bedroom, where he sat and thought about his Eastern journey by the low flame of his chamber-light. On the atlas in the library after dinner, tracing his intention across Turkey and Persia for his step-uncle, his very finger had felt lost and lonely amid these wastes and outlandish names. By its empti-ness and its hostility the atlas had chilled his blood as the most ferocious of travellers' tales had never done. The East! The East! His mind was as uncomfortably full of the glittery pricks of the idea as a pincushion full of pins.

*   *   *

Uncle Marcus next morning was solicitous over the breakfast table. 'They made you comfortable upstairs? Mrs Poynder has put you into the old nurseries, I believe.'

'They were your nurseries, were they?'

'We slept in one and played in t'other. Oh, always. You may have noticed, did you, letters burned in the chimneypiece? Initials? A.R.W. Your step-papa did that, one winter afternoon about 1802 or 3. With the poker. Queer thing, ain't it, to burn your initials – for how can you hope to get away with your crime? He didn't get away with it either, poor Dolly. He was awfully flogged. I often think of those initials, when I hear him complain of the way the world treats him. He used to say it was I did it – I burned his initials – but of course it ain't so. Dear, dear. He can't give you any money, I suppose, to carry you to India?'

'He might have paid a sea-passage, but I don't want that.'

Uncle Marcus drank tea in silence. Then he said, 'If you're set upon adventure, why don't you go and see some of these publishers, now, and arrange an advance of money against a book of your travels? That's what I should do in your place. If you are in earnest, that is.'

'I never was more earnest in my life.'

'Well, sir, I'll tell you what I'll do,' said his step-uncle after further deliberations in his tea-cup. 'If you can find the most of what you require, I'll round the figure out for you to what's needed to do the thing – that's if you remain in earnest about ending up a slave in the Bokhara market. Yes, yes,' he chuckled, gazing out of his tall bow windows onto his park, 'why, even working for old Gulliver would hardly instil as much steadiness into a man's character as working as a slave to the Kuzzauks, I suppose!'

Even on this half-promise of funds he wouldn't count, thought Tresham to himself as he walked out of the house later in the morning. He would not be part of the pattern of compromise and obligation with which his step-uncle netted down the parish and gelded his opponents. Look at the Tower, for instance, whose stone outline could be seen amongst winter trees at the head of the lake. As a library it had proved a failure, too damp for books, too chilly for readers. But Uncle Marcus did not by any means regard it as a failure because it had failed in its original purpose. No, no! It had provided work for masons and carpenters; he himself admired its Palmyra-tomb outline in his park; and in course of time it would become a picturesque ruin just where a ruin was required to dignify the lake shore. In short, the Tower was quite a success in the rector's view of things – a view which, rather than accept change, would tolerate a wilful curate who refused to bury a suicide, and a drunk sexton incapable of digging her a grave. Such imperfections were to the rector as necessarily tolerable as infirmness in himself – the deafness of age, say, or failing eyesight – for the parish was his, body and soul. Over farmland and church he had absolute power. The lake was his, and he made it. But, should the dam break and the lake melt away, why, the marsh that remained was his, and he had made that. Once netted into the pattern, it was impossible to escape his power.

The effect of the rector's 'repairs' had been to darken and enclose his mansion. Gothic windows and painted glass kept out the light. Creepers fingered the windows, leaves laid their hands over the panes, so that silence and shadow lay at the further side of every room, and at the end of every corridor. Outside, too, the crooked elms shut out the light from low green lawns, and all was shut in by the huge dark presences of the oaks in the park casting their network of shadows to the very walls of the house, for the midwinter sun never struggled high enough to look clear over their crowns.

Tresham now came to the edge of the lake in the hollow of the park below the house. Ruffled, cold, its lips of grey water lapped the shore at his feet. He saw it as an unnatural, ogreish presence summoned here by the rector's decree. Already it had devoured the woman and child he had helped to bury yesterday. He walked by the hungry water towards the Traveller's Tower. Gusts puffed dead leaves fitfully onto the waves, where fleets and squadrons took sail. Other dead leaves scratched against the stone walls of the Tower which he had now reached. It was here, so Mrs Poynder had told him, that the navvies' woman and her child had lived at the last. From this door she had walked out into the rector's lake to drown herself and her son. But had he made no lake, an oak would have served to hang herself from. And her son with her, whoever's son he was? He compelled himself against his dread to push open the wooden door.

The scrape of the door echoed in the stone interior. Like tremors of that echo a heap of rags under the spiral stair shivered apart. Out rushed rats in all directions. Sickening waves of smell broke over him. Liquid leaking from the rags had stained the floor. He shut the door at once before the rats rushed him. But he could not shut it before horror of what the Traveller's Tower contained had lodged in his imagination.

VIII

'PEOPLE SAY THEY WILL HELP US, but I'm hanged if I know when they'll begin,' complained Tresham Pitcher to Roland Farr as he lay in an armchair in Farr's rooms at Cambridge. It was a Saturday in early summer, and Tresham had run down from London in hope of persuading Roland to commit himself to making the Eastern journey next year.

Farr lay in another chair with his feet on the fender. He was most comfortable – not only comfortable at that moment, in these white-panelled sunny rooms looking out upon the fountain of Great Court – but comfortable in his life at Cambridge. He had many friends, and daily made more. All things that delighted him were close at hand amongst these streets and colleges. He was not teased by his mamma. Nothing impelled him away from the life he led, to travel to the East or anywhere else.

Nothing, that is, except Pitcher's influence upon him. This he felt strongly, and a trifle uncomfortably. Pitcher's knock upon his door that morning was the reverberant and not altogether welcome summons of the Traveller's oak staff conjuring him to keep an ancient promise. But the promise (if made at all) had been given by a younger self under other circumstances, and it was this alteration in himself that he found difficult to put to Pitcher. Christmas, when they had talked of going to these outlandish places, was so long ago; he had not known half of the fun of Cambridge then, let alone of London in summer. Old Pitcher was so strong at making him feel he owed a duty, where all he recalled was discussing an idea.

'I suppose if your uncle won't let you have the necessary, you must drop your plan, must you?' he suggested.

'I don't intend at all that that should happen,' replied Pitcher sharply.

'No, of course. And the publisher – did you take up his idea of getting money from a publisher for a book of your travels?'

'I did. I went to a publisher. At least, I went to your friend Mr Bounty and asked if he would introduce me to a publisher.'

'Old cat! I suppose he gave you letters to a dozen?'

'He did better than that. He asked me to his rooms in Albany and had this fellow Stourpaine along.'

'Of Buckle and Stourpaine? That was civil. Did it work, though?'

'Stourpaine was awfully jolly so long as we were drinking Bounty's wine and sitting on his gilt sofa talking about nothing. But all he'd say when I began about a book of travels I might write was to come and see him in Piccadilly some of these days – if I had the time, you know, with making my other arrangements for my journey. Fresh approach, young traveller, just the sort of thing that might go off well, old Bounty said. "Write to me, write to me," was all Stourpaine would call out as he swaggered off up the Rope-walk with his cape flying out behind. Such a vain fellow!'

'And did you write off to him?'

'I did, yes, and went to see him at the time fixed a week or so after. Do you know, I sat in his outer office forty minutes with the clerk looking on and sniggering in his sleeve. Forty minutes! Then out swings Stourpaine through the glass door with his hat on his head, evidently off to his dinner or his whist and forgotten clean about me. Of course he rowed the clerk, and took me in again, but it was only to be rid of me quick. I'd no name, he said, I was too young, I'd no experience of travel or authorship – all the points which had been my advantages in Albany, damned me in Piccadilly! No, not fifty – not twenty – guineas would he lay out in advance. His partner wouldn't hear of it. Then he pushed me out of doors and went off to his cards.'

'Oh Lord. So that's no good.'

'You don't know any publishers, do you, Farr? For I still think the writing idea is the best plan for making my uncle see I'm in earnest, when I'm sure he'll put up a hundred or two for our travels.'

'It wouldn't be the least use in life my going to a publisher,' said Farr, his heart rather sinking at 'our' travels.

'If you could put MA after your name, though. MA Trin. Col. Cant. looks better to a publisher than Esq., I suppose.'

'But I ain't an MA.'

'No.'

Each had sunk lower in his chair under wreaths of cigar smoke. Then Roland raised himself a little. 'What sort of a fellow do you suppose would have impressed Stourpaine to stump up the money?' he asked, the beginnings of an idea, or a joke, coming into his mind.

'Oh, some tremendously hard-bitten fellow, you know – one of those stray "captains" who knock about the world with a sword and a battered carpet-bag, and have just come from leading a troop of Lesghians against the Cossacks, or Cossacks against the Lesghians, and have a devilish knowing look about them, and a brown phiz with a couple of sabre-cuts upon it.'

'Yes, and speaks a dozen languages, and can tell you the jolliest place to dine in Vienna, and is known to have a romantic attachment to a certain Countess at Pesth – that's the sort of fellow these publishers swallow down whole, ain't it, and make fools of themselves half the time because the gallant Captain ain't a bit what he pretends. Well,' said Roland, 'I tell you what.'

'What?'

'Why don't you pretend you're a horse of that colour?'

Pitcher had pulled himself up in his chair too. 'And fool them, you mean?'

'Yes, make 'em put up the tin. Make 'em pay out for the "Travels" the gallant Captain Whatnot will send them when he gets to India. And the beauty of it would be, having made up your author, you make up his adventures too. You could make twice the book out of it you'd be able to make by sticking to your own name and the facts of your journey.'

'We could write it together. We could make the fellow up and write him in for just the sort of adventures a fellow ought to have in the East. Hair's-breadth escapes – wild tribesmen – '

'Secret visits to the zenana. My word, it would be a lark!'

'We'd make our name.'

'Make the gallant Captain's name, you mean. What shall we call him?'

Pitcher had got up and was pacing the room. Roland noted the shafts of sunlight loaded with dust-motes – this still summer air from the dear Cambridge world at the window – which was swirled into a maelstrom by his friend's heavy frame crossing and recrossing the open mullions. But the joke of his invention carried all before it in his mind. It was wonderful to have supplied a joke which had so caught on with Pitcher! 'What shall we call him? Pouter, Pepper – '

'Too like Pitcher. Could we bring it off, though? Suppose the publisher wanted to meet him?'

'Of course he'd want to meet him,' exclaimed Roland, loving the chance to lead, 'that's half the joke, that is. You'd trick yourself out like the Captain, and talk very gruff and knowing, and strut about with bandy legs like the fellows you see at Tattersalls. Do you know anything about the East?'

'Enough to take in a man who's never been there.'

'There you have it. I tell you what,' Roland went on, 'Mamma knows old Buckle, Stourpaine's partner, awfully well – I think he's sweet on her – so why don't I get her to write off to him to see this friend of mine, Captain Mustard, and hear all about the way he intends making a land-march to India?'

' "A land-march", that's good,' said Pitcher, praise causing Roland to flush to his ears with pleasure. 'Walking to India sounds a very cloudy sort of plan, but "land-march" – just the ticket! Ring of purpose to it.'

'Suggests the military man at once, don't it? And we'll – why, hallo, Easby,' called out Roland to a young face with large dandified whiskers which looked in at his windows. 'Coming in, are you?'

'Well, I, no, I ain't just coming in old fellow, no, I wondered was you coming along to the meeting and all that kind of thing. Didn't know you had company and so forth. Beg pardon, sir,' he added to Pitcher, who was casting upon him the gloomy, savage look which reflected his feelings towards upper-class people he didn't know.

'Oh, Lord – is it time for the meeting?' asked Roland, springing up from his chair and pulling out his watch. 'It is, too. I say, Easby, could I bring my friend along, do you think? This is Captain Vinegar, by the by,' said he smoothly, with a wave at Pitcher, 'Vinegar, old fellow, may I introduce Lord Easby?'

Gravely Pitcher extended his hand to the young man through the mullion. Roland could see the laughter in his eyes. There was real

condescension in the two fingers he held out over the window-sill –
the hard-bitten Captain to the callow undergraduate, however lordly.
Roland was delighted.

'Captain Vinegar is just back from Persia, you know,' he said, 'and
is come up to set some of our orientalists to rights. Are you dining at
the Lodge, Vinegar, or would it amuse you to come along to our
meeting?'

'I've rather a heavy hand at political meetings, Farr,' said Pitcher
in the deep, gruff tone appropriate to their invention, 'as you may
recall from my stopping with you down at Ravenrig.'

'Knocked a striker down at my father's place,' explained Roland to
his friend through the window, whose eyes widened.

'A strike-breaker he was, actually,' corrected the Captain.

'Well, one of those agitating coves,' said Roland, from whose mind
politics had rather faded as summer and London parties had come on.
'No, the thing is, it ain't a political meeting Easby and I have on hand,
it's a club we belong to, dining club, the jolliest thing out, and if you'd
care to come along I'm certain our President would be honoured to
have in a famous traveller, eh, Easby?'

'We should all be honoured, sir,' said Easby.

'Then I shall accept.' Pitcher stuck his cigar in his mouth and
looked keenly at Roland, as though to call his friend's bluff – if bluff
it was – by taking up the challenge to act Vinegar's part and carry on
in real earnest the idea begun by Roland as a joke. Roland did look a
little aghast.

'Sure you shouldn't rather lie down quiet after your journey?' he
asked. 'There may be a few bottles drunk, you know, and a good deal
of larks – that's if you think your fever's coming on?'

'My dear fellow,' said Pitcher, taking him by the arm and sweeping
him out of doors to join Easby on the cobbles, 'a man who has just
travelled from the Caspian don't need to lie down after railing from
London to Cambridge – though I confess I have been less shaken about
in an *araba* in the Kizil Kum than I was by your Eastern Counties
railway. Isn't it so, my lord?' he went on, catching Easby's arm as well
and marching the two young men towards the towered gateway and
the street beyond.

*   *   *

[145]

An afternoon a month later found Roland Farr walking with his friend Captain Vinegar along Piccadilly towards the offices of Buckle and Stourpaine beside the Egyptian Hall. Iron-grey whiskers and beard, a wide-brimmed hat with a low crown, a suit of checked tweed, a limp supported by a cane – beside the slender, blow-away elegance of Farr in his full London fashion, Captain Vinegar looked to perfection the part of a military man who has knocked about the rougher quarters of the globe. Farr was laughing.

'And don't forget to say that thing about "seeing a bit of the fighting in Beloochistan".'

'There ain't any fighting in Beloochistan that I know of.'

'He won't know that.'

'I say, Farr, it ain't entirely a joke, you know,' said the Captain in rather a strained voice, which allowed the diffidence of Pitcher to look out of the Captain's light-coloured eyes. 'I need the money from Buckle like the very deuce.'

'You shall have it, never fear,' Farr assured him as they came to the publisher's doorway. 'Here we are. In you go.'

'You're coming, though?' Pitcher clasped his arm.

'I'll come, but for Heaven's sake don't try and make me laugh as you did at Cambridge or we shall come unstuck.'

The evening spent with Farr's dining club at Cambridge had succeeded wonderfully. Enthused for his rôle by champagne in the conspicuous quantities which undergraduates like to provide (and still with the intention of paying out Farr for having pushed him willy-nilly into the masquerade), Pitcher's theatricals had surged from strength to strength until Captain Vinegar quite dominated the table, seated about the centre of twenty or so flushed young faces turned towards him to drink in the tales he related of his travels in Eastern lands. His step-uncle's library supplied the facts of the adventures – with wolves in the Carpathians, amid snow-drifts in the Taurus, or in ambushes in Koordistan – which only altered as Pitcher's imagination turned them into the adventures of Captain Vinegar. At the time Pitcher had gone ahead recklessly, amazed by the fluency of his invention, and gratified by the gullibility of these pampered young men whom he led about the East by their noses. He wished his account of his canal journey that night at Ravenrig might have gone off in such style! Later, he had worried that some of his audience might not quite have believed in the Captain; but Farr (when writing to say that he had fixed through his mother a meeting with Buckle) reported no suspicions in the club that Vinegar was anything but the genuine article.

However, a publisher at a sober hour in the afternoon was a different pair of sleeves from a Cambridge dining club with a bottle before each man's place. Farr, of course, didn't see the difference; but, then, it is the failing of undergraduates (as Pitcher had told him) to suppose that when their pretensions have taken in one another, or their dons, they have taken in any portion of the world at large. Pitcher's hands shook a little as he followed his friend up the stairs to the publisher's office.

The same clerk who had sat and sniggered on his stool whilst Pitcher had waited those forty humiliating minutes for Mr Stourpaine now darted away with Captain Vinegar's newly-engraved card. Almost at once Mr Buckle himself returned along the passage, a short, stout, beaming man in old-fashioned black clothes like a clergyman's, who first shook Farr's hand in both his own, and then grasped Vinegar's hand with a keen smiling upward gaze into the bearded face which the Captain withstood stonily.

'Most pleased, most pleased. Come along, my dear sir,' he said, leading the way down a passage narrowed by stacks of books lining its walls. At its end they entered a dingy brown room shaken by the rumble of Piccadilly's traffic below sash windows. They seated themselves, Pitcher choosing for the Captain an upright chair with its back to the light, Buckle taking the chair behind his desk and steepling his fingers upon a well-filled waistcoat.

'Lady Fanny well?' he began. 'I am in hopes of finding her at the Scratchwoods' tonight – do you go to them?'

'No, no, and if you do – if you do find Mamma, that's to say,' Roland said eagerly, 'pray don't tell her I'm in town, pray don't. I should be at Cambridge, do you see, but I ran up to see my friend Vinegar here whom you have to look sharp to catch, or he's off again on some of these journeys of his.'

'Quite so. Mum's the word, eh? Now, sir,' he said, swivelling his chair to face the Captain, 'may I ask in what way my firm may have the honour of assisting you?'

Pitcher put Vinegar's hat on the floor and dropped his gloves one by one into the upturned crown. Then he put the cane between his knees and stilled his shaking hands by clasping it. At last he said, 'The fact is, Mr Buckle, though I've knocked about the East about as thoroughly as any man alive, I've been for the most part acting for governments, if you understand me, and consequently I haven't been free to publish the account of my wanderings.'

'Ah,' nodded the publisher, 'ah, quite. Not free.'

'What I propose to myself now,' went on Vinegar, 'is to make a land-march from these shores to India, and in this I shall be acting for no Power, I shall be my own man, so that I shall break no engagement – no secret engagement – if I write up a journal of my travels and publish it after as a book.' This was the line worked out with Farr beforehand. He looked at Buckle to see how he was taking it. Buckle was polishing his eyeglasses on a silk bandana.

'I looked – forgive me, Captain – I looked you up here and there when I had Lady Fanny's letter,' said he, 'and I confess I found your name nowhere, not in the Army list, not at the clubs, not at the Royal Geographic. I confess I was puzzled.'

Pitcher said nothing. The incessant tinkling of the window-glass to the wheeled traffic in the street was like a nervous tic in his head as he watched Buckle hold up his eyeglasses to the light and look through them. Yet the edge of risk in the scene made his blood sparkle through his veins.

'But,' continued Buckle, 'what you say about "acting for governments" explains that, I take it.'

'Certainly the name Vinegar don't appear on such lists as the public is able to consult,' said the Captain haughtily, 'unless you can make your way a good deal further into the Foreign Office than most men.' Pitcher saw Farr's eyes widen in admiration for this high-and-mighty line. He was surprised by it himself.

'I see,' said Buckle, nodding his head, lips pursed, 'I see – so the name "Vinegar" ain't – ? Eh? Quite so. And I dare say your experiences, Captain, your former experiences – these could be let out into your narrative a little, eh, colour it a little? Could they?'

'Of course I shall betray no confidence, Mr Buckle, and you'll not look for me to do so, but yes – yes, there can't be a doubt that the queer things I've seen and been a part of must find their way into my writing, it is bound to be so. One tale will remind me of another, I don't doubt.'

'And the Foreign Office ain't going to come out with an embargo upon your publishing, I take it? That wouldn't do, you know.'

'Whatever you had advanced to me should be paid back in that event.'

'Advanced? Ah, you had an advance of money in mind, did you? Hum. I think we had better leave all that by for the minute, until – '

'For the right to publish the book when written,' said Vinegar heavily, 'I should expect the sum of 150 guineas to be paid to me before I leave England.'

The sum of £100 had been agreed with Roland beforehand, but Pitcher found Vinegar in full flow to be so satisfactory as to be worth another £50 at least, and rounding up into guineas. There was silence. Mr Buckle screwed up his face into as near an agonized expression as good humour and high living would allow, and seemed to be doing sums on a paper with the pen he had seized up.

'Dear me, dear me,' he said, sighing. 'Well, I suppose we might run to something like it, I dare say we might. I shall have to consult my partner, of course. We will step into his office on the way out – he deals more in your line, the travelling line, than what I do, and should be looking after you. He deals with the fact, and I attend to the fiction, that's about the way we break it up between us. Now sir, this journey to India – this land-march – you have a route in mind, I take it?'

Pitcher outlined the route he had planned long and carefully. The romance of the Asiatic cities' names, which he felt so strongly, filled the shabby London room like the colours of an Eastern carpet which he might have unrolled at the publisher's feet. As he talked, though, and spilled out the jewelled names and barbarous motifs to dazzle Mr Buckle, he considered with alarm the suggested meeting with Mr Stourpaine. Scant as had been Stourpaine's attention, he might even so recognise Pitcher behind Vinegar's whiskers.

'And you plan upon marching all alone through these wild lands, do you?' asked Mr Buckle, looking at his visitor respectfully. 'You speak the languages, I take it?'

'He speaks them to perfection,' put in Farr.

'A little, a little,' said Vinegar gruffly. 'Turkish carries you along

[149]

pretty well between Belgrade and Delhi, you know, that's if you go by the northern route. But no, I shan't be alone, for Farr here comes with me, don't you, Farr?' He saw the mischievous smile on his friend's face vanish.

'I certainly should like to, you know,' stammered Farr, 'if I could, you know. If I can get off, that's to say.'

'Oh, you can get off well enough if you care about it,' Vinegar told him, 'if you ain't to be tied to your mother's apron-strings all your days, that is. You have nothing to keep you in England that I know of, save a set of scamps up at Cambridge that would like you all the more for a few months' absence living hard. Ain't it so, Mr Buckle?'

'Certainly the opportunity of seeing the world with an experienced traveller don't come every day,' agreed Buckle with caution. 'Your people know of your intention, do they, Mr Farr?'

'Papa knows I should like awfully to go to the Levant,' conceded Farr, 'but pray don't speak a word of it to Mamma, Mr Buckle, for she would only make fun of it all, and say it couldn't be.'

'I don't know so much, Farr,' put in Pitcher, 'nobody better suited to present the plan to her than Mr Buckle here, who has met me and backs us up with an advance of money. She will see then it ain't just a lounge to Pera you're set upon, but a thoroughgoing march. Wouldn't you say so, Mr Buckle?' Pitcher was amazed how fluently he thought of ways to use Vinegar's strengths to advance his own schemes. 'Yes, Mr Buckle, you speak to Lady Fanny of it, that's my advice, and I'm sure your influence will procure young Roland's leave-of-absence. That's if you believe I am to be trusted with him, of course!'

All had a hearty laugh at the notion of the Captain proving untrustworthy, and Roland was obliged to agree that Buckle should urge his mother to allow him to join Vinegar's expedition. They rose to their feet. The threatened meeting with Mr Stourpaine could be neither avoided nor delayed. They filed between the passage walls of books as far as the outer office. Mr Buckle crossed it and rapped on the glass-paned door.

'Oh, sir, he ain't in,' sang out the clerk from his stool.

'Not in?'

'Mr Stourpaine ain't never come in from going out for a tick.'

'Dear dear. Has he not. Oh dear. Well then, Captain Vinegar, you see how it is, perhaps you'll look in again – when you wish for the advance of money perhaps you'll look in, and just meet my partner.'

'I shall be out of town a good deal, a great deal, I'm afraid – out of the country, in fact,' said Vinegar stiffly, 'so perhaps you will give me a draft on your bankers now, if it's convenient. Of course, if you have to ask your partner before drawing money – '

'Ask Stourpaine? No question of asking Stourpaine, I assure you, sir. If Stourpaine ain't here at this hour, why, he may like it or not, just as he chooses, when he finds I have advanced you £100 against the royalty fees on a book of your travels.'

'I believe it was 150 guineas we settled upon, Mr Buckle. But if you prefer the smaller sum it's all one with me,' Captain Vinegar added grandly.

*　　*　　*

Roland Farr was in his heart a little appalled at the ease with which Pitcher took up the ways and manner of this invention of his. Still, the imposture amused him, and he only regretted he had no one at Cambridge with whom he could share the joke of the thing; for he had a feeling that a practical joke which can't be discovered to its audience loses its humorous character and becomes in fact a fraud. He wished he might tell the dining club of it, and turn the invention of Captain Vinegar back into a joke again. However, he amused himself with carrying on a correspondence, in character, with the Captain in which he recounted his parents' reactions to the proposal of his journey. One thing after another – Buckle's advocacy with his mother, his father's wish that he should go to the scenes of his own labours in the Levant – had swept Roland along in the general direction of making the journey, without his ever having said to himself 'I will' or 'I won't'. He found when he talked of it that people rather envied him, which he liked. Girls seemed to think it was a tremendous thing to have on hand.

However, there came a development which brought matters to a head, and he wrote off to Captain Vinegar, c/o T. Pitcher, Esquire, at Creech Lane, Bishopsgate, to warn the Captain that he would have to be interviewed by his father, Sir Daniel Farr, in order to convince his parents that Vinegar was a proper guardian for their son abroad.

Pitcher at first gave the Captain no chance of taking in Sir Daniel. But he saw that if he succeeded, then Roland's company – and all the advantage of having with him in the East Sir Daniel's *fiat* and Sir Daniel's son – would be made certain. It seemed worth trying. Sir Daniel, he reflected, was extremely short-sighted, had no cause to suspect an imposture, was favourable to the idea of Roland's travels in any case. But he would pick the ground, and lay his plans, with care.

In late summer the day for the interview arrived. Roland and Tresham were together in the lodgings in Half Moon Street taken in Captain Vinegar's name. They had thought of taking a room at Limmer's in Conduit Street, where the sporting and military put up, but Roland had liked the idea of having a secret lodging, for his own use as well as Captain Vinegar's, and so he had engaged these Half Moon Street rooms indefinitely at six guineas a-week. Pitcher smiled rather bitterly to himself at Farr paying out, for a lodging he'd never use, just six times what he himself paid for a roof over his head in Creech Lane. Never mind, it gave their invention a wonderful credibility, to have his own accommodation. Whatever made Vinegar come alive was worth paying for.

Half-darkened by holland blinds, the sitting room was piled to the ceiling with boxes and traps and gun-cases – amongst them a mysterious object in a canvas bag called a "Levinge-bed" – all borrowed by Roland from friends, all now carrying labels marked VINEGAR in bold black letters. Roland lay in a chair waiting for Pitcher's reappearance from the bedroom, into which he had gone to change into Vinegar's check tweed, and to stain with walnut-juice whatever skin showed amongst his rugged whiskers. Roland Farr, at twenty, had himself a perfectly angelic ring of whiskers curling like gold shavings round his cheerful face. His mouth was small, the lips shapely, and a fresh colour in his cheeks set off the lively sparkle in his eyes. When thinking, he often sat as he did now, his fingers interlocked on top of his head, the bright hair curling between them, as though he was holding on a bonnet in a breeze. His smile at his thoughts showed his teeth, and it might have been said that there was something about so white and regular a set of little pearls that was almost too dainty for a boy. He wouldn't, of course, be in the room when his father called, but he intended listening to the interview from the bedroom next door, so as to miss nothing of the joke. He understood – it had taken him a little longer than it had taken Pitcher to see that if today's interview succeeded he was caught – that in his father tumbling to Vinegar's imposture lay his last chance of escaping this wretched expedition to the East. In part he hoped Vinegar might be exposed. It was on Pitcher, after all, that the wrath would chiefly fall – Pitcher who would suffer a bad quarter of an hour with his father – and then, if he knew Papa, there would be a side to the joke which would appeal to him after all: the extraction of 150 guineas from a pair of publishers, for instance, and Pitcher's performance to the Cambridge dining club. And there would be no question then of Roland leaving England, unless it were to run up to Scotland for Easby's grouse, or to run over to Ireland for the woodcock. In face of that dread summons to the ordeals of travel, he was ashamed of the pleasant occupations which would compensate him so thoroughly for staying at home. These rooms in Half Moon Street, now, could be developed into a very pretty attraction once he was acquainted with young ladies bold enough to take tea in a bachelor's chambers. He sighed, and stirred.

Another part of him wished to travel; or, rather, wished that the fag of it was over and he was well home again with a stock of tales which would set him above other fellows who had gone no further than Market Harboro' for the hunting. He wondered if the writer of *Eothen*, about the only book of travels he had been able to get on with, hadn't perhaps suppressed a certain side of his adventures, in Constantinople or Cairo. For he had talked loud enough of white slaves, and had described the slave-markets pretty thoroughly, but then he had got upon his high horse and censured the girls' plainness; was that really all the story? Had he stopped at the door, as he made out? Surely these fellows who travelled about the East weren't so very different from himself, for all their superior indifference, and found quite half the allure of 'the Orient' in such ideas as were summoned up by 'hareem' and 'odalisque' and 'bain turc'? Didn't Pitcher find it so – Pitcher with the girl at his lodging in Creech Lane all the while? The door of the bedroom opened and he looked up to find Captain Vinegar staring down fiercely at him. Roland started, then laughed.

'Capital!' he said. 'I should know you anywhere in that rig, for it's exactly how you appeared to me at school, but I'll lay a monkey to a dollar Papa don't cotton to it.'

'How I appeared at school?'

'Yes.' It was why he had started up in his chair, finding this fierce, admonitory figure from the past standing over him. 'Yes, you did, you know. Severe. Old. The master race. When I was lighting your fire and that sort of thing, or toasting your bread, I'd look up and that's how you would be. You and Cropper and those swells.'

'Well, I suppose it's where I learned swagger. Vinegar's swagger. I certainly haven't had any need of it since – not till you invented old Vinegar for us to fag for!' He cracked his cane down hard on Roland's chair, and they both laughed. 'I wish you hadn't called him Vinegar, though, I do indeed, for it don't sound much like the name of a real fellow.'

'Oh, didn't I tell you?' said Roland, jumping up and freeing himself from what had almost alarmed him in Vinegar brooding over him, 'I've given the Captain a noble papa, for my mamma's sake. I told her he was natural son to the Earl of Quenby. Just the dodge to make her trust him. And then you see it don't signify being called Vinegar, for she takes it to be a *nom de guerre*, as old Buckle did when you put in the beautiful stuff about acting for Foreign Powers.'

'Doesn't she know Lord Quenby?'

'No, no, he cut his throat years ago, and had bastards in dozens.'

'Your father ain't so easily fooled, though.'

'In ways he's easier fooled, sharp as he is about the shop. Anyway, he's all for Vinegar, and he'll find what he wants to find, you see if he don't. Wish I'd trodden on his eyeglasses in Berkeley Square this morning, though.'

Pitcher took out his pocket-watch. 'He should be here. Now then, old fellow, if we get well over this hurdle, I take it our course is fixed, is it? We leave England in April?'

April! Just when he should have liked to go into Aberdeenshire for the salmon. He went to the window and squinted down into the street. 'Here he is! – and, by Heaven, he has Enid with him!'

'We're done for! She'll be sure to know me!'

'Too late. Face it out. Good luck, Captain!' He darted into the bedroom and pulled shut the door, squeaking out a giggle of pure enjoyment at the turn the game had taken against them. He would see Aberdeenshire after all! And why was Pitcher so deuced confident his sister would know him?

Pitcher settled the blinds low on the windows and stood with his back to them while preparing in his chest Vinegar's voice, and in his mind Vinegar's outlook and vocabulary. He felt the brilliant tension of the actor in the wings. He felt too an actor's affection, an affinity, for the rôle of Vinegar which exceeded his attachment to the rôle of Tresham Pitcher. Let Pitcher rot at his desk at the Waterways, and Vinegar would rise from the ashes – Vinegar who had no Laidlaw Villa entangling his legs, no Charlotte-Anne in Creech Lane, no mother, no love, no loyalty, no burden. Of Pitcher, all Vinegar acknowledged was a foreign upbringing and his father's sword. A knock at the door!

'Come in,' called out Vinegar. He told himself how hardy he was, how self-reliant, and armed at all points, and subservient to no man.

The landlady showed into the dim room first the veiled rustling shape of a girl, then the short stumpy figure of Sir Daniel peering about him with his silk hat in his hand. 'Sir Daniel Farr,' she read from the card in her hand.

Having identified his host among the boxes and shadows, Sir Daniel walked towards him with hand outstretched. 'Kind of you to see me, Captain Vinegar,' he said. 'You'll forgive me for bringing in to you my daughter Enid, but we take you in on our way home from the Park, do you see, and I don't care to have her wait in the carriage.'

'Delighted to make Miss Enid's acquaintance,' said Vinegar, looking fiercely into her face. A hundred times Tresham had tried to recall that face exactly; now that he saw it again before him, the sweet oval, the slanting eyes, the mischievous mouth, he wondered that he had ever forgotten a line of it. Nor had she forgotten him. He saw the startled clouding of her eyes, the parted lips. She drew back. He did not know what she would do with her discovery. He turned to her father, who was fitting on his eyeglasses, pulling the gold wire over his large ears in the clumsy way he remembered, and peering about him.

'Forgive me,' said Sir Daniel, 'is it very dark in here? Do you find it dark, Enid?'

'Perhaps it only seems so after the Park, Sir Daniel.'

'Perhaps so. My eyes, Captain, suffered in the East. Ophthalmia.

[155]

Twice I was stone blind for a month, once in the Sinai desert and once at Baghdad.'

'I'm sure Captain Vinegar can have no objection to raising the blinds,' suggested Enid sweetly.

So she was going to tease him, not expose him. He ignored her, saying, 'Then you and I are in the same case, Sir Daniel, for I've a dose of the fever I took a year or two back in the Gulf of Scanderoon, and as I'm more comfortable with the light shut out we won't draw up the blinds, if you please. Now, sir, I think – '

'No more unhealthy place on earth than Scanderoon, I believe. Those marshes behind the town, eh? Never cared for having to go there – never knew why it was a trading station. However. Yes, sir, I have called on you because I understand that you think of travelling in the East next year and giving your protection to my son Roland and a young friend of his named – named – '

'Mr Tresham Pitcher,' put in Enid from her seat at the table.

'Just so – Pitcher. The fellow who came to us by the canals, or claimed he had. He is a friend of yours, is he?'

'I have met him right enough, but no – no, it is your son Roland I should claim as a friend, if it is either of them. I have been at Cambridge a month or two where a fellow making maps of Daghestan needed helping, and I have seen a good deal of your son, sir. A fine boy.'

Sir Daniel grunted at this. 'When his tutor was applied to, to know how they would take to his absence from his college on his travels, he said – what was it he said, Enid?'

' "Perhaps Cambridge will not be losing one of its future great men, but Cambridge society will be losing one of its chief ornaments." '

'Well,' said Captain Vinegar, 'I believe he has just the high mettle and fondness of new scenes which profits most from travel. Of course, I must go whether the boys accompany me or not, but as far as your son is concerned, sir, I should be most happy to have him with me.'

'How far do you go, Captain Vinegar?'

'I march to India, sir.'

'As does Mr Pitcher, does he not?' enquired Enid. 'You and he will be pretty well inseparable, I suppose, by then?'

'India, indeed!' Sir Daniel drew in his breath. 'A long march! I don't think Roland thinks of going to India, does he, Enid?'

'To tell truth, Papa, I don't believe Roly much thinks of going anywhere. It's his friend Mr Pitcher does the thinking, and intending, if you ask me. Roly would quite as soon stop at home and go to London parties.'

'Roland's thinking always was done for him by someone else,' said Sir Daniel, knocking his hat against his knee in testy fashion. 'Sooner you, sir, than that giddy set he's in with at Cambridge. "Chief ornament of society" indeed! His mamma – my wife – Lady Fanny says it don't matter a toss not taking a degree, half the noblemen in England come down without taking a degree, she says, but where's the point, eh – if you ain't a nobleman, where's the point of it all? Why, I'd a deal rather have him over ears in that Chartist fol-de-rol he afflicted us with, than running about to no purpose at all, I would indeed!'

'There's not a doubt about it, to my mind, he is just at that stage of life where the little *désagréments* of Eastern travel wouldn't do him an atom of harm. I should look out for him, of course, but I shouldn't be able to make all easy, or comfortable – I can't make the desert any softer a bed, nor stop the fleas biting in a caravanserai.'

'No, no – nor should I want it. His mother complains he's too young – but there, why, bless you, at his age I was overseer at some mines on the Black Sea, with a hundred Turks under me – and the Devil himself over me, too, as it seemed. Ever meet Herr Novis in your travels, did you? No? Fleas, aye – talking of fleas, Captain, I see you have a Levinge-bed there, am I right? Use it, do you?'

'To tell you the truth, it came up just before you came up yourself, and I haven't examined it. Heard of them, of course, but never had one. My hide's too tough for a flea to trouble me much. You used one ever?'

'Yes, indeed. I swear by a Levinge-bed on the march. You know how to put it together, do you?'

'Well, I haven't – '

'Shall we just look if it goes along the same line as mine?' Tentatively Sir Daniel half rose, peering at the contraption by his chair like a child at another's toy.

'I should be obliged to you, sir – if you've the time.'

'Oh, I've time enough,' said Sir Daniel, pitching down his hat and setting delightedly about unpacking the weird device of cords and

[157]

netting. Vinegar kept his back to the light and looked on. 'Yes,' Sir Daniel went on, 'in London an active man has time enough for any mischief, with nothing but Balls and driving in the Park to fill his days. But I'm off soon, I'm off soon. Now then, this wire goes like that, and you must push these cords through here – and all the while you're crouched in a hovel in Cilicia, eh, with a goat pushing at you from behind, and the village elders puffing smoke in your face, and half a dozen females trying to get a view of you down the chimney! Ah, this is your – '

'Papa,' put in Enid, 'perhaps Captain Vinegar has an engagement.'

'Have you, Captain?' He relinquished the toy. 'In any event I have a couple of words I'd like to say to you in private. Not to do with Roland – a matter I should like to commission you to look into for me, if you will.'

'A business commission, Sir Daniel? I hardly – '

'It is a little more than mere business, Captain Vinegar, and I need a man who ain't afraid of danger nor yet of mystery.'

For some reason Pitcher's mind flew at once to the headless statue at Ravenrig which Bounty had spoken of in the gig. 'Then fire away, Sir Daniel, for I'm your man.'

'Is there another room where Enid might wait for us?'

'Only my – my dressing-room next door, which she is welcome to.'

'Enid, my dear, I don't know what your mamma would say to your waiting in Captain Vinegar's dressing-room, but I hope she may never learn of it. I will be as brief as I can, but I must tell Captain Vinegar a longish story so that he understands me thoroughly. I shouldn't have thought of it, Captain, if I hadn't talked last night at a Ball with Mr Buckle, who gave me to understand that discreet work, and dangerous work, was altogether in your line.'

'Civil of Buckle, and I should like to be of use, of course. Now, Miss Enid, if you'll step in here – ' Pitcher had opened the door a fraction, and raised his voice – 'if you'll step in here, and forgive a soldier's bivouac.' He pushed wide the door and looked in. Roland must have piled himself and the clothes into a wardrobe, for the room was empty. On an impulse, as Enid brushed against him in the doorway, he leant forward into her fragrance and whispered, 'Roland is somewhere in the room'.

Then he closed the door, and she heard no more of his talk with her father, whose life had always been full of shady spots and mysteries in which men like Captain Vinegar might be asked to take a hand. Captain Vinegar – ! She had thought of him then as a real person, she realised, as though Mr Pitcher's masquerade had taken her in. She laughed to herself. All that she had feared from the imposture was that it might be a trick played by Mr Pitcher alone on her father; now that she knew from that whisper that her twin was in the trick too, she saw it at once from Roland's point of view, as just the kind of joke he liked best. To have Mr Pitcher – Tresham – whisper the secret so close to her, almost as if he had bent to kiss her, was pleasant too. It made her think of the time they had driven in the pony-carriage so close together, and Mr Pitcher had confronted the ganger just as Captain Vinegar might have done. How those whiskers would prickle! She looked half-nervously round the bedroom, as if searching for, and dreading, tokens of masculinity to shock her delicacy. It raised Mr Pitcher in her view, that he had such lodgings as these in Mayfair, when she had understood that he lived far from fashion in regions she would never penetrate. Or were they Captain Vinegar's lodgings? Was this his bed, or Mr Pitcher's? She found she did not quite know where one began and the other ended, and gave it up, and turned to hunting out her brother. She tapped on the wardrobe door, and called softly.

'You may come out, Roly. I am in the secret.'

He wasn't in the wardrobe at all, but under the bed, whence he rolled out at her feet with a bundle of Pitcher's clothes in his arms, muffling his mouth in a shirt to stifle his giggles. She caught him up and they leaned together whispering and laughing.

'They're fast friends,' she said, 'they're putting up the Loving-bed together, or whatever it's called. How did you think of it, Roly?'

'A fellow lent it me.'

'Not the Loving-bed – Vinegar, how did you think of him?'

'Oh, it's a long story. To take in old Buckle at first. But he's gone on from strength to strength.'

'He's no end of a swell – I'm in love with him already!'

'I tell you who is in love with him – Pitcher. I'm hanged if Pitcher don't like him better than he likes himself.'

'So should I. A dashing captain, if you was a clerk?'

'Oh, I dare say. But should you want to travel about the East with a ram-rod like Vinegar? There ain't much larks about him, you know.'

'But he's entirely a lark, Roly! He's a lark through and through.'

'I hope it may go on so, that's all,' said Roland, pitching his friend's clothes into a chair. 'A fellow may make up a thing in joke and find out his invention has a life of its own, you know. What's that tale about the Baron who brought a monster to life and found he wasn't its master?'

'Frankenstein.'

'Yes, well, I hope I shan't find out that's what becomes of me when I'm tramping about in the desert, that's all. Driven on by a monster. You know, you were right in there when you said I didn't want to go. I don't a bit. Is it too late to drop out of it, do you think?'

'But Roly, darling, what Papa said in there was true too, and what Captain Vinegar said – you should go, really you should. Shouldn't I just jump at it!'

'Yes, you'd jump at it to be with Vinegar, I suppose,' said Roland gloomily.

'Roly, if Mr Pitcher lives here, in Mayfair, couldn't we have him to dine? I thought you said he lived miles off.'

'Oh these – ' Roland stopped. He didn't care to let his sister know his plans for these rooms. 'Yes, we can ask him if Mamma doesn't mind it.'

'Why was Mamma so nice to him, when she speaks so against him?'

'Ah, why is Mamma Mamma? It don't signify, though. She speaks against everyone when they're not by. Wait a bit, though. Would it be Pitcher we'd invite, or Captain Vinegar? You can't separate them, now Pitcher's got Vinegar's whiskers, and Mamma would see through Vinegar in a trice. No, it won't do. Listen!'

Captain Vinegar's voice spoke loudly through the door, a warning to Roland to hide, and when the door was opened, out stepped Enid smiling. At the carriage she gave her hand with a warm pressure to the Captain, a pressure which Pitcher, toiling at his desk at the Waterways, would have given much to receive.

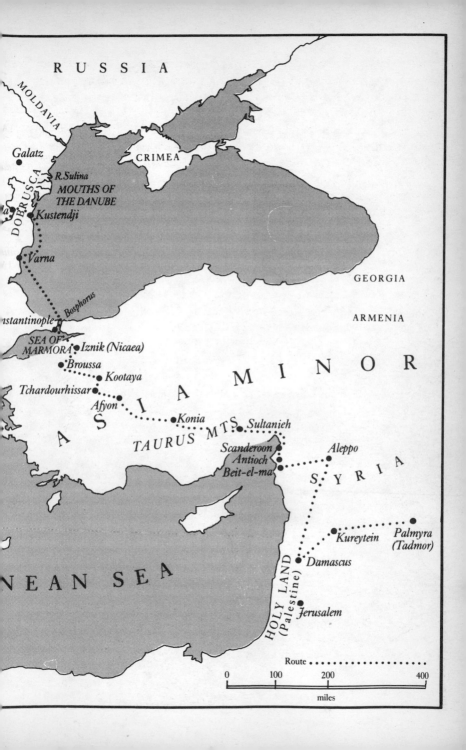

RUSSIA

MOLDAVIA

Galatz

CRIMEA

R.Sulina
MOUTHS OF
THE DANUBE

DOBRUSCA

a

Kustendji

Varna

GEORGIA

ARMENIA

Bosphorus

stantinople

SEA OF
MARMORA

Iznik (Nicaea)

Broussa

A   S   I   A   M   I   N   O   R

Kootaya

Tchardourhissar

Afyon

Konia

TAURUS MTS

Sultanieh

Scanderoon

Aleppo

Antioch

Beit-el-ma

S   Y   R   I   A

Kureytein

Palmyra
(Tadmor)

NEAN SEA

HOLY LAND
(Palestine)

Damascus

Jerusalem

Route • • • • • • • • • • •

0   100   200   400

miles

PART TWO

I
- - - - - - - -

IT WAS A PALE, MILD, rather melancholy afternoon at the beginning of April, 1850, that saw the steamer carrying Tresham Pitcher away from England beat a wake with its paddles through the glassy waters of the Harwich estuary. At the rail Pitcher watched the frothing commotion which rushed out of the paddle-boxes become mere ripples long before reaching the low, flat shore on either hand. Still the steamer, like a creature obsessed with its own rage, throbbed and thrashed and shuddered along, unconscious of its small impression on the face of the water, its furious black smoke, too, soon drifting away to nothingness in the vast sky. In the east hung a few clouds, their shadows bruising the sea.

Despite his liking for the fizz and rush of steam travel, Tresham couldn't help regretting that he had not slipped away from England under sail, at dusk, leaving the cliffs and high castle at Dover (and in it according to legend the skull of Sir Gawaine) to fade away together into night and the past: sail would have attuned better with his elegiac feelings at departure. The Harwich steamer was evidently full of trippers who would be back in England again tomorrow, or next week. Putting to sea had not been that decisive step into the future which he had imagined it would be when he had stood on the shore at Ravenrig. In all the scheming he had done since, to break free from England's constructions, it was the casting off from England's shore which he had expected to mark the moment at which the past ended and the future began. But the past had come aboard with him.

When would it come, the decisive step? Not in Holland, not in Germany, hardly at Vienna. His imagination probed the ground ahead. At Buda-Pesth? At crossing the Danube into the power of the Ottoman Empire at Belgrade? – yes, then, surely; whoever embarked from Semlin over the dark waters of the Danube to Belgrade would be

[167]

sure that he had taken the irreversible step which carried him out of his safe past and into a future as uncertain, and as dangerous to the traveller, as the tracts of the old afforested England to the knight-adventurers. The gloomy pool of the Danube expanded in his mind. He saw Farr and himself in the midst of it in their frail craft with their traps and their ferryman, the shattered towers and gilded mosques of Belgrade rising ahead – and he could not help his heart sinking. It was very real: his dread of it was the measure of its reality to him.

Tresham straightened up from the rail and walked rapidly along the deck, unable to be still. Anxiously he ran his hand over his beard and moustache – Vinegar's beard and moustache!

Vinegar's! At the joke of it his face – what showed of Tresham's young face between the Captain's whiskers – cleared at once, and Tresham's anxious light-coloured eyes lit with laughter. His pace slowed. Why, the Captain's bold heart didn't sink at the prospect of falling again into the power of the Turk at Belgrade! The Captain clapped him upon the shoulder and bade him cheer up, for the Turk can kill you but once, and at Belgrade the fun begins.

Smiling to himself, Tresham dropped onto a bench against the deckhouse and considered the Captain's feelings at quitting English shores for another of his Eastern journeys. For Tresham needed to understand Vinegar pretty thoroughly if he was to write up a journal of travels in the Captain's character. He was not concocting a subtle man, but Vinegar's feelings and reflections, however plain and tigerish, needed to be thought of, and must be kept separate from Tresham's own less certain and less vehement characteristics. Vinegar, for instance, was leaving behind him on that fading shore nothing in the world he cared about, save a box of papers establishing his noble birth in the strong-room at his bankers, a portmanteau of clothes at his club, and a decayed half-sister whom no one knew of kept by him in lodgings at Builth Wells. Vinegar was tied into no pattern, owed no loyalties, acknowledged no drag upon his independence, and feared nothing. These were the advantages of Tresham's hero, decided upon instinctively.

It was curious what a strong sensation of the real presence of Vinegar beside him – beside him and within him, too – Tresham had on the Harwich ferry. It was partly no doubt that they were alone together,

Farr having gone with his mother to Paris, where he was to stop at the Embassy and enjoy a thousand elevated gaieties before joining them at Vienna. It had not been possible, of course, for Vinegar-Pitcher to travel with Lady Fanny; besides, another of Vinegar's characteristics was his bearish contempt for the Societies of fashionable Europe where inequalities of money and social connexion serve to set the popinjay above the hero. Let Roland Farr enjoy the balls at Paris whilst he could, said Vinegar; once out of reach of his mamma's connexion, and soft beds and high living – once within the long shadow of the Turk at Belgrade – a very altered set of capabilities would be in requisition!

An action of Roland Farr's before leaving London had irritated Tresham exceedingly. What had happened was this. During the autumn Tresham had rather laid claim to Vinegar's lodgings in Half Moon Street, first staying there an odd night because he found the keys in his pocket, then using it as a store for the equipment he began to put together for the journey, at the last (Roland was in Wales, or in Scotland) more or less living there. He fetched up possessions now and then from Creech Lane until there was nothing much of his own left under the roof with Charlotte-Anne; but he shrank from the final confrontation with aunt and niece which he knew must come if he said he was leaving their house for ever. He had contrived to tiptoe backwards to the edge of the web he had walked into, but he recognised that to try and leave it altogether would cause such a convulsion of the gossamer as would be sure to bring old and young spiders down upon him with open jaws. He therefore asked Roland Farr (when he was next in town before the Cambridge term in October) if he would just run down to Creech Lane with a cab, pay off his landlady, and remove his last possessions with some excuse as to illness or absence abroad.

Roland had agreed readily. On the evening when the deed was to be done Tresham waited at Half Moon Street for the cab's return, half ashamed of himself, yet asserting that just in that manner would Vinegar have cut the Gordian knot of an entanglement with a Charlotte-Anne. Hours passed and Farr did not appear. The night passed. In the morning Tresham sent round to Berkeley Square to find if there had been some accident, and Farr came to him late in the day, brimming over with satisfaction at what he had to tell. Believing that

Charlotte-Anne had been Tresham's mistress, Farr had made up to her the minute he got into the house, had let her understand that he intended taking Tresham's place and lodging, and had ended up by carrying her off to Vauxhall, where they had drunk champagne and danced half the night, before he had ravished her in a four-wheeler on the way back to Creech Lane. He had forgotten to collect Tresham's possessions.

Tresham was outraged. He didn't show it, he laughed – after all, he had desired to be released from the girl's toils, and Farr had released him. Nonetheless, outraged he was. Farr said lightly, 'Knowing you'd ridden her pretty thoroughly, old fellow, I thought I'd try her over a furlong or two myself.' Farr – his fag Farr, whom he had thought was in awe of him! He couldn't be trusted, that was it. That was the outrage. And Farr hadn't an idea in life of having gone wrong. All unawares, the easy life and low intentions of his Cambridge set had eaten away his principles. What else in the moral storehouse might not have suffered from the same rat-teeth, and would prove Farr untrustworthy in the stresses of travel? That was what Pitcher (and Vinegar too) wondered, as they thought rather resentfully of Farr enjoying the pleasures of Paris whilst their paddle-steamer clanked into the grey German Ocean. Well, Vinegar would drop Farr mercilessly if he found he couldn't rely on his loyalty. 'I won't have amongst my people on a march (Tresham could hear him say) a man who might not be trusted in a tight place. It don't answer.'

Oh, Vinegar, Vinegar: how fortunate he was! Unmourned, unloved – paying that small penalty for their independence – such men as the Captain put to sea, leaving behind them with indifference England sinking into mist and marsh, looking ahead with equal cool indifference to the hazards of travel, being part of no pattern whose fabric is torn by their departure. If Tresham's spirits had risen on recognising the strengths of Vinegar's independence, they sank when faced with his own weaknesses in that line.

He watched the grey water slipping away, extending the gulf to the misty shore and the hardly discernible hump of Harwich church tower. On that island lay Rainshaw, its woods and lake, the old house on its crest in the parkland. He thought of his step-uncle's half-promise of inheritance.

> O fields! O woods! When shall I be made
> The happy tenant of your shade?

Well, he had accepted the gulf which that 'When?' of the poet's opened up at his feet between Now and such Hereafter as his step-uncle's half-promise had held out to him. For in that gulf flowed the torrent of life, the God-given gift. As for the Heareafter, let it come if it would. No, it was not Rainshaw, not 'prospects' or temptations which were the weak place. Love was the weak spot – attachment. Only his mother held him fast by that bond. He watched the water widening, widening, between himself and her.

> Love binds with cords of iron,
> But iron will part:
> Or, if the iron breaks not,
> Then breaks the heart.

He copied the lines into his pocketbook. He – Tresham Pitcher – wrote them down: in Captain Vinegar's Journal they had no place. It was only his mother who knew, she alone, that in his true nature there was no trace of a Captain Vinegar. So, in his own true character, always, he would write to her, pretending nothing. He swore it to himself as he copied down the lines. She had said once, long ago, stroking his hair in an Italian inn during the course of their wanderings, 'Wherever I am, there is a home for you.' He could see again the candlelight wavering on rough-surfaced walls, hear her voice, feel her hand on his hair. It was true. Only where she was, had he a home. Her very last words to him – they had said goodnight, and he was to leave Laidlaw Villa before she was up next morning, but she had come down again into the parlour with her grey hair loose and a wrapper round her shoulders, to put into his hands in its battered box his father's sword – her final words from the door, as she looked with a world of sorrow through the candlelight at him, were these: 'Only if you have a child of your own, will you know how I have loved you.'

The sword was with his baggage below decks. It was the weapon he had so longed to have a use for, left to him by his father, but kept by his mother in some secret place and never shown. 'When can I have my sword, Mother?' 'Soon.' 'How soon?' 'When you need it.' 'But I do need it for my game.' She had only smiled. When she gave it to him

[171]

at last she didn't smile, or weep, but she had looked strained enough to faint away, and old with sorrow.

The monotonous batter of the paddles on water pushed the steamer into the lifting swell of the open sea. This wide moat, the ocean river of the ancients, had to be crossed if England's constraints upon him were to be broken. If only he had never understood – never admitted – the bond of love binding him to his mother. If only she had died – the thought had come before he could be shocked out of thinking it.

He got to his feet. These were all Pitcher's worries. He would shake them loose by scouring about the deck in the character of Captain Vinegar, whose clothes and whiskers he wore, and within whose simple, gallant mind perhaps the susceptibilities of Tresham Pitcher could find shelter. Now, all round the steamer, the wide grey sea gleamed drearily to the furthest horizon. England was extinguished. On strode the Captain, looking fierce upon trippers and family parties. Safe in his box below he had a sheaf of letters of introduction to half the consuls and traders in the Levant – as well as a strange commission to enquire into certain private matters – given by the celebrated Sir Daniel Farr to Captain Vinegar. Such letters and commissions bolstered up the Captain's claim upon reality no end. It put a spring in his step as he walked the deck – and it made Pitcher laugh to himself at the solidity of the invention.

At Harwich, in the railway station, there had been groups of rough, dark fellows in ragged clothes staring about them. These gipsy-looking creatures (the porter told him) were Hungarians, remnants of Kossuth's beaten army, to be carried without tickets on the railway to London (to the porter's disgust) as a cautious gesture of Government support for Hungarian 'patriots' contesting Austrian rule. Their wild appearance had struck upon Tresham's heart like the drops of heavy rain you feel on your face when the storm is still distant, and his blood had quickened, not altogether comfortably, at the sight of their rags and long hair and dangerous eyes, for he was travelling towards the eye of that storm.

Captain Vinegar, however, paced the deck turning over in his mind a telling description of these brave fellows for the first item in his *Journal of a Land-March towards India.*

II

$\cdots\cdots\cdots$

Wilder Mann Hotel
Vienna

18th April 1850

My dear Enid,

    You will have heard all about my leaving Paris from
Mamma, who no doubt laughs at me awfully for making myself
a spectacle with my tears. But it seemed then so final, and I so
little wished to go. Will you remind her of the line in the poet
about Adam quitting Paradise? –

Some natural tears they dropped, but wiped them soon –

Of course my tears put her out of countenance before her friends,
as she said, but she would not let me take leave of her in private,
and I am sorry for it. There, will you make it up for me with her,
dear Enid, as you have had to do so often in old days?

    My low spirits were soon overtaken by the horrid dis-
comforts and frightful apprehensions of the journey to Vienna,
at one moment shaken to atoms by railway-speed, at another
half-smothered in a lumbering old eilwagen such as hasn't been
seen on our roads for a century. You no sooner surmount one
obstacle – removing yourself plus possessions from railway train
to diligence, say, in a foreign tongue and foreign tin – than up
looms another in view, of transferring yourself from diligence to
inn in another tongue and ditto tin. You cannot conceive of the
wear upon the nerves. Entering Vienna crowns all, though: at
the Austrian border-post you have had your passport taken from
you, and have been so poked about by officials and police-spies –
and so ferociously adjured to report yourself to the Police Office
at Vienna instanter – that I had resigned myself to thirty years
at least in a dungeon, or chained to a galley-oar, before ever the
city walls came in view. I must say, tho', that the first sight of

Vienna restored my spirits. You see a crowd of towers and steeples rising above its walls, the whole prospect ringed round with a park-like glacis of grass and trees, which makes it appear like a town in a German fairy-tale. Then you enter the city by a plunge through a long dark arch tunnelled under the Bastion, and arrive very much after the fashion of a prisoner of the old Romans, who has been obliged to bow his neck under a yoke. I went at once to a first-rate hotel (which a fellow in our Embassy at Paris told me of) called the Erzherzog Karl in the Karthnerstrasse, which I found pretty full of agreeable English, and quite comfortable enough to reconcile me to exile from Berkeley Square. Very far from being crammed with Turks and desperadoes, as I had expected, the streets look Londonish and familiar and even clean.

But I had a notion that my respite from 'the ceaseless toil of travel' (Ld Byron) would not outlast my joining up with Pitcher – or with Captain Vinegar, should I say? – which we had arranged to effect by leaving letters for one another at the Poste Restante Office. I was just finding my feet, and making acquaintance with some of the English (whom one mightn't have looked at twice in London, but we poor beggars of exiles can't be choosers), and thinking I would go along to the Poste Restante by-and-by, when there comes a note by a greasy servant – don't ask me how he had found me out – saying simply 'Pitcher and I are at the Wilder Mann, which suits our pockets and our inclinations, and have taken a room for you here – yours, O. Q. Vinegar (Capt.).' Of course I had to collect up my traps and move myself into the Wilder Mann, where I am not half so well housed. I have a pie-dish for a basin, and a handkerchief for a towel, which well shows how much washing these gentry like to do. However, Pitcher and I have settled that it is Vinegar's choice and we must put up with it (and of course it suits Pitcher's pocket, which I must think of always). We have a good deal of fun out of old Vinegar, coming out with his grim little sayings to each other, and thinking up the hard attitudes he adopts. He always sleeps on the floor without a mattress, for instance, 'so that I am no stranger to hardship when it comes'. We suppose that the Q of his initials is for Quenby (his natural father), but we do not know at all what the O stands for. Pitcher is adept at falling into his character, using his voice, etc. etc., which makes me laugh a great deal.

We dodged away from the Captain to go dancing last night – all Vienna is quite mad on dancing – at a café in the town, for though I am in hopes of working with Mamma's letters of introduction so that I may be invited to some of the Balls which go off every night here, it is plain that Society at Vienna is a hard nut to crack, especially if a fellow must crouch at the Wilder Mann hotel in place of the Erzherzog Karl. A Count I called upon with one of Mamma's letters made the excuse that 'Our ballrooms are too small to allow us the pleasures of a mixed Society such as you have at London' – this from a man living in a Palace, no less – and an Englishman I talked to at the Belvedere spoke of scenes of 'wild dismay' at a Court Ball last year where some Bankers' wives had been admitted. You may ask, What has become of my Republicanism, that I talk of trying to enter Society at re-actionary Vienna (a question Pitcher teases me with)? Well – I must confess my affection for the Cause is sensibly diminished since I have seen in real earnest the gentry a Republican is re-quired to share his views with, for the Students here look a very ragamuffin set, not at all our English idea of Varsity men.

But I was to tell you of our evening's dancing at the Sophienbad Halle. The etiquette is, that you may ask any lady to dance – many are masked – but you must put her back where you found her when the dance is done. Having gone through with this a time or two, we were recuperating at our table, when the band struck up a polka. Up jumped all, and in a twinkling the whole glaring, gas-lighted, gilt-mirrored café was one whirling mass of Terpsichoreans. The heat is terrific, the smell abominable (vide pie-dish, above). All was well until a red-faced German clutched by an enormous frau could be seen carving out a track for themselves through spilled dancers like a runaway steam-boat loose among wherries. Down upon us they bore, for she wouldn't answer to the helm, and crash! went her posterior into our table! Down it splintered with poor Pitcher beneath all, whilst I had sprang for a pillar and so saved myself from the general wreck. When picked up he was awfully vexed, poor Pitcher – quite missed the joke of the thing – and didn't take to it a bit when I put on the character of Vinegar and told him that this was the very kind of perilous mishap which we adventurous travellers must harden ourselves to withstand.

We have seen some of the lions, and I hope I shan't have to see many more. Pitcher is an indefatigable voyeur of all spots hallowed by bloodshed in the Rising of two years ago. We tramp to the spot where Latour was murdered, and to the scene of the Herrengasse massacre, or to any spot where he scents out blood, and there we stare at the paving stones. We even climbed to the top of St Stephen's spire, which gives a view of sufficient battle-fields to quiet the most sanguinary appetite, from the Turks' defeat of long ago, to the defeat of the Hungarians by Windisch-grätz last year. The view was indeed ravishing from that height – not of old battles, but of the city spread below, fair stone houses ringed by trees, and the butterflies dancing above the red roofs of the streets far below (for it was as warm as summer). I could hear a canary sing in its cage at a window, too, which made me think of the one we used to have at Twickenham before Papa moved us to Wales – do you remember? Then Pitcher called out to me, 'Have you seen the Danube?' I had not. I confess that when I did, and saw that width of serpentine river creeping so broad and dark through the landscape, and thought of how I must travel upon its current away from all I know and care for, into the barbarous East – I confess my heart sank within me. Pitcher of course is exiling himself, and must view with equa-nimity not only boating upon the Danube, but upon the Tigris too, I suppose, and the Euphrates and the Ganges and all other waterways of the accursed East. But I am not exiling myself – not I! Indeed I felt a very strong inclination to turn my back upon it all there and then, battlefields and Danube and East alike, and set out for home directly.

Still, in Vienna I have found my feet well enough – though this is the very deuce of travel, it seems to me, that you have no sooner dared to open your eyes in your present situation, and to take a cautious look about you, and to begin to get upon your legs, than removal elsewhere threatens you with just the same upset again. Pitcher is for ever gloating upon the removals and upsets and discomforts that lie ahead, in Vinegar's swagger-ing style which can't be talked to. Indeed, I confess it is a question with me sometimes, where Pitcher ends and Vinegar begins. I have just been out idling, for instance – coffee and kipfel at Kolczicky's, Jacquemar's gloves for Mamma from Lorbeer-kranze's shop – but Pitcher wouldn't keep me company in a lounge, choosing instead to pass his morning poring over maps of Transylvania and other outlandish regions which lie ahead of us, in Artaria's frowsty map-shop in the Kohlmarket. If he goes to a café, it must be in the Leopoldstrasse, where one must push through any number of shabby Turks and Albanians in their national dress, and sit at a dirty table remarking upon how cheap the coffee is. Of course, I must cut my coat according to his cloth, and share in his necessary economies, but it grates a trifle to have to hear lectures on my extravagance when it don't affect him, such as spending my money on gloves for Mamma.

We had a rather ludicrous example of what straits his miserliness may lead us into only yesterday. We had found out the house of the banker Herr Novis, to whom Vinegar had a letter from Papa, and I had made arrangements for a stadtlohn-kutsche – the proper kind of carriage to pay calls in – to take us there. When I come downstairs I find Pitcher has dismissed the stadtlohnkutsche as too dear and hired a fiacre in its place. Well, when we reach Herr Novis's mansion, our driver says he ain't permitted to drive into the courtyard, only a stadtlohnkutsche may do so, so that we must get down and tramp up to the door on foot like a couple of tinkers. The upshot was, that we weren't admitted! The servant said his master was out, which I don't believe, for the house was a blaze of wax tapers behind him.

Of course, I don't mean to say aught against Pitcher, who is a thoroughly good fellow and must make the little money he has last out ever so much further than I need think of. I still intend coming home from Constantinople, or from Jerusalem at furthest, though I have not said so. If I do, as I will, I might reach England before London quite breaks up in July. Meanwhile be sure to remind Lady Sophie of my existence – and I will make sure old Pitcher don't quite forget you!

Pray make my peace with Mamma over the scene I made her at Paris. The truth is, I was pierced by a ridiculous certainty I would never see her more.

Now I must go out and resume my machinations with Maginnis of our Embassy for inclusion on the list of invités for the Court Ball next week, which Pitcher growls at but counts upon attending nonetheless. There are, you see, one or two agreeable things in prospect before that brute Vinegar sweeps us off to be hacked into bits in Hungary.

yr. aff. twin
RF

PS I will direct this to Rawlins, as agreed, and trust her to see that it reaches your room without anyone knowing of it, for I can only write freely if you alone read the letter. RF

Hotel Erzherzog Karl
Vienna

22nd April 1850

My dear Enid,

My news in three words – there has been a quarrel, I am set free, I am coming home!

I only await the Court Ball to come off tonight, which I must attend if I don't mean to insult a fellow named Maginnis of our Embassy here who obtained cards for us at last – and then I shall set out for dear old England! My relief is extreme, for I had really begun to feel myself kin to the young lady gathering flowers in Sicily, who found herself snatched up by that grim old fellow in his travelling-chariot and carried off into the depths of Tartary. You will laugh at my characterising your kindly Tresham Pitcher thus, but I assure you you don't in the least know what changes may come over a fellow when he leaves behind him all the social niceties which must regulate our intercourse at home, and becomes a bear. We might never have left school, the way he sought to dictate to me. However – I write only that you may prepare Mamma, and Papa too, for my homecoming. I know Papa will huff and bang things about and tell me I have no steadiness of purpose, but I don't care much about it for he would say the same whatever I did. But Mamma's views I trust you to manage, for I will not bear it if she mocks me. You may let her know if you like the cause of my falling out with Pitcher, for it is a matter of correct costume in which I am sure she would take my side.

Actually I have been sucking my pen, for I find the quarrel a little absurd now I come to write it down. But you must understand that what would be a pebble in a man's shoe at home swells to a boulder blocking his path in a foreign land. I had got cards, as I say, for the Court Ball through Maginnis (an Irishman with a good deal of bounce, which Pitcher took amiss as condescending to him) and, when Pitcher enquired what I would wear to it, I replied naturally enough that I would put on an evening dress.

At this simple proposition he flew into a fury! I was good for nothing but to go to Balls like a Society miss – I never had intended to leave the pavements – I had betrayed the spirit of the journey from the first by going to Paris – what did I mean by encumbring his pack-animals with my suits of dress-clothes in snowy passes of the Caucasus, causing the failure of his expedition and the death of half his people? I thought at first he was affecting Vinegar's rôle, and tried to laugh him out of his tantrum by showing him in Murray that a dress suit is de rigueur for an audience with the Shah of Persia, and by accusing him of having a great sword in his own baggage (a fact!) which is a good deal less use nowadays than a suit of evening clothes. But he didn't like it a bit, and when I told him that if he was uncomfortable at not possessing correct clothes (which was the truth of the matter) then I would be happy to pay for a dress suit for him from the best tailor in Vienna – why, his fury knew no bounds! Be sure you tell Mamma that I found I couldn't travel about with a fellow who has no dress suit, and I'm certain she will understand the matter from my side.

Dear Enid – do you understand it a little too? I know that Pitcher had made an impression on you, but, really, friendship for you and me with such an uncomfortable sort of fellow is impossible. I am ever so glad I have found it out at Vienna, for I am not dependent upon him here as I would be once we were fairly inside the Turkish dominions, where I am sure he would have killed me at the least.

After our row he packed off bag and baggage to the Goldener Lamm, in unfashionable purlieus where he belongs, and I removed just as fast to the Erzherzog Karl, where I recline in comfort and content. Vienna is a tolerable enough town once you know you are to go home after. Not a noseless statue have I looked at – not a madonna with or without bambino – not a schedule of Danube steamers – not a map of Transylvania – all I have done is lounge about the cafés, and sit smoking with Maginnis, and make sure at the Police Office that my papers are in order to leave Vienna after tonight's Ball. Bless my luck that I am let off my ordeal.

Yr. aff. twin
RF

Danube Steamer
near Pressburg

Dear Enid,

I cannot just recall what I may have written in my last, but if I gave out the impression that I was coming home, then I write now to correct it. The truth is I had a fit of homesickness, and thought Pitcher had quarrelled with me, which was not at all the case. Now we are embarked on the Danube, and look forward to reaching Buda-Pesth this evening, where our travels proper may be said to begin. The steamer clanks down the river, pouring out smuts and black smoke over everybody, but fortunately we have been given one of the two cabins to ourselves. This came about – the cabin, I mean – thanks to Papa's name being well-known to the shipping company, and much being made of the honour of having myself aboard, etc. etc. I think Pitcher was gratified, though he rather made out that deck or cabin was all one to him. There are a pair of jolly counts, Count Veit and Count Bümm, who had made their way in and taken up residence. Pitcher affects to think they are called Feet and Bumm, and pretends to be very bearish towards them, but they are cheerful chattering fellows, one fat and the other thin, who are always running about and quizzing the females through their eyeglasses. They were in the party with which I went to the Court Ball.

I suppose you will want to hear about the Ball, which was rather a half-cock affair after all. There was much gas and gold, and brilliant uniforms, and no end of chandeliers and looking-glasses, but the effect was awfully vulgar. And then Maginnis gave himself such airs – quite as if procuring me entrance to a Court Ball signified that he was of the Blood Royal himself – that I understand why Pitcher had taken against him from the first. Pitcher, of course, was not of our party, though he had his ticket from Maginnis. My partner was a fine girl, a cousin to the Stahrembergs and so very bon ton, but lackadaisacal and unanimated according to the Vienna style. Dominoes and fancy-dress are allowed even there, and the uniforms of those Austrians, and Hungarians, and the court-dress of those Pumpernickel German princedoms, are so like the costumes at the Alhambra that one couldn't tell where reality left off and fantasy began. I was taking a turn on the floor with my fraulein when she enquired who was the stranger who looked so like 'votre Lord Byron' – and I found out she meant a tall, rather heavy-built fellow leaning at the door of the ballroom with his eyes evidently brooding upon us through his domino, and his person all decked out with swathes of silk, and turbans, and tassels, and high boots, like an Albanian desperado. It took me a moment to twig that it was Pitcher beneath the disguise, when I laughed aloud (which is unknown in a Vienna ballroom) and said I should be delighted to present to her 'Lord Byron', who was my own travelling-companion and school-fellow. She had already set a course towards him, and her ogling resulted in him leaving his door jamb (and leaving the squat toad of a creature in a Mephistopholean disguise who was beside him) and swaggering up to us to claim my fraulein in a waltz, as anyone may at these Balls. He carried her off in his arms with the gravest of bows to me, and the smallest of winks, with a flutter of his robes and a flourish impossible not to admire.

I must confess I was glad to see old Pitcher, after the increasing stiffness and we-are-great-people-ness of Maginnis's party, and when he brought the fraulein back to me (I had been left with the masked toad, who had waddled off after throwing some very venomous glances at me) we disposed of her to her mamma and had a long lounge and smoke together, in which it was possible for the first time to share one's amusement at the absurdities and pretensions of the scene. The toad, by the by, is none other than Herr Novis, the banker, whom we had tried to call upon, and to whom Pitcher had talked without disclosing his identity, which had elated him very much with his rôle of Vinegarish espionage on Papa's behalf, though what it is all about I do not know or much care for. His Albanian bravo's costume he had borrowed entire from an Englishman putting up at his hotel who is on the road home from Greece. This hotel, the Goldener Lamm, turned out to be a good deal nearer to the Danube Steamer Station than my own, as well as being the resort of real travellers in place of the tourists of the Erzherzog Karl, so I removed there next day, and this morning at an early hour we set out from Kaisermühlen on this steamer. Pitcher had already taken his ticket, and it was when I went to the Office to try for a ticket for the same boat myself that I found out what esteem Papa is held in by engineering and commercial circles at Vienna. Pitcher had only a place on board before, so he has found out some small benefit of my travelling with him by having this cabin to lounge in, even if we must share it with Feet and Bumm.

We have a very mixed cargo of races aboard as we rattle and splash down the river at racing pace on the spring current. We have just swept by the fortress of Pressburg, which Count Veit tells me was destroyed in the late war by its garrison of Italian troops who set fire to it rather than weary themselves further by carrying up coals and water to their officers billeted in its turrets! Warn Papa to employ no Italian coal-men at Ravenrig. I wonder if you are down there, or at Berkeley Square – I hope at Ravenrig, for it is easier for the far-flung traveller on the Danube to keep you in the compass of his thoughts, if you are amongst old scenes of shared memory, than if you are embarking on your own new adventures in Mayfair.

I drag back my thoughts from Ravenrig, to which they had wandered for quite half an hour as the steamer rushes on, to describe my fellow-passengers. There is a Countess Sturza going to visit her estates in Moldavia. There is a Russian invalid grandee, so abominably bullied by his uncouth servants that I should think he would greet Death with relief. There are some disagreeable French chattering like sparrows and finding fault with everything, especially with the victuals, which seem to Pitcher and me uncommon good, and come moreover in un-stinted quantities. In discussion of the armies engaged in the late wars in these parts one of the French said that the British army was a mere police force occupied fully in keeping down the natives of India – at which it was pleasant to hear Captain Vinegar growl out that on every single occasion when a British army had met with a French army, under both Marlborough and Wellington, it had defeated them absolutely. Of course this raised the chattering of the French into shrieks, but Pitcher merely pulled away on his cigar and looked very Vinegarish at the Danube scenery.

See – ! As I write, an immense barge, like the Noah's Ark we had at Twickenham (except that it is full only of pigs for German dinners!), is come in view being pulled up against the current by a team of horses splashing amongst the mud and reeds of the shore, and I wish you could hear the gunshot crack of the carters' whips, and the wild yells and singing of the men who urge on the horses, all coming over the dark water with an effect of dreadful savagery. Such spectacles, and my motley shipmates, are but an earnest of the barbarous lands we are bound for downstream, after quitting familiar comforts at Vienna.

Though my heart sinks at strangeness to come, Pitcher is in excellent spirits, seemingly, and to see him swagger about a Danube steamer you would put him down for a soldier-of-fortune who had left behind him in England nothing he cares a fig for. However, we shared a room at the Goldener Lamm (like Captain Vinegar he slept on the floor!) and he stirred about and called out most miserably, so his dreams are perhaps haunted by A Certain Phiz in Estregalles (as he tells me Wales was called in old times)? If only we were both well home again, I am sure we should overcome Mamma's objection to him, for it turns out he is in line to inherit a property in Kent from a step-uncle, which surely would allow him over Mamma's threshold if ever he does come back from India.

I have not as yet written to Mamma because, cast about as I may, I cannot discover anything in my travels thus far which would in the least bit amuse her. Perhaps if I am taken for ransom by Wallack brigands, or flung into a Transylvanian dungeon, she shall have a letter. Have you so arranged things that you can talk to them of my letters without being required to show them? If so, tell Papa that he may console himself for his impatience in London Society by the idea that he is famous at least in the Danube Steam Company, and that Captain Vinegar found out some deep facts or other about the Railway he is concerned with, from Vienna to Pesth, which is to be completed within a year or two. I do not know or much care what commissions Captain Vinegar was charged with in Half Moon Street – and Pitcher makes a great mystery of it, which is somewhat vexing in him – but I believe Vinegar wrote to Papa from Vienna, for I saw a package addressed to Papa on his table at the Goldener Lamm. If the matter concerns Herr Novis, I hope Papa (and Vinegar too) know what they are about, for a more repellent-looking and malevolent old devil I never saw. Count Veit is acquainted with him, and speaks of Novis's stratagems, and Novis's money, as having powerful ramifications in the lands of both the Christian and the Turk – Veit is evidently half-scared of his powers, though

[183]

of course making out that any mere banker must be small beer beside a foppish little Count in yellow gloves and a wasp-waisted jacket.

As I sit writing at such immense length to you, quite as if we were walking together under the beeches in the valley towards the sea, I am recalled to the rough reality of a Danube steamer by a great hallooing amongst the deck-passengers. We are just passing one of the floating water-mills you find upon the river, the mill-wheel fixed between two hulls which are the miller's home. All the common passengers run to the steamer's gunwale and halloo away at the miller whilst stirring their fingers round and round in the crowns of their hats. Why this should drive the miller nearly mad with vexation I do not know, but I see the poor fellow hopping and dancing and shaking his fists at us in a way wonderful to behold!

Veit tells me that the increasing number of these water-mills signifies our near approach to Buda-Pesth. How my heart sinks, for I had just got used to being upon the steamer, and found it was not so bad after all – and now I must prepare for my adventures to begin in these dark and perilous lands I see border-ing upon the river! Dear Enid, think of me, as you butter your toast or pour out your tea reading this letter in all the familiar comfort of the breakfast parlour, with the rooks building their nests in the trees at the window. How I should love to hear them quarrelling over their twigs!

Yr. aff. twin
RF

*   *   *

Darkness came on before the steamer reached Buda-Pesth. In the dusk, looking out over the water with apprehensive intentness, his writing-materials and his letter to Enid put away in the portmanteau at his feet, Roland had time to suffer ever-increasing nervousness as lines of moored barges, and islands with buildings upon them, encum-bered the river with signs of the approaching city. During the course of the day's journey he had come round to the view that a Danube steamer was a tolerable way of travelling; now he must quit it for unknown conditions which might be intolerable. Feet and Bumm, lucky fellows, were to stay aboard as far as Galatz, then to exchange into a Black Sea boat for Constantinople, whence they intended taking ship to Cairo, and returning by way of the Holy Land. That enviably modest itinerary (as it seemed to Roland) was exactly what he would have wished for himself, if he must go to the East at all, instead of Pitcher's far-ranging and uncomfortable plans to cross Transylvania and Wallachia by land before even reaching the Black Sea. But he felt that by abandoning the journey and then returning to it, as he had done at Vienna, he had forfeited any right to question the itinerary.

In the darkness the city itself rushed upon them. There against the night sky on their starboard quarter towered the Palatine Hill prickled with lights, and the further black outline of the Blocksberg. On their left a blaze of lights necklacing the quays was reflected in the water. Under the mighty Chain Bridge at racing pace shot the steamer, making half her passengers involuntarily duck their heads, her paddles flailing the water white as she ploughed across the gleamy-waved current to the Pesth bank. Smoking flares lit quays, and heaped mer- chandise, and façades behind them. What confusion awaited on that shore! Roland could hear the rattle of wheels on cobbles, shouts, the clatter of barrels rolled over paving, frightened animals. The commo- tion of water as the paddles reversed, and the judder of the steamer, was pierced through by sailors' shouts and the clanging of the engine- room bell. Agitation screwed his nerves taut.

How calm Pitcher looked, though, lounging amidst their baggage with a cigar in his mouth, watching the steamer dock as though the quayside, and the strange city behind it, and the dark leagues of Hungary behind that, didn't dismay him in the least.

Indeed there proved to be no hurry. Roland sat down again. Once the ferry was docked, and her paddles idle, a kind of serenity swam back into the lamplit scene, where bell-shaped lanterns glowed on the waterfront façades of fine stone mansions. But a porter unfortunately told Pitcher that the hotel where they had intended putting up, the 'Queen of England', had been demolished by shells in the war. Up leaped Roland again.

'Where shall we go, then?' he asked, all his apprehensions returning. He felt sure that the passengers now disembarking were intent on taking the last rooms in Pesth while Pitcher idled here. 'Shouldn't we go ashore?'

'There'll be room enough for us, never fear,' said Pitcher, who had an uncomfortable way of seeing into Roland's worries, and of laughing at them. 'Still, we may as well go, I suppose, if we ain't to be carried on to Belgrade.'

So they took leave of the two natty little Counts (who were to inherit their cabin) and Pitcher signalled for the porter to carry their baggage over the floating bridge to the stone quay. The Captain, a Pole named Lucowitz who spoke a little English (all the commands on the steamer were given in English, a fact which made Roland's heart swell with pride) – Captain Lucowitz came onto the quay with them, treating them as the most distinguished of his passengers, bowing deeply, even removing his hat when Roland offered his hand. As the Pole walked back to his steamer, which was making ready to depart, Roland said to Pitcher: 'There goes the last fellow in Hungary who knows who I am.'

'What Lucowitz knows,' said Pitcher, 'is who your papa is. I should be glad to try your paces beyond that sort of reach, if I was you.'

The gun fired, and the steamer cast off into the dark stream, its lights dancing yellow in the water, the splutter of its paddles glinting white, all clangour and smoke and purpose hurrying off into the night. Captain Lucowitz took with him the whole familiar world, leaving Roland as alone in darkness as a child may be left amid the horrors of night by the carrying away of a candle.

Roland followed Pitcher's easy stride behind the porter. Now that they were on the quay they found that it was mud and dung away from the waterside, and the smoking lamps showed them bullet-pitted walls and collapsed house-fronts spilled across the roadway. The 'Queen of England' hotel was indeed in ruins. The porter pointed further along the embankment, where the Chain Bridge vaulted away into darkness over the river, and they followed him. Bales and casks, and bollards, and the constant lapping of water, made the quay like a sea-port. Men loading barges, even children and stray curs, took little notice of the two Englishmen, and Roland was cautiously beginning to enjoy the walk, when out of a side-street issued a group of wild-looking horse-men who scattered across the quay with long ringlets floating out under their wide hats, and rode by Pitcher and Roland staring down with keen, haughty eyes. At once all that was ominous in the word 'Hungary' surrounded Roland in those curvetting hooves and the bravo-like arrogance of the horsemen, and his enjoyment shrank back within him again.

An hour later, however, established at the Emmerling hotel where he sat looking forward to a nine o'clock supper in as handsome a modern dining room as could be found in Belgrave Square, Roland's spirits had again begun cautiously to lift. The hotel at least was well enough. Such jolly rooms, and the prospect of dinner, tempted the hedgehog of his sensibilities to uncurl itself *pro tem*. The fact of the manager having urged them to take tickets for the theatre, which was tonight giving *The Old Curiosity Shop*, had also helped assure him that all was not barbarity on the banks of the Danube – though the idea of Dickens in Pesth had made Pitcher puff out his whiskers, or Captain Vinegar's whiskers, in great disgust. Tomorrow no doubt would reveal to Roland that he must resign himself to every misery of travel: tonight he was sufficiently content.

Pitcher's first objective next day was the 'Casino of Nobles', founded by Count Szechenyi before the war upon the plan of a London club, and thither they walked through a brilliant spring morning which brightened the colours of the town. The light, the very air, seemed refreshed and made vivid by the presence of the river. What a presence! As they walked beside its wide hurrying waters, Roland discovered in himself a feeling – an affection – for the Danube which surprised him. He remembered the dread with which he had first seen its far dark coils from the spire of St Stephen's at Vienna; now, at Buda-Pesth, he walked beside it arm in arm as if it were an old companion. Now it was not the river, but unknown lands lying behind this façade of Pesth, which struck the ominous note.

Nor was the city quite the flourishing capital it had appeared to be by lamplight. Buildings which had looked handsome enough by night were revealed by the sun to be ruins behind façades riddled with the cannon-holes of bombardment. It became harder to place much trust in *The Old Curiosity Shop* as a measure of civilization amid such earthquake-like destruction. Across the river, too, the summit of the Palatine, once crowned with its Italian palace, was a jagged black outline of ruin. Not a wall they passed that was not pitted with bullet-marks. Yet life (to Roland's surprise) seemed to go on well enough in the bustle of the quays.

'None of these fellows seem to care tuppence that the place is in ruins,' he said to Pitcher as they waited whilst a team of eight horses turned a waggon with much whip-cracking and shouting between the shelled house-fronts and the river.

'It pretty well always was in ruins from one cause or another,' said Pitcher. 'My word, though, it gives an idea of the war, don't it? What I should give to have been in it!'

'Which side should you have taken?' Roland asked, a little aghast at such Vinegarish fire-eating amid the ruins.

'Which side?' It was as if he hadn't considered that sides much mattered. 'Oh, I suppose these Magyar nobles must get the vote.'

'At Vienna you were hot against them. At Vienna you said Palffy and Zichy and Esterhazy and the rest didn't stir a hand for their people.'

'Look at that fellow now! Do you see? On the grey? Look at those moustachios – wicked, eh? – and his slashed jacket, and the whole style of the man! Wonderful! You can't resist them.'

The waggon was turned, and they walked on to the splendid stone front of the Casino, which had escaped destruction. Up the marble steps ran Pitcher, and spoke in French to the black-coated servant who opened the doors to them, giving him an envelope to be conveyed within.

Roland said, 'You don't need any introduction here. I asked at the hotel. An Englishman gets in gratis.' When Tresham ignored him, he asked, 'Who is the letter from, anyway?'

'It's from your father. It's made out for Captain Vinegar. I thought it was about time he was brought to life, eh, now our travels have begun in earnest?'

Roland shrugged, slightly irritated. He was irritated by the way Pitcher had arrogated Vinegar entirely to himself, so that the Captain was fast becoming an oracle whose utterances only Pitcher could divine or voice. Pitcher's command of French, too, rather put him out – as if it was a capability discovered in Vinegar – and he hardly knew whether to believe what Pitcher claimed, that he had learned French before he had learned English, in his childhood at the court of King Bomba at Naples. The link with foreign scenes and adventures (in a mere clerk at the Waterways) rather disquieted Roland. When the black-coated servant returned they were invited to sign their names – Pitcher signing 'O. Q. Vinegar (Capt.)' – and at once made free of the spacious rooms, with wide windows on the Danube, and gazettes and easy chairs, which comprised the premises of the 'Casino of Nobles'. Whether Tresham Pitcher would have been made as welcome as Captain Vinegar, it was impossible to know.

They had taken up copies of Galignani, and had ordered coffee, when Roland observed a short, somewhat dilapidated figure of fifty or so, with a grizzled set of moustachios and a brown bald head, sauntering towards them with his arms under the tails of his coat. He came to a stop in front of them and examined them both out of hooded eyes. Then he held out his hand as though he had decided, on balance, in favour of noticing them.

'I am Count Giza,' he said in a hoarse voice, 'and I am content to velcome two Englishmen, as I think, to our Casino.'

Farr and Vinegar introduced themselves, and he listened closely, leaning forward lest he missed a syllable, afterwards straightening his back again with the air of a master who had not heard all he had hoped for from two boys answering a test question.

'No,' he said, 'I do not know these families. Still, you are many in England – many names, eh? Many not known names. *Si, tanti.* You know, with us a little time ago, *tre anni fa*, it was always English this, English that – everything English, *tutti*. Orses, steamboats, coats, ounds – we were crazy for English, *pazo*. Then, *mes amis*, if you have come to Ongry you have been appy. Now is not *così*. But I velcome you. I ave not lost ope in England.'

'Devilish good of you, Count,' said Vinegar fiercely.

The fierceness was ignored. 'So, what appens now? Since you give us no elp to struggle against Austria? Why, now is Ireland all Magyar is crazy for. Now is Irish orses, ounds – and Irish men, *même ce monsieur* Oke Onnell *qui* struggles against England as we Magyars aganst Austria. But I ave not lost ope in you, *come ho detto. Poiché? Poiché* I know you, and I never expect your help. *Ecco la mia ragione!*'

[189]

He gripped Roland's elbow warmly as he said this, pleasure at predicting English perfidy evidently outweighing any grief it caused him. His fine large eyes opened, and his ruddy-veined countenance lighted, when he smiled. 'Come, when you are at Buda-Pesth you treat me as your friend – your dragoman – your *lacquais de place*. Let us have an English breakfast brought – an Irish breakfast!' He called out to a waiter, and gave orders, keeping Farr by the elbow and then walking him over to the window, where he expatiated on the scene.

The Count's apparent frankness and good humour worked at once on Roland's eager nature. Despite a rusty coat, and boots rather the worse for wear, here was a Magyar nobleman taking them under his wing! His eyes were hooded by lids so heavy that to raise them sufficiently to look out at all seemed to confer an honour on what he noticed. Roland found himself carried along by the Count's plan for a sightseeing tour of the two cities, pleased with their good fortune in having fallen in with so amiable an acquaintance straight off. But Vinegar soon put in his oar.

'I don't at all know if we shall have time enough for it,' he objected. 'We have a good many arrangements to make for our journey.'

'*Dove andate*? Wien, *ou* Belgrad? You go up the river, or down her?'

'Neither,' said Vinegar shortly. 'We leave the river and strike out for Debrecen and Transylvania.'

The Count's gaze wandered over Pitcher's face in wonder. 'Impossible. To Debrecen? Across the *puszta* – in *aprile* – do you know ow it is? Impossible. Is not a *partie de plaisir*, Captain Winegar. Stay with your English steamboats, I beg of you.'

'We are not making a *partie de plaisir*, Count, and the steamboats don't take us where I wish to go.'

'What can take an Englishman to Debrecen? Or to Transylvania? Is nothing, is a great crowd of fat ugly Germans, *niente più*.'

'Do you know the name of Novis, Count?'

'Hush, Captain Winegar!' The Count's hand was held up, he looked round to see if the name had carried to others in the room. 'Do not speak that name aloud here! And that one is not to be found at Debrecen, *je vous assure*.'

'Maybe not, but his works are.'

'The works of the Devil are everywhere, *partout, ça ce voit*. They are ere in this room, men that one is ruined, many many works of that Devil. Ah, if you go to concern yourself with that one, I agree with you, Captain Winegar, you are not upon a *partie de plaisir*. The *puszta* in *aprile* – pouf! is nothing to you. But today, come, let us make our tour, all gay, eh?'

Roland felt Pitcher's eye still coldly upon himself and the Count. He separated his arm from Giza's grasp, in case it was that connexion that Pitcher disapproved. 'Come on, Vinegar old fellow,' he said cheerily, 'why don't we let Pitcher stop at the hotel with his nose in the maps just for today, eh, and let him worry about the *puszta* and so forth? And you and me look about the town with our friend here?'

'You ave so another gentleman with you?' asked Giza uncertainly.

'Yes,' said Roland, 'yes, we have, but he's a dull dog and we shan't give him an airing today.'

It was not clear at the outset whether the calèche, into which they settled themselves at the foot of the Casino after their breakfast, belonged to Count Giza or had been hired by him. Roland didn't care a straw either way, but Pitcher's questions showed his concern.

'Useful little trap for this work, Count.'

'Is not so bad,' agreed the Count, who was disposing of rugs and cushions with a grand proprietory air. '*Allora, andiamo fare nostra gira!*'

'Stable the nags at your town house, can you?' persisted Tresham.

'In town I am at the Casino.'

'Ah, keep 'em at livery, I suppose?'

'Now, gentlemen, first to the otel to find your friend?'

'Friend?' asked Pitcher.

'No, no,' said Roland, laughing, 'old Pitcher won't want to come, will he, Vinegar?'

'Ah, no, I daresay not.'

'Pitcher – Pitcher – this name I know,' said the Count, '*ho sentito questo nome, sono sicuro, ma dove?*' He gave it up, and directed a torrent of Hungarian at the coachman's back, who put the horses into action.

Roland settled back. He was amused. It gave back to the idea of Captain Vinegar some of its original humour, that Giza had been knocked off balance by suspicion that another Englishman, and one perhaps more socially elevated, was being concealed from him.

Pitcher's efforts at nonchalance, too, as he tried to discover whether he would have to pay for the calèche, were comical to Roland. He was amused, and when amused he was happy.

Giza's air of magnificent ownership extended to everything they saw in their drive through Pesth. Since the great floods of 1838 the town had been much rebuilt, and had then been severely knocked about in the last years' fighting, but of new buildings and of heaps of ruins the Count was equally complacent – in the very shell-holes in the road he took a patriot's pride.

'Tell me, Count,' said Pitcher as they drove into a square of new stone houses, 'how is it that Herr Novis has ruined so many men?'

'A fine square, you see.' The Count waved his hand towards the mud and puddles at its centre. 'Statues, of course, are needed. Eroes of our nation. When it is decided.'

'When it is decided who are to be the heroes?' asked Roland.

Giza answered the earlier question: 'Ow does he ruin our nobles? That one buys their souls, Captain Winegar. For a noble Magyar, is lands, is people, are *son âme*. *E quello diavolo ha comprato tutto*, at Vienna he buys mortgage, always mortgage, to give Magyar nobles money in city, at court, to live. Then, *vieni la guerra é* – snap!' Giza clapped together his hands like jaws closing. 'When comes the war, that one – *come si dice*, closes, shuts?'

'Forecloses,' supplied Pitcher. 'So Novis sold them up, did he, and ended owning their estates?'

'And, so, worse things too,' said the Count, waving his hands, '*come ho detto*, in Transylvania *si trova qualche* – '

When Roland (who couldn't understand Italian) heard the name of Transylvania coupled with these dark deeds of soul-selling, he shut out the Count's voice. Transylvania lay in the future. For the moment, driving amongst these raw squares with their flocks of sheep and croaking frogs, he felt quite easy, even condescending, towards Pesth as a country town. It was not the alarming or outlandish place he had dreaded from the Danube steamer. If travel consisted only of this, he might even enjoy it. He looked out for the river everywhere, glad to see yesterday's companions at a street's end, or beside them again when they emerged from the town onto the quayside, and Count Giza proposed crossing the Chain Bridge to Buda. Of this bridge too he was very proud, expatiating on its length and magnificence as they approached it, and taking from his purse some coins which he flung at the soldier in Austrian uniform in the booth at the bridge's end. Annoyed that the Count had not mentioned that the bridge had been designed and built by Englishmen, which for Roland was its chief interest, he said rather waspishly, 'I thought you paid no tolls or taxes, you Magyar nobles?'

'On the old bridge of boats was true, was the old ways, we pay nothing. Now, this new one, *pagiamo tutti*, we pay like the *canaille*.'

'The war made you? The war changed it?'

'No! The war change nothing. Is little rule of the bridge, all pay.'

'It was the rule of the banker who financed it, I think,' said Pitcher. 'A little rule, but a beginning.'

'Excuse me – a beginning?'

'Yes, towards the nobles paying taxes. Towards the peasants' freedom and equality.'

'Ah – Freedom! Equality! Ah, you Englishmen!' The smile of an old race, an old tyranny, curled the corners of Giza's mouth downwards.

'We English, Count, might have helped you against Austria,' said Pitcher, 'if we had found you intended setting your peasantry free.'

'Free? Excuse me, Captain Winegar, what is "free"?' Giza's fleshy nose broadened as he sneered the word. '*Quando arriva il giorno* – when the hour comes for you English to make free Ireland, *allora, anche noi facciamo qualcosa*. And, one thing, sir – do not go about the world knowing already what should do every nation. *Non siamo tutti Inglesi*. You say you go by Transylvania. *Allora, guarda un po'*. Look at the Wallacks. Look at the Saxons. *E poi*, when you come to Bucharest, tell me if you believe an English ruler would allow to these peoples any more "Freedom" than what is allowed by an English lord in Ireland to his peasants, or a Scotch lord. *Questo è vero*, that the English, excuse me, make free only the English, whom they do not fear. The Celts they do not make free. And our Wallacks you know are Celts. Yes, is true, your Welsh is our Wallack. Now, sir, no more talks of "Freedom" *per piacere. Guarda – guarda la città rovinata* – look there in front at the castle all ruins – you see the truth, is Peace is more needed than Freedom in my poor Hungary.'

The calèche was on the Chain Bridge about the middle of the

Danube. The blackened ruin of the Elector's palace on the heights ahead was a graphic warning of the ills of war. In England Roland had never thought that buildings would burn, and palaces fall, and houses collapse into ruins, if peace was disturbed. He saw in his mind's eye Mr O'Connor helped into a cab by a policeman that wet day at Kennington. It was like a scene at an immense distance away from him. That was England, little England, far away. He did not feel that he had truly left it till this moment, when Giza's words had shown him how far it was away. The wind sang in the ironwork of the bridge, so cold, so cold. Over the hurrying current it looked so distant to either shore. The span of the bridge vaulted the river like a miracle, and in the remote midst of light, and water, and the cold wind singing in the chains, the buoyancy of his heart suddenly flung him upward into freedom like a seabird from the deck of a ship.

He did not listen to the Count's voice. Across the river in Buda the calèche soon began to climb the Blocksberg at a crawling pace, the road winding upward through tiers of hovels. Roland got out to walk, impatient of sitting still whilst the sense of liberty sparkled within him. Up the road he strode ahead of the poor toiling horses.

From the summit of the crag an immense landscape of forest and plain filled his view, here darkened under clouds, there brightened into greens and browns by broad moving tides of light which travelled across it. Through this landscape – through the towns at his feet too – rolled the Danube. So central was the river to what it passed through, and so vital was the light, that it seemed certain that river and light gave existence to the earth and the towns on it; that the moving water, and the moving light, were the essence of creation. So it seemed to him, watching those two prime movers flowing onward with grand indifference below him. Change, movement, the flux of light and water, is at the centre of all things, makes all things. So the traveller creates what he sees, and possesses the world in moving through it. Something in what the Count had said – he didn't know quite what, except the tone of it all – had cut the painter tying him to England's shores, and set him free. He heard the calèche approach behind him.

Count Giza stepped down and invited them to admire all over again his country and his cities spread below, those un-Hungarian façades of Pesth catching the watery light from the river, the English Chain

Bridge, the English steamers smoking at the quays, and the far yellow Hungarian plains to the east diminishing into mist and oblivion. Into that doubtful east, away from what was certain – away from the gentle green-mantled hills of Buda rolling away to the west – they must travel. Roland tried out the idea on his new-found liberty and buoyancy, straining his eyes to pierce the haze. But nothing to the east was clear. As he came upon it, so would it exist, league by league, day by day.

'What is that building, Count?' He pointed at a curiously-domed octagon of white marble gleaming in a shaft of light on the green Buda hills nearby.

'Is our Toorkish tomb, very fine.'

'You had the Turk here a good many years, Count, eh?' said Pitcher, his thumbs in his waistcoat-pockets as he looked about.

'*Quelques ans, quelques ans.* But,' he said, raising a finger and letting sly humour show in his yellow eyes, 'but, they go away at last, which, I think, the Norman never do from England, *davero*? Come, my boys, *vieni, andiamo giù*, I will show you what else of Toorkish we ave in Buda.'

In the calèche they descended the steep hill into the swarm of hovels clinging to its flanks where lived, Giza told them, the pariah caste of *Rätzen*, more miserable, and dirtier, than any slum-dwellers Roland had seen. Below the huts of these wretches the calèche soon brought them to the Saracenic arch of a dilapidated brick building at the foot of the hill, where they followed Giza to a low green door. Payment was demanded, and the Count, who had out his purse, paid for all. Then the door creaked open, they passed through it, and were plunged at once into a surprising scene.

It was a Turkish bath. Wraiths of vapour reached out for them, close and sticky as the brush of feverish hands, horribly tainted with foul smells. The sweat broke out on Roland's body, and damped his hair. In dim rays of light which wandered through the mists from the domed roof it was possible to make out the shapes of poor shadows struggling amid splashings and echoes and watery dissolution, before steam engulfed them. He had just grasped that there were women as well as men half naked in the water, and the idea had shocked its way through him, when Pitcher's hand fell on his arm.

'Come away,' he said, 'do come away.'

But Giza stood watching the scene, and Roland stood by him. The heat now was fierce, sweat clammy upon him, his ideas as clouded as the steamy bath with figures ungraspable in vapour. Flesh, and shaggy hair, water washing over bodies, glistening, splashing, the dome rolling back the echoes and the vapour till all was an infernal confusion of tantalising hints and unfocused lust.

'Do we go in?' he shouted through the pandemonium to Giza.

'Not I,' said Pitcher.

'Go on or go back,' the Count said, 'just ere is wet and nothing good.'

'I go back,' said Pitcher.

'Hang it, Vinegar,' said Roland, shaking Pitcher's hand off his arm, 'I thought we left old mother Pitcher at the hotel!'

But Pitcher was already opening the door to go out. Roland followed him. The air struck through his clothes and chilled him like frost, and the rapid beating of his heart subsided. Was a fellow like Pitcher not plagued by lusts? Or was it that fellows like him lacked the aplomb to throw off their clothes and plunge into that mêlée? He wondered how it would be amongst the silken houris of the East, at which the writers of Travels hinted between their lines. Meanwhile the calèche carried them towards the Chain Bridge once more, and Pitcher tried to pay the Count for their entry to the bath.

'You are kind enough to take us in your carriage, of course I must pay, I insist upon it.'

'*Non è la mia carrozza*, Captain Winegar, no, mine is all at my country house. This one I ave – *come si dice, louer?*'

'Hired,' said Pitcher grimly.

'*C'est ça* – I ave ired im for you, is yours as long as you stay at Buda-Pesth, *enfin si paga, e finito.*'

'Thank you, Count, kind of you,' said Roland, turning away to hide his smile from Pitcher.

'*E niente, prego.* And the money for the bath, Captain Winegar, if you insist, is one dollar.'

'A dollar?' Pitcher's hand froze in his pocket. 'But I saw the price written up, it was – '

'*Aiee, prezzi, prezzi!* These price is for peasants, gentlemen give one dollar, two, three – *non importa* how much gives a gentleman. I gave one dollar, of course I am happy to pay for you.'

[196]

Pitcher's dollar made its way reluctantly from his waistcoat pocket into the insouciant and straining waistcoat of the Count, where it had (Roland thought) few others to clink against. Teasing Pitcher about money was Roland's resource when Pitcher irritated him; mean, perhaps, but he promised himself that Pitcher should never really go short of money as long as they were together, so his little fussing worries where chimerical, and amusing, to his younger and richer companion.

However, when they reached the Casino again, where they were to dine, Roland's irritation over the Turkish bath incident still rankled, and he was moreover pretty well weary of hearing his friend talk big all day to Giza in the accents of Captain Vinegar. So, when Pitcher swaggered up to him at a window of the Casino where he was standing looking at the Danube, and banged him on the back with *The Times* newspaper just in Vinegar's overbearing manner, and drawled out just in Vinegar's self-satisfied voice: 'One may as well never have left the clubs in St James's, eh, old fellow, one is so devilish comfortable here.'

'I didn't know you ever was in a club in St James's,' retorted Roland, walking off to where he might watch the darkening waters of the Danube undisturbed.

III

·-·-·-·-·-·-·

Kronstadt
Transylvania

May the 12th 1850

My dear Mamma,

You must picture me wrapped in my 'bunda', a kind of travelling rug (shared with a thousand fleas!) which it is impossible to live without in this draughty and comfortless land, reclining amongst a few cushions in a bare wooden room of the Gasthof Romischer Kaiser at Kronstadt, the capital of Transylvania, and a cobbled, slate-roofed little German-looking town clasped in a crook of the Carpathians, whose crags and forests rise abruptly into clouds at the town gates. Picture me also quite as fiercely bearded and bewhiskered as Captain Vinegar, for I have not been shaved since quitting Buda-Pesth twelve days ago, and am so bumped and bruised by those twelve days of travel that I can only sit down on my 'bunda'. Pitcher has gone out alone, as is very often his way when our day's journey is done, to walk about the town, and to peer into its churches and odd corners, as if he was hunting out a clue in a paperchase. He is a good fellow, but will make a mountain out of a mole-hill, by agitating himself about what's to come, in a way I have quite left off bothering with now we are fairly launched upon the flood and still well afloat. Vinegar I believe is in his bed asleep, which is his recourse whenever no action is required of him. And so you have us!

We travelled across the Great Plain of Hungary from Pesth to Debrecen on a system which is called, rather absurdly, 'Fast Peasant'! You are shut up in a box without springs, and dragged through the mud for ten hours by a team of dirty little ponies, which are changed pretty often at staging-posts where the peasants themselves supply the cattle. The day's journey is pretty dull, of course, and I should have drawn the sack over the window and slept, and so would Pitcher I believe, but Vinegar would whisk it back again to peer about the desolation outside in search of 'the facts' – as he calls whatever is dullest or least agreeable in our circumstances. At night you come to a 'csarda', or inn, in the midst of marsh and mud of the 'puszta', and there you may be lucky enough to find a free table to sleep upon, and a helping of Hungary's interminable gulasch (a thick spicy soup) for your dinner. Eight days of this we had. A kind of little Count we met at Buda (you know that Maria Theresa ennobled every Magyar who killed his man in battle, so that the country is consumed by a legion of impoverished nobles) told us we should not get through the 'puszta' at all, but of course we did, for travel seems to me a constant process of exploding gloomy prophecies.

I will tell you about the third of these 'csardas' we stopped in, where the landlord was a Hungarian (ordinarily they are Swabians) and so wore spurs, and kicked everyone, and was a great man. He brought in a message to us after our arrival, which was sent from the local landlord, and invited us to supper at his house. After a day of scraping the mud from our cart's wheels when they had seized up, and of being jolted to death in the intervals, such an evening of rustic boredom was the last thing I wished for. But you would have thought from Tucker's response – who had been so bearish, mind, about seeing any company at Vienna – that he had received an invitation to sup at Stratfield Saye! I hope you will agree with me, that a dull fellow does not become interesting because he lives in the midst of the 'puszta', nor a country boor any less boorish because you cannot understand a word he says – but Pitcher's idea of it seemed to be, that here was a great chance of making his way into society, so off went himself and the Captain, with lantern-men wading beside the cart sent for them through the mud by this squire, for of course it was raining.

I passed the evening with a one-legged soldier who spoke fair French. He had lost his limb against the Russians, under the General Bem who is now fled to Turkey and become a Mussulman, and had been left for dead on the stricken field under a heap of cadavers. At first he had not dared move for fear of the Russians bayoneting him, as he saw them serve many another wounded wretch. Then the dark came on, and the warmth began to go out of the corpses piled upon him, and he thought himself safe enough from the Russians to attempt a move. But he found, to his horror, that the wolves had stolen out of the forest, and were beginning to pull off the dead men from the heap above him, and would soon reach his own living flesh. I am ashamed that I cannot tell you how he resolved his dilemma, but the truth is, that the heated atmosphere, and the slivovitz, and my defective French, combined to keep the conclusion of his tale from me. He was an ill-favoured, low-looking brute, as are all the Wallacks, with a vegetable sort of face gashed like a Hallowe'en pumpkin for eyes and mouth, with a very dim candle of intellect flickering within. One can well imagine them murdering their masters wholesale, as it is said they did in the late rising. Indeed, Pitcher made sure that we was all to have our throats slit, in a hovel where we were obliged to stop three nights back with a broken axle-tree, for I loosed the baby's clothes to stop it screaming so (which of course succeeded) and attracted some very black looks and growls from paterfamilias!

Though I let slip the chance of meeting with the rural landlord, I did go with Captain Vinegar to call upon a Saxon family at Hermannstadt, another of these Transylvanian towns, whom I believe he wished to see on Papa's business, only the gentleman was out. Their salon would have amused you, I think. Imagine a narrow curving street of old-fashioned houses with plastered fronts painted the colour of a pistachio ice, or eau-de-nil, and deep slate roofs pulled down like nightcaps – the roofs mossy, the bell-tower of a Lutheran church looming above them, and the mountains above that – and imagine in one of the houses a first-floor drawing room with four crinkle-paned windows admitting dusty sunlight, and a creaky parquet floor, and upright French chairs with tattered silk covers, and in the chairs Vinegar and myself leaning forward to make uncomfortable conversation with stout, breathy Frau Danzige and her two flaxen-ringleted daughters. Can you credit my part in this scene? – knowing how cordially I detest morning calls! But I have been so persuaded by Vinegar of the dire strangeness of all things awaiting us across the Tamesche Pass of the Carpathians outside this town, where Turkish rule commences, that I feel I am taking leave of the last drawing room in Europe as I sit there chattering French with my gloves in my hat, and the shadow of the Turk already lengthening to engulf us. Frau Danzige's salon is dull enough, but it is a familiar dullness, and I almost feel nostalgic about such dullness in anticipation of how I shall look back upon that last morning call, in that last airless drawing room complete with albums and fringed tablecloths and pianoforte, when I shall be squatting on my haunches in some Mussulman's tent, as Vinegar is constantly threatening. And the owners of the flaxen-ringlets are perhaps the last young ladies I shall gaze upon without the yashmak intervening, so of course I ogle them disgracefully. They understand the game, and simper, and tinkle with laughter, and shake their ringlets, in a manner which contributes to my anticipatory nostalgia quite as much as does their pianoforte, or their mother's indulgence when she sees a well-bred young fellow making up to her daughters with his flat little jokes and his gossip of the latest theatre at Buda-Pesth ('The Old Curiosity Shop', no less!) or the last Court Ball at dear Vienna, for of course these Saxons supported Austria in the war, and even called in the Russians to aid them against the Magyar, a case I fancy of calling in Bruin to chase out the mice.

My penchant for doing the sociable in Transylvanian drawing rooms is anathema to Vinegar, who comes into the ascendant when we are in some woodcutter's hut, and he may pretend that we should all be murdered were it not for the cuffs and curses he deals out. The truth is, he understands better how to behave towards inferiors than towards equals, and, since he looks upon most foreigners as his inferiors, the further he is from England, the more content with the society does he become. Still, I was glad of his company when we were benighted in the woodcutter's cottage with our axle-tree broken, and my own loosing of the baby's clothes was so ill-received. I did it without thinking, for the little fellow was half-suffocated, and bawling like a pig, which you know has always upset me. I behave everywhere as if I was at home, as Vinegar says, for I never can believe that anyone means me harm. Perhaps (as he also says) I am better fitted to extract another cup of tea from a matron, or another smile from her daughter, than docility from a hut-full of savages. Very probably his sharp orders and cuts with his stick brought us safe through the night where I alone should have been murdered. The Wallacks are frightened by bullying – indeed they are frightened by everything, including (if you will believe it) by vampires!

Our party is much intrigued by rumour of these corpses which rise from their graves with the moon and suck blood from the living. About here, every house, almost every person, is protected from the attack of vampires by (most improbably!) a sprig of garlic. I believe a law of Habeas Corpus would protect them better than all the garlic in the world against the blood-sucking propensities of the nobles, whom folk-lore has no doubt transformed into these monstrous bats, but there! – it is a pretty legend. At Fagaras, where we stopped a night, it seemed at one moment we had come upon a vampire-hunt. We had eaten our supper, and had strolled out to take the air before turning in, when we heard a mighty commotion in the town square. Before we could reach the square by the narrow streets, there came a rattle of horses' hooves towards us, and we had time only to fling ourselves against a mouldy wall before ten or a dozen horsemen dashed by us, long hair flying, wild cries urging their horses on, the blaze of their pine torches throwing crazy shadows on street and house. We followed to the town gate, which had been opened for them, and watched the horsemen rush towards a large gloomy castle which stands behind moat and walls a few furlongs from the town. It was a moonlit night. The horsemen milled round the castle gateway, their lights reflecting in the moat, whilst a good deal of hoarse shouting was directed upward at the fortress. The meaning of it all, of course, we did not know, but we amused ourselves with concocting a yarn about the posse rattling off in pursuit of a vampire sated with some poor maiden's blood, as we walked back to our inn. There the landlord told us that our posse had in fact been called out to apprehend brigands who had robbed the mail of 7000 florins, and had ridden to the castle to put themselves under a leader. Since the brigands had operated on the very road we had ourselves travelled that day, I had almost rather it had proved a vampire-hunt after all.

I would tell you of our encounter with another of the perils of the road, a wolf, but I am sure you will say that my letter is already too long, and too dull, to admit of another incident so lacking in drama, and so full of anti-climax (though Vinegar in his usual state of high alert of course fired off pistols in all directions), that I will not risk you falling asleep altogether over my 'adventures' by narrating it. There is such humbug talked about danger. In Pesth I was told that the Wallacks would certainly

[202]

murder me if I crossed the 'puszta', and now I am told that, having escaped the Wallacks by the skin of my teeth, the Turks will undoubtedly finish me off – and I dare say the Turks will prove as affable a set of rascals as the Wallacks. One cannot always be in a state of alarm. I have an idea that by nature I am pretty well adapted for the traveller's life – better so than Pitcher, certainly, with his forebodings of giants and dragons to be encountered on the road – for I can forget to be frightened, drift with the stream, sleep in any corner, and wake ready to· enjoy whatever offers.

We shall soon learn whether the Turks are as black as they are painted, for we have taken the coupé of the diligence to ourselves for the run over the Carpathians tomorrow down to Bucharest, and one enters Turkish territory at the top of the pass. I look round my bare little wooden bedroom in this gasthof as if looking my last on all European comforts. There is no bell, but a wooden dial on the balcony at the door, on which one turns a pointer towards one's room number, which I must go now and do, in hopes of hot water for that very un-Hungarian purpose of washing myself.

Farewell, dearest Mamma. Here amid strange scenes it is hard to discover what events might interest or amuse you in your little upstairs sitting room at Berkeley Square, where I I suppose you are, and where my letter must compete against the news and gossip of London. Pray give my best love to Papa, and to Edmond and Lucy and, of course, dear Enid.

Your loving and affectionate son
Roland Farr

*   *   *

From *Journal of a Land-March towards India*, by O. Q. Vinegar (Capt.), 2 vols, folding map, 8vo, London, 1854

Fagaras, May 10th, 1850
We were partakers in a fine scene of Wallachian savagery tonight. The moon being at the full, or nearly so, F— and P— and I took a stroll from our Inn through the curious old streets of Fagaras lighted by its silvery beams, and we were thus wandering, and smoking, and discoursing, when certain shouts and halloos from the town square, and a firing off of guns, made us prick up our

ears and hasten to the scene of the entertainment. Crooked old German-looking buildings of the Middle Ages are hunched round the square, all black and silver in the moon, and these sleepy dwellings, together with the grotesquely-carved front of the town hall, and the dark bulk of the church, were now made to ring again in the night with the yells and screeches of a dozen or so desperado-looking horsemen clattering their steeds about the cobbles. Lifting our gaze to the first-floor window of one of these old houses, which seem to have survived out of some of the old German tales, we beheld 'what the fun was about'. An old man in a close-fitting cap stood in the window, his extended arms burdened with the limp and beauteous form of a young girl. Fair she was – nay, did I say 'fair'? Alas, surely here was the pallor of death, or worse than death, for the utter translucent whiteness of her bosom and limbs shone through the gauzy garments which but half-veiled the lovely lines of womanhood. Had she been carved from alabaster, the moon's light could have blanched that flesh to no more bloodless a hue.

I pulled F— and P— into the shadow of a doorway, for it was plain that an ugly mood prevailed. I know a little of the Wallachian tongue (which indeed any fair Latin scholar may make a tolerable fist of understanding), and I learned that the old man at the lattice was urging his fellow-townsmen to ride 'ere set of moon' to the Castle, there to demand revenge, or satisfaction – the last of his speech was lost in wild huzzas. The horsemen, who seemed as eager for all kinds of sport as a set of Meltonians outside Scraptoft Gorse, cheered him to the echo – or, rather, roared and bayed in a manner to chill the blood – as they caracol'd about the square and caught up pitch-pine torches flung to them by some other fellows stirring up a great fire at the church door.

'Do you remark that they are all bearing crosses?' whispered P—. It was so; each had a cross of wood or metal slung about him, as well as the torch he brandished, and a rusty old firearm, and the long butcher's knife these ruffians are never without.

Well, it was inconceivable that we should forfeit whatever fun was up, so, chancing pursuit, we made a dash to the stables of our Inn, where, flinging a ducat to the ostler and our legs over three of the nags that had drawn our conveyance that day, we were soon riding for dear life after the 'young bloods' of the town, bareback and with a rope halter for bridle.

They had rattled away through the narrow streets, wild hair flying, their torches flinging shadows on the houses, and now, beyond the town gate, they rode a ragged charge over the greensward towards the grim bulk of the Castle, which awaited them with the moon sinking behind its embattled towers. As its long shadow engulfed them, so the bravado seemed to go out of them, until, under the very walls of the fortress, one fierce cracked voice alone hurled up its wild tones at the impassive stone.

We three had drawn rein – or, rather, drawn rope – in the shadow of a group of trees whence we could watch the outcome. Now – and I cannot account for the horror I felt at that moment – there broke away from the Castle of Fagaras a *fragment* of the darkness of which it seemed made, and that *fragment* – a monstrous, winged fragment – flapped low over the greensward *towards us!* I looked round – I suppose to see how we might escape – and saw that the trees which sheltered us, sheltered also a *graveyard*.

I suppose there are men cool enough to face out whatever horror it was that flapped towards us – and to face out the charge of the village posse who were now in full cry after IT – but, if we were those men, our mounts let us down. Putting down their heads as only ponies can, and very little influenced by the rope halter, they fled under the trees for home. As they dashed among the tombs I felt my pony leap, and, looking down, saw that he carried me over *an open grave* . . .

* * *

Gasthof Romischer Kaiser
Kronstadt
Transylvania

May 12th 1850

Dearest Mother,

We are at this Saxon town which is a last outpost of Christian Europe. In hopes of settling my thoughts before quitting this known world for that other across the Pass I have been out wandering. Farr as usual sleeps or idles or makes up to the innkeeper's daughter as if no care burdened him. I walked outside the gates at first, before they were closed. In some of

[205]

those old monkish illuminations of a 'fair castle' you have the picture this walled town presents. Massy walls and bastions, steep wooded mountains close at hand – all that is wanting is the fair lady in her steeple headgear waving a kerchief to the departing knight. The mediæval sense is very strong here. These Saxons are descendants of those Hamelin children spirited away by the Piper in the legend, and indeed a legendary Gothic air still hangs about the place. I came in and walked about the streets when the town gates were shut up for the night. What I was to leave behind me at quitting Europe was very clear to me in those candle-lit windows of handsome houses I passed. Clearer yet was my idea of it on entering the Black Church (as it is called), which I did at dusk. Far, far away, and encompassed by the infinite darkness of the nave, burned a single candle. Yet it was not extinguished by the darkness. It was a gleam which I put whole into my heart, to take into the darkness ahead. I came away at once to tell you of it, since it has brought me peace. I may as well tell the wall as tell Farr, good fellow as he is.

My responsibilities towards Farr are a burden. Like my commissions from Sir Daniel (which I told you of), looking out for Farr makes me into a person I am not, and sometimes wish I had never attempted to be. You would not know me. An instance is this. We broke an axle-tree in the peasant's cart we were travelling in through a wild country of oakwoods on Transylvania's western border, and were obliged to pass the night in a woodcutter's hovel. Had I been alone, I should have wrapped myself in my 'bunda' and lain down quietly to rest with a pistol under my hand. But Farr has no notion of danger. So far as he cared about it, our hosts might have been foresters or gamekeepers on his father's estates. A baby was squalling in a box, and Farr started in to unpick its wrappings (which were cruelly tight, and alive with lice) for all the world like a nursemaid in the Kensington Gardens. I should tell you that of all the low and brutish ruffians ever intent on the murder and pillage of all who fall into their hands, the Wallack must come first. They wear fur hats like thimbles pulled down over matted hair, and have sullen, cruel countenances, and cloaks of sacking, and are besmeared in mud, and wear large boots like the ogre in a child's tales. Amongst these beasts Farr with his pretty ways, and smiles at the girls, and winks at the children, seemed to me

to have the chance of a bright little songbird in a den of cats. So
I found myself striking out left and right with a cudgel to clear
the room of them all, and setting the table against the door, and
lying awake with a pair of pistols in my hands, just like the brutal
travellers you read of, and despise. Farr of course laughed at me
for my trouble, believing himself on very good terms with our
hosts, and dropped off to sleep instanter. See him in a front
parlour buttering a fat Saxon frau and her two giggling daughters,
or see him in a den of Wallack ruffians, it is all one to Farr, who
is convinced (by his privileged youth, no doubt) of the bene-
volence of all the world towards himself. Meanwhile he tells me
that I like to invent dangers so that I may congratulate myself
on overcoming them. Maybe so.

After the thousand imaginary deaths I die on his behalf,
a real danger comes almost as a relief. We were driving at dusk
over a spur of low hills on the skirts of the forest three days ago.
Out of the dark of the trees came a number of village dogs (as I
thought). They came nearer, a pack of them. At the same moment
as I recognized their gaunt grey flanks and quick-trotting action,
out sprang our carter to seize his lead-pony's bridle and control
the animal, which of course had known the wolves instantly, and
had reared up screaming. I fired off a couple of shots. This woke
Farr, who had been sleeping on the straw in our cart (as he will
sleep anywhere). 'What's up?' he asks. 'Wolves,' say I. He peers
out towards the famished brutes watching us with muzzles raised.
'Ain't they rather small for wolves?' he enquires. Well, after a
moment or two trotting in circles, and sitting down to scratch
like any old Towser on the Clapham common, and a few half-
hearted moans, they melted back into the forest again. So much
for wolves! I wish all our fears and perils would prove as timid
as the wolves of Transylvania.

Sir Daniel's commissions too have aged me by fifty years.
He asks me to look out a banker at Vienna and enquire what has
become of certain projects begun before the revolutionary wars,
in which Sir Daniel had sunk money. Simple enough. I expect
'a banker' as you and I understand the term, but I find a man in
the circumstances of a Prince, appearing and vanishing mysteri-
ously, who carries me into deep water at once. An agent of his
was to have met me at Hermannstadt (husband to the fat Saxon
frau with the daughters) but did not keep his appointment, and

was killed by brigands robbing the mail near Fagaras. Now I am to meet another emissary, or perhaps the Prince himself, at Kustendji on the Black Sea, the port to which Sir Daniel's railway from the Danube was to have been constructed, so as to shorten by many days the transport of goods and passengers from Vienna to Constantinople, had the wars not intervened. What am I to gain from these meetings? I feel myself a cat's-paw poked out by Sir Daniel into the unknown to see how his adversary may react.

Well, tomorrow we cross the Pass into that unknown. Towards the world I must wear a savage mask not my own. Towards you only I may turn my own true face unchanged. I take forward with me that candle-gleam from the Black Church, and thoughts of home.

Your ever-loving son,
Tresham Pitcher

IV

'Come, hurry, I believe that's the steamer come in now!'

'I'm sure there's no hurry, Pitcher old fellow. What time is it?'

'Do come along. What does the time signify? It don't work to a schedule, you know, like the Greenwich ferry.'

'Oh, very well. Have you seen my – ah, here it is, after all.'

The scene was the corner of an ill-lit, crowded room of the 'steamer-station' at Rustchuk, on the banks of the Danube about thirty miles from Bucharest. A crowd of merchants and soldiers and peasants, either fighting for space or already squatting on the floor, intensified the atmosphere with clouds of smoke from their pipes and the hubbub of their voices. Through this confusion of noise Pitcher shouted down to Farr, bending anxiously over the corner in which his companion had been wrapped in his *bunda* and apparently asleep.

'I've got our traps together and a *hammal* to take them aboard,' Pitcher went on as Farr pulled on his boots. 'Aren't you eaten alive, though, down there?' he added as he watched Farr scratch his chest.

'Pretty well gnawed.' Farr grinned. Not his unclipped beard, nor the dirt of his face, nor his greasy furs, took away the ready cheerfulness of his smile, or the whiteness of his teeth, in that filthy corner.

He got up. He had not slept, but had closed his eyes in preference to extending *ad infinitum* Pitcher's speculations as to the arrival or non-arrival of the steam-ferry from Belgrade. The drive from Bucharest had been rough work: a cart made of wood, three feet high by four long, filled with hay and pulled over the roadless plain by four little nags at a gallop, with the coachman astride the wheeler. Still, he had endured it, and it had ended: he did not want to talk over again every bump and jolt of the drive, with effusions of the rage and contempt which Pitcher had kept up against all aspects of Wallachian life. After the frantic drive, they had found that the steamer was seven or eight hours late, so Farr had lain down in his corner and drawn his *bunda* over his head. Now he followed Pitcher outside through the crowd.

'Watch your feet!' called Pitcher sharply. 'These filthy brutes have made a latrine of the place.'

Indeed there was a slop of mud and filth underfoot. But Roland noticed mostly the clearness of the air after the foetid hut, stars above; and, gleaming and glaring through the dark from the river ahead, the wonderful blaze of light centring upon the steamer. She smoked and steamed, and the beat of her engines filled the night.

'My word!' said Farr. 'We've seen the world a bit, haven't we, since we were last aboard a Danube steamer? Remember it going off from the quay at Pesth and leaving us? I'd have gone on with Feet and Bumm for two pins.'

'And so we might have done, for all the good we've got by going round.'

'Oh, I don't know. We've seen the country a bit, and we're alive. I call that a good.' When Pitcher said nothing, Farr went on, 'And what does old Vinegar think about it, I wonder? "After my long tour I rejoiced to see – "'

'He thinks we ain't come far yet.'

However, when they reached the busy, bustling deck of the *Argo* steamer it was evident that Pitcher, like Farr, had the feelings of a hero come in from the night, and from far-flung adventures, to such tame domestic shipboard scenes, where they had the right to swagger and expect attention. Through the cabin window, as Pitcher oversaw the unloading on deck of their luggage and its placing in the public saloon, Farr had noticed that a cold pair of eyes, in a clean-shaven pale face, was appraising him. The man seated at his ease in there was surely an Englishman.

'Stay with the baggage, Farr,' Pitcher said. 'I'll see if I can get us cabin places from the steward. Stay there.'

Off he went. Roland accepted that Pitcher rushed about on their behalf – not sent like a servant, of course, but self-impelled by the wish to lead. The crowd of Turk and Greek and Wallack and German, with all their attendant women and children and baggage, and all their shrieking and smoking, had transferred itself from bank to steamer like an ants' nest removed on a shovel, and was now spilling out across deck and saloon into every corner of the boat. Farr was amazed at the awkwardness and delicacy of the objects which these people tried to take about with them. Next to him a furious old Turk was remonstrating with a German who had sat upon what appeared to have been a geranium in a pot. He watched the wrapped and swaddled women carrying elaborate tea-kettles, and he watched a man set down the flask of his water-pipe in a space in the hurly-burly, and settle down beside it himself to pull away with every appearance of satisfaction. Meanwhile the steam-whistle shrieked, and the engines pounded, and the press of people onto the boat in the flaring lights became more urgent still.

How thoroughly he would have hated it (thought Roland) if he had been shown this scene a few months since, and told that he must be part of it. And how he now enjoyed it! He felt, and saw, and smelled, and heard – and he was perfectly well, perfectly content. But then, so had he been quite well and quite content at Cambridge.

'Wretched creature says the cabin is taken. Some pasha, I suppose.' Pitcher was back, with his usual agitations and resentments.

'Never mind. We'll do all right here.' When they had settled their baggage so as to make seats for themselves in their corner, Farr said: 'In fact the fellow in the cabin looked very like an Englishman.'

'Did he?' Pitcher was lighting a cigar. 'I wonder if he'd let us in with him.'

'We'll do very well here,' Farr repeated.

Pitcher smoked in silence, restlessly. 'I'll just take a turn and see if I can see this Englishman,' he said presently, and went off again.

Gradually the crowd sorted itself into less furious and less noisy knots, and settled about the steamer. Renewed frenzy broke out when the ladder abruptly rattled up the ship's side, but at last the shore-bound were off, and the passengers were on. Answering the jangle of the engine-telegraph with a deep rumble which sent a shudder through every plank and rivet of the steamer, the paddles began to revolve, water to churn, and the mean lights of Rustchuk to slide away astern.

'I'll tell you who it is who has taken the cabin to himself,' said Pitcher's voice behind Farr, who was looking out at the scene of departure. 'It's Lord Vauchurch.'

'Lord Vauchurch?'

'Yes. Who left the Ministry.'

'Oh, I know. Wasn't there some row he made, or some other fellow made?'

'His wife went off with that fellow who won the Derby. Now, is he a friend of your mother's, do you know?'

'I never heard of him being.'

'Dammit.' Pitcher thought a bit. 'Tell you what, though – if you can make your mark upon the Captain of this boat as you did upon the Pole in the last one – as being Sir Daniel Farr's son, I mean – then he might give us a leg-up with Vauchurch.'

Roland remembered an exchange on the Pesth quay, when Pitcher had mocked his dependence on being his father's son to give him an identity with Lucowitz. It had rankled. 'Do we want a leg-up with Vauchurch?' he said.

Pitcher stared. 'Well, I do,' he said. After a moment he added, 'I tell you what it is, old fellow, I can put up with rough quarters about as well as any fellow going, so long as I know nothing better is to be had. But I don't care to put up with the second-best if a little work will get me the first-rate. So why don't you talk to the Captain? I dare say he'll be on his bridge. I'll stop with the baggage.'

There was no help for it but to go. Roland got to his feet and picked his way amongst possessions, and sleeping forms, and the flasks of water-pipes, until he was on deck. Clear night air swept past, the steamer hurried along spilling light over the black waves. He walked forward. Through the cabin window he saw the grave, clean Englishman seated in a chair with his leg cocked on his knee, reading a blue-bound book in a pool of steady light, while behind him a respectable-looking servant, evidently English too, was laying a table. To Roland, the glimpse carried him home across such gulfs of space and time, from the deck of a Danube steamer, that he might have been a ghost looking in through a window at the living. Before his lordship could look up, Roland walked on. Why should he and Pitcher disturb that careful ease? He walked the whole way round the deck, and came in to the saloon again.

'No good, I'm afraid,' he said to Pitcher.

'Why not?'

'The Captain don't speak much English, and I don't think he ever heard of Papa.' After a few moments, when he thought the matter finished with, he suggested making a meal of the food they had brought with them from Bucharest.

'We're not beat yet,' said Pitcher, springing up and stepping over encumbrances to the door. In a moment he was back, 'I say, Farr, have you got 50 or so piastres? A dollar would be better.'

'Here you are.' Farr pulled out his purse and gave it unopened to Pitcher, who made off again. Though teasing Pitcher with extravagances, Farr was anxious to pay as many of the expenses of the journey as possible, partly because he knew that Pitcher had little money, partly so as to feel he pulled his weight in the expedition, which he seemed always to be taking too idly. In Pesth he had paid the hire of the calèche, though not before Giza and Pitcher had fallen out over it, Pitcher's recital of the incident always ending with him wagging his head angrily, as old Giza had apparently done, and crowing out the words *En magyar wagyok!*, which never failed to make Roland laugh. Waiting for Pitcher, he counted up how long it was since that day at Pesth. Three and a half weeks: it seemed a lifetime away, those incidents historical, himself a man looking back on his youth. Only three and a half weeks, less than half a Cambridge term, in which span, usually, no change took place in himself whatever.

Presently Pitcher stalked back over passengers and baggage to settle by Roland with an air of satisfaction. 'I think we shall see some results now,' he said, handing back the purse.

Roland, who was hungry, didn't like to suggest again that they should eat. Pitcher had a daunting capacity for going without meals – it was part of his display of hardihood, which withstood sleepless nights with the same indifference – and had indeed lost all excess flesh from his face and large frame, so that now a leaner, harder, grimmer man (well suited by Captain Vinegar's clipped whiskers) had superseded the gauche and rather heavyweight youth with uncertain eyes whom Mr Gulliver, for instance, would have described if depicting his clerk. They sat side by side. Roland had pulled a grimy book out of his pocket, but didn't open it. The steamer juddered and rattled and shook in every particle of plank and iron and glass. Through the open door the beat of her paddles splashed like mill-wheels in the dark.

'When we get to Kustendji – '

'Do you remember the – '

They had started together, Pitcher looking forward, Farr looking back. Before either could go on, they saw a man in a dark uniform signalling to them through the door. Pitcher sprang up.

'Come on,' he said, 'that's our man.'

Roland followed him onto the deck. No one but themselves, he reflected, had come and gone from the saloon with such ceaseless discontent: all the other passengers remained where they had first settled. However, they now looked up without interest or irritation at the two Englishmen tramping yet again amongst their feet and wives and pipes and possessions. The uniformed man led them forward along the deck. At the door of the cabin he paused a moment. Behind him, Pitcher smoothed his face and beard with both hands. Then the man threw the doors open and entered.

The scene within was as Roland remembered it through the window – calm, quiet, orderly – except that the grave Englishman was now seated at table, a white napkin tucked into his dark clothes. In the draught from the open door his peace, like his candles, had been rudely startled. However, he showed the minimum surprise of a lifted eyebrow and a hand stayed on its way to his wineglass.

'*Encore deux anglais, milor, qui sont – *' began the uniformed man.

'I most sincerely beg pardon, my lord,' broke in Pitcher, pushing the man aside and entering the cabin. 'I had no notion we should find Lord Vauchurch already here when this fellow insisted upon us taking up our quarters in the cabin. Of course we will go back to the public room at once. Again my apologies.'

'Just close the door, would you?' asked his lordship in rather a mild, high voice. Perhaps he had intended that they should close the door on their departure; the steward, however, at a glance from Pitcher, closed it with them inside the cabin. Pitcher now took Farr by the arm and brought him up to Lord Vauchurch's table.

'May I present my friend Mr Roland Farr, of Trinity College Cambridge, to your lordship?'

'Very pleased, very pleased.' He touched his napkin and held out two fingers to Farr. 'Trinity, eh? I was at the other place.'

'Farr is a little knocked up with our journey from Bucharest, you know,' said Pitcher, in the rasping tone which Roland knew was meant for Captain Vinegar's *persona*. 'Indeed, a rough time of it we've had all the way out of Transylvania, devilish rough, which is why I should have liked a wholesome meal and a cabin place for him now we are aboard the steamer – but there, we shall do well enough in the saloon, I suppose.'

'Dear, dear. Transylvania! Dear, dear.' Lord Vauchurch was looking about the cabin under cover of these remarks, evidently judging the effect upon his comfort of sharing the space. 'Well,' he said, 'well, well. I don't think we can have a Trinity man roughing it in the saloon, I don't indeed. Could you squeeze yourself in here, Farr, do you think? And I daresay there'd be something to eat for Mr Farr here, wouldn't there, Dommett?' he suggested, leaning back in his chair to communicate with the silent, watchful servant who had remained in the shadows.

'Enough and to spare, m'lord.'

'Well done, Dommett. There now. So.' Then a thought, a fear, seemed to strike him. 'You're not ill, are you, Farr? Because I haven't brought a doctor with me. You've no . . . symptoms?'

Roland spoke for the first time, rather irritably. 'I'm perfectly well, sir. I wish you wouldn't put yourself out by our coming in here. We shall do very well in the saloon. Come – '

'It's all settled.' His lordship raised white hands to still this dissidence. 'Your friend too must keep you company. Whom have I the honour of addressing?' he asked, his cold eyes taking in Pitcher with no more expression in them than if they had been looking over an envelope to find the address.

'Vinegar,' said Pitcher without hesitation, extending his hand, 'Captain Vinegar, at your service.'

'How do.' Again the two fingers. '*You* are not a Trinity man?'

'No, my lord, I am a soldier making a land-march to India.'

'Are you, by Jove? Now, let your people bring your baggage in, and Dommett will show them where they may put it. Dommett, bring up chairs for these gentlemen, will you? And see what can be done in the way of victuals. Yes, yes,' he said, turning his faint smile on his new companions, 'this is the sort of pell-mell way of going along that we Eastern travellers must accustom ourselves to, I suppose.'

It was not very long before Pitcher and Farr were seated at two newly-laid places – silverware from his lordship's canteen – with a bowl of *ragout* in front of each of them, whilst Lord Vauchurch watched them fall to. Unwilling as Roland had been to suffer disturbance from his tolerable berth in the saloon in order to intrude on this grandee, he was now thoroughly pleased with their new surroundings, and with Dommett's *ragout*. It made him smile to remember how he had looked in through the cabin window at that remote scene of tranquillity and order, which Pitcher's conjuring trick had enabled them to join. What, though, had been Pitcher's idea in introducing himself as Captain Vinegar?

'Simple, is it, the journey from Bucharest?' enquired Lord Vauchurch.

'Ay, simple enough. A cart. And then over the Danube from Rustchuk, you know, in such a lamentable old punt with a lateen sail I was sure we should upset, or be run down by some of the barges.'

'But we weren't,' added Roland, 'it was safe as a house.'

'I had thought of taking in Bucharest myself,' said Lord Vauchurch, motioning to Dommett to refill their glasses, 'but my fellow, my *cavass* you know, believed there might be a difficulty about procuring a carriage to take me there.'

'I suppose our Consul at Bucharest would have sent a carriage for you.'

'Oh – I'm travelling in quite a private way, you know. No fuss made.'

'Well,' said Pitcher, taking up the wineglass, 'had the Hospodar known of your wish he'd have gladly sent one of his carriages for you, I'll be bound. If I had known of it myself I'd have asked him.'

'You met the Hospodar?' Interest, for the first time, lighted his eye.

'Met him, yes, twice.'

'Stirbe Barbey?'

'Barbe Stirbey, my lord.'

'Barbe Stirbey, just so.'

They looked at one another. It seemed the cards were suddenly in Pitcher's hand, or perhaps in Vinegar's. Though curious, Lord Vauchurch asked no further questions as to the Captain's dealings with the ruler of Wallachia; and Vinegar's courteous smile gave nothing away. Turning to Farr, his lordship announced, 'Now, *I* am on my way to look into the Sulina Mouth.'

'Really, sir?' Roland pictured the peer on a ladder gazing into some orifice of antiquity. 'Where do they keep the Sulina Mouth nowadays?'

Pitcher laughed. 'Really, my dear fellow – '

'Well, what do *you* know of the Sulina Mouth?' retorted Farr.

'A good deal less than his lordship, I don't doubt,' said Pitcher, 'but, to be brief, the Sulina Mouth is the chief channel by which the Danube reaches the Black Sea, and is under Russian control.'

'Ah, you've seen it, I suppose,' said Roland. 'Been there, have you – Captain Vinegar?'

'I've seen it a time or two in my wanderings, yes,' replied Pitcher with a boldness amazing to Farr.

'Ah, have you now, Captain?' Again the calm lordly eye brightened with interest in the candlelight. 'I should be disposed to welcome your opinion upon it if you was there at all recently.'

'Well, my lord,' began the 'Captain', leaning back with his wine, 'there ain't a doubt about it but the Russian don't stick to his bargain. What they agreed with Austria in '40 about the dredging they don't perform. Oh, they sent dredgers in, two of them, saw them there myself standing idle. But how much work did they do? Two days! Two days dredging out the channel since '40. Why should the Russian do more, what's the Danube to them? The Danube, my lord, is a mere European waterway, and the more the Russian can cause it to silt up, why, the more damage he can do to Europe's trade. In the old days, now, under the Turk, before the war of '38, there was a constant sixteen feet of water at the bar there – sixteen feet, and kept clear by ships being obliged to drag iron rakes behind them. That was the law. And what is there now – what depth is there now at the bar?'

'Oh, I couldn't tell you. But I have it in my Reports here, I don't doubt.'

'Nine feet, my lord. Under the Russian there's nine feet and not an inch more. That means lighters are needed, of course, to carry out goods from the river ships to the sea-going vessels over the bar. Well, how much does that increase the charges, should you say?'

'Oh, a great deal, a very great deal.'

'By five shillings and sixpence a-quarter. Freights for England at Galatz here, on the river, are at 13 shillings a-quarter, while at Varna on the Black Sea they're no more than 8/6d, 8/– even. So, the Russian by his non-dredging policy is able to put a surcharge of 5/– on every quarter of goods sent from the Danubian provinces to the English market. It ain't a bad method of carrying on a war against us. It ain't at all.'

Roland was so astonished by this performance that he simply stared at Pitcher in amazement. Then he looked to see how Lord Vauchurch had taken it. His lordship was moving a silver fruit-knife about the cloth in front of him with a sagacious, downward stare which gave nothing away. Without meeting Pitcher's eye, he said, 'Yes. Yes, you hold my view of the matter entirely. Entirely. Tell me – what sort of a place is it down there at the delta?'

'Abominable.' Pitcher shot out the word, which took effect.

'Ah. Yes. Marshes and so forth, I suppose?'

'Marshes! You may say so! – marshes without end, and swamps, and lagoons, and reeds, and mosquitoes, and channels in a maze to lose yourself among, and nothing but the pelicans and the buffalo to watch you die. Upon my soul, a man must be deucedly hardy if he is to visit the delta! I shouldn't care to go through it again, I confess, for it beats the Sea of Azov and the Scanderoon marshes to nothing.'

Lord Vauchurch looked considerably shaken. 'But the garrison lives there, I suppose?' he suggested.

'Dies there, rather. The Russian picket would sooner be sent to Siberia – he'd live longer down a salt-mine! The huts they have! Built out over some stinking pool, and as cram-full of mosquitoes in as out. They aren't allowed to build a fort, as you know, by the Treaty, so they live in huts, poor wretches, and die by the score.'

'Die of – ?'

'Why, of the fever, my lord. Danube fever. It don't come out for weeks after, very often, but it's sure to be fatal at last.'

'Bless my soul. But surely quinine – '

'Not a bit of use against the Danube fever, they say.'

'Bless my soul,' repeated the shaken peer. There was a silence while he pondered the terror of the marshes. Roland kept his eyes on Pitcher's face, still astonished as much by 'Captain Vinegar' 's knowledge of Danubian commerce, as by the aplomb of his friend's acting, and was rewarded by a wink flashed to him over the back of Dommett, who was again refilling the glasses. The wink relieved him. As a joke rather than an impersonation – rather than a fraud – of course he could enjoy Pitcher's performance.

'An excellent ragout, my lord,' said Pitcher.

'And an excellent claret,' said Farr. It was just a bravura performance of Pitcher's, surely, with no motive but amusement behind it. The idea made him happy. 'You have fed us like aldermen, sir,' he said with satisfaction.

'Yes, yes,' said Lord Vauchurch absently, and then went on, 'You two gentlemen are not travelling so far as the Sulina Mouth, I take it? Do you leave at Galatz and go to Varna? Forgive my asking, perhaps your plans are private.'

'Not the least bit,' said Pitcher. 'No, we go ashore at Cernavoda.'

'Really.' There was a silence. Sure that Lord Vauchurch had never heard of the place, Roland saw his chance to recoup a little credit for Trinity after his ignorance over the Sulina Mouth.

'It's the point on the river which is closest to the Black Sea if you was to go overland, you know, and not go round by the delta,' he said. 'There's a ridge of high ground which turns the river eastward there. But from Cernavoda to the sea direct is only – only how far, Vinegar?'

'Forty miles.'

'Thank you for the lesson in geography, young man,' said Lord Vauchurch, dropping the words on Roland like stones. Then, when Roland flushed, he went on with a little more warmth, 'But I confess my ignorance – I never had heard of your Cernavoda. I know of the mountain which keeps the Danube from entering the Black Sea for another hundred leagues. There have been schemes for bursting through it, I believe. Canal schemes. But I dare say you know all about it, Captain?'

'A little. Sultan Mahmoud measured out the ground for a canal, oh, as long ago as '35 or 6. Then came the Russian war and nothing was done. Now all is changed.'

'Oh. How so, pray?'

'Railways, my lord.' Vinegar was cryptic, looked as if he wished to say no more.

'You mean – ?'

There was a silence between them, into which the steam-thump of the engines, and the clap and rattle of the steamship as it bustled along, intruded itself like a suggestion.

'Yes, my lord,' admitted Vinegar, as if the beans had been spilled for him, 'you have guessed it. A railway is planned. You shorten the Vienna–Black Sea journey by a hundred miles, and you cut out the Russians. So the great men plan a railway over the high ground from Cernavoda to the sea. The work is begun,' he said, leaning towards the candles and speaking low. 'Oh, all you may see of it if you ain't in the plot is a leetle enlarging of the sea-port at Kustendji where the line will run out – a leetle widening of quays – a leetle dredging of shoals – but up there above in the Dobrusca, and down about the Karasu lake, why, the work goes at it hammer and tongs! Hammer and tongs!'

'A plot you say, eh? What's the plot? Who are the plotters?' His lordship leaned in towards the candles from the other side in his intentness. 'Though I have no right to ask, of course, none in the world.'

Vinegar leaned back. 'I wish I could answer you plainly, my lord. If plain answers were known, I shouldn't be about to land myself at Cernavoda and make a reconnaissance of the matter at first hand. No, by George, if I hadn't interests to look after in the matter, I should have gone on in the regular way to Constantinople, from Galatz to Varna, and let Herr Novis and his plots up there amongst the wolves and eagles go hang. I should indeed.'

'Novis, you say? Is he at the back of it?'

'I never knew of an affair in this part of the world Herr Novis was not at the back of.'

'No, indeed. Why, I remember when I was – but that's another matter. No, if Herr Novis is at the game, it will surely come to something.'

'Novis, of course, was to be expected in such a scheme. The question is, my lord, shouldn't England take a hand at the game too?'

'England? In building the railway?'

'Building it is controlling it. The thing would be about as valuable to commerce as any of the schemes for driving a railroad across the isthmus to Suez. Look at how close to Trebizond you are, where all the Persia trade goes nowadays!'

As soon as the word 'England' had come up, Lord Vauchurch had turned very judicial and impenetrable once more. 'Well, sir,' he said,

[220]

'Herr Novis is no friend to England, as I dare say you are aware.'

'For all that, he is using English money and English machinery up there on the Dobrusca,' said Pitcher.

'So there *is* English participation?'

'Stolen English money – stolen English machinery – that's what the matter is, my lord. You know the name of Sir Daniel Farr, I dare say?'

'Naturally I do, but – wait a bit! You, sir – ' He looked at Roland.

'Is Sir Daniel's son,' said Pitcher.

'So . . . And you act . . . I see. I see. Stolen, you say? From Sir – quite so. Well, well. And if Novis was to accept your claim upon the railway, then there would be an English stake in the venture.'

'Exactly so. A patriotic Englishman – ' here Vinegar bowed to Roland – 'a great English contractor, would hold a stake in the enterprise, and ensure safe passage for English goods. If we succeed with Herr Novis, that is.'

'I wish you well of it. He is a formidable adversary, is Novis – formidable. Well, well. Fancy.' Lord Vauchurch sat back. It was as though a certain enthusiasm for these young men and the scene in the cabin of a Danube steamer had brought him to the edge of the leap, whereby he might have joined them; and then a habit of fastidiousness, and passivity, had held him fast by the coat-tail, and kept him from committing himself. The little warmth he had shown now waned. Pitcher looked disappointed, though Roland could not guess what he had hoped to secure, beyond the interest of a political nobleman.

Later, when Dommett had cleared the table and set up his master's travelling-bed, and Pitcher and Farr had made their simpler arrangements of cloaks and rugs in two corners of the cabin, Lord Vauchurch looked up from washing hands and face in the canvas basin erected for him, and said as he took the towel from Dommett, 'Do you know, I believe I shan't go into the delta after all. I believe it would serve no purpose. I should learn nothing more of the Sulina Mouth by looking at it, and I might . . . no. No, I believe I shall go ashore at – where was it? – with you gentlemen, if it is at all possible to get over this mountain to the Black Sea. Do you propose hiring a carriage, or horses, or what do you propose for yourselves?'

'There is no comfortable way over the Dobrusca, my lord,' said Vinegar's voice from its dark corner.

'Comfortable, no, I suppose not. I dare say not.'

'But if your lordship is going on to Constantinople, you may very easily go across the spit of Moldavia from Galatz, you know, to Varna, and from Varna take the steamer to Kustendji, where we should meet up with you.'

'Ah yes, yes, very likely.'

From his own corner Roland listened sleepily to their conversation. It was quite as if Captain Vinegar were a real personage over there in the dark, for he knew things, and talked of things, which surely Tresham Pitcher was ignorant of? After dinner Vinegar had discoursed on the state of Hungary since the war in a manner which sounded as though he had lived months in the country, and Roland, recognising some of the material as having originated with Count Giza – 'take the tolls on the Chain Bridge, my lord' – was the more impressed that the man at his side on their travels had accumulated so much information, whilst facts and figures had merely floated past himself and left no residue. Nor did Vinegar stick to the facts of their journey; again, it was as though he was a real person, who had made real detours from the route followed by Roland, and now sat in the cabin of a Danube steamer recounting them. It was necessary for Roland to remind himself that Captain Vinegar had been invented as a joke that day in his rooms in Great Court, and had been introduced to Easby to see what Pitcher would make of it.

Well, now he had learned what Pitcher would make of it. There was the interview with Buckle! – the meeting at Half Moon Street with Papa and Enid! – now he rather wished the joke might have been ended at that point. But of course in Half Moon Street the die was cast. The letters of introduction from his father were all in Vinegar's name, and could only be used by Pitcher if he assumed Vinegar's identity. No doubt with that in mind he had introduced himself as 'Captain Vinegar' to Lord Vauchurch, seeing possibilities of confusion ahead at Constantinople if his introductions should be to people known to his lordship. 'A tangled skein we weave (what was the line?) when first we practise to deceive.' Deceive! The word rang uncomfortably in Roland's mind, who had never deceived anyone but in jest. Ah, but wasn't it the trouble with these fellows like Pitcher, with their way to make in the world, that they used such tricks and deceptions to advance

[222]

themselves, which a gentleman used as a lark? It had been his mother's objection to Pitcher all along, that a man of that sort from the middle class was always endeavouring to put butter on his bread.

Ah, well, it was lark enough to be dropping off to sleep with the throb of the paddles coming up through the planking, and the mighty Danube hurrying them down through the night towards Moldavia.

V

––––––––––

Misseri's Hôtel d'Angleterre
Constantinople

May 28th 1850

My dear Enid,

When you see the heading of my letter, you will look forward (or not, as the case may be) to several pages of my raptures on first beholding the stupendous spectacle through morn's pearly mist of the Sultan's city brooding upon the Bosphorus. Alas, you must apply for such raptures elsewhere! I confess it, I was fast asleep when our Black Sea steamer dropped anchor in the Golden Horn. Partly it was on account of a storm in the Euxine, which had kept me on deck most of the night previous to see the fun, and partly it was that I suffered (at the expectation of really landing at last in a real Eastern city) a sort of climax of reluctance to go on with it – to go on with the journey, I mean – from the moment I saw the coast of Asia loom up in the night on our steamer's port bow as she nosed her way into the Bosphorus and I heard the wild waves breaking on the Cyanean Rocks, which are the Clashing Rocks of antiquity. Few travellers survived the Clashing Rocks, and it appeared to me suddenly on that Stygian deck (just as it did when I bade farewell to Mamma at Paris) that I, too, would never escape their jaws, or see Europe more.

However, of course when I awoke to find the steamer anchored off the Galata quays in the broad sunshine of a May morning, and was tumbled ashore with Pitcher and two or three 'hammals' to carry our baggage, in a little cockleshell of a skiff, why, rapid action quite dispersed my melancholy forebodings! So it is with me: ever reluctant to exchange a tolerable present for a doubtful future, yet ever discovering the future to be altogether jollier once one has plunged in.

[224]

And so it is with Constantinople, the very name of which (on Pitcher's lips) had begun to fill my dreams with Haroun-al-Raschid-like ideas of mystery and barbarism. Instead, what do I find? Believe me, the streets and mansions round about our hotel (which is in Pera, the Frankish 'quartier') might be in Tyburnia, except they tend to a steepness not found in London's new-built districts. The hotel, too, is perfectly comfortable and London-like, and is kept up by Misseri, the fellow who was dragoman to the author of 'Eothen'.

Whom should we discover in Misseri's coffee-room but the Counts Veit and Bümm, of old Vienna-to-Pesth days, whose necks I fell upon quite as upon the necks of childhood's friends, for a day's companionship on the Danube puts one upon an intimate footing not achieved in a hundred voyages on the Thames. Pitcher greeted them pretty gruffly, being unwilling to find anything familiar at the Turkish capital. Pitcher – or perhaps I should say Vinegar – is the very reverse of myself, ever wishing that all things new should be outlandish and strange, and without connexion with aught that has gone before. As soon as outlandishness fades, and the place we are in becomes just that familiar lounge I care for, he agitates to be off somewhere else. So, though we have been at the Sultan's capital but four days, poor old Pitcher is out fussing himself over arrangements for our onward journey through Asia Minor into Syria. Firmans, buyuruldi, teskerés, and such outlandish Turkish passports without number, as well as horses, saddles, servants, victuals, medicine-chests, beds – there is no end to the items he has found to fuss over and sigh about. Veit and Bümm, who project a comfortable tour to the Holy Land and Egypt, seem to fuss about nothing, and lounge about Pera and Stamboul without a care in life. When I told Pitcher that they had kindly included us in their party to view the mosque of Santa Sophia, for which the mere hotel waiter had obtained them a firman, he flew into a rage that anyone may achieve a firman so simply! They have engaged a Greek as dragoman, who attends to everything for them, and of course robs them mildly, but the sums are so pitifully small that it is absurd to care for them. The awkwardness of travelling with a fellow so much less well off than oneself may become, in a great city, the irritation which it is not in a hovel in Transylvania.

To add to his air of mystery and bustle, our Captain

Vinegar is become a man of affairs, a diplomatist, a visitor at foreign chancelleries, all of this entailing meetings (which mostly fail to come off) and mutterings, and ponderings over notes, which would be excessive in the plenipotentiary of Pumpernickel to the Porte. Like his wading off through the mud of Bucharest to see the Hospodar, or his riding from the Danube forty miles over a wild mountain to see a parcel of navvies, it all has to do with his pursuit of this fellow Novis, whose shadow is to be made out (selon Pitcher) behind every scheme and stratagem. It was Papa set him on Novis's trail that afternoon in Half Moon Street. I sometimes regret we did not step in from our giggling next door and scotch Vinegar while he was yet scotchable. Now, as you will see from what follows, Vinegar has a life all his own, and so we are caught up willy-nilly in these tiltings and jousts between Papa and Novis.

So far as Bucharest, Vinegar's enquiries turned up a blank, for those he wished to see had invariably flown the coop or (in the case of a poor fellow at Hermannstadt) been murdered by brigands the day previous. But at Rustchuk, on a Danube steamer, he fell upon his feet. There in the cabin, and quite as comfortable as if he was aboard his own yacht between Westminster and Greenwich, we found Lord Vauchurch, late Minister-for-I-know-not-what in Lord John's ministry. Now, attend to this: for Vinegar it was the work of a moment to establish himself (and me) in his lordship's cabin, and, whilst eating up his lordship's dinner, to hold forth on Danubian affairs to such effect that by morning old Vauchurch had given up his visit to the delta, and become a dyed-in-the-wool supporter of the scheme to build a railway from river to sea with Papa's money! (Money I think which is owing to Papa from Novis.) You would have been astonished to see our friend Pitcher, the Waterways clerk, wrap Lord Vauchurch round his finger! – or perhaps you would not, having felt the wrapping-round powers of that finger yourself?

At all events you would be sure to laugh to see how a Great Man of Lord V's stamp proceeds on his Eastern travels amidst his flock of cavasses and servants and dragomans, enquiring into this, looking into that, making up his mind about t'other – and all the time he is so managed by his attendants that he can go nowhere they don't choose to take him, and he may, moreover, be utterly gulled by such a mountebank as Captain Vinegar.

Well, it didn't suit his lordship's attendants that he should ride over the mountain of the Dobrusca with us – or else Pitcher didn't care for him to see for himself the very half-cock state of the railway works between Danube and Black Sea – at any event Lord V went round by Galata and Varna, and met up with us when his steamer put in at Kustendji. Here Vinegar showed him (as if it was a desperate secret) the iron rails stacked on the quay, and the dredging of the port to receive the railway traffic, and one or two British navvies reeling about in a state of intoxication, and persuaded his lordship that the scheme was really a great deal further advanced than the random diggings in the interior would confirm.

When we got aboard the Constantinople steamer at last, I thought we should come unstuck, for there we found a rascally Irishman on his way to fight for the Shah (or against the Shah, I forget which) who was so very like the article our Captain Vinegar pretends to be, that I made sure he would sniff Vinegar out, and turn him upon his back. But our dinner was scarcely on the table before Captain Hoolaghan had set upon Lord V for the mismanagement of his lordship's Irish estates, which he claimed were in a worse state of impoverishment and starvation than anything beside the Danube (over whose miseries, as seen from a steamer, Lord V had been wringing his hands). When Hoolaghan averred that the half-underground hut of the Wallack was a palace compared to a Connaught cabin – and that even these cabins were fast being thrown down by Lord V's agents, or burned over their tenants' heads – Captain Vinegar weighed in with a very vigorous defence of evictions and rent-raisings as methods of increasing the tenants' prosperity, so that old Vauchurch came as near beaming upon him as a Great Man can. When Hoolaghan was gone to his bunk (for the arrack did for him at last) Lord V warned Vinegar and myself very gravely against being deceived by such mountebanks as he!

I expect you will be surprised that I did not join in with Hoolaghan and go for his lordship myself over his Irish estates, as I would have done a year or two past, when I had seen neither the world, nor great poverty nor great riches; but the effect of my travels has been, that in a woodcutter's hut I feel myself a democrat, and in a prince's palace at Vienna I feel myself an aristocrat. Again, Pitcher is nearly my opposite: antagonistic to princes when in palaces, and to peasants when in huts. He has a bitterness, as if all systems were designed to exclude him from benefit. I had no idea, until I was so much in that kind of fellow's company, how the iron of narrow circumstances may enter a man's soul.

This bitterness of Pitcher's was given much to work upon by Lord V's treatment of him when once we were arrived at Constantinople. As soon as the steamer had dropped anchor (according to Pitcher's account of it) a pinnace manned by British tars came alongside, and carried his lordship to Therapia, where the British Ambassador's palace is. From that privileged haven a few miles up the Bosphorus Lord V sent neither invitation nor message to Captain Vinegar about Kustendji railway or Sulina Mouth or any other of the topics discussed between them. When I remarked that, after all, Vinegar was a piece of fun, and we had had our run out of him with Lord V, Pitcher scolded at me that I knew nothing of Vinegar's importance in the scheme of things (which I confess I don't). Anyway, having been, as he thought, thrown over by his lordship, Pitcher was at once reduced to the pre-Vauchurch straits of applying to the Consul-General (who is a great swell here, and thoroughly contemptuous of Trade) and to the commercial gentry of Pera, all of whom he reports to be either very frightened of crossing Herr Novis, or else very indifferent as to recovering Papa's money (if it is indeed money, and not something more ominous, that Papa has lost, or is owed, in the East).

Poor Pitcher, in fact, was quite at a standstill until, by chance, I ran against Oscroft, who was at school with me, and who is now an attaché to Sir S. Canning at the Embassy. By this means I was invited to Therapia, and, when Pitcher heard of it, he flew into a fury that I had not contrived an invitation for him. I said that another meeting with Lord V would surely lead merely to a repeated disappointment. I will show you how calculating a fellow he is (or has become) by giving you, as near as I can, the very words of his answer: 'Oh, no (says he), for it is not in managing a first meeting with a powerful man that the difficulty lies, it is in contriving a second encounter. Anyone (he said) may meet Lord V by chance, or so the Lord V's of our 'democracy' flatter themselves; but you must meet him twice before he will say to himself, Here is a man who knows how to come in upon me by more doors than one, so I will give him my attention.' Well, of course, I took him with me to Therapia, and we were able to feel quite as caught up in the bowstring-and-Grand-Vizier atmosphere of Eastern intrigue as anyone could wish. You should have seen your friend Pitcher seated on a satin sofa at a window above the Bosphorus, toadying some Teheran mirza in a tall lambskin hat and a dressing gown, or deep in whispers with a Periote banker amongst the Ambassador's rose-trees, or agreeing with Lord V's views (which he has just put into Lord V's head). Still, the poor fellow has his way to make in the East, and I suppose we are arrived at the scene of operations, so I must put up with it.

And what, in all this Vinegarising, has become of the true Tresham Pitcher? Having told Oscroft that I was travelling with Pitcher, whom he remembered only as having been taken away from school over some mishap, I ran a risk in introducing 'Captain Vinegar' into the Embassy (as was necessary with Lord V of the company). But Oscroft did not twig to him. Pitcher, I said, was sick in bed – too sick to go out – and I fear secretly, such is the awkwardness of having Pitcher to conceal, that we may have to prepare ourselves for our sick friend's demise.

Meanwhile I contrive to find amusement with Veit and Bümm. The 'horrors' of Stamboul turn out of course not dreadful at all, any more than the wild Wallack, or the little Carpathian wolves one would have liked to carry off for pets, or the Transylvanian vampires, or the tribe of Montenegrin navvies in whose camp we bivouacked on the Dobrusca – or any other of our 'adventures' to date. Always Pitcher is threatening me with what is to happen next, promising me that, if I am happy now, I shall be miserable in a moment. But I begin to allow myself to believe that I may be perfectly happy anywhere. Certainly Bucharest was amusing in its half-barbarous, half-civilised way. For your hotel room, which is an attic over the stable without furnishing of any kind save the filth left by your predecessors, you are charged just what you would pay at the Hôtel Meurice at Paris. Mind you, you get more for your money: would you, for instance, in your room at the Meurice, be kept awake by the howling of imprisoned gypsies? Perhaps you would not wish to be, but you must agree that it would certainly appear on your bill as an extra charge, in the Rivoli. These gipsies, who may be bought on the hoof for £10 a-piece, live in crowds round the town, and are charged with every kind of vice, cannibalism, etc. The mastication of eighty-four travellers a few years ago is laid at the door of one tribe which, not satisfied with that, proceeded to swallow down a great many of the guests at a wedding feast – but we escaped their jaws just as we have escaped the jaws of all other phantasmagoria of travel.

My idea is, to declare against toiling across the Syrian wastes into Persia with Pitcher, like the poor fellows in Xenophon, but to dig in my heels at Damascus. Thence I may join up forces with the jolly Counts at Jerusalem, or come home directly from Beyrout, which is most probable. I would go off with Veit and Bümm now, if I had the courage for it, but I hesitate to tell Pitcher I think of defecting, for I do so hate a row. I wish he would accept a gift of money in my place, but I suppose he is too stiff-necked for it. Prepare Mamma for the news that I am no longer with Vinegar, though, and speak highly of Austrian Counts when she is by. Dear Enid, I know you cared in quite a special way for Pitcher when he came to us at Ravenrig, but he is now so thoroughly Vinegarised that I know you would declare for Veit and Bümm if you was in my shoes. I know you would.

yr. aff. twin
RF
PS Count Veit is having his portrait taken by Signor Preziosi, who does all the travellers and has an immense stock of costumes in which one may dress up – I have just looked in on his studio with Bümm, and rather thought of having myself done in an Albanian outfit. I wonder if Mamma would care for it?

*   *   *

A few days after the date of this letter, Roland Farr, wearing a fez, occupied himself with his packing in a sitting room at Misseri's hotel quite as snug as that other sitting room in Half Moon Street where this same collection of baggage, then somewhat less stained and scratched and knocked about by the last two months of travel, had watched Captain Vinegar come alive and begin to take his first steps towards an independent life.

Bother Captain Vinegar! Roland left off dropping books into a carpet-bag and went to the window. The city would have been so jolly without Vinegar. Red roofs dropped steeply to the Bosphorus. Behind the queer round night-capped tower of Galata, which poked up near at hand among the roofs, stretched blue water and the hazy Asian shore wooded with the cypress-groves of Scutari. This wasn't 'the East', of course; this was comfortable Pera with its Italian houses, and boulevards, and Consulates and clubs, which could have been so jolly. But across the Golden Horn – and his eyes followed the thought over that lagoon within the teeming bridge where swam the ponderous Turkish three-decker men-of-war amid swarms of kaiks like water-boatmen – across the Golden Horn began the Orient. Stamboul's skyline of domes and minarets satisfied all expectations of an Eastern city's carapace. Old towers, and latticed kiosques, and gleams of marble amongst green gardens where the Sultan's seraglio rambled down to the water's edge; this, what he saw, touched glints on all the equivocal ideas which 'the Orient' started in his mind. What he saw tantalised him. When the sun sank behind Stamboul each evening, such shadows came into being under the roofs of the old houses and khans across the water, that you could imagine heavy-lidded eyes, darkened with kohl, opening at dusk to watch Pera . . . It was not comfortable. He went back to his packing. The old city across the Golden Horn struck an unsettling note that he did not want to hear. The sense of place does not usually penetrate so sharply as to be disturbing into the mind of a rich and cheerful young man intent on enjoying himself; but Stamboul penetrated Roland Farr's mind with uneasy forebodings.

In his packing Roland took only what was essential to him, left behind anything whose ownership Pitcher could conceivably dispute. Dreading the accusations which would surely come when Pitcher realised he was to be deserted, Roland hoped that liberality over cigars and writing materials would allow him to escape with a belief in his own generosity.

The trouble was with Stamboul, that even walking through it by day with Pitcher, on his excursions to equip for the journey ahead, Roland felt on the verge of being shown, at every turn, more than he wanted to see if he was to keep his peace of mind. The dark, rat-filled confusion of lanes and ruins and tottering houses was how you might illustrate the mind of a madman, or a mind in the grip of nightmare, or fever . . . He and Pitcher were walking down the stone-arched passage of a bazaar. Now and then a sunshaft fell by a roof-aperture through the shadows, lighting by chance some heap of merchandise, or a coloured turban, or a donkey, or striking upon themselves as they strode through the echoing, patter-footed crowd, in boots of English leather ringing loud amongst the slippers. This was pleasant to Roland. There was the prospect of spending money, which he loved to do, and was kept from as much by Pitcher's force of character, which made the money blush in Roland's pocket, as by Pitcher's poverty. It was amusing to walk through the colour and crush and scent of 'the Orient', especially with Misseri's good English breakfast inside him. Suddenly the air was saturated with the stench of blood met like a flood from a side-alley. Pitcher paused, laid his hand on Roland's arm. At the end of the side-alley lay a courtyard beyond studded khan gates. The heavy wet thud of some instrument in there seemed to pump the reek of blood over them. On his arm, Pitcher's hand compelled him towards it. Was it the source of all his fears? He did not want to be challenged. But Pitcher did, always did. Challenge was the most fascinating issue in Pitcher's mind. What might it not lead to, at the end of blood-soaked side-alleys in Eastern cities, if he did not give up travelling with Pitcher?

As he packed, Roland heard a step on the stair, and his heart bumped. It was a slow and weary step climbing the stairs, each foot sliding onto a wooden tread, then a pause, then another sliding step. Roland snatched off the fez he had been wearing and hid it in the carpet-bag. The tired steps mounted towards the room. He changed his mind, found the fez and jammed it onto his curls again. Then he waited with a book in his hand until Pitcher entered the room, when he dropped it into the bag to make clear that he was packing. However, Pitcher said nothing. He leaned at the door with his eyes closed recovering from the climb. His linen jacket was darkened between the shoulder-blades with sweat. His eyes, when he opened them and sat down in the chair nearest the door, stared with unhealthy brilliance out of a face white as dirty paper on which beard and whiskers looked ragged. Still he made no comment on Roland's occupation.

'Pitcher – ' began Farr, 'Pitcher, I'm thinking of removing to the Hôtel Byzance.'

Pitcher was silent. Then he drew a short breath and expelled it, an exhausted man's laugh. 'To Giuseppina's! You know it's a brothel.'

'If you say so, old fellow.'

Pitcher sat thinking in his chair. Then he rose, and said without troubling to look at Roland, 'I'm afraid you can't go. Mayn't go. And do take off that fez, it don't suit you.'

'What do you mean, "Can't go"?' He kept the fez on with an effort, unreasonably hurt to hear it didn't suit him.

'I am responsible for you.'

'Veit and Bümm will be at Giuseppina's.'

Pitcher only blew out another weak, contemptuous laugh.

'What is your objection to Veit and Bümm?' asked Roland, stung.

'What is not my objection! Idle, ignorant jackanapes. Running about chattering as if they'd never left Vienna. Your precious Feet and Bumm are just what a man leaves Europe to be quit of! How do you suppose little Veit with his mincing airs is going to support desert travelling, if it comes to the test, eh?'

Roland turned away. 'I dare say it won't come to the test. It never does with Veit, why should it? We ain't all obliged to make an ordeal of it, you know.'

Pitcher was at the window, his back to the room, looking across at the wrinkled old city over the water. When he said nothing more, Roland hoped that objection to his going to join the Counts was withdrawn. Anxious to dispel ill-feeling, with that excess of good-nature which blinded him to incompatibilities between his friends, he said, 'We plan to run over and see the Slave Market by and by – will you come? Veit has been and says it's a great curiosity.'

'I can't, Farr,' said Pitcher over his shoulder. 'And to tell truth it don't much interest me. Besides I have just been over there at the Horse Auction.'

'Don't interest you? Oh, come, that's great humbug! You may write in Vinegar's journal the slaves don't interest you, but you know they would. Greeks? Circassians? Come!'

'You're not let see the white girls.'

'That's all you know about it. Without a baksheesh you ain't. But Veit says he saw, and touched – '

'Oh – Veit! Ain't we never to hear the end of Count Veit? Don't you weary of those simpering – '

'On the contrary,' broke in Roland, 'I think of going with them as far as – ' he stopped.

'As far as where?'

'Well, quite as far as the Slave Market, at all events.' About to tell Pitcher he was going with the two Austrians when they left Constantinople in a few weeks' time by sea for the Holy Land, Roland shrank from the row it would make. 'You should come with us and see the girls.'

'The truth is, Farr,' said Pitcher in a strained voice, 'I have a thousand things to do without running after girls at the Avrat Pazari. A march across Asia Minor takes some planning, you know. I have been out this morning looking at horses. We shall need three, I suppose, and it seems they'll cost £10 or £12 each if they're to be the sort of beasts we can count upon to stand the conditions.'

'Oh, the conditions – !' Roland's heart sank at the word, and he flicked back the tassel of his fez with a jerk of his head.

'Yes, when we are upon the plateau round Konia we will find it pretty harsh going, I should say, in June. Hot. Dry. Long marches between the caravanserais. And then there are the Taurus to be got over on our way down to Antioch. The Cilician Gates. That will be rough work, make no mistake.' His eyes stared unseeing past Roland into what lay ahead. 'And food. I've got the biscuit and the arrowroot and the portable soup, and – '

'And I'll get a dozen or two of those race-glasses you want for presents. I know the shop,' said Roland, eager for shopping that was not for necessities, and anxious to heap extravagances onto Vinegar's expedition in place of accompanying it himself.

'And a servant,' continued Pitcher. 'I think I am on the track of a fellow your friend Oscroft told me of, who might just suit us, a Greek. It seems you must pay a dollar a-day for a good fellow.'

'Have a good fellow, Pitcher, by all means.'

'And then a firman Oscroft seems to think may be managed with the Porte, which should smooth our road if we get into a difficulty. You see,' he said to Roland, whose heart had continued to sink under the network of these plans which seemed to bind him prisoner in Tresham's train, 'you see, there's a thousand things to think of. And the Slave Market is sure to be a great deal more lively at Baghdad, or Ispahan, or some of those desert places where the Turkestan traders come. At the Mashed slave market there won't be any fellows like Feet and Bumm making a peepshow of it! I say,' he said suddenly, opening his jacket and showing a shirt soaked with sweat, 'ain't it awfully hot? Do you feel it awfully close?' He sat down, and got up again immediately. 'I must get away to Therapia, though. Lord Vauchurch has promised he will have talked over the whole plan of the Danube Railway with Sir Stratford. We are asked to dine. Lord Vauchurch – '

'Oh – Lord Vauchurch!' exclaimed Roland, dropping another book irritably into his bag. 'I tell you what it is, Pitcher, I'm quite as weary of that solemn owl Vauchurch, and dining at Therapia, as ever you can be of Veit and Bümm, who at least look jolly and try and enjoy their travels. There ain't much in the way of larks at Therapia, that's certain, with old Canning and his glooms and rages. "I have had the honour of conferring with your father," he says, giving me such a glare. Oscroft says it, and I feel it too, as if we was all back at school and may be flogged if we don't know our lesson. "The honour of conferring with your father"! I suppose he intends to quiz me.'

'Listen, Farr.' Pitcher staggered as he turned towards Roland, but put out his hand on a chair-back for support. 'Listen. You don't care much for the place your father has made for himself out here. The name he has made. I see that. And I dare say you find Veit and Bümm agree with you. I saw the sour face your fat Bümm pulled when he was obliged to touch the hand of Robinson from the Sultan's iron-works. I saw it. But Sir Stratford Canning don't agree with you. Hang it, Palmerston himself don't agree with you. They don't sneer at Trade. They know right enough it's at the foundation of all England's power, Trade is – and men like your father, and Robinson, and Hanson the banker there at Candili. Canning and Vauchurch – all the lot of them – they all sit upon the back of your father and men like him, believe me. Merchants, traders, bankers. Just as your Counts Veit and Bümm seat themselves on Herr Novis's back, if they would but acknowledge it.' He seemed to have gathered his failing energy into the speech.

Roland said mildly, 'I didn't know you would come out so strong for Papa and trade, I didn't indeed.'

'I tell you what it is, though,' said Pitcher, rubbing the centre of his forehead with his fingertips, his eyes closed. 'Ever since I saw your father up there in the rigging in the storm I've – '

'In the rigging?'

'On the roof, that's to say. Strange,' Pitcher added, opening his eyes, 'd'you know, I'd swear to it I'd seen him in the rigging of that sloop he said he'd sailed on in the Black Sea.'

'A brig it always was in Papa's tales, not a sloop. A Smyrna brig – full of currants, Enid and I used to suppose. But there,' he added slyly, 'I dare say what you've made up in the way of adventures mingles pretty freely with what you've really done, don't it, by now?'

'What do you mean to say, Farr?'

'Adventures for Captain Vinegar I mean, of course.'

'For him. Of course. Yes. Making up a life for Vinegar is the very deuce. The very deuce.' He sared for a moment, thinking. 'But it wasn't Vinegar but myself was so struck by your father up there on the castle roof taking in sail while the snow came down and the wind blew . . . do you remember how the wind blew among the chimneys and the canvas pulled in our hands? And he – he defied it all. The storm and the men who'd struck work and every damned thing that came in his way. I'd never seen it so clear, a man who wouldn't let his destiny go out of his own hands. I'd never seen it at all, except where the giants and enchanters in the stories stand up there against the elements and make things fall out as they choose. It was very fine. I often think of it – think of him in the storm. And if I've the chance to carry on your father's interest a little, with Canning and Vauchurch and the rest against Novis, well, why, I'd a good deal sooner be at Therapia than at the slave bazaar, yes, I would.'

'Between Papa and Novis I should say you would need to look alive to keep your feet.'

'Oh, I expect to be nimble. I expect to need to keep on my toes. I know well enough your papa sent Vinegar on his errands because he knew there'd be few questions asked if Vinegar's body should turn up floating in the Bosphorus. That's Vinegar's use. Of course it's a risk. But if he can make something of it – if Vinegar can keep your papa's interests afloat, and dodge his enemies, well, he would have a more thoroughgoing life of it here in the Levant than ever Tresham Pitcher is offered in India.'

'Lord,' said Roland, 'surely Papa has plenty of tin without risking fellows' lives!'

'It's more than money with him.'

'Oh, with Papa it's always only money, you know.'

'There you mistake it. There's always more than money. Money's only the beginning.'

'How should you know more about my father than I?'

'It would be hard to know less.'

After a moment Roland asked, 'Who was it told you all about Papa, for I never did?'

'Bounty talked of him first, the day we went over the moors in the gig together. He told me of your father being turned out of Turkey and how he'd given the fortune he'd made into Novis's charge to keep it from the Sultan. And he told me about the statue. The headless statue at Ravenrig.'

' "My Phidias"?'

' "My Phidias".'

Roland's face cleared. 'Oh, Lord, is this to be the great coup, then? Your great coup in these parts? To find Papa's head?'

'It would be the making of Captain Vinegar.'

'And what of Tresham Pitcher?'

'Captain Vinegar would have a better life of it in the Levant than ever Tresham Pitcher was offered in India,' repeated Pitcher, as though it was a maxim he had formulated, and had often used to himself.

'So Pitcher would . . . ?' wondered Roland.

'Oh – ' Pitcher made an impatient gesture – 'do you know, I believe I may have to knock Tresham Pitcher on the head, if he ain't to trip me up between one thing and another. You see – ' He leaned anxiously forward, as if now he would explain it all – but instead he fainted. He swayed forward and collapsed, half in Roland's arms, whose fez fell off as he caught him.

VI

- - - - - - - - - - -

Hôtel de l'Olympe
Broussa

June 14th 1850

My dear Enid,

No doubt you have been long supposing me lost to
civilisation in the midst of Asia Minor, a spavined quad carrying
me behind the ramrod back of Captain Vinegar through flood,
desert, brigand's ambush and mountain pass? Not so. All the
while I have been living the most agreeable life imaginable, of
picnics and water-parties, first at Constantinople, and now at
Broussa where the silk comes from. The Counts Feet and Bumm
have been my companions, and continue so. Only one thing has
distressed me, and that is the loss of the little silver vinaigrette
which Mamma gave me in Paris at parting, which I grieve over
quite as if it was an amulet or talisman I had lost. But I hope it
may be found at one or other of the baths or pleasure-resorts of
the town, and returned to me.

And why (you will ask) have I frittered away half the
summer at Constantinople, instead of attending to my travels?
The answer – don't laugh – is that my fire-eating travelling
companion of the ramrod back went down with the fever!

At first I was dreadfully alarmed, and ran about the town
looking out doctors and surgeons and hakkims ad lib, but the
calmness with which all these medical men took my news, and
viewed the patient, persuaded me very soon that he had taken
an ague on the Danube, and would live. He had some bad times
at the beginning, and the doctor being very much addicted to
bleeding, they drew countless ounces of blood from him with
the largest leeches I ever saw, which come from Trebizond. It is
a curious fact that, so horribly real has Captain Vinegar become

[238]

to me, I found myself wishing to consult him as to Pitcher's treatment, and half expected to find his upright form and clipped whiskers standing across Pitcher's sickbed from me, looking down upon his victim. Vinegarish as Pitcher had become over my diversion with Feet and Bumm at Constantinople, there was nothing Vinegarish about the poor fellow lying so ill in his bed, and rambling of old days with his mother in Italy. It is monstrous odd, to see upward of fifty leeches attached to one's friend's stomach, for it seems that with the fifteen or so ounces of blood they suck from him, they must surely suck away his life. I was sure that Pitcher would not survive the attack, and, as I say, I had too the parallel idea that the fever had not touched Captain Vinegar – that he stood at the bed and watched Pitcher's sufferings with the grim satisfaction of such ironclads as he.

A poor dear fellow Pitcher was, though, when the height of the fever gripped him. I had no idea I should be so distressed to hear his ramblings – the tears ran down my cheeks as he talked with that urgent innocence of the madman about 'old forgotten far-off things'. Do you remember the morning walk we made once to the sea with him at Ravenrig? He talked of that, and of old M. at his cottage door showing us the 'lobsters' in his basket! And of driving in a chaise with you – he talked of that. Oh, and a hundred things that meant nothing to me, but how I wished to understand, and to be of comfort, as if to make amends for the impertinence of overhearing the poor fellow's intimate thoughts! There was a horror, too: a tower by a lake holding some horror I could not make out – a dead woman, a dead child – which he wanted tools to bury. Then in the midst of his burying he would suddenly shoot upright in his bed and shout out 'Arrowroot now – have we enough arrowroot?' and I would be surprised into laughing aloud at such worries mingling with terrors. He stuck it all like a trump, and would mutter to me in lucid moments, 'I haven't fussed, have I, old fellow?', and clasp my hand.

But just when I thought he should have been better, and the doctor declared him so, he seemed to relapse into low spirits, and an apathy, which made it hard to get along with him. At last I left him, and came on here with the jolly Counts, to try if it wouldn't shake him into life. I have said to him, that I remain here a fortnight, and that if he comes up with me in that time (of which four days remain), I will go on south and east with him

[239]

into Syria. If he does not, I shall be free of obligations to him, and will join the Counts' tour to the Holy Land by sea. So I have left it up to him what I do, which is always the best plan in making decisions.

Here we are comfortable enough, in a hotel on a hillside looking down upon a long green valley, with chestnut woods above us, and the snows of Olympus above that. We are half a mile from the town of wooden houses, where there is a castle to walk to (as prescribed by physicians in all spas!) and any number of mosques, and chalybeate springs just like the ones at Tunbridge. The youth of Broussa (unlike Tunbridge youth as it could well be) disports itself very freely in the baths, which are magnificent affairs, though highly indelicate. Dear Enid, I run on because I am so well-lodged, lounging on a divan in my robe of Broussa silk, with my water-pipe at hand, and a slave to bring me coffee. Yes, the Counts and I have gone over to Oriental ways in all things, some very wicked and others less so. So here I sit doing nothing at all, which is very Oriental. Shall I describe the view to you? Our hotel, which is built of wood on a kind of Swiss-cottage plan (some sorry-looking pine trees which shade it add to its sombre Swiss air), seems to be slipping down the hillside of rough grass onto the hump-back roofs of a *hammam*, or bath, below. We share the hillside with a busy little farm, where morning liberty has just been given to a dozen cocks and hens fluttering out of a fowl shed. At the farm door sits an old woman crooning to herself as she spins silk, and, all around, children tumble and screech in sunny dust. On the road which winds down the hill a wayfarer has just stopped by the yard to light his pipe and retie his turban, and to bawl out the news to the old lady, whilst below them two milk-white oxen may be seen slowly and creakingly plowing under the mulberries. All over the hillside the wild broom flowers as yellow as butter, and scents the breeze which comes in at my window.

Well, does it sound to you in the close air of Berkeley Square, where I suppose you are, an agreeable manner of passing the forenoon, to watch such a scene? With the prospect of a pleasant sea voyage to the Holy Land ahead of you? – for I am sure that Pitcher will not come up with me now, and has probably already set out for Konia on the direct road. I think you may tell Mamma of my changed plan – I have sat wracking my brain these ten minutes for one single circumstance of my life here at Broussa which you might tell her with propriety, but there is none.

Farewell dear Enid.

Yr. aff. twin

RF

Do not on any account tell Mamma that her vinaigrette is lost. RF

*   *   *

Although the sun had shone that day upon Roland Farr, a wet evening was closing in upon a wet day as Tresham Pitcher approached the walls of Iznik, only a day's march from Broussa, on his road from Constantinople to catch up with Roland. Out of mist and rain clouding the landscape there rode first Pitcher, then his Greek servant Giorgio astride a little nag well laden with baggage. No other creature disturbed the monotony of rain and emptiness through which they had ridden from the Sea of Marmora, which they had crossed the previous day by boat from Constantinople. Poor little Giorgio splashed through the mire on his wooden saddle, round-backed as a monkey, and moaning to himself, or singing sadly, as the rain streamed from his black curls. Ahead, looking over-tall on the quick-actioned little horse, Tresham rode as stiffly as a man in a trance, who cares neither for his whereabouts nor for the small miseries of wet knees and a wet saddle. One thought tapped in his mind like a loose shoe with every step:

I could not be more miserable than I am.

When, however, the walls of İznik showed their gloomy outline through the mist, his spirits fell a notch lower. His expectation, without his intending it, had projected forward to journey's end the comforts of a bright fire and a cosy parlour. The disappointment of a subconscious hope strikes a blow a man has not guarded against, and the ruinous outline of Iznik now struck such a blow at Tresham's hopes. Out of puddles and heaps of filth the ruined walls rose, ponderous, useless as a whale's carcase on the shore. Between bastions the arched gateway was so silted up that his head would have struck the keystone as his horse carried him under it, had he not ducked.

[241]

Ducking his head snapped him out of the trance in which he had ridden for hours through the rain. He saw an old woman with a staff leading through the mud a cow, a white cow of beautiful and gentle appearance. These were the first creatures he could remember seeing in all the dreary landscape of the day. He noticed too that within the walls, though the rainy wastes stretched away almost as desolate as the country outside, swallows and martins swooped and sped over the puddles.

Still the rain fell small and fine, misting the scene so that huts appeared one by one as he rode towards them, wretched dwellings which looked likely to collapse into the pools of water around them, and nowhere was there even what might be called a village, where once the temples and palaces of the great city of Nicaea had stood. Now and then appeared a single tree, a ghost in the mist, seeming in its loneliness to stand sorrowfully as a *revenant* in scenes of past grandeur. Past heaps of ruin, past carcasses leaking into the puddles, past a roofless mosque, and a shattered minaret, Tresham rode his pony along the wretched track. *I could not be more miserable than I am.* Under him the pony's feet slid in the mud. In what hovel would Giorgio lodge him, with the authority of the *teskeré* which it had seemed such a triumph to be granted at Constantinople before his illness. Probably the fever would return now and kill him here. This was what it had all come to – his 'adventures'! He had not even spirit enough to laugh bitterly at his end.

An hour or two later Tresham stood looking out into the softly falling rain from the door of the poor Christian's house in which Giorgio had installed him. He had been unable to eat the meal Giorgio had cooked for him. The weakness of fever had left his bones like twigs and his muscles like cotton, so it felt. To rise from a chair, or to walk upstairs at Misseri's hotel, had meant sitting ten minutes beforehand collecting his strength. Only loneliness and self-pity, and the fear of dying alone at Constantinople, had compelled him to start on the three-day journey to Broussa. Now he would die at Iznik, and be put into this sodden ground to rot. He thought of what hard work it had been to dig the poor girl's grave at Rainshaw, and the tears ran down his cheeks into his beard. He stood against the doorpost because he feared the finality of lying down.

And he should write another letter. Having left Constantinople, he must write in Captain Vinegar's character to Sir Daniel to make the most of what he had achieved at Therapia over the Danube Railway. How was he to find strength even to mimic the Captain's energy of thought and expression? He had already written to his mother, so that she should have his last words if he sank into fever and death. The letter was in his hand.

Iznik, June 14th 1850

My dear Mother,

You will see from this address that I am again a wanderer, wishing I had never begun my journey. You knew that I had the fever at Constantinople, for Farr wrote, I believe. He considered every debt of friendship paid by having called in an inhuman doctor to kill me by bleeding, and never came near me save two or three times, in intervals of licentiousness with two Germans. They soon went off to extend their vices to Broussa and left me hurrying to the grave. Added to my weakness this betrayal reduced me to lying weeping in my bed. I could not endure to confront Turkish life. My tears flowed for hours together at seeing from my window a kid-goat taken from its mother and slaughtered before her eyes. My spirit, like my health, is broken.

If I am to regain Farr's company I must reach Broussa by the 18th, or he will have quitted that town with the two Germans. So I have dragged myself onto a boat from Tophane to Yalowa, and thence to this miserable hut in a swamp, where from weariness and want of strength I cannot endure the very barking of the dogs at the door. When I remember how unkind I was to Eliza and Walter on the score of their snug cottage at Sydenham, I consider that I shall have deserved to die in such wretchedness as now surrounds me. Pray beg them to forgive me. My only companion now is a Greek servant, whom I expected to murder me for my purse before we were well clear of the burying-ground at Yalowa.

He is a good fellow, though. He has held me on my horse when I would have fallen from weakness into the jaws of the dogs,

[243]

and uses every exertion of a cheerful nature to dispel my despair, though himself shaking with fright at every horseman on the road. When I thanked him for his care to me in my abject state, he replied (in Italian), 'We are two Christians'.

Here, where our hut stands amid the ruins of the once-great Nicaea, hardly two stones of Roman building remain upon one another. This is Asia. Such scenes make my own poor life, and mankind's history, alike insupportable for want of purpose. Tomorrow's ride, let alone the extent of Asia before me, seems utterly beyond my strength.

Adieu, my dearest mother,
from your ever affectionate son
Tresham Pitcher

The letter finished, he looked between the hut's doorposts into the stillness of neglect and decay, and the veils of rain drifting over the ruined walls. The quicksand of Turkey, which had sucked down mighty Nicaea almost without trace, he could feel sucking at his own feet. It would kill him, and he had no courage left. Courage was no use against the ruin and fever and swamp of Turkey. In its box in his baggage was his father's sword, but cold steel was no more use than courage, unless he turned the blade on himself. These were not the enemies he had imagined, when he had so longed to possess his father's sword.

He tried to remember his father. But there were only stories. There were only stories in his mother's voice, in the dark, out of which the heroic figure loomed. No doubt put into his mind by the sight of the vast stork's nest spilling off a column in his view from the hut door, Tresham thought of his father descending a cliff-face in a basket let down by rope to take eggs from an eagle's nest in Scotland. The old birds had returned to attack him; wielding his sword (surely a knife?) against them, he had accidentally cut through all but one of the strands of the rope. Wildly the basket bumped and banged against the rocks – fiercely the eagles attacked – whilst a ghillie above sought to draw up the rope without severing its final strand . . . ah! (thought Tresham) if only he had such perils as that to face, instead of the weariness and fever and mud and rain of Turkey. The eddying basket, the abyss below, the rope's last fibre twisting unbearably taut – even thinking of it quickened his spirit within him. Perhaps it could be put into Captain Vinegar's Journal? 'Slashing with my sword at the lammergeyer, I had inadvertently cut through all but one of the rope-strands by which my frail aerial basket depended. My position was now a perilous one. Above me the crags of the Caucasus, below me the rushing Terek . . .'

Yes, it could be done. Heartened by the flow of blood into Vinegar's veins, Tresham felt himself capable of writing the letter which the Captain owed Sir Daniel. Thinking of it, he stood a moment or two longer at the door. The rain fell less hopelessly from a lightening sky. As his mind filled with ideas and phrases for Vinegar's letter, so the miseries of Iznik, and of Pitcher's situation, receded from foreground into background. His father's spirit had put into his hand a weapon of more practical use against the enemy than a sword. Turning back into the hut, he surprised little Giorgio by calling out loudly for lights and writing materials.

Iznik, anciently Nicaea
Pashalik of Broussa

June 14th 1850

To: Sir Daniel Farr, etc. etc.
Sir,

     Having quitted Constantinople yesterday I halt upon the march to write you an assurance that the affair of the Danube Railway is pretty well settled to your advantage. In consequence I felt no further obligation to 'kick the heel of idleness upon the carpet of impatience' beside the Bosphorus, and have satisfied a soldier's restlessness by setting out at once for Broussa, where I rejoin your son and young Pitcher.

     As I informed you in my last despatch, I had turned aside Vauchurch from visiting the Sulina Mouth, and had persuaded him well enough of the advantages to Great Britain of diverting the Danube trade across the Dobrusca by railroad to Kustendji – so long as that railroad was in British hands. Vauchurch will instil the need for Government support into Sir Stratford's head, and I think we may be tolerably sure that His Excellency's despatches to Downing Street will be as satisfactory to your interests as if you was to have buttonholed Lord Palmerston yourself. The Fleet which so over-awed the Greeks, in that absurd affair of Don Pacifico in January, can no doubt do the same service against Novis and the Bulgars!

What Herr Novis may have made of my successes in this affair, I hardly know, or much care. I believe I caught sight of his face by light of a paper lantern as he was hustled into his sedan-chair outside the Austrian legation one night, when he bent upon me a look of the utmost ferocity; which compliment I returned with the tightest of bows. I heard he had been at Candili, no doubt brewing up mischief with Hanson, and it was evident at Therapia that a certain counterswell against the Danube Railway, and in favour of the Sulina Mouth party, had been set going by unfriendly interests. Now, I am reliably informed by certain useful spies I have long employed at the Turkish capital, our adversary is gone South, no doubt to the Orontes, where I purpose next to encounter him or his works. As to those Orontes works, on the quays at Tophane a day or two past I fell in with an English navvy (the worse for liquor) who had got off the packet from Scanderoon, and had come from 'digging out a channel' in the vicinity of Antioch. Surmising that he had been employed about the Orontes navigation scheme which you told me of, I was putting some questions to the rascal, assisted in my investigations by a stout stick, when he left the pothouse into which I had drawn him, to answer the call of Nature. He did not return. Enquiry in the street suggested a scuffle, blows, a limp figure carried away – but you are as familiar as myself with the mishaps so apt to befall any witness one has laid hold of in these regions. The incident determined me to march South.

I should have set out before this, but suffered a return of the intermittent fever, my old enemy since Sea of Azoff days. It proved a sharp bout, but with practice a man is able to doctor himself tolerably well, and although my symptoms no doubt alarmed the two boys pretty thoroughly, I sent them on to amuse themselves at Broussa until I should be well enough to come up with them.

This I did since illness prevented me from overseeing their amusements and guarding them sufficiently well against the moral dangers of the Othman's capital. The sloth, and luxury, and depravity of the Turk is a fascinating magnet to the unformed Anglo-Saxon mind. I need not remind you of how, on every hand, lie slave-markets, and resorts of vice, and dragomans eager to act the pander to weak youths with long purses. The boys, too, have met up with a pair of mincing little 'counts' of Vienna, one of whom exhibits in his amatory tastes 'the disgrace baboons are free from'. I hope that by sending them off to Broussa I have restricted the mischief, and shall find them unharmed, and ready for our severe march across the Anatolian plateau.

It is with the utmost relief that I am quit of the streets of Pera, and the niceties of Therapia, for, however fulsome the compliments of diplomatists and men of fashion, it is a man's own estimate of himself that must be the basis of his confidence, and where better to form that estimate, than upon the lonely march, the solitary bivouac, the sturdy existence far from all those props of privilege which can make the weak appear strong in England? I know of nothing else in life which so quickens a man's spirit, as the knowledge that his security – his very existence – is dependent upon boldness and self-assertion, rather than upon gas-lamps and constables. In the midst of the ruin of the Roman city of Nicaea, from which I write to you, one sees plainly enough what may become of a world over-dependent on gas-lamps and constables, when the barbarian decides to foreclose. Etiam perieri ruinas.

I must now proceed to kick my servant out of bed, for the Sun will be up in an hour, and I have passed the night in writing reports for friends at Therapia who were kind enough to think a plain soldier's views on the Eastern Question worth canvassing, since I know the Russian end of the Black Sea rather intimately, and flatter myself that my advice will be of use at Downing Street. Now for Giorgio, and a start! He is a lazy fellow, cowardly as all his race, and with feet as flat as a shark's fin flapping on a dhow's deck in the Arabian gulf, but I have administered sufficient cuffs to his head to persuade him that he has an old Eastern hand to deal with, and not the 'greenhorn' Pitcher who employed him whilst I lay sick.

Believe me to be, Sir,
your etc. etc.
O. Q. Vinegar (Capt.)

Before he climed into the glimmery white contraption of mosquito netting which Giorgio had made ready for him – the famous Levinge-bed brought into use at last – and before he blew out his candle, Tresham read through both his letters. He found that Captain Vinegar's brisk spirit had dried up his tears. In consequence he put the letter to his mother impulsively into the candle-flame. It showed him a creature too weak to survive the journey ahead. So he burned the paper, and blew out the candle.

He lay in the dark listening to the mosquitoes outside his netting, and managed even to smile to himself at recollection of Captain Vinegar's vigorous phrases. Strange that he found it so easy to concoct attitudes for the Captain, as if the work was exactly what his education had prepared him for. He had only to stifle what was naturally in his heart – burn the letter to his mother and deny the self that wrote it – for Captain Vinegar to tramp into his head fully armed and begin dictating. He slept sounder than on any night since the fever had attacked him, with a weight off his mind.

In the morning he found his resolution confirmed. At the door the rain had ceased some hours earlier, for a clear, pale sky awaited the rising of the sun, and shadowy hills enclosed a vast, pale lake which gleamed over the ruined western walls. His spirits rose.

'Giorgio!'

'*Ecco mi qua. Mi dica, signore.*'

'Giorgio, *mi porta un colazione o qualcosa – cosa c'è?*'

How the Italian language came back into his mind, like the heat and light of Italy itself, from early wanderings and other days! He wished he had time to write to his mother now, with his recovered spirits. She knew how a fine dawn had always made him cheerful. But he had no time this morning. The parent's heart which is burdened by the child's complaints is rarely relieved by his rejoicing. In came Giorgio with water in a pail.

'*Eh, signore, come sta stamane? Ieri sera ho pensato io –* '

'Hold your tongue and bring my breakfast.'

Tresham saw from the man's idle manner and insinuating tone that it would not do to talk Italian with him. His own vocabulary and demeanour in Italian was that of a child, for he had learnt it as a child. Evidently (he saw at once this morning) Giorgio had taken advantage of this, and of him, to lounge into a position of equality, and probably of contempt. He remembered the man's sly smile as he had said, 'We are two Christians', as he might have said, 'We are both outcasts, slaves, *giaours*, together.' Today he must set about correcting a relationship which had begun so ill, with weakness and dependence on his part. Indeed, today he must set about correcting his own attitudes altogether, if he was to survive the journey ahead. The pitiful creature who had ridden into Iznik last night in the rain would not reach any of the objectives of the journey. He splashed water from the pail over his head, and shook the drops vigorously out of beard and whiskers.

By the time he rode ahead of Giorgio towards the ruined Yenisehir gate, the sun was up, flooding light and the first warmth of day upon walls and lake and mountain. Such works of man as existed, ruined or entire, were shrunk to insignificance in the wild and far-flung grandeur of the landscape. What were the walls of Nicaea, in light of the hills ranged above the lake, and what did it matter whether they enclosed the temple and palace and paved street of Rome, or the swamp and hovel of the Turk? The conquerors' splendour had vanished with the conqueror, leaving his marble to serve the peasants' lime-kiln, his temple and palace as stone-quarries for hut and stable. The European painter, or poet, or traveller, bathes the ruins of antiquity in the westering light of sunset; now, with a wrench of his understanding, Tresham turned himself round in his saddle to view Nicaea's ruins not by the light of the Western sunset, but by the dawn of an Eastern day. He pushed on his horse resolutely between the bastions' broken parapets, under the gate's shattered arch, into Turkey beyond the walls. 'I know of nothing in life which so quickens a man's spirit as the knowledge that his security is dependent upon boldness and self-assertion, rather than upon gas-lamps and constables.' Vinegar had struck the note, and he must attune to it.

'In the ruin of Nicaea one sees what may become of a world dependent on gas-lamps and constables, when the barbarian decides to foreclose.' Yes (he thought), and in the ruin of Buda-Pesth, and the Paris massacre, and in the quaking condition of all the European capitals, under the threats of the '48. Two summers ago, from his desk at the Waterways he had watched the flame of revolution run from one settled city to another, with the eager interest of a prisoner in irons in a ship's hold, who hears the storm and hopes that the foundering of the vessel may set him free. He recognised now, riding out of ruined Nicaea, the hope he had nursed, that order would collapse.

But in England it had not. The gas-lamps still lit the secure streets of the rich. In the June of '48, on Clapham Common, an entertainment had been given to five hundred and fifty Special Constables who had volunteered for duty on the day of the Chartists' march on Kennington Oval; military music had sawed away amongst the tents and trees, audible from Laidlaw Villa, whilst toasts had been offered to The Constitution, The Industrious Classes, and The Friends of Good Order. The ship had not foundered, the barbarian had not foreclosed, and Eliza and Walter had returned from that June celebration in perfect safety to Sydenham.

The vessel hadn't gone down, but he had freed himself of his leg-irons and jumped clear. Here he rode, in an Eastern dawn, mist clearing off the lake to reveal a vast calm only troubled here and there by waterfowl, hills tipped with sunlight, the track mounting ahead through fruit orchards and olive groves, his little horse lively under him. Yesterday's misery, like yesterday's rain, was forgotten. Here he rode, part of the wild Turkish scene.

The lake fascinated him continually that morning as he followed the track of the Roman road along the hills' flanks above its reedy shore, and the sun steadily rose, and the heat increased. The lake's size, and the occasional far-heard splash, or the sudden furrowing of its glassy surface by a monster of the deep, made him speculate upon the silent companion of his ride almost with fear; then, from the road, he would look down into the clear sunlit water of a cove below, and long to plunge into the cool subaqueous world it promised. Again, so beautiful a prospect would now and then strike him, of wooded capes reaching far into silver water, or the dark cypresses of a burying-ground outlined against the shimmer of olives, that no idea of Turkey's malevolence, so strong a sensation yesterday, and still to be discerned in the eye of the lake watching him, could subsist in such a view today.

At mid-morning they came to a place where the track had been swept away by a landslide. Although the collapse had happened ten, or twenty, or maybe fifty years before, no repair had been attempted to restore the line of the Roman road. Instead a slippery, narrow, treacherous path wound over the landslip. How Giorgio abused the Turks as his horse slithered and slipped amongst the stones! But Tresham checked impatience, murmured his *mashallah*, and freed his horse's rein to let it pick its way over the obstacle. He would unite himself with Turkey. In Giorgio's complaints he recognised the note of fear underlying his own complaints of yesterday at the ruin and disorder and indifference of the land into whose power he had committed himself. He would not be afraid.

'Giorgio,' he called back, 'I am going to swim.'

'To swim? Ah, no, *signore*, I beg, is impossible. Is very much dangerous. Big fishes, bad current, water very very deep.'

'Follow me down through the olives.'

By plunging into the lake he would unite himself with Turkey. Or, if it was a challenge, he would meet this eye of the underworld which watched him.

*　　*　　*

For a good many hours of the afternoon Tresham had been aware of the presence of Broussa on the hillside at the head of the long valley up which he rode. Through the haze which blued the mountains, and vaguened the sprawl of houses indented on their flank, the declining sun struck many domes, and lit many slim white minarets. Above all was the rosy flush of snow on the summit of Mount Olympus. It seemed to be an enchanting town he was approaching.

Apple orchards, and fig and olive, were planted on the slopes he began to ascend. Under the trees he passed an old man scything the grass, and the patches of poppies so brilliantly scarlet, the thrust of the scythe's sweet edge through stems, and the rasp of the whetstone behind him as he rode on, now added to the scene that element of husbandry which he had missed all day. For the land, though fat with summer grass and summer flowers, and watered by fine rivers, was almost empty of people. On the road pack-animals came and went, in the charge of drivers shuffling along in their ragged dress and turbans; or a group of armed horsemen dashed by in a rattle of speed; or a grander and more leisurely merchant would pass, smoking his pipe at ease on his donkey, while a string of laden mules pattered through the dust behind him; but only the road was a ribbon of life across a forgotten land.

Near Broussa, however, the thickening life of the countryside, and the increased bustle of the road, prepared Tresham for immersion, once within the town, in the noise of carts and hooves and feet and sharp cries which filled narrow streets and echoed off blank walls up into the blue strip of sky amongst domes and minarets above. He had told Giorgio the address of Farr's hotel, and had followed the little Greek about the streets as enquiries were made. Now he rode behind Giorgio, outside the town again, along a road which traversed the hillside in silence and evening light.

They had ridden half a mile when a cluster of houses appeared ahead, under a dome and minarets, and Giorgio pointed to a group of gloomy trees, firs, in whose shadow stood a fantastic wooden structure of galleries and gables and jetted balconies.

'*Ecco, signore – albergo tedesco!*' he announced like a conjuror.

It was an extraordinary place. They rode down to the terrace on which it had been built in the side of the hill. Tresham dismounted and gave his reins to Giorgio. No dog barked, no servant appeared. The ricketty pile of starved-looking timbers stood before him, hurriedly contrived into the resemblance of a Swiss cottage, its gables rough-cut where they should have been carved, the balusters of its balconies mere struts of wood, the whole improbable heap of planks having the air of being about to slide down the hill to destruction. The overshadowing firs, in which the evening breeze spoke of faraway northern forests, dropped upon this retreat a deeper and more sinister shade than lay beneath plane-trees shading the road. A footstep creaked on wood. Tresham was aware of a man at the door cleaning his hands on the dirty apron tied round his belly. Though his head was shaved and his skin swarthy, he was plainly European. Tresham said in Italian that he was looking for Signor Farr. The man's rude stare collapsed into servility. 'For the Counts and the Milor?' he said in German. 'Please, sir, please come in.'

Inside the Swiss cottage, where the light was faint and the smell unpleasant, he learned that Farr and his friends were out, though expected back 'from the bath' within the hour. No, nothing had been said of 'milor's' arrival – but a room would be prepared instantly, the largest and best remaining, if 'milor' would honour the German hotel . . . the resentment Tresham had felt on finding himself unexpected gave way to a grim satisfaction at having reached Broussa before the birds had flown.

He had himself shown into Farr's rooms – the rooms occupied in common by Farr and the Counts, as it appeared – while Giorgio oversaw the carrying-in of his baggage by Turkish servants who had now turned out and were screeching amongst themselves under the pines. The low large room, darkened by a verandah overhanging its window, was furnished in uneasy mingling of Europe and the East: stiff-backed chairs at a table littered with books and journals; raised, carpeted benches covered with cushions round the walls; a galleried dais strewn with more cushions; here and there the glass flasks and snaky tubes of narghiles; and everywhere a heavy, oversweet fragrance which cloyed the nostrils and puffed suggestions of sensuality into the mind. Here, in short, was 'the East' of the Turkish Smoking Divan in the Strand.

So thought Tresham as he kicked about the room. This was what Farr wanted of Turkey – this set-dressing and paraphernalia. No doubt he and his friends wore little velvet caps with tassels as they sat smoking in their Swiss cottage. Tresham would not wait for them here. He wouldn't be found by them on their territory. Besides, certain squeakings and rustlings and patterings behind thin walls made him uneasy. With what creatures might they not share these couches and these cushions?

He walked out, and found the greasy German, whose half-leering watery eyes made the same suggestions of depravity as his hotel, and, having learned from him that a coffee-house was to be found among the dwellings of the village a quarter of a mile along the road, told Giorgio that he would stroll there to stretch his legs.

He would storm in upon Farr and his two fancy Counts with the dust of real Eastern travel upon him, and stamp about their kickshaw-looking 'oriental' hareem with an energy that would let them know how fully he had recovered his health since riding into Iznik twenty-four hours before. He took with him his whip, to ward off dogs, and set out for the village.

The coffee-house was pleasant and beguiling. It was tucked into the hillside below a dilapidated mosque, and possessed a terrace under a vine pergola where Tresham sat against a couple of bolsters, his coffee on a stool at his side, and quietly observed the scene. To one group a garrulous old man in a vast green turban laid down the law in a voice like a cracked bell. Yet he seemed to be persuasive: men moved themselves and their whole apparatus of narghile and coffee to be within earshot of his oratory. Meanwhile a boy carried water in a vessel from the mosque fountain and splashed it into the flowerpots which stood about the terrace, a cool sound refreshing the air of evening. Other grave figures sat as Tresham did, pulling occasionally on their pipes, gazing out at the view. There was an air of comfortable dignity, even of luxury, in the way they sat and smoked so peaceably, which the greatest nobleman in England, at ease in his library, could not have matched. Tresham copied them, and looked out across this tract of Turkey which they contemplated with such satisfaction.

Below the terrace the hillside fell steep and rough into the plain, which the mists of evening now made vague. Still the rich yellow of marigolds patched the slopes, and the rich scarlet of poppies; beyond, on the line of march he had followed all day, the lines of further hills faded into dusk. Of course, rubbish and refuse had been flung out of the village onto the slopes below, where it rotted malodorously, but Tresham set his mind against complaining of this, even to himself, just as he had set his mind against complaining of Nicaea's destruction once he had thoroughly knocked into his head the Asiatic point of view as to the dispensability of temples, and paved streets, and gas-lamps and constables. What was Captain Vinegar's phrase? – 'boldness and self-assertion not gas-lamps and constables'. He smiled. He would show Farr the Captain's letter to Sir Daniel, and make him laugh. They would concoct the Captain's Journal together just as they used to do. He considered the scene before him through the Captain's eyes:

I know of no activity, or inactivity, which adds so mightily to a man's gravity as smoking the narghile: observe the unmoving head bent down as if in sage ponderings, the bubbling rose-water obedient to meditative sucks, and one would suppose old Moostapha there, who is very probably a mendicant tinker, to be the greatest philosopher since Avicenna. Watch, too, those

[254]

Turks playing at backgammon under an ancient *cinar*, one of them smoking a narghile and the other not: is it not easy to believe that the impassive smoker has the dice all his own way, while his Latakia-less opponent throws none but twos and threes? Tobacco reconciles the Turk to every defect in life, for, so long as he may smoke, he will sit staring away by the hour together at any view which offers, however noisome he may have made that view with his refuse, and you may imagine, to watch him stroke his beard, and pull away at his amber mouth-piece, that he is enumerating in his mind, as he tells over the beads never far from his fingers, the many and immense superiorities which this his native heath possesses over all other localities upon the face of the globe. For this, I must own, I love him. Next door to the café we see the tomb of some worthy who, having in life sat many hours together gazing upon this view, has said to himself 'Hang it! I shall be buried here', and so, having cleared a space in the rubbish, and planted a few cypresses and a dozen roses, has in due time planted himself, too, under that stone canopy, with the view everlastingly before him – and, no doubt, a goodly number of the black-eyed houris of a Mussulman's paradise to light his narghile for him as well as attending to his other wants.

In this style they would put across the Captain's view of Turkey. It would make Farr laugh. He suddenly looked forward warmly to Farr's good-natured laugh, and to his cheerful face in its golden fleece of beard, and to Farr's company altogether, so that he half rose from his seat intending to go back to the hotel. But he sank down again. The Counts! The wretched Counts. In Vinegar's letter to Sir Daniel he had mocked them, as well as accusing Bümm of buggery. What would be Farr's response, if shown the letter?

His eye fell on the bulbous roofs of one of Broussa's famous, or infamous, *hammams* which bulged out of the hillside below the village. Perhaps Farr and his little Counts were under those domes now, sharing the intimacies of the Gehenna he had glimpsed in the vapours of the bath-house at Buda. No – he would not think of it! Naked imps in the steam with triple-tined spears like leisters. Enid's form confused with her twin's. No! – he would not let ideas crawl into his mind out of that pit.

His mind darkened. He would not show Vinegar's letter to Farr. He would take Farr from Broussa just as he had taken him from Cambridge, and isolate him alone with himself in the uplands of Asiatic Turkey. Vinegar had promised Sir Daniel that he would do so, for his son's benefit, and would subject the boy to the rigours of the long march and the soldier's bivouac, in place of the squeakings and whisperings of that depraved Swiss cottage, or the heat of the *hammam*, or the posturing young noblemen of Cambridge and Vienna. It would not be necessary to show him Captain Vinegar's letter, for he would show him Captain Vinegar's face.

VII

WHEN ROLAND FARR AWOKE to early light in the travellers' room of
the village of Tchardourhissar, his first thought was to try over his
state of mind in order to discover what was painful, or wretched, as a
result of this precipitation from Broussa's pleasures into long marches
and rough quarters. He had not thought it worth the trouble to bring
his Levinge-bed, which he had never put up at Broussa (its constric-
tions not being adaptable to the habits of the hareem), so he awoke
rolled in his cloak on a couple of thicknesses of carpet. He had not
been very much bitten. His neck was stiff, but that would wear off in
the warmth of the sun, whose beams he could already see whitening
the dust below the ill-fitting door. He turned over. Against the light of
the window there hung from the ceiling the muslin bird-cage which,
sewed to his sheets, made up the Levinge-bed within which Pitcher
slept. Roland laughed silently: to his eye, Pitcher's solemn antics as he
climbed nightly into this contraption and drew tight the strings over
his head were as ridiculous as they were elderly. His Levinge-bed,
though, was of a piece with his other cares and precautions against the
terrors of travel which bore so heavily upon him. Had Roland not
laughed him out of it, Pitcher would have strapped to his saddle the
old cavalry sabre he had suddenly produced from the baggage! What
were these perils? How tiresome he was!

Good-nature instantly suppressed the spurt of pique, which only
flickered through Roland's mind like the scream of a swallow through
an arch, and was gone into sunlight.

Instead what was comic came into his head. For instance, on quitting
Broussa, leaving the German hotel and the jolly little Counts smoking
amongst the girls on their verandah, Pitcher had led the party straight
up the hill above, by a kind of goat-track, the climb so slow and arduous
in the heat of the sun, and the track so tortuous, that for hours the

[257]

Counts and their pipes and their *amorazzi* were clearly visible to the toiling climbers making their zig-zag ascent of Olympus, until it became perfectly evident from the lie of the land that ascent and descent were alike unnecessary, for, having laboured over a spur of the mountain, they rejoined the road they had left, and were obliged to bivouac a mere stroll from the German hotel. These were the difficulties Pitcher was determined to encounter!

Roland had hardly regretted leaving Broussa, which had begun to grow a little tedious with its round of baths and smoking and debauch. The food was so poor, and there was no champagne. Besides, some creature in one of the baths (or, worse, in a brothel) had stolen the silver vinaigrette given him by his mother at parting in Paris, which had soured him with them all, even with the girls he and Veit kept at the hotel, and Bümm's catamites. He looked at them as if they might be thieves, and saw how repulsive they were. That they should touch his mother's present – given him as a prophylactic against the smells and fevers of the East – was a desecration of herself. Shame, and the tremor of disquiet at losing a talisman, made him now sit up abruptly in his cloak-wrapping in the *oda musaffir* at Tchardourhissar, and wish for the day to begin. He got up and went to the door with the intention of waking Giorgio to make him breakfast.

'Where are you going?' asked Pitcher's voice from within the muslin, which made him invisible to Roland.

'To wake Giorgio.' Roland disliked the idea of having been watched unawares.

'I have told him to have our coffee prepared at seven today, as we're not marching, so I shouldn't disturb him, old fellow.'

'Hang it, he's servant to both of us, you know.'

'Just so, but someone must give the orders all the same.'

'How long is it till seven?'

Told that he had thirty-five minutes to wait, Roland lay down again in his cloak with a carpet-bag for a pillow.

There had been no quarrel over his rejoining Pitcher's march instead of taking the Counts' tour to the Holy Land. Before Pitcher had appeared in their midst from Constantinople, recovered from his illness though plunged into a harsh and unappeasable mood, Roland had rather hoped that he and the Counts might escape before Pitcher came up with them, and that he would thus be let off the crossing of Asia Minor to the Syrian coast, of whose severities so much had been threatened. But when his gloomy Mentor had knocked at the gate, Roland complied with the summons without repining. One companion suited him pretty much as well as another. He objected, though, to its being made out that it was a matter of duty to march to Syria so as to deliver a letter from his father to a Mr Mangles at Antioch.

'I don't give a rap for Mangles, or for Papa's letter,' he had said. 'Pray don't make the journey for my sake.'

'It ain't for you and it ain't for me,' Pitcher had replied. 'It's Vinegar must meet Mangles, it's Vinegar's got your father's letter to him about the Orontes navigation scheme.'

'Oh, Lord,' said Roland, blowing out smoke from his narghile where he sat among silken bolsters in the German hotel. 'We're to run all over Asia to please Vinegar now, are we?'

'I suppose what it is, Farr, you don't care to leave Veit and Bümm.'

'I don't care a pin who I leave – that's to say, I don't care for one fellow's company more than another. We'll go and see Mangles, if Vinegar wants it.'

So Pitcher was jealous of him taking up with the jolly Counts! Jealousy alone explained his bitter tone. It gave Roland a shock, as though he found himself tugged at by a dangerous current whilst intending, as usual, merely to paddle in shallows and to bask. At Cambridge surely there were no jealousies? But at Cambridge there were none of these uncomfortable fellows of Pitcher's sort, and class, for ever imagining slights. Roland hardly cared: it was perfectly true that one companion suited him pretty much as well as another. Men as widely liked as Roland, and as affable, and as good-natured, are not often found to apply a high standard in choosing their companions.

The first three days of their journey from Broussa had been perfectly tolerable. Ah, but the terrors and trials would begin later, beyond this park scenery, beyond the Black Castle of Afyon, on the high salt wilderness around fanatical Konia – so Pitcher threatened. However, these threats and terrors ahead were becoming, for Roland, less features of the topography of Turkey, than a feature of the topography of his companion's mind. It was a part of Roland's amiability that he didn't consciously analyse his friends' mentalities, or indeed his own; as a result of experience, though, he found himself possessing certain rather altered opinions of Pitcher. For the moment they masked themselves in the amusement he took in Pitcher's gloomy prognostications of hardship to come.

'Come on, Pitcher, it must be seven now. Do go and wake Giorgio, there's a good fellow, for you're a firmer hand at it than I.'

They had arrived the evening before at Tchardour at the end of a ride which had carried them forty miles south from Cotyaeium, in Phrygia (as Pitcher's *Useful Knowledge* map called the little town of Kootaya below its castled rock). It was a fine landscape. There had been in the dawn a valley of grass fields, with a swift little river running full between leaning willows, and fishermen out netting the stream; above this, and above a rocky gorge holding the headwaters of the river, they had crossed a high, lonely tract of dust and stone, its whitish volcanic soil dotted with a scrub of evergreens, and had made a long descent towards the plain of the Rhyndacus with, always in their faces across the levels below, snow-covered mountain ranges in Pisidia and Pamphilia lying across their road to the south. Now and again a wayside fountain, so worn as to resemble natural rock, showed that the track, lonely now and broken-surfaced, followed the line of an ancient highway.

It was the ruins of Azana that they had stopped at Tchardour to see. This purpose Roland accepted, as he accepted all else in the job-lot of travel, but he found that he cared awfully little for 'ruins', now that breakfast was done – bread and *kymak* and *yahoort* supplied by the villagers – and he looked forward to an idle day with perhaps a little fishing in the stream which he had noticed flowing through the village on their arrival in the dusk last evening. So, when Pitcher came to the door with his hat on his head, and looked in to enquire if he was ready for the ruins, Roland replied from his seat against the wall:

'I thought I might try a little fishing before the sun's too strong on the water.'

'Fishing? But we don't need fish, I've had Giorgio buy a sheep for our dinner, I told you at breakfast.'

'I know we don't need it – I should like to do it, that's all. Can I take one of those lines you brought? Where are they?'

'I don't want those lines used up playing about here, you know, Farr, I don't indeed. There may come a time when we shall need to depend on them.'

'I shan't use them up, never fear. I'll ask Giorgio to look one out, shall I?'

'For Heaven's sake don't let Giorgio pull everything about! And you haven't a rod. I should give it up and come along to the ruins.'

'What became of your passion for fishing, eh, Pitcher? In your grandfather's rivers in Scotland, wasn't it, that you used to tell me of?'

'In Scotland is one thing,' said Pitcher rather hastily. 'Besides, in Scotland there aren't classical ruins to look at.'

'Well, I should rather fish than look at ruins.'

'You never saw a Greek ruin yet.'

'Well, did you? Where have you seen any ruins?'

'You forget I've been at Rome. Besides,' Pitcher went on, 'my uncle, you know, my uncle at Rainshaw, has a library full of ruins and travels to ruins – why, there's Sir Charles Fellows's book has two or three drawings in it of these ruins at Azana, which I've looked at a dozen times at Rainshaw.'

'Oh, well, if you've got it all up from books then I dare say . . . but I shall try a little fishing first, if you'll just be a good fellow and look out a line for me. I shall catch you up. And some flies, too, if you please,' he called after Pitcher, who had stamped away.

These Scottish grandfathers with their rivers, and Rainshaw Park uncles with their libraries, and this knowledge of Rome and ruins, rather irritated Roland with the false notes they seemed to him to strike in a Waterways' clerk. Never mind – poor fellow! When Roland had obtained the line and two or three flies which Pitcher had left for him with Giorgio, he set out for the course of the stream above the village, which willows marked. A wand from these willows he cut for a rod, and was soon dabbling a Marlow Buzz in the sparkly runs of the Rhyndacus, here very little wider than the stream which ran more loudly over its stones between Ravenrig and the sea. But he was not keen on fishing. He found himself forced into fishing so as to avoid clambering over ruins – which he pictured as the heaps of dark stone which had frequently bored him in Wales – when all he wished for was to idle about and smoke cigars. If fish there were in the bright water, they would not take the fly. He was picking his way along the bank into the village, occasionally throwing out a line, when he saw the bridge.

Its seven stone arches crossed the stream, and the seven arches, and the cut piers, and the face of the bridge carved into garlands, showed such workmanship amongst the mean dwellings that Roland stared in wonder. His rod trailed in the water. His first thought was to tell Pitcher what he had discovered, so that the poor fellow should waste no more time climbing over ruins when he could see this masterpiece of antiquity entire.

Not quite entire, he now saw. Some of the moulding, and much of the parapet – more and more was missing the closer he looked – had fallen into the water. A length of carved masonry was being used by washerwomen in the shallows to thump their laundry upon, and another, in midstream, served as a roost for a party of ducks. He saw this, but still the impression remained with him that the bridge was perfect. What it had lost, it could afford to lose without losing its beauty and its dignity, which made up its perfection.

He climbed the mud bank into village lanes. Dogs woke, hens scattered, children's dirty faces looked over walls under fig trees, and out of the black holes of doorways. Eyes looked at him out of the quickly-muffled faces of women. He smiled at dogs and children and women alike, and walked on with the willow rod dancing in his hand. Houses faced one another across narrow lanes of dust and shadow. He noticed now, as though the marvel of the bridge had opened his eyes, that the masonry foundations of these dwellings, on which stood the mud-brick upper storey, was formed of cut stone and marble, and even of entablature and metope, taken evidently from some fallen city. Where a wooden doorpost had rotted, the drum of a fluted column, or a Corinthian capital, supported it: at a corner, with goats drinking from it, stood a carved sarcophagus full of green water: the commonest mud-wall of a yard rose upon a marble base. He found the house where they had slept, larger than most, with a wooden outside stair and a vine on its wall, and there he left his rod and line before following the direction he had seen Pitcher take.

He saw his friend on the slope of a low hill outside the village, and hurried towards him. Pitcher waited, seated on a block of marble. 'Well?' he called out. 'Sick of fishing?'

'Have you seen the bridge?' called Roland in reply. Too impatient to wait for an answer, he went on as he approached up the slope, 'I was fishing and I just found it. Really, you must come. It's perfect.'

Pitcher looked out at him from the shade of his wide hat. 'A bridge?' he said with gentle amusement, and made a gesture of his hand inviting Roland to turn and look back from the hillside.

Roland turned. 'Oh,' he said, as the prospect broke over him, 'my word. My word. I say, does anyone know of this, do you think?'

Below, near the village, the ground swelled into a dais, and on this green lawn arose the columned stone, and light and shadow, of a temple. It was the most glorious work he had ever seen. It was sublime. But there was an austerity about the worn lines of column and pediment – a purity of sun-bleached stone – which confronted Roland's mind as severely as a proposition in Euclid. When a stork flapped off its nest on a broken column of the peristyle, Roland's eye followed the bird's flight gratefully into the empty sky, resting his mind from the severities of the temple.

Ah, yes, the temple was beautiful, of course – but see how the little parties of goslings bowl about the green around it, with mother-goose jogging after them and little goose-girls with long wands marshalling their charges! See the older girls, too, muffled in veils in the temple's shade, perhaps worth strolling to look at . . . So his eye set to its work of trivialising, so that the sight before him would fit into a shallow mind without disturbing it. How jolly it would be to have bridges and temples at home in one's park as the great houses do. He would suggest it for Ravenrig. So his eye came back to the temple, and withstood another confrontation with that austere geometry. He had taken off his forage cap. A touch of colder air from the far-off snows behind the temple stirred through his curls.

'It is awfully grand,' he said, 'most awfully grand.'

Pitcher rose from the stone and took his arm. 'Come,' he said, 'I'll show you more.'

They climbed to the crest of the mound and looked down beyond into the glimmering half-moon of a marble theatre sunk into the flank of the hill. Tier upon carved tier of steps rippled down into the depths, the happy light flowing over them like a torrent over falls. At the bottom, where the stage had been, willows grew in water which lapped the lowest seats. The old earth clasped the theatre's foundation and slowly pulled it down, cracking the marble, sinking it, engulfing this brilliant plaything which seemed to Roland to utter the cry for pity of Persephone in the grasp of 'the gloomy monarch'.

'Well?' asked Mentor at his side, still holding his arm.

The theatre's beauty, or its plight, had touched Roland's heart so that tears filled his eyes. He turned his face to Pitcher and shook his head. 'Oh, the waste,' he murmured, 'the waste!'

Pitcher pressed his arm. 'You see how earthquakes have shaken the benches out of true?' he asked almost eagerly.

'I know, I know,' Roland replied, as if that was the very point he mourned in the theatre's slide towards the underworld.

'And you see the detail of the carving?' Pitcher continued, touching with his foot the baluster supporting a bench-end. 'See it? Everywhere the detail! Marvellous detail! And all of it useless. All of it useless,' he repeated on a note of triumph.

Roland disliked the note. 'Useless? I don't know so much – '

'Useless because it ain't what counts, that's why. Detail ain't. Details don't stop the barbarian, when he decides to shut you down. Carving your bench-ends don't stop the earthquake swallowing down your theatre whole. No, no!'

Roland heard the exultation in Pitcher's voice, and was affronted. He felt himself attacked in the attack on pretty details. 'Well,' he said, 'we have the plays that were performed here, earthquakes or not. Ain't that something? The theatre may go to the Devil, if we still have the plays that were given here.'

'Plays? And what in perdition is the use of a Greek play, to that fellow ploughing down there, and cursing at the bits of Greek marble for getting in his way?'

'Of course it ain't any use to a beastly Turk,' exclaimed Roland, 'of course it ain't. It's our history, not his. The plays and the temples and the details and everything about it – it's Europe's history, not Asia's, not these people squatting in the ruins here. And what counts we've taken away with us. What counts we've already got, and have based ourselves upon. Based our ideas on. Marbles and carvings and such is all detail, yes, and it don't matter a hang what becomes of it, if the thrust behind it carries on. Elgin there, taking the Parthenon marbles there was such a fuss about, he was only like a fellow collecting the title-deeds to the property he's been living upon for generations by right of inheritance. Of course it's nothing to a beastly Turk, for it ain't his history, all this. The soil is his history, and there he is down there ploughing it, as I dare say he was when the Greeks was up here carving swags on the benches and looking forward to hearing the *Medea* when they'd done.'

'Oh – !' Pitcher turned angrily away. 'I hope you'll find such rubbish a comfort when London lies in ruins! – and when they come for your head with their scythes to Ravenrig! Then you'll see how much use your gas-lamps and constables are, and your Greek plays.'

He had walked off down the steps between the marble benches, and shouted up the last words over his shoulder, so that they came to Roland magnified by Greek acoustics and very clear. Pitcher's bitterness was very clear. Roland turned the other way, and walked back to the top of the hill.

He looked out over the landscape so gracefully decorated with the wreckage of grandeur, over hillocks and dells encrusted with fragments of marble and cut stone which showed the vast extent of the vanished city. Swallows chased over wheat and grass brilliantly enamelled with the colours of wild flowers: from a distant tomb arose the clatter of a stork's bill as her mate came wheeling and dropping through the blue sky to her nest: a hoopoe ran quick about the stony ground: near and far there was peace. In the midst of all, cynosure of all, stood the temple on its green dais, which communicated to him again its high, severe idea of purity, and which appeared perfect, despite all that it had lost to earthquakes and Turks and time. Around the temple the goose-girls watched their charges, and around the Greek city's ruins lay the village landscape of orchard and pasture and wheat. Each part fitted into each in harmony. By hearing the harmony, he himself was attuned to it. This was what he had discerned, which Pitcher was blind to, and deaf to, in the bitter solace he drew from destruction. The only sound from the landscape below was the insistent unmusical clink of a ploughshare against stones, or fragments of marble, where the man Pitcher had pointed out was ploughing behind three little ponies harnessed abreast, under some orchard trees.

Thinking that he would walk back and see what was proposed for dinner, Roland began to descend the mound towards the village. He soon found himself in a narrow valley cut into its flank. Perhaps it had been a stadium, its steep sides once banked with seats, like the theatre, for masonry arches which might have supported such stands could be seen in the scrub and bramble at the foot of either slope. They showed dark, like the mouths of caves. The air was hot and still. Intrigued by those half-buried Cyclopean arches, which had once perhaps upheld thousands cheering a chariot race in this silent arena – or had even been the dens of wild beasts to be loosed on poor Christians – he thought he would explore them. The idea of snakes occurred to him, and he broke off a dead stick from a thorn-tree to rattle on stones as he climbed towards the half-silted openings into the hillside. He had reached such a cave-mouth, and was banging his stick on its masonry, and peering into its earth-dwelling dark, when a lion slipped between further arches and bounded away. A *lion!*

He knew instantly, amazed as he was, that it was a lion. Yet it wasn't what he expected a lion to look like. Out slipped this lean, tawny beast, almost the colour of the stone, thin-flanked and somehow slight, with the mere sketch of leonine mane, and was gone in a ripple of light on muscle up the hillside. It was gone. But it was a lion, without doubt.

'Pitcher!' Excitement filled the hollow inside him. A lion! He must tell Pitcher – if only Pitcher could have seen it! 'Pitcher!' Calling his name, Roland scrambled and slipped and clambered up the steep where the lion had bounded, losing his forage cap as he went, and was soon running along the crest between theatre and stadium. When he saw Pitcher down below amongst the tiers of marble benches he shouted: 'A lion! A lion!'

Pitcher too was shouting something, which Greek acoustics brought clearly to Roland's ears: 'Hat! Put your hat on.'

'Lion!' Roland shouted back, cupping his hands to his lips. Perhaps Greek acoustics prevent the audience shouting at the actors on the stage, for Pitcher appeared not to hear, but climbed the steps calling out at intervals:

'Hat! Wear your hat, you ass!'

'Lion! I've seen a lion!'

* * *

[266]

From *Journal of a Land-March towards India*, by O. Q. Vinegar
(Capt.)
Azana, June 28th 1850

It is not, I suppose, quite every traveller whose sword has been
stained with a lion's blood, but such was my case today. We began
peaceably enough, for, although the boys tossed and turned a
good deal in endeavouring to sleep in a Turkish *oda musaffir*, I
confess that I, wrapped in my soldier's cloak upon an earthen
floor, there reposed myself more soundly in Morpheus' arms
than ever I did among the silken hangings of an Emperor's Court,
and I awoke to make a hearty traveller's breakfast upon the simple
fare offered us by these wild villagers.

After breakfast the boys were at me to show them fishing.
Never loth to practise 'the gentle art', I soon led the way to the
Rhyndacus where, offering up apologies to old Izaak for the
roughness of my tackle, I made a few casts in the *un*-blushful
Hippocrene, and soon had several brace of fine chubb, of two or
three pounds weight, upon the bank. Tiring of such easy sport,
I left P— to tempt the fishy denizens, and wandered with F—
upstream. So closely sowed is the ground with ruins, and fragments of ruins, that here the very moles pitch up antiquities in
their hillocks, and, when one needs to pelt the village dogs, it is
fragments of the antique that lie ready for use – a finger following
a nose, say, or, in grave cases of attack, an entire hand may be
thrown at a persistent cur. Following the stream, we came plump
upon a rousing sight: ten or a dozen village maidens were dis-
porting themselves in the fluid, having cast aside, with their
chemises, every vestige of feminine attire. Loud were their
shrieks as some half their number plunged up to the neck in the
now *blush*ful Hippocrene, whilst their bolder – and, dare I say,
prettier – sisters remained standing very much as Eve must have
stood when holding out the apple with a roguish smile to Adam.
It was, no doubt, only my grizzled whiskers which made them
suppose themselves safe in focusing their smiles upon me, and
ignoring young F—, rather to his discomfiture. We beat a retreat,
but I warrant those unclothed Nereid forms will swim oft times
before my companion's eye, when he pines amid the crinolines
and hoop-petticoats of May Fair. When P— heard of our
adventure, he voted angling poor sport after all (for he had
caught nothing) and wrapped up his lines in disgust.

It was now the turn of antique beauties to beguile the eye. The bridge we came upon, which carries the village traffic, a Roman work of Adrian's time, and well enough in its florid way, made a vast impression upon F—. One forgets that an eye unused to stumbling over these wrecks of Roman ambition, in the midst of vigorous Turkish life, cannot interpret them aright, and F— was ready to mourn the decay of Roman grandeur, when he ought more properly to have mocked the absurdity of Roman pretension, and, indeed, of Imperial pretension altogether, in having believed it possible to export into the midst of Asia Minor, or any other Colonial possession, a tax-farming middle class to live at the expense of a local population.

Despite location in a hostile land, Azana was evidently a city of no military strength, having neither a position of natural defence, nor artificial fortifications. No, a pretentious ambition had erected those palaces and temples, and theatres and baths and stadia, in the open plain, and a complacent arrogance had neglected to fortify them. Well, we saw their wreck – the wreck of that selfsame conceit which might, in our century, build a Tunbridge Wells, or a Cheltenham, upon the open plain at, let us say, Caunpoor or Lucknow, and then affect surprise when the native *sipahi* forecloses (as he will!) upon frivolity and idleness lacking armed strength to back it, and throws down our pleasure-domes, and massacres our women and children.

The boys were delighted with the ruins, and ran about imagining picnic-parties as if they were amongst the follies of an Oxford-shire park; meantime the stoic Turk, an object-lesson in *quieta non movere*, ploughed his ground with an instrument identical with the cashcroom I have seen in use by the stoic Caledonian in the wilds of Wester Ross, and I meantime made experiments with a thermometer to ascertain our height above the sea level, a point which the few earlier travellers to this remote spot had not established.

I had climbed for this purpose the Hill of the Theatre (as I have named it), and the two boys were idling after me, poking into holes and thickets among the masonry, like a pair of spaniel-puppies nosing through a West Cork cover after woodcock, when I heard a cry of alarm – nay, of deadly fear! Back I rushed, supposing that some accident had occurred. Picture my dismay when a shaking and white-visaged P— informed me that young

[268]

F— was held prisoner within a cavern of the hillside by – a lion!

A few strides brought me to the cave entrance, and I looked in. Sundry growls betokened that Leo was at home. I have brushed with him often enough in the thickets by the Tigris to respect his indomitable courage, and to have a right knowledge of his ferocity. Our assailant here was a large male, of a peculiarly yellow tinge, and he had F— fairly pinned within, whilst switching his tail and growling and rolling his eye from one of us to the other with a growing impatience. Knowing that he might at any instant spring upon his victim, my only thought was not of 'heroism', or of risk to my own life, but of extricating the boy in my charge from his deadly peril. How often must it be that a man dubbed 'hero' will look back in fear and trembling upon the very action which won him that honourable sobriquet? I had stuck in my sash that morning – for I wear the native garb – an old cavalry sword, once my father's, which completes my dress in the wilderness, and this weapon I now drew, and closed with the adversary.

I had never before fought with a lion beard-to-beard, and would have supposed that courage and fortitude of a do-or-die stamp is required of he who would challenge the King of the Beasts within his den. However, whether it be that the same grizzled whiskers, which had made the Adamite village virgins feel themselves safe in smiling upon me, now alarmed the lion, I know not; at all events, the battle was a brief one. A few snarls, and lashings-out with his formidable pads, which I was lucky enough to parry; a few cuts of my sword which fortunately went home, and Leo made off by a back-door onto the hillside, and was no more seen. F— had stood like a trump throughout, with never a whimper, and now both boys made a great to-do of their 'salvation', and, Giorgio learning the news, the whole village was soon apprised of my 'heroics', allowing me not a moment's peace without the hallooing and stamping and wagging of heads which is the tribute these rude fellows, who live by courage, will pay even to such a trivial case of audacity as my own.

I believe that songs were made up impromptu commemorating the event, which will doubtless perplex later travellers to the spot, who may wonder as to the identity of this foreign lion-tamer in the song, and will suppose him co-eval with Hercules. I regret that a lack of printing-presses at

Tchardourhissar prevents me from appending a copy of the verses to the present page, to be sung *con vivace* in rectory drawing rooms by the young ladies in hoop-petticoats aforementioned.

*   *   *

Captain Vinegar's characteristics, and his views and ideas, were very much in Pitcher's mind in those days of travel onwards from Azana by Afyon and Konia across the high Anatolian plateau towards the Taurus and Syria. The events of the day began to somersault themselves ever more rapidly into the form of Vinegar's Journal. In Vinegar's eyes everything that happened – and the native population, and his companion, and all aspects of Turkey – was background and supporting cast designed only for the purpose of displaying the Captain and his rugged virtues in their best light. As he worked his way into Vinegar's mind – or as Vinegar worked a way into his – Pitcher too came to see all that happened through Vinegar's eyes. And Vinegar became increasingly independent: on a day when both Pitcher and Farr were exceedingly low, owing to an attack of dysentery, and hadn't the strength to visit some fine lakes south of their road from Afyon which Giorgio told them of, still Vinegar wrote an account of the lakes into his Journal, and swam in them, and noted the quantities of magpies and irises round their shores. It was just as if the Captain's eye did remain lively in Pitcher's sick head. By describing the weather that day as 'akin to the most perfect English summer climate imaginable, which I alone, alas, could enjoy', an uncanny impression was produced, even in Pitcher's mind as he wrote the words, of the detached and superior existence of Captain Vinegar.

Now, two days to the east of Konia, about six in the evening, Pitcher and Farr were riding across a dreary tract in the kind of waking trance which settles on men who have ridden long hours across weary flats towards a horizon which does not change between dawn and dusk. As the sun declined behind them, and his horse's shadow lengthened on the sour tussocks of the steppe, Pitcher looked earnestly into the dim wastes ahead for the sun's low light to show him the walls of some khan or caravanserai that they might reach before night. Something malignant in the shadows and mists of evening, and in the failing power of light to keep them at bay, made Pitcher anxious. A phrase jogged in his mind read long ago in an old book of knights' journeys: 'Their desire is ever to reach the monastery ere the bat hath flown his cloistered flight.' Farr rode ten yards behind him, and they had not spoken for an hour at least. The two of them were quite alone, hastening across the vast landscape.

Giorgio was no longer with them. Pitcher had parted from him at Konia, without consulting Farr, after falling out with him very much as Vinegar might have done. At Konia they had used their *teskeré* to quarter themselves on a Greek merchant chosen by Giorgio in a half-ruined mud hovel with the meanest furnishings imaginable; both Farr and Pitcher had been unhappy to impose themselves on such evident poverty, telling Giorgio to assure their host that they would pay him well. No need, said Giorgio, for the man is rich, only here in fanatical Konia no Christian dare display wealth for fear of martyrdom. What! protested Pitcher, this creeping, abject wretch in rags a rich Christian? Ah, we are all Christians (said Giorgio) and must all take care.

In the collusive tone of this, Pitcher felt himself smeared with these rayahs' abasement. He remembered his disgust at Iznik with Giorgio's sly saying, 'We are two Christians'. Such spiritless humility was intolerable. Besides this, all memory of Iznik was uncomfortable to Pitcher, who had suspected (from looks shared between Giorgio and Farr) that the little Greek had betrayed to Farr his nadir of misery and weeping amidst the rains and ruins of Nicaea. So he was in a touchy mood in Konia, and ready to resent all slights. He bore with being jostled in the streets by fat Mussulmans on donkeys, for the hatred and contempt in the crowd's eyes warned him to take care. But when a gob of spittle splashed on his boot he swung round with a clenched fist, and found himself looking into flat uncivil eyes willing him to strike a blow. He saw, as he thought, Giorgio smirk at Farr. His clenched fist struck the Greek servant in the face. He persuaded himself that it was unwise to trust their safety to this creature whose fawning notions of Christian humility, and disrespect for his masters, might well cause him to sell them to the highest bidder amongst the robbers of Anatolia. Disrespect (as he told Farr when informing him of Giorgio's dismissal) is, in the East, a sure precursor of danger.

Farr, therefore, was quite alone with him as the sun sank upon them in the midst of nowhere two days east of Konia. No doubt Farr was apprehensive. Pitcher felt the responsibility of leadership not as a burden but as an accolade – a promotion. He said nothing to reassure Farr, imagining for him the disquiet, and dependence upon his guide, which Vinegar usually soke of as characterising 'the two boys'. With Vinegar's eye he noted a 'solitary stork, which, crossing the darkening sky, emphasized the lateness of the hour and the loneliness of our own position'.

Then, suddenly near, from a gully in the plain which the misty twilight had hidden from them, there emerged a train of eight or nine camels stalking along in the same easterly direction as themselves. Farr spurred up to him and spoke, cheered by the companionable sight of the soft-footed tall beasts hastening over the ground towards shelter which must now surely be within reach before dark. There was comradeship in hurrying towards the lively bustle of the caravanserai, where there was always an empty niche for the latecomer to make his hearth and smoke his pipe.

And now, as if the camel train had supplied its objective, a more solid shape appeared in the low dim wastes ahead, and hung there, and wavered, and changed its form in the mists as Pitcher stared at it. Was it a hill? Had it the broken outline of rocks, or of a ruined castle of the Middle Ages? At one moment he could make out towers, a keep, the gleam of sunset on western walls: at the next, all he saw was a low hill. Dusk advanced as fast as they advanced themselves, so the object grew no clearer. It was a disappointment when, after an hour's riding, the idea of towers and keep sank back into the mists, and all that remained of their hopes was a small, lonely hill looming out of the misty steppe.

Still the camels continued in line ahead, and still Pitcher and Farr followed. Close under the hill its shape divided itself into two, their route evidently lying between. The camels filed up a shallow pass, and Pitcher felt his horse quicken and brighten under him as he followed them between the volcanic hills. Revealed in the hills' hollow was a round and death-still lake of black water. But beyond, at the base of the volcanic rocks, stood the strong, square walls of a caravanserai, and the deep gate-arch under its stone lantern, and the glimmer of fires from its court.

'Here we are,' said Pitcher.

It was what he meant to say, casually, keeping surprise and even pride out of his voice at having conjured up this castle of refuge out of the Asiatic plain, but he had been silent for so many a long and dusty *farsakh* that his voice only croaked like a raven's.

An hour later, in the smoky dusk of the caravanserai's court, Pitcher made his way amongst the groups of men and animals with a bag of English gunpowder in his hand which he intended exchanging for eggs and bread when he should see what he wanted at one of the firesides. In place of his wide-brimmed hat he had wound a turban round his head so that he should be less stared at, his loose shirt was belted with a sash, and altogether he cut a large and imposing figure moving between firelight and shadow.

He had watched Giorgio barter for food, and now found himself obliged to plunge into the midst of things and make his own bargain. Having sacked Giorgio, he could not complain to Farr of doing Giorgio's work, and so he had set out into the hubbub of the courtyard with his bag of gunpowder as though it was the most natural thing in the world, leaving Farr in their niche to make up the fire to cook what food he might procure.

In the crowd of firelit faces, and the colours and scents and voices through which he passed, Pitcher guessed at the presence of half the races of the East. By one fire little camels lay among silk-bales and slant-eyed Chinese-looking drivers, by another squatted white-robed Egyptians, here a tall Persian lambskin hat nodded beside a turban, there a skullcap talked with a fez, men sold firewood, bought fodder, quarrelled and screeched – within the walled court, under the stars, was brought together the wide East from Roum to Cathay, and he walked through the midst of it, and was part of the immemorial scene. His position enchanted him. The scene through which he walked was delectable to him, the feast of existence. He felt himself to be the individual he had so long wanted to become. *I am here*, he said to himself, as if he had reached at last the centre of his being.

It still remained to buy food. He rather shrank from accosting these wild Asiatics, who were so busy, and noisy, and fierce. Captain Vinegar would have dropped on his haunches by that fire where the fellow was cooking rice, or beside those two raking their bread out of the fire, or he would have picked a chicken from the bunch that Mongol-looking rogue was swinging upside down from his hand. What the Captain would have done, he must do. It was not enough to be here, a spectator; he must act.

At last he succeeded in exchanging his powder for a basket of eggs from a barefoot trader with long matted hair on his shoulders like a dervish, and mad cross-eyes. Some of the eggs he pressed on a party of quiet country travellers for two flaps of the bread they were baking on an iron dish in embers of their fire. One of these old men had the fragments of a red rose in his hand, which he pressed to his nose now and then, picked God knows where in the desolation stretching away from the caravanserai's walls.

The eggs and bread which Tresham carried back through the crowd towards his and Farr's quarters seemed to him the first food he had ever earned in his life. His heart expanded within him. All the vexations of cities and society – all jealousy and irritation – cleared from his mind. Things were again as they had once been, and he was independent, and free, and he had Farr with him safe. He understood the satisfaction of the bridegroom who finds himself alone at last with a much-courted bride in the closed carriage that dashes them away from the wedding-breakfast.

But what was this, in the cave-like niche in the stone wall which had been allotted to them? No fire? He saw their two horses eating chopped straw, his own still saddled, Farr's unsaddled. A candle lit the interior of the niche and showed their belongings strewn about. But there was no fire. There was only Farr's bent back, and the soles of his boots, as he knelt and blew at the blackened sticks.

'That won't do,' said Tresham cheerily. 'That'll never burn.'

'I'm sorry, Pitcher.' Farr got to his feet. 'I never could make fires go.'

'Never mind.' Tresham patted his arm. 'But be a good fellow, do, and put the saddle back on your horse.'

They had disagreed about this each evening, Farr insisting on following the European custom of unsaddling, Pitcher urging the Eastern usage of leaving the horse saddled day and night throughout a journey. Now at last Farr complied, resaddling his horse while

Tresham dismantled the fire, rebuilt a pyramid of sticks over a little of the horses' straw, took a hot coal from a boy carrying round a tray of embers as lights for travellers' pipes, and soon had flames crackling brightly. Farr had come back, and lounged watching on his carpet. 'We've got a slave-merchant three doors down,' he said presently, taking the cigar from his mouth. 'You should go and look.'

Tresham said nothing, breaking eggs into the cooking pot.

'Or perhaps he's just a Turkish gent taking his hareem for an airing,' Farr went on. 'He's got the girls tucked up in one of those travelling contraptions with curtains to it, but if you walk by it's like throwing a fly over a trout, and you're sure of a pair of eyes at least.'

'You'll be sure of a knife in your back.'

'I'd risk that if it would get me feminine company.'

'You keep clear. You ain't at Broussa now, you know. You can't run about here in a fez and curly slippers between the slave-market and the brothel, or you'll get a knife in your back as sure as fate.'

'Well, I'm not going about with a long face expecting to be murdered every minute, that's certain. There's no fun in that.'

'Fun!' Tresham beat the eggs in the pot.

'Yes,' said Farr, 'fun.' There was a silence, Tresham stirring the eggs over the fire, Farr watching him with his hands interlocked on his bright hair, and his cigar glowing in his bearded mouth as he breathed. 'No,' he said at last, as if he had been trying over a conundrum in his mind, and gave it up, 'no, I can't take it seriously. It ain't any more real than a page in the Arabian Nights. Compared to Ravenrig, I mean, or Berkeley Square, or Great Court. It just don't ring true, somehow. It's as if all these fellows were dressed up to look like fellows in the East. Don't you find that? The last thing in life they are is frightening. If one of them was to take out his knife, it would be sure to have a paper blade like a knife in a pantomime. But I'll take care, never fear,' he said amiably, pitching his cigar-butt into the fire and looking eagerly at the cooking pot.

They ate the eggs folded into the flaps of tough bread, as delectable in Tresham's mouth as the whole scene to his senses. Farr boiled some water and brewed tea afterwards, which they sat drinking by the fire. Shared food and firelight and casual talk smoothed Tresham's ruffled feelings. Of course, Farr did not really think the caravanserai, and their

[275]

situation in its midst, 'unreal' in comparison with an absurd castle in Wales! Between puffs at the long cherry-wood stem of his *tchibouk* he said, 'You know, there's very likely goods of your father's amongst the merchandise in the court here. Did you think of that? Very likely. Or ventures his money is behind, at least. And I'll wager there's merchants here his name is known to.'

'Well?'

'Well – don't that convince you of the reality of it all? I remember you believed in the Danube steamer, when you found the Captain knew of your father.'

'Yes, and you said I should try my paces beyond where my father was known. Well, I did. I have.'

Tresham puffed derisive smoke. 'You haven't yet put a foot beyond your father's sphere of influence!'

'My father's sphere of influence don't define reality any more,' retorted Farr. 'I work by quite another map. It's what I've found out on my travels – that I may navigate by quite another map of the world than the one my father drew out. That's growing up out of childhood, it seems to me. What's most real to Papa ain't real a bit to me. Never was. Bolt Court where he has his shop in the City never was a place I could believe in – not like the West End, I mean. No, no. And now I shan't care that it's so, as I used to. He shall keep to his map, and I to mine, and we shall both be happier for it. Now, old fellow, I believe I shall turn in, for I'm devilish sleepy all of a sudden.'

Long after Farr had rolled himself in his cloak, and laid himself down on his carpet within the niche, Tresham sat smoking at the door over the fire's embers. The caravanserai slowly resolved itself into stillness and sleep, and darkness under the stars. Brought together to withstand the night, its elements would disperse across Asia with the sun's earliest rays. Each on his own adventure, whether occasioned by pilgrimage or by trade – or by the mere restlessness of the wanderer which was like the windblown dust percolating into every niche of the caravanserai – each traveller would resume at first light his own journey under the sun's eye. Tresham lived over again in his mind the dawn starts of his own march, saw again the misted hollows of a valley at a hut door, and minarets and poplars insubstantial in early haze, and a mosque dome lighted by the first beams of the sun through the smoke of breakfast fires, and the path up the mountainside ahead. He felt again the heat of the sun at noon overhead, and saw the caravanserai's walls far across the steppe at dusk. Surely no life so freed the soul of man – out of the shadows into the brilliance of reality.

It came into his mind that no spot where he had ever stood – not the mountainside in Scotland, nor the navvies' camp, nor his bivouac under a hedge on his trip through the canals – would so suit his father as the spot where he now was. His father was a wanderer, at least his son's idea of him was that. Had he himself been searching always to find the place where his father would have been at home, and would most readily have joined his son? – and did his happiness now consist in having found it?

He lay down to sleep, aware of the immense sweep of the world away from the caravanserai's walls on every side. The night sky above, with its space crossed by the stars' journeys, was a metaphor of Eastern travel graphically before his eyes.

*　　*　　*

Caravanserai of Sultanieh
Middle of Nowhere, July 12th (I think) 1850

My dear Enid,

Here I am, a dot in the immensity of Asia, a long day's ride having effected no visible change whatever in our surroundings, just as if we had been riding round a treadmill from dawn to dusk! I am crouched outside a kind of den in the caravanserai wall, our lodging for the night, blowing at a fire of damp sticks – or I was, until I rebelled, and took out the pen and ink of civilisation to remind myself that such accomplishments as writing still exist, and that a letter penned here, in this grotesque mediæval phantasy, may yet be read at a Berkeley Square breakfast-table, and be spattered with real English marmalade.

Have we been a month on the road? – a year? – four centuries? There is no future, no past, only the dot of existence amid nothingness. The plain extends for ever, in all directions. In the dark of each morning we set out across a landscape which dawn reveals in all its hopelessness. Perhaps, far off, a leaden mist hangs about low hills: how eagerly I spur towards such incidents – such hopes – which will surely exchange the weary plain for broken country, and trees, and streams! Alas, after two or three hours we climb through that rim of rocks to find ourselves merely upon another and more dreary plain at a higher and more barren level. Here and there a sour marsh-pool reflects the sky. In the shape of humankind, for which I pine, all that exists is the occasional dark outline of a Turcoman shepherd in his cloak of felt, which makes a kind of triangular sentry-box he stands in. So still does he stand, and so long is he in view amid the flatness, that he has taken on the character of an ancient watch-tower, hoary with age, by the time he sinks from sight into the wastes behind us. Meanwhile his dogs, great brutes in spiked collars to preserve them from wolves, may or may not have made a furious attack upon us, at the caprice of their master.

Well, will you continue our day's march with us? When we have done thinking over the shepherd and his dogs, we ride some hours without thoughts at all, before stopping by some brackish puddle to make tea (the one luxury in our baggage) and chew at a flap of leather bread; then we ride on another few hours, nothing in our view changing save the sinking of the sun behind us, and the thickening of Tartarian shades ahead of us, until eyes tired with staring into dim emptiness fashion the outline of a rock into the lantern over a caravanserai's gate, or the shadow of a cloud into a grove of trees. Is it? – Isn't it? – Hooray! – At last the irrefutable fact takes shape, of walls, trees, shade, water, rest. It is at this moment of certitude that Pitcher always announces the caravanserai out loud over his shoulder, like the guard on the railway train, as though he had invented it especially. Under the gate-arch we ride into the courtyard, which is about the size of Trinity Great Court as a rule, with smiles cracking our dusty burnt faces.

Then it is that my keenest disappointment of the day is felt. For what have we arrived at? A verminous, half-ruined fortress of the Middle Ages! That is the goal we have attained with excitement throbbing in our bosoms over so many a weary league! I repeat, it is the worst moment of the day. In England, now, if you exert yourself thus – find yourself cast loose at the end of a long hunt, say, and must ride ten miles home through cold rain, or tumble in a sea-channel stalking geese on a December

[278]

marsh – in England when you attain your goal, why, you are HOME, and you will find a hot-water bath before a fire of sea-coal in your bedroom grate, and the dinner–gong sounding as you button on a clean shirt. I suppose I am always half-persuaded in my mind that I shall reach home at the end of each day, and so I am always disappointed.

Not Captain Vinegar, though – or Tresham Pitcher if you prefer that name for my travelling-companion – no, not he! He is come into his element. He bustles his way into one of these wretched stone dens in the walls, and busies himself unpacking his traps and setting them out in just the same nice order as he set them out last night, and the night before, and will no doubt continue to set them out in niches in the walls of caravanserais all the way to India. To Vinegar we have reached a very satisfactory goal. But then I suppose he never did go out hunting at home, and get rained on, and know the comforts of a country-house; no doubt if a man's idea of home is Clapham, or Creech Lane, he will reconcile himself a good deal sooner to a stone cave amongst a set of savages in the wilds of Asia. Once his belongings are set out to a T, he dresses himself up like a native and off he strolls into the crowd to 'hear the news', as he puts it – though in reality, of course, he cannot exchange a single word with the dirty fellows swarming in the court.

To the groans of camels (which I echo inwardly) I set about lighting a fire. But of course the fellow has sold us damp wood, since we are giaours and deserve no better, and moreover have no Giorgio to bargain for us any more. Yes, we have 'let Giorgio go', as Mamma says of the footmen, and our kind, timid little Greek is gone, turned off by Pitcher for the offence of being a Christian, and therefore inclined to sing too small to suit his swagger.

Dear Enid, you will think I am hard upon Pitcher, and mock him unfairly, and that all the while you would take his side if you was here. Earnestly have I pondered his character, as his ramrod back recedes ahead of me hour after hour across the wastes of Asia, as oversized on his little quad as a Turk on a donkey. What drives him? Discontent with what is, and longing for what might be, those two elements called by the Greeks $\pi o\theta o\varsigma$, which together make up that curious animal, a traveller. $\pi o\theta o\varsigma$: it affected Alexander the Great, and it affects the wandering beggar-

[279]

man you throw a sixpence at in the street – and I, who haven't got it a bit, am attached to the coat-tails of a fellow with a raging case of the disease!

Whilst I am writing, the fire has quite gone out! Up I spring full of guilt to repair my fault, just as I used to do when I heard his step upon the stair at school when the same calamity had occurred in his grate. Farewell! I am in good health and spirits, repining only occasionally – when I see amid the wastes a poor little wheatear, say, who seems as much an exile from our Welsh moors as myself – or when I think of the paved streets and gas-lamps of May Fair, which seem to make a charade of what we endure, as though a man was to choose to live in the Middle Ages. But – here comes Captain Vinegar stalking home through the crowd, and I must act my part of fag and go down on my knees and pretend to be blowing humbly at his fire.

Yr. aff. twin

R.F.

PS I add a line next morning whilst Pitcher is scientifically loading the horses – with poor Giorgio we had to abandon many comforts, such as the portable soup and the green umbrella which Pitcher bought at Pera, yet I retain my dress-clothes for interviewing potentates, and Pitcher retains his sword-box and his Levinge-bed, so our nags are as well laden as tinkers' ponies. I forgot to tell you (it seems so long ago) what occurred when I was poking in the old ruins at Azana, and roused up – what do you think ? – a LION! A small and shabby lion, to be sure, but lion it was. Why, I felt quite like Captain Vinegar for an instant, before it cantered off ever so quick. Pitcher, who hadn't seen my lion, denied its existence. He said there are no lions in those parts. Of course, I let the matter drop, but it was provoking in him. Tell Mamma that her son has faced a lion, and see if she don't drop the coffee-pot! R.F.

PPS While Pitcher yet struggles with straps and buckles I will tell you our great news: by the earliest light this morning mighty mountains well splashed with snow have appeared to the south, the Taurus, giving us hope that we will soon be quit of these plains, and will descend through the Cilician Gates to the Mediterranean, and Scanderoon, and Antioch. R.F.

VIII

————————

Beit-el-ma (formerly the Grove of Dafne)
near to Antioch, in Syria

August 7th 1850

My dear Mother,
    I wrote you such a gloomy account of myself from Iznik,
as I tried to prepare myself to cross Asia Minor, that I did not
send it. Since that place there has been no chance of finding a
post-bag for England until this, when my letter will join the
despatches of Mr Mangles, our host, the British Consul at
Antioch. For here I am in the Elysian south after my crossing of
Asia Minor, tested and tried by near two months' hard marches,
and better content with myself than I ever was in my life. From
its nadir in the marshes of Lake Ascania, my strength has
mounted with the sun to a zenith in this southern clime.
    A day-to-day account of my journey you will one day
read in a book of travels issued under my pseudonym of 'Captain
Vinegar'. Now I will try to give you a glimpse of myself as I settle
into my berth in that entrepôt of Eastern travel, a caravanserai
on the wild steppe of Anatolia. Imagine an old stone courtyard
like that of a mediæval castle, half in shadow from the declining
sun. Fill it with such clamour and diversity as only the furthest
corners of Asia can supply. Under the gate-arch arrive camel-
trains from India on the road to Smyrna, or mules from Russian
Tartary on the march to Egypt, or slaves from black Africa en
route for Constantinople. By one fire you see the shaggy little
Bactrian camel, by another the Arab's gleaming flank, by a third
is lighted the mild superior eye of the desert dromedary, who
seems ever wishing to raise himself above the paltriness of things,
and become a philosopher; surely such a scene, to a soldier –

[281]

Tresham stopped writing. He was not a soldier. He laid down his pen and read over what he had written. Captain Vinegar had crept into his hand, and had taken over writing this letter to his mother, as if it had been an entry in his Journal. Since the only writing Tresham did was in the Captain's character, in the Captain's Journal, this was not surprising; but it wouldn't do. Yet he was half-ashamed to remember the halting, disjointed sentences in which he had tried to express the truths and fears of his heart, from Kronstadt and from Iznik, in contrast with the Captain's ornate prose.

Ah, it was too hot and lazy here in the Consul's garden to rewrite. He listened to rushing waters which plunged into the gorge below the vine-arbour where he sat, and looked out from its shade over garden-walks, and shimmering evergreens clothing the hills, to far blue plains and heat-hazed mountains between Antioch and the sea. It was a paradise. And it was familiar to him, as a paradise foreknown in a dream. He would not rewrite, but he would put down if he could his own true feelings in the court of the caravanserai:

> . . . surely such a scene, dear Mother, is a wonderful thing! I walk in it as if on tiptoe in deep water, so conscious of the fullness and frailness of life. For I never was so aware of existing. Did you ever see a solitary tree struck by one wandering shaft of light in a dark landscape? I am that tree, so singled out by the vivid finger of life. When I ride into those caravanserais at dusk, as a knight-errant into a castle courtyard of old, with darkness and the threat of death all around, I am what I have ever longed to be. I am –

A movement at the further end of the garden-walk caught Tresham's eye so that he looked up. Farr had come into the garden from the mountain slopes beyond, where the fountains of Dafne's grove dashed down their green gorge to the Orontes, and was strolling through sunlight and shadow under the cinnamon-trunked arbutus trees which shaded the walk. At his side, in her diaphanous cloud of muslin, walked the Greek girl. Seeing them together, Tresham's heart took the short, unhappy step from solitude to loneliness. He looked back at his letter. He would give Farr the character he deserved.

[282]

I see [he wrote] that I have described it all as though I was alone, but of course Farr was always there. I would stroll back from bargaining for food for our dinner, and from hearing The news from a Tatar 'sureji' riding post from Baghdad, and from listening to the story-teller begin his tale, to find young Farr huffing away at a dying spark like the good fellow he is, though no better a hand at making a fire than he was when he fagged for me at school. I believe he can't puzzle much sense out of it all, though trying his best to make himself useful to me. Onward he drifts, wishing that our cosy niche was a room at the Hotel Meurice, and regarding a Kalmuck merchant offering him Bokhara plums with about as much curiosity as he would show the delivery-boy from Fortnum and Mason's. One touching little dart he made at establishing his character for a bold traveller occurred when he ran up to me in Phrygia shouting out that he had seen a lion! Unfortunately he had chosen a province where there are many dangers, but no lions. It was rather typical of him, to dream up an imaginary antagonist, where he certainly would not notice a real one. Of course I pretended no end of interest in his pet lion, and poked about sufficiently thoroughly to have discovered the Chimaera itself, had it been at home. Now, however, he is happier. I see him at the end of the garden-walk in which I write, making love to a Greek slave-girl whom our host rescued when an infant from a Turkish massacre of Greeks in some island or other (he bought a basket of infants on the sea-shore, rather as we buy a basket of lobsters, and this dark-eyed houri is the last left with him, the rest of the catch having been given away to friends). She is —

Tresham stopped writing. He would not describe the Greek girl. He would not think of her. He would not think of the lips in Farr's curling beard which had the dampness and coolness of a spring in a wood, surely irresistible to the Greek girl in this heat. He would think of the garden, and describe it in his letter. Pen in hand he surveyed the scene. Where should he begin?

Now that he looked, with a view to writing, the beauties of the garden seemed to withdraw, and hide themselves. The flowers, profuse in his mind's eye, were in reality dusty and scant, the grass rank, the heat lying heavy on the glitter of leaves. The loveliness of the garden as it had seemed when they had first come upon it existed for him more graphically than this reality. To be truthful, he must describe a garden which worked upon his reader that wonderful effect which this garden had wrought upon him: he must paint an imaginary paradise, if he was to convey a true picture of this real garden. So he closed his eyes, the better to see again the Eden he remembered, with its attendant ideas, from the evening of their arrival a week ago. Having descended the Taurus, and spent many days of fever-heat circling the marshy bay of Scanderoon, and climbing the sun-cracked rocks of the pass of Belen, they had ridden into half-ruined, dusty Antioch to be told that even now there was no rest, for Mr Mangles had removed to his summer cottage in the hills west of the city, and they must ride after him. On they had ridden, and in the evening light had climbed onto the shoulders of the hills, under the settled azure radiance of a classic sky which he recognised as the very sky he had loved in the library painting at Rainshaw, and had found at last a shadowy garden where . . .

Grapes ripen upon the trellises over my head [he wrote], everywhere fruits grow in profusion: the citron, the mulberry, the peach, the nectarine, the loquat, all are ripe, and all are of finer taste than those from the hothouses of the richest nobleman in England, while from arbours devised under the arbutus-walks at vantage points about this Eden you may glimpse through fangs of tawny rock the distant plain of Antioch, a world away amid its heat and dust and toil. Close at hand is the gorge of Dafne falling towards the plain, crossed most picturesquely at a mile's distance by a dark cape of rock deckled with the cypress-tree. Overhead, the tall whispering planes conspire; below, groves of bay-laurel and orange planted on terraces drop away into the gorge; fig, and olive, and myrtle, too, all swaying in a warm wind – but swaying unheard, for the spirit of the place is running, rushing water – water whose clamour fills the air, its silver streams creeping over ferny rock, its showers veiling grottoes, water falling in bright unending streams from height to height, the rush of it moving the ferns in passing, plunging into the depths at last, where the river foams over boulders, and the roar of its silver cataract over rose-red rock comes up to my ears in the garden above. Far off, under the thickened tight and smoky clouds you see in Claude's landscapes, rise rumbled blue ranges of mountains whose peaks are flushed with snow; for here is achieved in Nature all that Claude attempted in Art. Nor is there any work done in the garden, save the rustic work of Arcady, pruning the vine, gathering its fruits. From above dash down the streams and cascades which water the garden, and refresh the noonday, and spangle up rainbows against shady recesses. Within our Eden is one natural spring, a copious one evidently known to the ancients, for it gushes forth under a pavement of marble which it is certain the Greeks laid in place. Thus the pact between Arcady and Eden – Vergil and the Bible – is sealed in our –

Again he stopped: he had heard through the fountains of his vision the low, liquid run of the Greek girl's laughter from the arbour which hid herself and Farr. In closing his mind to her, he shut out one half of Paradise.

      – our Elysium. We have too in our Paradise, in deference to local belief, one of those houris Mahomet has promised his followers, the poor slave-girl upon whom Farr forces his company at all hours. I shall not upset him by cutting him out, for I am a good deal too much occupied with the cares of Sir Daniel's Orontes navigation, but you and May might be interested in her costume, which is that of the Aleppo Christian: a cloth jacket embroidered with gold thread, open to the waist, is worn over a white chemise of more than risqué décolletage, whilst wide silk shalwars, and dear little yellow slippers, clothe the nether person . . . On her well-made figure the dress sits enchantingly, and, were it not for treading upon poor Farr's toes, I should be inclined to draw her into an arbour myself, as I see he has contrived to do, to while away the heat of the afternoon. I wonder if she knows the fate of Dafne, pursued by Apollo in this very grove? – and whether she has Dafne's remedy against capture at her finger-tips?

      In frondem crines, in ramos bracchia crescunt –

As he wrote down the line of Ovid, he recognised that it was again Captain Vinegar who was writing in his Journal, not he himself writing to his mother. Could he no longer strike the heartfelt note, without Vinegar's swagger, and Vinegar's artifice? He re-read the letter. All, save a few words, was in Vinegar's character. Well, it was of more use in this life of travel than was the other. His mother might like his letter or leave it, for these, now, were the thoughts in his head. So he finished it with a sketch of his plans to march within a week for Aleppo and Damascus, and signed it, and sealed it up. All the time a resolve was forming to leave this place forthwith. Farr was not to be trusted. Look how he had served poor Charlotte-Anne, attacking her in a four-wheeler after filling her with gin at the Vauxhall Gardens! Wherever there was society, he was not to be trusted.

'Farr!' he called, recapping his ink-bottle, 'Farr, come a minute!' No answer from the arbour, where the giggles had ceased. 'Farr!'

'What is it you want?' Farr appeared alone at the further end of the garden-walk. He had in his hand a branch of bay-laurel torn from a tree, perhaps to switch away the flies. 'What is it you want?' he repeated.

'Just come a minute, there's a good fellow.' Pitcher busied himself moving papers about his table and didn't look up until Farr stood near. 'Ah. I've had some intelligence from one of Mangles's people, and he thinks we must move quick if we're to be on the Orontes in time to make out what Novis is about. So tomorrow we march.'

'But you said we'd stop another week. I thought you liked it here.'

'Likes and dislikes must play second fiddle, I'm afraid. The fact is, Novis has – '

'Oh – Novis! The fact about old Novis, Pitcher, is I don't believe it a bit about him being such a bear as you make out. I believe you've made him up as a what-you-may-call-it, an antagonist, for Vinegar. I do indeed. I have it from Veit and Bümm, who ought to know, that Novis is a perfectly civil little Vienna banker – with some rather large ideas as to what's due to his social position, that's all. As to his being this monster you make out, I think it's great humbug, I do!'

'The little Counts! Aye, they would see only a want of social position in the Devil himself. It is what I should expect of them exactly.'

'I suppose we must allow they know Vienna society as well as you do, at least.'

'Just so! Vienna society! Well, now, Vienna society, and little sprigs like your Veit and Bümm, are about of equal concern to Novis, let me tell you, as Berkeley Square and snobs like Bounty are to your father. Let them meet with Herr Novis on his own ground – on the Orontes, or at these excavations Mangles talks of at Mucksureyah – let them face him far from their gas-lamps and constables, and then let them tell you all he cares for is his position in Vienna society!'

Farr only laughed, and turned away. 'I tell you what it is, old fellow,' he said over his shoulder, switching his sprig of laurel. 'Your view of Papa on the roof at Ravenrig gave you quite a wrong picture of his character, you know.'

'You may say so.' Pitcher was taken aback. 'You may think so. But whatever you think about it,' he called after Farr, who turned into the arbour again at the walk's end, 'I should like you to make ready to leave this place tomorrow.'

*   *   *

Because Captain Vinegar took away his party so precipitously from the Grove of Dafne he missed the mails which came up from Antioch next day. One letter, addressed in a female hand to 'Mr Pitcher, c/o Capt. Vinegar', Mr Mangles judged probably harmless enough to be forwarded to the Consul at Damascus, a man named Jenkins who was in the pay of Novis and would certainly open and read it. The other letter, however, which was addressed to Captain Vinegar himself in a hand well known to Mr Mangles, he thought it best to destroy, knowing that it would be unsafe to send it either to Damascus or Aleppo. It shall be given here.

To Capt. O. Q. Vinegar, at Mr Mangles, Antioch
Bolt Court, London.

July 23rd 1850

Sir,

I have received by certain Parties intelligence of your movements, and corroboration of the results of your enquiries into matters spoken of at Half Moon Street prior to your departure. Thus the Pesth Railway, and the Kronstadt concern, and matters in Transylvania generally, are to be abandoned. But in the Dobrusca an energetic policy will be pursued, facilitated by your enterprising visit to Barbe Stirbey at Bucharest, and our interests in that peninsula may very possibly carry the day. So much for the ground you have already travelled over. Now for my purpose in addressing you at Mr Mangles – whom, by-the-by, you may trust with your life, for I could not write to you thus freely at any other Consulate in the Levant.

I learn from my son Roland's letter of June 4th date, at Constantinople, of his intention to separate from yourself and travel by sea with a party of Austrian nobles directly to Jaffa to make a tour of Bible Lands, and thence home. I will say nothing of this, since I do not know the grounds of separation, which I hope was amicable.

However, with your responsibilities towards Roland at an end you will feel yourself freed doubtless to face the greater hazards, and larger rewards, of an exploration of the enemy's line-of-march between the Orontes and Aleppo, and of his intended route eastward by way of Halebyah. Halebyah is the crux of all. If our own interests may be substituted for his at such an entrepôt, what matter if he holds Trebizond? – for we shall have an equal, if not a superior, route to the Persian and Indian market open to us in winter as in summer, which the Trebizond–Erzerum road is not. To give the Devil his due, Novis has established a pretty control upon this Southerly line, suborning Consuls, bribing Pashas, employing bashibozuks to terrify merchants, etc, etc. The advantages, and dangers, of challenging him without delay will be apparent to you.

You will study his navigation works upon the Orontes, discover at Aleppo how far his interests may be secure against attack, or counter-bribery, and decide there upon your next action. Should enquiries lead you South to Damascus, or East towards Halebyah, I need not caution you that your life will be at risk every moment, for I fear that you must assume by certain signs that have reached me that our adversary has unravelled your identity and your design, and will have put his assassins upon your tail.

Roland did not write of Mr Pitcher's intentions, so I do not know whether that other boyish companion with whom you left England still remains in your care, or whether he too has been sloughed off somewhere along your march, and has left Captain Vinegar alone.

Believe me to be, sir, yours very truly

D. Farr

* * *

At the House of the British Consul,
Aleppo

August 20th 1850

My dear Enid,

'Her husband's to Aleppo gone, master of The Tyger' – do you remember our schoolroom readings with Miss Marbelow? And wouldn't you expect to find Aleppo upon the sea-coast, with a port for The Tyger? Not a bit – you must come at it by the most tedious days' travel in life, over a treeless waste, and hills of a stoniness inconceivable, all the time with a violent southeasterly blowing in your face. The singular feature of the town is the steep hill at its centre, white and dry as a mound of ashes, which is crowned with a citadel to be seen ever so far off above the mosque-domes and minarets, and even above the green gardens which surround the city walls. I may say I saw it with relief on the evening of our arrival. You ride through the gardens, and come upon the old stalwart walls facing the sunset, the rubbish of ages heaped against them like suspended waves against old sunburnt cliffs, and there stands open the stout, copper-sheathed Antioch Gate, which you enter, and find yourself in a tunnel twisting this way and that in the dark thickness of the arch. On top of the arch, I may say, crowds a row of urchins shooting with slings at the myriad of swifts which scream and wheel above the roofs – and a stone-shot or two is sure to surprise yourself or your horse, which 'accident' the giaour is obliged to take in good part.

We are stopping with the Consul, to whom Papa gave Vinegar a letter (in explaining the absence of T. Pitcher from our party, who is named in all these letters introducing 'Captain Vinegar', we are obliged to say that he imbibed a fever at Constantinople, and stopped behind, which is not very far off the truth). You may picture us altogether caught up in Aleppine circles, which consist of three or four brace of half-bred Levan-

[289]

tine families like our host's, who have about as poor an idea of fun as a set of Welsh baptists. Their houses are well enough, in an Oriental way: I am seated at this instant on the shady side of a courtyard paved with rose-and-honey-coloured marble tessellation, whose fountain is full of petals fallen from the bougainvillea-tree, whilst opposite to my seat, on the fantastically-carven upper storeys of the house, appear the windows of the hareem as if veiled in lacy stone. Two levels of cellars, descended to for coolness in the heat of summer, lie beneath the house and hold (it is reputed) the treasures of these Christian merchants which so excite the piety, or envy, of the Mussulman mob. The interiors of the rooms, every door frame and shutter as well as ceilings and walls, are painted and fretted and chased beyond endurance, so that no undecorated surface anywhere serves to rest the eye.

I fear their society is not unlike these painfully over-wrought interiors. Last evening, in Vinegar's honour, the world came to us, and sat smoking on couches under the hanging lamps until a yellow tobacco fog enveloped all, which was pierced by cunning-looking Levantines talking prices, and their wives whispering scandal, and their daughters looking down at their boots. I expected even Pitcher to find it a trifle slow, but he puffed away at his narghile with the best of them, as if such society was the very summit of a man's ambition. It is, you will say, the best society in Aleppo, and doubtless that thought compensates, in the case of fellows like Pitcher, for the hurt of their less-than-best position in society at home. There is a mighty air of self-importance, and much talk of 'telling the pasha' this or that, about the most underbred of Englishmen out here, who would scarcely find himself invited to dine with the Mayor of Bangor at home. Pitcher has been careful to tell them that Mamma is an Earl's daughter, so I, in riposte, have whispered in our host's ear that Vinegar's soi-disant papa, too, sports a coronet.

I am pretty well used now to the company of Levant traders, for we came to this from stopping with another friend of Papa's named Mangles in a little wooden shed on a mountain between Antioch and the coast. Such rusticity! The fellow had planted up a roughish sort of plot, and we were asked to believe that this, with a few rather seedy bay-trees and some very moderate fruit, amounted to 'Eden', as he had named it, whilst a sluggish sort of spring under a stone in the hedge was made to serve for the 'Grove of Daphne' of the ancients! To one familiar with aristocratic pleasure-grounds in England, these contrivances are as trumpery as Aleppine 'society'. Do you think, by the by, that Mamma quite knows the level of society that Papa kept in his Eastern days? – for I had always imagined him as having audiences of the Sultan, and riding finely-caparisoned Arabs in select company, and sipping sherbet with a vizier or two in latticed kiosques upon the Golden Horn; and it turns out he was the intimate instead of ever so many of these pinchbeck pedlars. Mamma would not care for it, I may as well tell you.

As for Papa's works, or money, or lost statuary – or whatever items it was that he commissioned Vinegar to look into at that interview at Half Moon Street a lifetime ago whilst you and I giggled next door – well, I am as much in the dark as ever I was. Works there undoubtedly are on the Orontes to improve its navigability since poor Chesney's day, for we rode some miles beside the river and saw the evidence, though not the work going forward, or the navvies carrying it out. 'We are too late! It is just as I feared!' Pitcher kept muttering between his teeth, like the hero of a melodrama. What he had hoped to find I do not know, and was too vexed by his manner to ask, but my opinion is, that his quest after Novis is a will-o-the-wisp, and he might as well engage in the hunt for the Holy Spear of Longinus (which by-the-by Mangles interests himself in, and which is heard of in these parts about as regularly as the antiquarians turn up King Arthur's chattels in Wales). I have about as much belief in his Chimerical Austrian banker, as he has in my fabulous lion!

Poor little Mangles has suffered from the Aleppo Boil, and consequently has no nose to speak of, whilst for a wife he has a vulgar native female with a screeching voice and transparent blouses, who sat torturing us with the dulcimer, if she was not pulling away at her pipe like a navvy. So much for Eden! However, you may be sure I make the best of it, as I believe I would be sure to make the best, nowadays, of any company that lived in a house, and spoke in English, and understood one in fifty of my jokes – none of these conditions being met with in a Turkish caravanserai. Besides regular Aleppo society, there is a class of rather sporting gentry, called 'dellals', who race doubtful-looking screws round the citadel, hoping for a sale, which makes a morning lounge for Aleppo's knowing set, and would bring a lump to the throat of any exile from Tatt's. Pitcher, who accuses me of being a snob towards his Levant pedlar friends, objects to my intimacy with these rascals as infra dig. But still I go, for there is a café under an old tree looking out upon the scene, exquisitely dirty and filled with Arabs in night-shirts, which serves the finest-tasting thimblefuls of coffee I have ever savoured (you may tell Papa that I have come round to his view of how coffee should be made, which I somehow never could abide at home). That done, there is the town to saunter through, for I am reduced to sad straits to find amusement now that I keep out of Pitcher's way. It is a town of hot, still, narrow lanes lined by windowless walls, with every now and then a door, its wood worn to a polish by the fumbling hands of centuries, each door furnished with a bronze knocker in the form of a charming little female hand grasping a ball. These lanes, paved with stone, lead you (or, rather, draw you as a current does) into the great khan's covered arcades, whose sudden coolness and darkness is quarried into a thousand recesses, where a thousand-and-one merchants sit cross-legged on their benches amongst their wares, and eye you sleepily as you ride by.

Dear sister, does it sound awfully dull? Remember, you can walk out of the door by way of Bruton Street and Bond Street into Piccadilly, whereas I am condemned to wander eternally through no better thoroughfare than the khans of these savage towns. On I go, and on. To left and right are glimpses between the great studded doors of courtyards; whenever I look in, it is always to see some sanguinary ruffian skinning a sheep; or you meet with a pile of sheep's heads, or a slithery heap of offal, or find your nose banging against a bunch of bloody hearts hung from a butcher's hook – incidents unknown to the Burlington Arcade idler. The crowd is immense, a shuffling, echoing, padding sort of crowd pressing through the half-dark tunnels of stone which are here and there pierced by sunshafts, some fellows dragging carts, many burdened with sacks, a few riding. At a crossing of ways sits a desert-looking Arab on his pony, turning this way and that with slack rein, with the air of a dandy on a corner in St James's with two Clubs to choose from – and past him ride I, wandering on until the time comes to set out for home, and pretty certain to have lost myself in the great khan, so that I emerge, like as not, to be confronted once more with the blinding-white stone citadel rising on its ashy hill, just where I parted from it an hour or two since.

There is nothing worth buying, though I pick over the wares to pass the time. Apropos of Longinus' spear afore-mentioned, it is amusing that the 'sacred relic' amongst the Imperial Insignia at Vienna (the lance of St Maurice), and Mangles's treasured lance-head, said to be that found by the Crusader Peter Bartholomew, could be bought by the gross at any weapon-stall in the great khan here, not as 'holy relics' but for immediate use in war! It is rather a charm of the East, I confess, that the remote past goes on all about one, and articles such as Longinus' lance, and vessels much like the Holy Grail too, I don't doubt, are in everyday commission. It gives one a sort of notion of living in the midst of a Romance, even if one does not go so far along the road to the ridiculous as Captain Vinegar.

Meanwhile I count the hours to Damascus, when I shall be free. I wonder more and more at having ever set out with such a fellow as Pitcher proves to be. You should have been by to see the truculence and bombast he used towards a little orphan Greek child in the Mangles household! She was a dear creature, and we had become fast friends, when along comes Pitcher with his swaggering ways, and uses her just as if she was his slave, on account of some fable as to her origins. At first she was too timid to be disobliging, I suppose, and soon she found she couldn't be rid of his importunities, which were of a monstrous kind. Very far from a slave, she was the nearest thing to a London miss I have found since I left home – though I dare say a London miss don't wear her bodice open to her waist, and inexpressibles that may as well be made from cobwebs, unless fashion is much altered in my absence.

Alas, the truth is that I (like the Greek orphan) allowed my good-nature to comply with a proposition I should have turned down flat when Pitcher came to see me at Cambridge. I had supposed till then that one was bound to knock under when a fellow with Pitcher's bounce made his appearance at one's door with his plans made. I wish a thousand times a day that I had gone home from Vienna, when he flew into a rage over possessing no dress-clothes. But I shall leave him at Damascus, never fear.

Two days past I shot a woodcock in some gardens outside

the walls. Will you tell Edmond? When I held the little brown dead exile in my hand, and heard the water-wheels groaning in the dusk, and the muezzin from the minaret – when I saw the barbarous walls and citadel of Aleppo, and thought how far were the bird and I from our beloved dark woods under the moor at home – why, I half wished myself dead in its place, that I might wing home at once in spirit. I have only to reach Damascus, and I shall have my freedom. Farewell, dear sister.

      Yr loving and aff. twin
      RF

IX

THE ROOM OF THE HOTEL PHARPHAR AT DAMASCUS in which Roland
Farr lay in his cloak on a divan was dark and full of shadows. In one
sense this comforted him, for his eyes hurt him exceedingly. They had
been injured, he supposed, by the glare of the light travelling south
from Aleppo through the gaunt plain of Hamah and the rocks of
Shemsyn under a brass sky. In another sense, however, the shadows
alarmed him; by the sudden malignance of the shapes they assumed,
and by their Protean images, they put into his mind a fear that he was
sickening. The worst they had done to him, these shadows, had been
to come together into a cloaked and turbanned bulk bending over him,
so real that the creature's venomous breath had touched his face like a
toad's tongue, and had spat out the words 'Where iss Winegar?' Even
now Farr's head rolled on the dirty cloak to escape this phantom, seeming to hear the hiss of its voice in the shadows still. If only he had
his vinaigrette, and could inhale from it that sharp, clean essence of
home, such chimaèras would vanish. Tears for its loss ran down his
cheeks.

The room was earthy, like a cave in a mud cliff, a raised earthen
platform around its walls, and a mud floor half covered with shabby
rugs. A mat hung over the doorway: the heat of the day outside could
be guessed at by needles of light piercing the mat. On Pitcher's advice,
Roland had stayed indoors to recruit his strength after their dawn
arrival at Damascus, but as soon as he had lain down had come this
ominous propensity of the shadows towards masquerade, and these
sudden little spills of incoherence inside his head, which frightened
him awfully.

Besides these ills he had a toothache. Though it had for the moment
left off devouring him, the wild beast of pain crouched in his head. He
feared to move in case it sprang. He wanted a drink, but lay still. The

[295]

sound of a fountain spattering on stone penetrated from the courtyard, but the image that it threw into his mind was not of water, cooling, but an image of fire: he imagined a huge candle burning down so rapidly that the splashing of its wax caused the sound he heard. Down burnt the candle into its socket, then another, and another. The light of them hurt his eyes, their heat parched his tongue. If only he could force them to be water, he would be well. But, burning ever faster, candle succeeded candle from the magician's store.

Pitcher's strength grew and grew. He was out now, walking about the town in the heat of noon. Looking for what, finding what? What did he want of these squalid ruins of cities, that he found by walking their streets with that long, tireless stride, looking into every corner so eagerly?

It was true that the far-off first sight of Damascus had cheered Roland's spirits. After a ride of seven days from Aleppo, to rest his eyes on a drift of green gardens in the desert, from whose foliage rose minarets, and towers, and violet domes tipped with the golden crescent, was wonderful. Damascus! Alas, instead of a nearer view surpassing the distant prospect, as rewarded the traveller coming down from the heights of Hampstead into the magnificence of Regent Street, the illusory distant delight of Damascus, as of all Eastern cities, soon vanished in blank-walled lanes and heaps of ruin. They had ridden directly from the gates at dawn to the Consul's house. Here they had stopped long enough to enjoy in anticipation the fountains and orange-trees they saw, and the open rooms shaded by reed-mats which servants were drenching with water, before a clerk had brought Pitcher a letter forwarded from Antioch, and had told them that the Consul found it impossible to accommodate them. The clerk had recommended them to the Hotel Pharphar.

Riding behind Pitcher through the alleys, rejected alike by Christian and Mussulman, and tired to death, Roland's heart had sunk through apathy into apprehension. He was within the grasp of the Orient, and he feared it. He could not pretend to ignore that he was ill. Even resting at the Consul's house he had felt stiff, and sick, with a headachy pain creeping about in his limbs and suddenly squeezing him in one place or another. He complained most of his toothache, which was the only pain he could describe, but his fears, and his feelings of misery, were general. Never having been ill in his life, he had no defence prepared against illness.

On the mud wall above his head clustered patches of bugs. They only waited for his eyes to close before crawling down onto his body to sup up his blood with filthy suckers. In the insouciance of health he had never cared about the bugs before, but now he had collapsed into such vulnerable terrors that he wept for fear of them. At Hamah, in a Christian's hut in a swamp of abominations, they had slept in the vilest quarters yet offered them anywhere, where the rats had run over his very face, and he had conceived there a horror of the dirt, and had wished very heartily that he hadn't disdained to bring on his Levinge-bed from Broussa, as Pitcher had done, who slept protected from Hamah's rats and fleas alike. So he lay on his mud shelf at the Pharphar and wept, in utter dejection. Why did Giorgio not come near him?

'Giorgio!' he shouted with sudden anger.

Silence closed in on his cry immediately. Was this how Giorgio repaid his kindness? Was Pitcher right, that charity was merely a weakness in the East? Was Pitcher right in everything? – in Vinegar's proud, cold manner – in wearing flannel underclothes – in possessing no dress-suit? If only he would come back, surely he would concoct some powerful draught from the little medicine-chest, which would restore Roland to that steady lost world where fountains were not of fire and shadows did not terrify. Perhaps he would have found the vinaigrette, and would put its worn, cool silver into Roland's hand. If only he would come back. The slips into incoherence in his head frightened Roland. He pictured his brain missing its footing on steep stairs within a dark tower, and falling . . .

He became aware of sounds in the courtyard. There was the mutter of Arabic, the shuffle of Arab feet; and then the sharp steps and voices of his own race. Europeans! He heard the voices nearer. Germans! His brain recovered hope in its prison tower, and shouted down the twisting stair for help:

'Veit! Bümm! I am here!'

Tresham Pitcher meanwhile was seated quietly amongst the striped bolsters of a café under willow trees overarching a channel of the river

Barrada which waters Damascus. He sipped his coffee, the very essence of taste, and smoked the narghile which had been lit for him by a black little imp with a tray of coals, and was perfectly content. He felt not in the least tired: curiosity gave him energy, and satisfaction gave him rest. Face and figure alike looked lean and worn, by exposure to the sun and rain of experience, an identity refined out of that clumsy Waterways' clerk who had stood so many hours looking out of his window into London's smoke, and wondering what he should do with himself. Now he had learned the answer. This was what he should do with himself. He was perfectly happy.

Disregarded in his hand was a letter. Addressed to 'Mr Pitcher, c/o Capt. Vinegar', and forwarded from Mr Mangles at Antioch, it had been given him by the Consul's clerk that morning. The clerk had made no apology for the letter having evidently been opened. Pitcher did not recognize the handwriting, a careful but uneducated script, probably feminine. The letter was dated July 5th, from Rainshaw Park, Kent, and began:

My dear Tresham,

You will forgive me for employing Mrs Poynder's hand to write on my behalf, when you learn that I have suffered the Affliction of a seizure which has restricted my use of the pen. I am informed by your Step-father, to whom I had applied for intelligence of your whereabouts, that a letter sent to the care of Capt. Vinegar at Antioch would intercept your Eastward roaming before you have (so to say) crossed the Rubicon of Tigris and Euphrates. Now to my Purpose in thus writing to you.

My dear boy, I have afforded to my intention long and hard consideration. Give to my Proposal, I pray you, equal attention, before you place the Desert, and those mighty Waters, betwixt yourself and England.

I must now consider it unlikely that I shall wed; or, if I should wed, improbable that I shall produce an Heir of the body for my House and Estate at Rainshaw. Indeed, a further seizure may carry me off at no distant date.

I am anxious to settle the question as to who is to succeed me here, but no less anxious to assure myself that my choice has been made with wisdom and discernment; which proviso may only be satisfied if I survive long enough to preside over a term of trial, in which such an Heir as I had chosen would make his Residence here as my Son, and learn his Duties.

Evidently my choice could not well fall upon a Nephew who had elected to roam about the Eastern deserts all his days, till some Tribesman or other shall decide to knock him on the head. It is one thing to manifest the virtues of independence; quite another to sever yourself out of perversity from your true interest. Should you think it politick to turn back before the Rubicon is crossed, you may be assured of a hearty welcome from

yr affectionate Uncle,
M. Wytherstone

postscriptum: I wd write more, but I grow weary of the work of spelling out each word, and good Mrs Poynder grows weary of the work of amanuensis.

Beneath the shaky signature and postscript was added a further note in Mrs Poynder's hand:

I beg to add respectful compliments and asure that Squire do go about well enough in himself for to see the Places and to Church though slow. In Church helping himself up from Prayers has pulled off wing off carven angel on his Stall. Has had a Craft builden for to row on Lake which Tom does who you will remember who makes a Capital boatman though abused by Squire if ever the Craft rocks. Squire think much of Yourself and how you will perhaps come. Repairs is all compleat. With humble duty, Alice Poynder.

The letter lay in Pitcher's hand as he sat among his cushions in the café beside the Barrada, but his mind was not upon its contents. It had indeed, as he read it first in the weary disappointment of being turned away from Consul Jenkins's house, opened a window in Pitcher's mind giving upon the remote pleasaunce of Rainshaw; but it was a window that Captain Vinegar had very rapidly shut. What did the letter amount to? Hints and half-suggestions, that he should give up his adventures to go back and lie under the plum-tree with his mouth open in a kind of dream. Tom? Mrs Poynder? And what had been the sexton's name, and the Curate's? How dim and faint seemed their grasp on life, compared to Vinegar's in this brilliant present reality. His thoughts had returned to Damascus.

Farr was only a little tired, perhaps sunstruck. He would not wear flannel, he would not wind a muslin turban round his hat, he would not trouble with his Levinge-bed. Tresham could not help feeling the satisfaction of the man whose precautions have been justified, in weathering an ordeal better than his companion. Here beside the flowing water all was cool, all was peace. Light reflected from ripples trembled on the undersides of vines and of a willow which shaded the café. Not far off a cascade tumbled into a pool. He watched stout silhouettes crossing the bridge over the pool at the meditative pace which rests the eye that watches them. Here was a scene which answered every eagerness to reach Damascus, and fulfilled all promises held out by a first sight of the gleaming city in its island of green gardens amid the desert, and made the traveller content with his journey. The stories and tales which in England had filled his heart with unaccountable longing for strangeness, and mystery, and long-ago, might here prove true. Turning a corner in Damascus that morning he had thought of Pastor MacPhee's story of a madman of the parish whom he had found making his meal within the carcase of a dead horse, for he had come upon three children squabbling with dogs inside a dead camel. Fantasy, grim or gay, here found its setting. As Farr had remarked of the bazaar at Aleppo, you might well put your hand on the Lance of Longinus at the Armourers' Khan.

He was aware of the *tchiboukji* with his tray of coals at his elbow. The child's fragility, and huge eyes, made its sex questionable, and there was an indelicacy in this question which made Tresham avoid looking at the creature now. But a thin brown hand reached a folded paper onto his lap. When he turned, the child was gone. He opened the paper. Written across it in a strong foreign hand were two sentences: *Look at the gate. Look into the basket.* At the gate of the café stood an old man carrying a wicker basket such as fishermen use, who was apparently resting for a moment on his stick. Only when he had looked at the old man did Tresham turn his attention to the other patrons of the café, to see which one of them had been curious to watch him open the paper. All had resumed the musing stare-at-nothing of the Turk at his ease. Should he look in the basket?

His heart beat a little quicker than was comfortable. He thought how content he had been just now, with the idea of mysteries and adventures. He connected this incident of the note with the only thing which had annoyed him in Damascus, the Consul turning them out of his house that morning without so much as the offer of breakfast, and he determined to look into the basket.

He rose to his feet and walked to the café's gate, where he stood by the old man. In the basket nothing could be seen but folds of blue cloth. He looked into the ancient face, seamed with lines, the beard white and scant. The eyes were blind; opaque and filmy in sockets of wrinkles. Should Tresham speak? He felt his fingers seized and, looking down, saw his neighbour's withered claw guide his hand into the basket. Under the cloth his fingertips met a shape so cool and firm and fine that the sense of touch transmitted the idea of beauty to his mind, like a hand which brushes a loved body in the dark. Parting the cloth he looked into its folds. A head of the most exquisite beauty lay asleep in the basket. He touched the lips, eyes, the curls on the wide brow. The marble seemed to yield like flesh to his fingers, white as milk, the very veins tinged blue under the silk of the skin. He knew at once what it was. But what was he meant to do? He looked about the café to see if some signal would be given him. The little *tchiboukji* was standing by the place he had left, a paper in his hand. Thinking he would take the old man with him to the place, he turned – and found the blind messenger vanished, his basket with him.

All that he could do was stride towards the androgynous imp with his infernal tray of coals, and hope to seize him. But the child slipped off, and couldn't have been chased without making a row – already he felt himself watched with disdain, and even with gleams of hatred, from many a heavy-lidded eye. A second folded paper lay on his bolster, which he snatched up. Again the heavy black writing: *It will be to you restored at Tadmor. Take it home. Claim your reward. Tell no one, as you fear Death.*

Enjoyment of the tranquil shade under the willows was gone. The place held watchers and spies. He considered the message, uncertain what to do. The head, the Phidias, would be given him at Palmyra (as Europeans call the village of Tadmor three days' march into the desert from Damascus). Why not here? Palmyra was lonely, exposed to a trap, a perilous meeting-place at the end of a hazardous journey. That should not stop him keeping the tryst! Indeed the danger of it resolved him. Glad of an object for immediate action, he determined to go back to the Consul's house, and find out what was needed for an expedition to Palmyra.

So he set out, leaving behind him his step-uncle's letter to join the refuse of the café. How wonderful it was! No tourist concocting adventures for a Captain Vinegar now! Better than looking in on the Eastern scene, he was a part of it. No two desperadoes by the café gate muttering together under their enormous turbans, and fingering their Damascus blades, could be deeper in intrigue than himself! Through the great city he walked, by narrow lanes roofed over with matting against the sun, or past flaky walls with the sun's heat full upon them, where an arch or a door gave promise of courts and fountains within, havens concealed from the passer-by like the women in their cloaks and veils; deeper and deeper into the city. He relished the clamour of life in the bazaars, and the rustling robes, and the dark faces so close to his own, and hot gusts of spicy air, and the tinkling of the sherbet-seller's cups – even the sudden violent smells, or ghastly spectacles which jumped on him from side-alleys, gratified him by not shaking his nerve. As he walked he turned over the message in his mind. 'Take the Phidias home.' To England, it must mean. Why should he go back? To 'claim the reward'? Sir Daniel no doubt would behave handsomely towards whoever restored his chief treasure's head to its body. What would he give? What had he in his gift that Tresham would care to possess?

He found himself at last within the Consul's gate again, waiting in the anteroom, with its view of the shaded courtyard, where he and Farr had waited just after dawn that morning. Yesterday's march had been so much slowed by Farr's weakness that they had reached Damascus to find its gates shut for the night, and had been obliged to sleep on the ground outside the walls, and enter the city with the sunrise. It was now after midday. The thought struck Tresham that whoever had sent him the note at the café, and had placed the blind man at its gate, must have followed him since he had entered the city. But no one save the Consul had known of their arrival.

An Arab servant now appeared to lead Tresham along stone passages which, with their sharp turnings, make attack upon an Eastern house difficult, and the ambush of a guest easy. He was shown into a fountained courtyard where the Consul half lay upon a silk divan in an arbour of orange-trees. He was a purplish, plethoric-looking man with a rough ginger beard, and little eyes creased into the fat of his face. He did not rise, but held out two fingers to Tresham, and let the smoke of his narghile dribble out between meaty lips.

'Captain Vinegar? How do.'

'Good morning, Mr Jenkins. I called on you earlier with Mr Farr and sent you in his father's letter. Sir Daniel Farr. I don't know if you received it?'

Jenkins removed the amber mouthpiece of his pipe. 'I received it. Thank you, Mister Postman. Now then, I won't ask you to sit down, for I've a devilish lot on hand, but if you'll state your business we shall get along.'

The phrase about sow's ears and silk purses occurred to Tresham as he stood before the fat man rolling in his cushions. 'Yes,' he said. 'I have the intention of visiting Palmyra, and I suppose you can arrange it.'

'Out of the question.'

'It ain't a bit out of the question, Mr Jenkins, for I shall do it,' said Tresham, summoning all Vinegar's grimness and gruffness to his aid. 'The question is, shall you help me to it, or must I find out all about it without you?'

'Look here, Captain – ' Jenkins flung himself back in his cushions with a weary note in his voice – 'it ain't Surrey out there, you know, or Aldershot heath, or wherever it is you do your soldiering. Out there we've the Druse, we've the Maronites, we've the Aneyzeh – we've enough tribes to frighten you into fits, sir, and just at present they're all at each other's throats. Which you don't know about, no, no. None of you tourist gents ever do know anything about it, that's of course.'

'I doubt if your tribesmen are more to be feared than the Tcherkess of the Caucasus, Mr Jenkins, whom I've lived – '

'And if the tribesmen should be merciful and let you go, there's a pack of Arnaut deserters from the nizam who won't – aye, and a squadron of bashibozuks out a-hunting the Arnauts, who'll be sure to mince you up small!' He laughed at the idea of this operation, good humour restored by the Captain's certain misfortunes. 'Lord, man, you'd be fortunate if you was to come back alive in anything but your hat, you would indeed, like a fellow a year or two back. Just his hat!

Not a stitch else. Just his London hat, and some of his robbers had pinched the band off of that! No, no. You put Palmyra out of your head. The pasha won't have it – and I won't have it. You cut along to Jerusalem, that ain't dangerous. They treating you all right at the Pharphar, are they?'

'Tolerable. Tell me, though, the pasha don't give out passes for Palmyra, ain't there a sheikh of the Aneyzah one applies to? For safe passage?'

Jenkins struck a cushion angrily. 'You can throw your money at any of a dozen sheikhs, it won't bring you safe through. It's the pasha and I have to pick up the pieces, you know, when some Cockney who wants to cut a dash at home goes out and gets himself killed. I don't care a hang if you're killed, Captain Whatsyername, but pray have it done elsewhere. There's nothing to be seen at Palmyra you won't see quite as well at Baalbek. Nothing at all.'

'Can Edessa be reached from Palmyra?' asked Tresham suddenly.

'What? What do you want with Edessa?' The amber mouthpiece smoked unregarded in Jenkins's hand. 'Why do you ask?'

'Can it be reached from Palmyra?'

'Look here, Vinegar. Look here. You cut along. Unless you mean to pickle a rod for your own back, you cut along to Jerusalem, or Baalbek, d'ye hear? Now then, if you don't mind I've much business and I'll have you shown out.' He had leaned forward to deliver this warning, anger squatting red on his face. Now he leaned back and clapped his hands for a servant.

Tresham allowed himself to be shown out. He had become aware half-way through the interview that a listener was concealed among the orange-trees – he had seen the leaves shake, and the fruit tremble on the branch. Perhaps there always was a listener in the East, but he connected this eavesdropper with himself.

The tremor of alarm sent through his veins by the idea, as he found himself once more in the silent streets, could not be distinguished from a tremor of pleasure. He had tried the name 'Edessa' upon Jenkins, and upon the unseen listener, because Edessa had recurred in conversations with both Mangles and the Aleppo Consul, when the whereabouts of Herr Novis's stronghold in these parts had been discussed. He knew that it was a town on the edge of the Anatolian escarpment, overlooking the desert between the Tigris and the Euphrates, which had once been the capital of a Crusader kingdom. Jenkins's reaction showed that Edessa had significance. Yet if it was the hand of Novis which had shown him the Phidias, and had promised to restore it to him at Tadmor, why should Novis's creature, Consul Jenkins, forbid his journey to Palmyra? There were more parties in the plot than appeared. He thought of it all as he walked through the streets towards the Pharphar Hotel. The sense of deep water enlivened every stride, and quickened every apprehension of the reality of the moment, with himself in its midst. He would enquire of the Pharphar dragoman for the Aneyzeh sheikh who provided a safe passage through the desert. To Palmyra he would go.

Outside the Pharphar's shabby wall he thought for the first time of Farr. Should he come to Palmyra? *Tell no one, as you fear Death.* Better leave Farr; then, if he returned from Palmyra with the head, they would travel home together. *Claim your reward.* The message spoke as though the reward was a known object – a prize – but his mind would not select a prize. Inside the gate he remembered that he had promised to look out a barber to attend to Farr's toothache, so he roused the sleepy little Cypriot dragoman and sent him off to bring in such an operative from the bazaars. Crossing the paved court, he heard through the wavering splash of the fountain a German-accented voice coming from Farr's room. Novis? He paused, listening. The voice chirruped on. Veit! That wretch had caught up with them! He pushed aside the matting over the doorway and went in.

There was Veit in full chatter, strutting about the shabby den, describing to Farr on his mud shelf the most amusing of his experiences in the Holy Land, whilst fat Count Bümm listened and wheezed from his seat. Veit was a sharp, restless, glossy little starling of a man, bird-thin shanks encased in shiny boots, a close-fitting jacket sleek as feathers, his head pecking about rapidly to correct the fault of having lost his left eye in a duel, which made him suspicious of what might be all the while occurring on his blind side. When he caught sight of Tresham he broke off his chatter, and glittered a rather horrible smile at him. Bümm, too, looked uncomfortable, and clicked his heels and bowed. When Tresham had shaken their hands, Farr said from his shelf:

'They saved my life, I believe. Lord, but I was low when they came! I thought I was awfully ill, Pitcher, when you were gone.'

'I've sent out the fellow to bring in a barber to look at your tooth,' said Tresham. 'I daresay that's what's poisoned you. That's all it'll be. Now then,' he added, turning on the Counts, 'are you stopping at the Pharphar?'

Roland said, 'No, lucky beggars, they've got themselves a billet with some friars.'

'Oh?'

'Yes, so,' chirped Veit, 'Terra Sancta conwent, is clean house, bed witt sheet.'

'And, also,' said Bümm in his slow voice, 'cellar full witt vino d'oro off Liban. Ve drink.' He tipped back his head to show how this was done.

'Another thing with these friars,' put in Farr, 'they have crowds of girls come to Confess. Come right in and upstairs.' His unsteady feverish eyes watched Tresham tugging at the strap of a saddlebag in their heap of baggage. He was lying on his side, the damp curls stuck to the pallor of his face. He said, 'I wonder if I should be better off there? With these friars. If I'm to be not well.'

In the suggestion Tresham saw his chance of making for Palmyra unimpeded. Yet he was unwilling to surrender Farr to the Counts again. He weighed the question whilst asking them where they had been since leaving Broussa two and a half months ago. After a sea-voyage from Ismid to Jaffa they had toured the Holy Land, and had then come north by leisurely stages to Damascus. They had met neither with difficulties nor with hardships; indeed, in the whole course of their travels of four months from Vienna, they had progressed as smooth and easy over the East as if they had flown through the air.

'Your dragoman vill show vot you must see,' Veit said to him of Jerusalem, so as to save the need to disturb a sluggish memory.

'They say it ain't worth our trouble going to the Holy Land,' said Farr.

'Ah, well then.' Tresham exclaimed. 'And I had always been told how much of interest there was to be seen!'

'Not so much,' said Bümm heavily, 'unless you are wishing to be make Graf – how you call Graf?'

[306]

'Knight. What do you mean, make knight?'

'Knight, right so. At Jerusalem you can be make knight of St John. For this nothing needed, no quarterings or coat of arms, nothing to show. Ve are noble, for us is not necessary, but for you maybe iss good.'

Knights! Like the funnel of a steam-engine driven through realms of romance, the Counts sprayed out smuts over every landscape. Before Tresham could show his annoyance, the matting was pushed aside to admit a glare of light with the little Cypriot dragoman. Behind him there darkened the doorway, quite as effectively as the matting had done, the gigantic figure of a Negro.

There he stood, and gazed at one after another of the Europeans with the curiosity of an anthropologist entering a cave of savages, whilst the Cypriot laid his credentials as a barber-dentist before Tresham. The difficulty had been to find a barber who would touch a *giaour*'s tooth. This giant was an Abyssinian, or had first been enslaved by Abyssinians perhaps, and so professed no particular disgust at the idea of putting his hand into a Christian mouth. 'Deuced good of him,' said Farr rather faintly, 'damn his cheek. I suppose I must put up with him, must I?'

'If you look at most of the Christians these fellows have had to judge by,' said Tresham, 'I shouldn't care to put my hand in their mouths either. Let him look, at least, now he's come.'

The Negro, who had wrapped a length of scarlet silk round his colossal frame for the visit, smiled to reassure them as a doctor does among children. When Farr was pointed out as his patient, he smiled with particular ferocity at the invalid, and strode across to pin him to the mud shelf with a terrific grip. Finding he couldn't see well enough, he picked Farr up and carried him to the doorway, where he set him down against the doorpost and kneeled beside him to peer into his mouth. His show of authority had its effect upon his European watchers. The Counts hung together, and were silent.

Poor Farr underwent the torture. It happened too rapidly for Tresham to see what the Negro was about; perhaps he wouldn't have interfered anyway. Out came a pouch, and from the pouch he took an instrument like an awl. With a change of grip of Farr quick as a wrestler he had his head locked fast under one arm. A black hand held the awl-point to the boy's gum, whilst the other palm struck the awl-handle three mighty buffets, the barber shouting aloud at each blow. Blood and screams squirted between the black fingers. After the third blow he seizèd the loosened tooth and ripped it out of Farr's head. It was as quick and bloody a deed as an execution. Poor Farr's head flopped forward with moans and bubbles of blood as if it had indeed been severed.

Tresham obeyed an instinct not to comfort Farr, not to touch him, till his tormentor had been paid by the Cypriot and had stalked off. He would not show concern. Let the Counts' weak nerves make them chatter and cringe. He took Farr's ordeal as a challenge, and was careful to show only Vinegar's stony indifference to pain.

As soon as the scarlet-decked barber had gone, and the two Counts after him, Tresham lifted Farr onto his cloak on the mud shelf again, and sent the Cypriot to dampen cloths in the fountain whilst he knelt by the victim's head. Eyes opened, and sent mute messages from the immense distance and isolation of pain. The stained lips moved, and words fell painfully out of them: 'Why did you set that creature at me?'

'I didn't – ' Tresham leant forward urgently to explain, but the eyes had closed. The tongue moving restlessly in the parted lips was swollen and whitish. Again the eyes opened, again words dribbled out:

'I shall go no further.'

'You shall, old fellow! Indeed you shall!' Tresham leaned over him.

'No!' He rolled his head as if to avoid Tresham's shadow. 'I shall go home.'

Though Tresham remained looking into his eyes, the light had gone out of them like a candle-flame guttered out in a hood of wax. His skin was a rotten white. Sweat trickled among the roots of his beard. Blood caked the corners of his mouth.

Suddenly Tresham felt frightened – inadequate, and frightened. The Cypriot had put a wetted cloth into his hand, and he knelt by the mud-shelf to sponge away the blood with desperate care. It was all he could do. He hadn't meant the barber to draw the tooth, only to look at it. But he knew in his heart that he had meant to startle Farr into silence on the subject of his toothache, which had been a maddening refrain since Aleppo. Poor fellow! Tresham's fingers felt the shapely lips under the cloth he cleaned them with, felt the bones of the cheeks, the clear broad brow. He felt with his fingers what he had never quite seen, or never quite admitted: the resemblance between Farr and his twin sister. In the heat of his desperate feelings, one loved face elided into the other. And perhaps it was his fingers' memory of the touch of the marble head in the basket, at the café gate – the head of Dionysus, both male and female – which now put into his head the riddle *Claim your reward*. Of course. Enid!

He ceased the tender work. He got to his feet and gave the Cypriot the cloth. Poor Farr! Still, he had only had a tooth drawn, as hundreds do each day. I will leave him my Levinge-bed when I go to Palmyra, thought Tresham, that's what I'll do. He was so much agitated by ideas of his 'reward', and by the prospect of Palmyra, that he had to go out and walk about the courtyard.

*　　*　　*

From *Journal of a Land-March towards India*, by O. Q. Vinegar (Capt.)
September 6th, 1850

A curious adventure befell me today, which, with P—'s little incident at the Barrada café yesterday (of which more by-and-by), persuades me that we are hot upon the trail of what we seek.

Young F— had passed such an uncomfortable night at the old Pharphar, where I always prefer to put up when at Damascus – and this in spite of my having looked out the Negro Rastas from the bazaars to attend to his tooth, who is I suppose the best dental operative in all Syria, and moreover owes me his freedom after an incident in the Houran some years back – that I searched about for some superior accommodation for the poor fellow, and found it at last at the Terra Sancta convent, with some friars whom I prevailed upon to take him in, and there he may remain, lapped in all possible luxuries, until he is quite himself again, and able to rejoin P— and myself after our expedition to Palmyra, which promises to be very full of hazards, and of an outcome impossible to predict.

[309]

These hazards received a very hearty increase by my adventure of this afternoon. After making my usual arrangement with Miguel (who is, of course, the son of the sheikh of all the Aneyzeh tribes) to conduct myself and P— to Palmyra – the fee asked, I should add, reflects either a sharp increase in tourist traffic, which I doubt, or else an increase in the dangers of the road, which the inhospitable J—, Consul of a certain Great Power, hinted at in the interview I had with him – I was idling over a pipe with the good friars, who are jolly fellows, and not averse to cracking a bottle of 'best ordinary' with a companion, when a message was brought in to me by the little Cypriot dragoman of the Pharphar, who is as devoted to me as a spaniel. I found it to be a note in a strange hand, advising me to attend a certain *hammam* at an hour named, where I would be sure of learning facts to my advantage. Now, I have many acquaintances amongst all classes in Damascus, and a hand in a goodly number of intrigues in this city of secrets, but this summons I connected instantly to the incident of the Phidias head at the café, and to my suspicions that old N— himself had been concealed amongst the oranges at J—'s.

Aut Caesar aut nullus. The hour named found me entering the *hammam*. As I waited in the spacious entrance-hall for the *hammamji* to show me into the closet where I might undress, and contemplated the festoons of ropes draped with blue towels a–drying, and the glassy, skating-rink sort of floor reflecting light from on high, I wondered if I might not be delivering myself literally naked into an enemy's hand. There is something awfully naked about the nakedness of a Turk: his frightful baldness, save only the tuft in the midst of the shaven skull, makes such an alteration in his proportions after the voluminousness of turbans; and then again his fatness, once unrobed, has none of the dignity of the stout Turk-in-the-street. However, when I too was undressed, and draped in my two blue towels, and clapping along on my wooden pattens towards the *tepidarium* with an eerie sense of nakedness being spied upon, I comforted myself with the reflexion that, if I was as unarmed as Daniel entering the lions' den, then the lions too had had their teeth drawn, for no man can conceal a weapon in a Turkish bath. That my calculations were a little out, will be shown in the event.

The *tepidarium*, where I expected to be approached, or

attacked, seemed indeed like a den, dark, and oozy, and filled with the echoes of shouts and frantic laughter arising from certain profligate sons of Allah who make these places their resort of vice. Finding myself ignored, I pushed on to the *sudarium*.

When the sensations of being choked by heat had passed off a little, and I could look keenly about the narrow marble chamber in which volumes of steam made ghosts of the inmates, I tried in vain to identify which of these spectres might have summoned me into this simmering-pot. I felt intelligence melting under the ferocity of the heat, and was ladling water from the fountain over my limbs with a great iron spoon, for all the world like Cook basting the Sunday roast, when I was seized from behind in a grip of steel and thrown down on a stone bench upon my face.

Now, it is small use struggling in the pinion of one of the *tellahs* of the bath, who *will* massage you, and *will* crack your joints for you, whether you like it or no. They are as used to protest under their attentions as was old Keate when I was an Eton boy, and they put it down with the same strong hand. I knew this, of course; and yet I felt a horrid premonition that this fellow who had seized me, and was now squatting with all his weight between my shoulder-blades, was no *employé* of the *hammam*, but one of Herr Novis's lions aforesaid. He spoke no word, and nor did I, but he began his work upon my joints with the utmost cruelty. Soon I heard the clack-clack of a heavy personage approaching my torture-bench on his pattens. Looking as much sideways as I could, with the incubus crouched on my back and operating upon my neck and spine, I saw a pair of white, hair-covered legs with the veined fat wrinkling down over the feet like a pair of loose stockings, and heard the hoarse German voice I remembered from the Court Ball at Vienna.

'Ah, Captain Vinegar! You put yourself quite into the hands of the *tellah*, I see, despite your untrusting nature.'

'Perhaps you will inform me what it is you brought me to your infernal den to tell me, and then your assassin may leave off strangling me,' I gasped out.

'I will be brief, if you are uncomfortable. Captain Vinegar, I am prepared to concede that you have stirred up a hornets' nest for me in the Dobrusca, in the matter of gaining British concessions for the Danube navigation. You have played a bold hand. I congratulate you.'

I saw his heels click his pattens together, and could imagine the toad's body creased over in a bow beside my bench. I said nothing, for it was all I could do not to scream out with the pain of my wrenched joints.

'But' – went on the German voice – 'that was in Europe, Captain. We are now in Asia. Your capacity for mischief-making ceased when you crossed the Bosphorus, as your powerlessness to interfere with my scheme for the Orontes will have made you understand.'

'I don't know about powerlessness,' I jerked out, but he broke in with:

'Powerless, Captain – as powerless as you are upon that bench. Now, if you wish to make your fortune in Asia, Captain, where the field is a very wide one for an enterprising man, you would be wise to commence by exchanging sides. Farridam – F—, as you call him in England – can do nothing for you in Asia. Except (here he laughed a few unpleasant notes) to make certain you are killed! I, on the other hand, can do everything for you.'

'And if I don't care to exchange?'

In answer, an excruciating agony shot through my frame from some cunningly applied pressure by the devil crouched upon my back.

'What then must I do?' I groaned out, as if resistance was at an end.

'First,' he responded eagerly, 'you will use your influence with your friend T— P—, to persuade him that he must give up India, and go home and pay his court to Miss E— F—. Then you will persuade her papa that P—'s suit shall succeed. It will not be difficult. Your success upon the Dobrusca will give you influence with him.'

'And then?' enquired I, for the pressure had in some degree been lifted from my aching back.

'And then, if you like it, you shall come back to Asia and govern a province under me – and, of course, your inseparable friend P—, and his bride, will come too. We must be sure to have the bride.'

'And what of the statue's head?' I suddenly asked, to see what he would reply.

'The statue!' He was contemptuous. 'His aspiration after higher things than money was ever the soft spot where Farridam might be hurt! Who cares for the statue, Captain Vinegar, if you and I have the daughter?'

'If you and I have the daughter!' I seemed to look into the abyss, as I repeated the dreadful words.

'Remember, Captain – the choice is yours. Power, riches, fame, or – '

I heard no alternative, for an agony so searing tore through my nerves from a jerked vertebra that reason took flight, and I swooned.

How long I may have lain senseless I know not, but when I came to myself it was to find my body, and head, enveloped in a froth of soapsuds swamped and lathered over me with all the abandon of washday. I turned myself over, and, finding that I was no longer in the power of N—'s attendant demon, and that N— himself had withdrawn from the hot chamber, I soon kicked the soapsud enthusiast out of my way, and returned to the cooling room to recover myself with tobacco and coffee. So easeful is that dreamy langour as you lie shawled and turbanned in this state, that, by the time I came to dress myself again, and to put the price of the bath, which is here 40 paras, or about fourpence, onto the looking-glass brought to me by the *hammamji* so that I could adjust my turban before leaving, I could scarcely believe that my rough handling in the *sudarium*, and those insinuating suggestions, had not taken place in a dream. Certain lingering shoots of pain, as I walked through the streets towards the Terra Sancta, persuaded me, however, of the truth, and, moreover, N—'s extreme measures in the bath assured me that we are close upon the track of some secret he desires to conceal. Clearly, if J— is his tool, as I suppose, N— wishes to keep us from visiting Palmyra, and therefore knows nothing of the promise made to P—, that the marble head would meet him there. Who, then, offered P— the marble?

Go to Palmyra we will, P— and I, but N—'s antagonism to the project will add mightily to its hazards.

*   *   *

[313]

Palmyra! Pitcher's heart bumped against his ribs with the double pulse of excitement in the name as he entered the gate of the Terra Sancta convent. He and Farr had removed there that morning. Coming in from his meeting with Miguel, son of the Aneyzeh sheikh who claimed control over the passage of the desert to Palmyra, he had found the Armenian proprietor of the Pharphar shouting loudly at poor Farr's huddled form, and kicking together their possessions into a heap. Farr was lying curled up small on his shelf with his hands over his face, either trembling with fever, or sobbing. It had not been worth putting him into the Levinge-bed after all, which was only a trouble to pull him out of for his bouts of vomiting and diarrhoea throughout the night. Pitcher had seized the Armenian by a handful of his robe, and demanded an explanation from the Cypriot, who had attached himself to Farr's helpless state and now fluttered in the background like a little bantam hen that sees her nest broken up. He replied that the proprietor insisted on them leaving his hotel on account of 'milor's' illness.

'Illness? He has the toothache. Tell the fool. The toothache! Why,' added Tresham, 'what does he fear?'

He looked at Farr, who had taken away his hands from his ghastly face at hearing his friend's voice. Before answer could be made to his question, and alarm confirmed, Pitcher changed his tack: 'Come, we will go to the convent,' he told the Cypriot. 'Make the arrangements. It will answer better. And tell this wretch,' he added, turning fiercely on the Armenian, 'that if he don't leave off this instant I shall pitch him into his fountain.'

So they had removed to the convent of Terra Sancta, where a bare, swept upstairs room had been given them, with a terrace over the gate. It was in this room that Farr lay when Pitcher walked upstairs with his mind so uncomfortably full of the journey ahead to Palmyra. He hoped that the invalid would be asleep in his rugs on the floor whilst he began putting together the few necessities he could take with him on tomorrow's adventure. All that could be done for Farr, surely he had done. He had tried him with calomel, with tincture of catechu, quinine, cream of tartar – with everything the medicine-chest contained, except rhubarb and magnesia. He could do no more. Excessive concern would only alarm poor Farr. Besides, there were the Counts in the convent to look after him, whose company he was so keen upon, and surely one of the friars would bleed him if it was thought necessary – if, that is, a friar could be spared from making wine or listening to girls' confessions. The Counts had spoken of going off to Baalbek, but even Germans, surely, would not be so heartless as to leave a friend quite alone, and unwell, for a mere pleasure-tour?

So Pitcher assured himself of his freedom to keep the tryst at Palmyra. To draw back was cowardice. The thrills of fear with which it filled him were the measure of its necessity to him. Such thrills of fear, and the furious brilliant eyes of the Arab, Miguel, to whom he had entrusted himself, beckoned him on. He would recover the Phidias, and claim his reward. The reward! He had so worn away in his mind's eye the sharpness of Enid's image – had sucked her bird-bones so dry of flesh – that he looked involuntarily at her brother as he thought of her. Roland was not asleep after all. How that face shocked him! – shaking hands clasping haggard cheeks, the damp beard, the wild bright eye! He went across and kneeled by the pallet.

'You are in good hands here, old fellow,' he said tenderly. 'I shall be gone a week at most, and in that time you'll get quite well again.'

'I say, Pitcher,' muttered Farr, looking out at him earnestly with eyes which had sunk so far into his skull that they glimmered like puddles in exhausted wells, 'I say . . .'

'Yes, old fellow?'

He tried again. His words were muddled and thick, and he tried to fumble out a hand to lay hold of his friend's arm: 'I say, don't go, Pitcher. Pray don't go.'

'Oh, I shall do well enough. I shall come through, you see if I don't. I daresay they exaggerate the danger. Don't you worry about me, old fellow, but get well yourself while I'm gone.'

Farr's hand dropped away from his friend's sleeve frustrated. He sighed deeply. Pitcher stood up, and again busied himself sorting amongst his possessions, beyond reach of the invalid's eyes. All that was unnecessary, or cumbersome, in his luggage must be stripped away for this passage through the needle's eye of the desert. A cloak, a water-flask, his double-barrelled gun, a rug to fold behind his saddle – and his father's sword. This weapon he took softly from its battered box and hid from Farr under the cloak and other things put ready for the morning. No question but that it was essential.

He sat in the fading light writing rapidly in Vinegar's Journal, to bring the Captain's account of events up to date. 'Having performed for young F— [he wrote finally] every duty of friendship, I now throw my mind forward to tomorrow's adventure. I am to encounter my wild escort, and their lawless chieftain, before dawn at the Aleppo Gate.'

He closed the book, and placed it with the possessions he was leaving behind. Who would open it, if he did not return? He walked out onto the terrace over the convent gate. Above, in a violet dusk, stars had begun to twinkle. When these stars paled, he would be upon the desert road! The sword was out of its box at last.

X

_____

At FIVE NEXT EVENING Tresham Pitcher was resting in the shade of a palm-grove at Jerud, where the Eastern deserts begin. At ten they would leave for a ride of another twenty hours into the desert, to Kureytein, where he understood that Miguel's tribe was encamped; and there the party would exchange horses for camels for the last, waterless, fifteen-hour stage to Palmyra. That was what lay ahead. His tired mind considered this future as tired eyes look out into the dusk at a mountain range to be attempted tomorrow, before the curtain is drawn across the traveller's window, and he sleeps.

Already accomplished was a ride of nine hours from Damascus. Fears – that he wouldn't be well enough mounted to keep pace with the Arabs, that he would tire before they did, that they would blackmail him for more money – had been settled by the day's work among these wild horsemen. In a situation of utter strangeness he had held his own, quite as if he was that old campaigner, Captain Vinegar. Let the next days be strange as they will, he had learned that he could deal with strangeness. This knowledge allowed him to rest under the palms' leaves sawing at one another in the desert breeze. He wore the Arab turban and _abba_ over English trousers and boots, and was comfortable, and lay on the ground knowing he would sleep, and ate dried apricots. These, with biscuit and raisins, and a quart of water in a Russia-leather flask, made up his stores. Earlier a meal of boiled wheat had been prepared, which he and the horseman had shared with three old men of Jerud, the headman possibly amongst the three. Speaking no Arabic, Pitcher learned only from their behaviour, not from their lips. All day he had been watching them, following their glittering lance-points and flying robes mile upon mile into their own territory.

He had met with them as arranged, outside the Aleppo Gate before dawn. In the half-dark, horsemen had milled round him, voices as

[317]

sharp as the bark of foxes, hard to count, their spears brandished against the gold of dawn like the black lance-points in the Crucifixion scenes of the Gothic painters upraised against a gold-leaf sky. He identified Miguel amongst them. No one spoke to him. Then they had set off, at the hand-canter of their Arab mares, in a cluster of drumming hooves along the walled lanes between the gardens which extend a mile or more from the walls of Damascus along her rivers. Once out of the shadow of the trees' heavy foliage, with the sun pouring light into their faces as it rose above open country, Pitcher counted four horsemen besides Miguel. They ignored him, the expression in their black eyes changing no more when it fell upon him than when it fell upon rock or tree. Occasionally one of them screeched out a remark, sounding as though a fiery temper was strained to its utmost, but for hours they rode in silence under the shaking tufts of ostrich feathers on their bamboo lances. Pitcher felt able to settle into their company without the awkwardness of silence amongst Europeans. He watched them carefully. All were dirty, and fierce-eyed, with well-formed faces etched by the clear light.

Their road lay over a wide level of grass, and patches of wheat, with far, bleak mountains rimming it to the north – as far as the village of Kutefeh it was the road to Aleppo by which he and Farr had approached Damascus a few days ago. Pitcher imagined to himself his feelings of envy if he and Farr had seen this party of Arabs around a single hardy European riding so fast and far. It was Vinegar, surely. He had caught up at last with that fugitive and doughty figure whose Journal he had kept all the way from England's shores! When they left the Aleppo road, and branched away north-westward out of Kutefeh, he felt wonderfully lightened of all inessentials, and become his true self alone against the landscape, and against the task, and against his wild companions. His sword thrust through his belt, his double-barrelled Manton on his back – the brilliance of the traveller's armour gleamed against the real storm-clouds of adventure, as no gilt armour ever glittered on the pretty noblemen at the Eglinton Tournament! He thought of the day's ride behind him with the utmost content as he stretched under the palms at Jerud to sleep.

Eight o'clock the following evening found Pitcher and his Arabs at Kureytein. Numbers had altered during the day, a man now joining them out of the wilderness for a few hours, another two or three galloping off into the limitless wastes. Receiving no sense of 'protection' from these horsemen, Tresham was well-satisfied to feel that all rode together as equals, he with the rest. Admiring them as he had admired no other Eastern people he had seen, he wanted no superiority over them, only to ride as their comrade-in-arms. The £40 in gold that he had paid them he forgot as an irrelevant factor between them.

Now they scoured through the village of Kureytein, low mud oblongs of huts, a well, a scatter of trees, and rode out towards a declivity in the desert beyond, where the rakish tents of the Aneyzeh were pitched like black-tailed feluccas in a creek of the sea. The camels, too, were tethered against the fallen stones of some building or other as if they were ships moored to stone quays. Their gallop ended amongst the tents and camels when Miguel drove his lance into the ground at the entrance of the largest tent, and leaped down. He gestured Pitcher off his horse. When Pitcher's boots hit the ground, he thought he would fall from exhaustion. But he forced himself erect, and followed Miguel into the eclipse of the tent.

He received a wonderful impression of coolness and the glow of colours in this lantern-lit interior after the desert. It was a pavilion he thought of, not a tent, so marvellously excluded was the desert's harshness of light and heat in these cavernous depths which lanterns hung from posts revealed. Carpets covered the floor. At the end of the vista sat four or five Arabs older than the men who had ridden with Pitcher. With a gesture one of them indicated a place near himself. Walking towards it, past a black boy pounding coffee beans, Pitcher felt himself assessed with a shrewdness very different from the bovine stare of the idlers in the travellers' quarters in a Turkish village. Though it was painful from stiffness to fold his legs under him, he managed to drop down pretty neatly into his place. The old men were all armed with long-barrelled matchlocks, as well as with the knives stuck through their shawl belts. He kept his own double-barrelled Manton across his knees, the browned metal still warm from the desert sun.

Miguel talked for a few moments with the old men in their screeching fish-wife voices, then he took the gun out of Pitcher's hands.

Pitcher controlled his urge to snatch at it or to protest, but his heart beat fast. The gun was only to be shown to the greybeards, who clustered together and squawked over it. Arms and horses were the passions of these men's lives, Pitcher thought, just as they had been in the brave days of old in England. What nobler passions were there, and what race was finer, and of higher caste, than that of this desert sheikh with whom he rode and sat as an equal? Coffee was brought to him, and he took the nice care in drinking it which showed his appreciation.

The thin reedy cry of the muezzin disturbed the examination of Pitcher's gun, and drove all the inmates of the tent to its opening, where they washed their faces with handfuls of sand before making their devotions. Pitcher did not move, but listened. *La allah illah allah* . . . Add to those high-bred passions for horses and arms, the passionate faith which had once, too, been a thread of gold through England's days of castle and tournament. Faith! He felt very far from an English church, as he listened to the mutterings of the Arabs at the door into the desert – as far removed as he had felt from any of the dirty and degraded Christians of these Eastern lands, whose toad-eating ways were so contemptible to an Englishman. The prayers were over. Miguel brought him back his gun and, as he thrust it into his hands, spat out some English words:

'Soon eat. Rest. Moon rise, ride on camels. Goodbye.'

The old Arab whom Pitcher took to be Miguel's father fell into a perfect transport of delight at this, his withered dignity of expression cracking up into cackles and twinkles as he twisted this way and that to show his pride to his fellow-elders among the bolsters. Pitcher was disappointed. Even though Miguel had managed to keep all his scowling ferocity as he barked out the English words, yet the accomplishment, and the high value set on it by the old sheikh, were as disappointing as a Brummagem pen-knife where you look to find only Damascus blades.

However, he was not disappointed with the scene when he lay down to sleep rolled in his cloak on the tent floor, after a meal of mutton seethed with rice, and allowed his mind to range back over the incidents of the day's ride. If there had been danger from Arab tribesmen he had only felt it as an excitement in the blood. Twice horsemen had appeared, unnoticed until lances and horses, made spidery and shaky by the heat-haze, had risen from behind low escarpments; but they had vanished again into the brown wastes. These figures, this touch of fear, made the landscape very real. At an oasis of a dozen trees and a little grass beside a well, amongst the tumbled stones of some building thrown down centuries before, they had come up with a group of dismounted Arabs holding their horses in a circle. Peering into the circle, Pitcher had realized with a shock that a corpse was being lowered into a grave. Their robes flapped out round them in the breeze blowing through the trunks of the trees. An arm of the corpse trailed out of the blanket like a sleeper's, the limb unstiffened by death, and bluish in colour. A few words were shouted between Miguel and a mourner. Then they rode on, trees, and well, and grief, soon hull-down on the plain behind them. Riding alongside Pitcher, Miguel yelled at him,

'Plague!'

It was another tincture of fear – of reality – in the landscape of the desert, another touch of blackness in the storm-clouds against which the traveller's armour gleamed. Plague! It added a zest to the sense of abounding health with which Pitcher had ridden stirrup to stirrup with Captain Vinegar all day, and with which he now settled in his cloak to sleep until the moon rose.

Touched on the shoulder a few hours later, he awoke to immediate awareness of his position. Only the journey existed, and himself in the midst of it, absorbed in flight like the arrow in its rush through the air. Outside the tent a large, low moon silvered the scene. Three camels casting long shadows stood very black against the sky, armed Arabs already mounted on them. His own camel kneeled nearby. He thrust his sword through his belt and slung his gun on his back. A hundred times, in caravanserais at dawn in Asia Minor, he had watched how a camel is mounted, and he now climbed for the first time himself onto this essential figure of Eastern journeys, and settled his water-bottle and saddle-bags, and crossed his legs over the beast's hump, and took the braided cord in hand to set this new chapter of the adventure in motion. The creature groaned, rose to its knees – he was flung back – hoisted itself from hocks onto back legs – he was flung forward – and jerked him up nine feet all at once into the night sky. At first the height seemed tremendous, but as soon as he was amongst other camel-riders, and the lanky-paced camels had carried them away from the tents into the desert, there was no mark to reckon his height by, and he was able to look about at the desert. Away to the south-east the moon revealed a low spur of hills unseen the evening before.

They rode in silence at the camels' wrenching stride. After an hour, although not comfortable, Pitcher knew that a long camel-ride was within his capability, and settled to defeating the hardship of it mile by mile, hour by hour. To ride downhill felt most precarious, for the beast had no front, as a horse has, but the desert fortunately was tolerably level. The moon crossed the sky above them as steadily as the camels crossed the wastes beneath it. With dawn came the weariness which early sunlight reveals by prying into faces, and into minds, which the moon has not disturbed. For the first hours of the day Pitcher felt as tired as death.

At about ten in the morning Miguel halted by a solitary ruined tower in a dip of the desert which they had come upon suddenly. The Arabs squatted in the tower's shadow eating bread and drinking, a tattered huddle of men beside that finger of crumbled masonry. Pitcher, too, sat on the ground, chewing *mish-mish*. The worn bare earth was so old: the tower looked old enough, old beyond and before the ages of Europe, but the earth seemed to have been pounded and powdered intolerably by time. On a high, lonely stone of the tower's face a Cross was cut. Deeply etched, it was deeply shadowed by the sun. Pitcher's tired mind registered the Cross as a tired runner notes a clue in a paper-chase, and knows himself to be on the right track. He watched a scorpion crawl out of a cracked stone and totter towards him. For some reason he moved away rather than killing the creature, and, walking round the heap of stone at the tower's base, found that further ruins existed in this dry valley, an arch or two of an aqueduct as well as other remains.

As he stood wondering whether to walk down to them, there issued out of the shadow of the aqueduct a singular figure. Cadaverous, stooped, leading a sorry-looking camel laden with sheep-fleeces, and with two greasy locks of black hair dangling down under his hat to frame Semitic features, he climbed the slope. Pitcher put his hand on his sword: he did not know what form Novis's emissaries might take, and this wandering Jew seemed a likely manifestation of his adversary, if any had been sent to stop himself and Captain Vinegar reaching Palmyra. He stood alert, and nodded to the creature. The man, and then the camel, passed him by in a clatter of cooking implements hung from the pack, and plodded onwards into the brilliant space of the desert. So that was not his assassin.

In the saddle again, riding onwards through the heat of the day, he thought once more of the scorpion, and the Cross cut in the tower, and the wandering Jew. Such images, in all that emptiness of desert, seemed full of significance, if only he understood their meaning. Miguel, who could explain nothing to him in words, could not be asked to explain how that one old pedlar came to be on the road to Palmyra with his camel-load of fleeces, like the ghost of all the rich caravans which had thronged the route in days of Palmyra's wealth, nor why the solitary tower was marked with the Cross. He puzzled over the clues as he rode.

They had ridden their camels for five hours through the fierce glare of the desert when the landscape began to alter, and to throw features in their way close enough for it to seem to Pitcher worth screwing up aching eyes and staring into the dazzle of light to see more. What was at first a shallow trough in the levels became a valley. An escarpment approached their road from the right, its curve apparently closing the valley ahead of them. They rode nearer, saw more clearly. The stony hillside seemed built with towers, whose faces the sun lighted – towers, or tombs, in an elegant state of ruin, like the follies in a nobleman's park. Strange buildings! He looked at them, aware that he had seen some such tower somewhere before. But there now came in view on the brow of the hill across the deepening valley into which they rode, the dark stone mass of a castle overhanging the road. The silence was absolute. They rode into the pass between castle and tombs as if between enemy outposts into an ambush. Why was it familiar, Pitcher wondered? His camel was alert under him, its pace quickening. Dust rose in clouds from the beasts' feet, and hung in the blue air undispersed in the shelter of the pass. Then the hills fell away to left and right, and Palmyra lay before them.

Such a vast sepulchre of bone-white ruins! At Azana Pitcher had seen one temple, a theatre, a few heaps of marble; here was stretched the colossal destruction of a metropolis, white, silent, vast. Lines of mighty columns marching away in rank upon rank mazed the eye. Here amid general wreck rose a single column; there, and there, and far in the distance, stood others in isolation, or in groups supporting entablature. All was open, and arched, and airy, and as white as picked bones: and behind the silent, airy, bone-white wreck of all this magnificence, the yellow sand of the desert stretched illimitably away.

As he let his camel follow the others down into the Arab village among the ruins, the name 'Senaudon' spelled itself in Pitcher's mind. The crumbling towers, the broken gates and deserted streets, the marble palace lighted with corpse-candles – was it the wasted city of Senaudon lurking in his memory which had made the approach to Palmyra familiar? – Senaudon, where the dragon turned into putrefaction when his challenge was met, and where the knight in the story at last learned his own true name. The camels were urged to their knees among the huts by their riders' sharp cries, and the goal of the journey was reached. It now remained to achieve his purpose in coming. Somewhere in all this broken marble was the beautiful head of Dionysus. And one among these wild people clamouring round them, the only inhabitants of Palmyra's ruins, was charged to restore the head to him.

As the last light of evening, flooding between dark hills, flushed the milk-white columns of the ruined city, Pitcher sat in the doorway of the hut assigned to him and watched the onset of night. He was profoundly discontented. Nothing had come of the journey. He had waited, expecting to be approached, if not by the old blind man with the basket, then by an emissary in some other form who would give him the head of Dionysus; but no one had come.

At first he had waited in his hut, pleased with the cut and figured stone it was built of, and sure that his arrival would be met at once with a response. But two hours had passed. The hut he had found to be so infested with fleas that he had been driven out, to sit where he sat now, wrapped in his cloak against the marble doorpost, watching the sunset. Even the sense of danger, should the tryst be a ruse of the enemy, or should Novis have discovered it – even this pleasure had gone, and his gun now leaned against the doorpost beside him. The arrow had rushed through the air and fallen to earth, but it seemed that it had not struck the mark. Palmyra might be the target of all the world's travellers, but was it his? If it was not to be the scene of his tryst, its fame was nothing to him.

True, the island of wrecked marble afloat in its desert sea had astonished him at first. Destruction on so Titanic a scale, fragments so Cyclopean hurled down with such fury, seemed the work of giants and dragons, and had kept alive in his mind the idea of legendary ruin, and of Guinglan waiting in the waste city of Senaudon for an outcome to his adventure. But astonishment will not last. The eerie sense of second-sight soon evaporates.

An awful stillness and silence lay upon the scene, save for the chip-chip-chip of a cold chisel where Miguel, in Pitcher's view, was attacking the base of a standing column as a woodman attacks a tree. Here, unlike Azana, there was no continuity of life among the ruins; no goose-girls, or clink of ploughshare, no birds even, or wild flowers. There was only desolation and emptiness, and the disappointment of all hope.

He sat alone at the end of the world, every ambition frustrated, every reward withheld. A profound sadness weighed down his heart. 'You speak as if one summer was all we might have' whispered the voice close beside him in the pony-carriage, which had so often quickened his heart with its hint of promise since that snowy day. But there was to be no reward now, or second summer. It was over.

Crash!

Pitcher's hand leaped to his gun. Not a shot, but the fall of stone on stone had split the silence, and now rang against colonnades, echoed, echoed again, and volleyed away into the desert. The crash was succeeded by silence more profound: the chipping of Miguel's chisel had stopped: the column had fallen. One column's fall was such an event? They lay in his view in thousands. Yet each one's fall had been an event like that resounding crash which had startled him! Where an extensive graveyard will incline the mind towards comfortable generalities on the subject of Death, one funeral will remind the watcher that men do not die in general, but singly and alone. So the fall of one column struck Pitcher, in that whole ruined city.

The scutter of bare feet approached in the dusk. Was it the messenger? He gripped his gun. Alas, only Miguel appeared before him. The Arab held out to him the coin found beneath the column he had thrown down. Disappointed to see only Miguel, and contemptuous of so base a reward for the destruction of a column, he pushed the hand away. Miguel squatted on the ground, pulling his *abba* round him as if intending to stay some time. Presently he barked out, 'Tomorrow on?'

'On where? Tomorrow I go back.'

'Not Zenobia.' The Arab shook the greasy locks he had freed from his *keffiyah*.

'I don't want to go to Zenobia.' It was a site he had heard of on the Tigris. At Aleppo the Consul had spoken of rumoured excavations being made there by Europeans.

'Not Zenobia,' repeated Miguel in his high sharp voice, 'is finish Zenobia. Now is at Halebyah.'

'What is at Halebyah?' Pitcher had never heard the name. Something in him – a Vinegarish instinct – pricked up ears to it, as though it was a challenge, and should be met. 'Who is at Halebyah?'

'Feringhee. Many men, many camel. Dig. Much gold. Dig.' He dug with his hands in the dust. 'Today he go from here.'

Alert, Pitcher asked, 'Today the feringhee went from Tadmor? Did he leave nothing for me here? Are you sure there is nothing left for me here?'

'Is nothing for you here.' He parted his hands and let the dust fall. 'Tomorrow on? To Halebyah? To find the feringhee?'

'No.'

Pitcher had spoken out before he was aware of having considered the question. No; he had come far enough, done what was required. This place, and what he had been through to reach it, were within his capabilities; more than this was not. The challenge had been to reach Palmyra. This he had done. Now the adversary altered and extended the challenge, and tempted him on into the desert. A wise man must know a challenge from a temptation. Ah, though he wore many masks, Pitcher knew his adversary in the Bedouin squatting before him in the ruins of Palmyra, and tempting him on to some unknown or even legendary city, perhaps Senaudon itself, deep in shifting desert sands where he would assume another mask, and issue a further challenge. Whatever Halebyah might be, he would not go there.

'No,' he repeated. 'Tomorrow I go back.'

It had been arranged that a start would be made for Damascus in the evening of the following day, which was a Sunday. It was a weary Sunday to Pitcher, wandering amongst ruins which had scarcely sustained his interest for an hour. Only as the background to action could he care for a scene; inaction made everything at Palmyra dull to him. After sharing the Arabs' midday meal he had set out to climb the slope to the north-west of the ruins, towards the Turkish castle, merely to put in the time with exercise. He had not climbed far before his eye was caught by a figure moving rapidly over the slope on the other side of the valley, amongst the tower-tombs. It was a young Arab, perhaps even a child, who hurried over the ground leaning very much to one side to counterbalance the weight of the basket clasped in his arms. It was a deep wicker basket, of the sort used by fish-sellers in the market.

Lethargy left Pitcher in a moment. All at once the scene became vivid with excitement. He took the direct line towards the hurrying child, plunging down into the valley over steep rough ground. He watched the fluttering robes which moved quickly amongst the tombs above him. The evident weight of the basket made him sure of its contents. In a minute the boy had disappeared into a tomb. Fixing his eye upon it, Pitcher climbed with long strides towards its entrance. Now he knew where he had seen such a tomb, or tower, before: beside the lake at Rainshaw. Of course; Uncle Marcus had designed his Traveller's Tower from Wood's engravings of Palmyra. There was released into his mind, too, by recognition of the tomb he was approaching, the horror which the Rainshaw tower had contained when he had pushed open its door. Still he climbed the slope at racing pace. The child had not emerged from the tomb. He must be within, in the darkness, perhaps not alone. Pitcher realized that he had left his gun behind. The entrance-mouth was now close, and infernally dark. He drew his sword and let the impetus of his climb carry him without hesitation between the breached stones into the tomb.

It was empty. Light from a chink in the further wall showed him where the boy had escaped. And that chink of light showed him too the basket on the earth floor. He kept his sword in his right hand, still fearing the rush of feet, shouts, an ambush, and knelt by the basket. He put in his left hand to explore the vague glimmer, as he thought, of marble. Hair met his fingers, and a chill colder than marble. He looked. Shrivelled, blind, dead – it was the head of the old man who had carried this same basket at the café gate. The smell of putrefaction filled the tomb. Tricked, perhaps trapped, Pitcher grasped his sword and prepared to break out of the tower, and to sell his life dearly amongst his enemies if need be.

Towards sunset Pitcher and his escort of Arabs started for Damascus into a stiff wind. There had been no enemy to fight outside the tomb. He wished that there had been. He had met the challenge. He had been perfectly sure of himself – sure of his courage – with that enlarged and vivid self-awareness flashed into the mind by danger, and by the mastery of fear. But there had been no adversary, no fight, only the bare hillside and the tombs. He had left the head in its basket inside the tomb, and had told no one of it. He had failed.

All that night, and all the next day and the next night, the wind continued to blow in their faces like divine anger. During halts, it was necessary to squeeze down between two kneeling camels for a few minutes' respite from the pitiless blast, or the mind of a European could not have endured it. All day the sky was a cruel blue, and the sun's heat was buffeted into their faces by the wind: at night the wind drove darkness over them out of infernal gulfs, whilst stars and moon shone down from tranquil realms unclouded by the miseries of earthly life.

As a storm isolates from one another the ships of a convoy, so the desert wind isolated each man alone on his camel within wrappings of cloak and *abba*. There was no communication, or companionship; only a few thoughts blown into tatters by the wind. Round and round in Pitcher's head, like the clicking of a metal vane driven by the wind, spun the thought that he had failed. His failure had put the old blind man's head into the basket, where the marble head of Dionysus should have been. His failure had been to refuse the challenge to pursue 'the feringhee' to Halebyah. That was where he should have gone, even if he had ridden straight to his death. Failure had cost the old man his head, Sir Daniel his Phidias, and himself his 'reward'.

At Kureytein they ate, then lay in the wind-battered tents. No interest was taken in Pitcher by the sheikh, as though his failure was common knowledge in the desert. When the moon rose they remounted their horses for the journey to Damascus. In the early light of dawn they passed through Kutefeh and rejoined the Aleppo road. With scrub-trees and bushes to give it a thousand complaining tongues, the wind swelled in power and insistence. Between cloak and scarf Pitcher's eyes were no more than a crack in his burnt face, and took no delight in what they saw.

At sunset they entered the gardens of Damascus. The walled lanes, and the shade of the gardens – the groaning water-wheels and whispering trees – oppressed him after the desert like the images in a dream. The ceasing of the wind, too, took away a dimension of reality. At the Aleppo Gate he parted from Miguel.

He rode alone through the narrow roofed-in streets. It was the hour of curfew, and he had no lantern, so he was obliged to make haste. But an urgency which had nothing to do with curfew suddenly seized him as he approached the Terra Sancta, and made him push his little horse along. The black crows of Eastern towns flapped across the strip of sky between housetops. Ahead, at last, rose the convent gate. From the terrace over the gate – the terrace outside Farr's room – smoke ascended in a column, the clean smell of it pricking Pitcher's nostrils through the stench of the town. He saw a cowled figure tending a fire. As he watched from his horse, the friar poked his staff into the fire and held up a smouldering European shirt to make sure the flame consumed it.

XI

————————

IN THE DUSK OF AN OCTOBER EVENING the intricate masonry of Raven-rig's western façade glowed richly as it received the sunset gleams along the valley from the sea. The ridged and cushioned outlines of the beechwoods, too, were encrusted with the gilt of this light, and, above the vanes and turrets and twisted chimneys of the castle, above the beechwoods and the crook-backed oaks, the profile of moor and mountain was edged with rose against the darkness of the east. Only one of the castle's hundred windows was lit within, red light from that one streaming forth like blood from a stab-wound.

The light issued from a turret corbelled out from the North Tower, whose stained-glass window tinged it red. In the large room behind this window, of which the turret formed merely an alcove, Lady Fanny Farr lay still as death in a canopied bed in shadows stirred by firelight, whilst the short, stubborn figure of Sir Daniel tramped between fire, and bed, and turret. The room's ceiling was supported on clustered oak columns twined with carved ivy, and everywhere the intricate *boiserie* of Lady Fanny's taste, and the armorial glass of her breeding, filled and darkened the chamber. Wherever Sir Daniel's hand fell in his wanderings, it fell upon some carved finial or fretted pinnacle or elaborate grotesque. At this terrible moment, nothing was simple.

In the turret-alcove stood a writing table on which was placed the only lamp lighting the room, and beside the lamp, held down by one of those bronze door-knockers in the shape of a lady's hand which Roland had noticed in Aleppo, lay a letter. When his tramping brought him into the alcove Sir Daniel did not read the letter, but peered out of the turret windows in all directions, like a man expecting enemies.

The letter behind him on the table was dated from Damascus fifteen days earlier. He knew that it would have crossed the Lebanon to Beyrout to meet the French mail-boat for Alexandria, whence the

English steamer would have brought it home. He had told Lady Fanny several times that this was the route the letter must have taken, and each time the recital had irritated her more. But until he could decide who was to blame for the catastrophe, he had nothing else to say.

Dear Sir Daniel [the letter began]

It is with very real regret that I must inform you of the death in this town of your son Roland Farr, from the plague, on September 10th. I offer you and your family a soldier's sympathy.

Since it is my belief that a man may as well lie where he falls, I have caused your son's body to be interred in the Christian burying-ground outside the walls of this city. If, however, you prefer it, I will give orders for the remains to be disinterred and placed in a cask of spirits for shipment to England. Not by any instinct or wish a Traveller, perhaps after all poor Roland would rest easier in English soil.

Certain Friars, in whose convent of the Terra Sancta your son died, attended to the last needs of both body and soul. The duties of friendship and affection were, I believe, carried out to the best of his abilities by Mr Pitcher, who was with him to the End. It is perhaps a pity that Pitcher sent for no medical man other than the Syrian hakkim, who might have lightened the ignorance of the Friars, and applied such modern resources as the burning of oil-soaked cotton on the patient's stomach, etc. etc., but you will know that Consul Jenkins is unfriendly to your interests, which circumstance is as much to blame as Mr Pitcher's youth and inexperience. Two Germans who had professed friendship for poor Roland of course ran off as soon as his disease was confirmed.

Pursuit of duties entrusted to me by yourself had obliged me at that critical time to make the hazardous journey to Palmyra, and it was only on my return that I learned the tragic news of your son's demise, whom I had left in perfect health but a week before.

At Palmyra I had almost laid my hand upon your Phidias, but the prize was snatched from me by your enemy, who has now retired further into the desert. I remain at Damascus only long enough to hear your wishes in the matter of the corpse, when I will fit out to pursue the enemy on to the Tigris and beyond. Whether Mr Pitcher will now come home, or continue Eastward with myself, he seems at present too distressed to determine. Negligent as he may have been, you will I am sure acquit him of all blame for the Tragedy.

No doubt you will already have discovered that my poor efforts in the matter of the Danube–Black Sea Railway have more than fulfilled all hopes in that direction. The scheme upon the Orontes I advise you to drop, for I believe it never will come out as you wish, as I indicated in my despatch from Aleppo.

Believe me to be, with deep regret,

yr obedient servant,

O. Q. Vinegar (Capt.)

Two subjects occupied Sir Daniel's mind as he paced about the room. One was the question of bringing Roland's body home. Knowing well Damascus, and himself quite as much upon familiar ground there as in Wales, he had no preference as to which earth received his son's body; but in the arrangements, and orders, and permissions, which would be needed to bring a corpse from Syria, he foresaw a means of busying himself and his especial capabilities in a matter relevant to Roland, which was what he longed to do. However, he was uncertain whether Lady Fanny would think it the correct course; Vinegar gave his opinion that a man 'should be buried where he fell', and Vinegar was an officer, who probably expressed the correct view of the matter in the best society.

Working powerfully in Sir Daniel's mind also was the inclination of his temperament, under distress or misfortune, to lay the blame upon someone, and to look for revenge. Though by no means a weak-minded man, he allowed himself to believe that no enterprise of his could go wrong except by the malignity of his enemies. Therefore he had gone over Vinegar's letter twenty times to ferret out where blame might be laid for Roland's death, and he intended finding a scapegoat. The Consul? – the two Germans? – the Friars? – Pitcher? – or Vinegar himself, who smeared all these others with blame, while claiming for himself the alibi of having gone to Palmyra on a wild-goose chase. Scrutinising it so closely, as he had never scrutinised Vinegar before, Sir Daniel at last smelt something a little rotten about the Captain's letter – some little breath of treachery or deceit.

'I believe Vinegar is the man to blame, after all,' he decided aloud into the recesses of the four-poster bed. 'I don't blame young Pitcher.'

From her pillows, open-eyed, absolutely still, Lady Fanny said in a perfectly controlled voice, 'I don't think it is quite manly to look out always for whom you can blame.'

'Where there's misfortune there's fault, Fanny. And where there's fault there's blame. Manly? – I don't know. Not gentlemanly, I suppose you mean. Well, I don't care for that. In this I don't care a hang for what's gentlemanly. Did you suppose I should be content with putting up a monument and calling it all square? If Vinegar's to blame, I shall hunt him into his grave. He shan't hide from me, no, not in all the deserts of Arabia. He talks of enemies. By Heaven, he shall learn what an enemy I can be! We are but half way in this story.'

JOURNAL OF
A LAND-MARCH
TOWARDS INDIA

by O. Q. VINEGAR (Capt.)

Third Edition, post 8vo.

'Remarkable' – *Pall Mall*

Ready shortly: by the same Author,

ADVENTURES
IN THE CAUCASUS,

at the time of the

CRIMEAN WAR

BUCKLE AND STOURPAINE, 105 PICCADILLY, W.